IN THE CAPTAIN'S QUARTERS

Nash carried Columbia, arms crossed over her chest, into his cabin and tossed her down on his bed. To her chagrin, he swung a chair in front of the door and straddled it, leaned his chin on the chair's straight back, and stared at her without saying a single word.

It seemed like an eternity, as she sat cross-legged on his bed staring back at him. She realized that the first move was hers. Lifting her chin in a display of bravado, she said, "Now that we've sat here long enough for my ardor to cool markedly — you can remove your person from the door and let me get on with what needs doin'."

She cautiously rose and moved within a foot of him. His body language did not give anything away as he rose and moved the chair between them aside. Now she stood face to face with him.

"It appears that against our wills, our lives have become irretrievably entangled," he murmured, in a voice heavy with the unbidden promise of passion. "Yours with mine; mine with yours," he added in a husky whisper.

"So it appears," Columbia managed past the furious pounding of her heart between her ears. Her earlier determination was abandoning her, leaving her with that recognizable craving she thought she could ignore. She could *not* ignore the man in front of her.

Slowly, his hand came out and lifted her chin. He dipped his head and brushed her lips with his. Gazing into her turquoise eyes with an untamed intensity, he breathed, "What do ya'll think we should do about it?"

"What we *should* do?" she echoed, struggling to keep her wits about her.

"Forget all the shoulds in the world, Mary Catherine. Want. What do you *want* to do about it?"

This time, both hands came up and inched her jacket from her shoulders, letting it slip down her arms . . .

GWEN CLEARY

RIVERBOAT TEMPTATION

ZEBRA BOOKS
KENSINGTON PUBLISHING CORP.

ZEBRA BOOKS

are published by

Kensington Publishing Corp.
475 Park Avenue South
New York, NY 10016

First printing: August, 1992

Printed in the United States of America

Chapter One

Nash Foster lay sprawled on the hurricane deck of his paddle wheeler, naked as the night he'd entered this world. One hand rested on the ample bosom of a woman he'd picked up earlier, in some saloon along the docks. With his free hand, Nash took a final drag on a cigarette, blew a smoke ring into the warm night air, and flipped the butt over the side.

"Hey, sweetie, you might've offered a girl a couple of puffs first," the painted woman whined from the crook of his arm. She sat up and craned her neck over the side into the inky waters rippling against the boat. Rolling her eyes at the waste of a good cigarette, her vision caught on the elongated silhouettes of three huge, foreboding men striding along the dock toward the gangplank.

"You expecting company?" she sniveled, scrambling for her clothing strewn about the deck.

Nash pulled his gaze from the woman's generous fig-

5

ure, and noted the three men boarding below on the main deck. His face impassive, Nash slid muscled thighs into his trousers and tossed on a shirt.

"Guess we'll have to call it a night, honey," he said in a dismissive drawl. "Seems as if I am about to be otherwise engaged."

The frizzy redhead threw her hands on abundant hips. "But I haven't been paid yet."

"And you probably ain't gonna be, either," George Garrison announced in a sly gruff voice, as he took the last step to the top deck and emerged into the flickering light lent from the wheelhouse. "Foster ain't got much of a reputation for makin' good on his debts . . . or promises. That's why we're here."

The woman's eyes shot to Nash. Without hesitation Nash turned his pockets inside out and shrugged. "It was mighty entertaining while it lasted, darlin'. But I am afraid all mutually pleasurable moments must come to an end at some point," he said in an easy Tennessee drawl.

Contorted in rage, her glare raked the ruggedly carved, ebony-haired captain. "Pleasurable? Entertaining? You may be one of the best lookers I ever bedded with—and I am not saying you weren't a good roll—but I got bills to pay. I am not leaving here till I get my money, fair and square!"

"I would be most happy to oblige, if I had any. But fact is, life generally proves to be anything but fair."

Growing impatient with such prattle, Cliff Sherman adjusted the belt beneath his big gut, stepped forward next to George, and gave the partially clad woman a shove. Then he shifted his jacket and flashed a badge. "Get going before we run you in."

6

His eyes hiding hatred of the Yankee lawmen, Nash helped the woman to her feet. Despite a reputation as a no-account captain, Nash considered himself a Southern gentleman where the fairer sex was concerned. "Ya'll right, darlin'?"

"I will be once I get my money," the woman snorted.

"Go below and see Bartholomew McGraw, my first mate. Barth will see that you get your due."

The woman wiped her arm where the lawman had touched it. Looking down a prominent nose at the fat man, she snipped, "I'd rather give it to a flat-broke captain for free, than to the likes of your kind flush with cash."

Nash watched the woman scoop up the rest of her clothing and disappear down the stairs, before he shifted his attention back to the lawmen. "And to what do I owe the pleasure of ya'll's late-night excursion aboard my vessel, gentlemen?"

The third bulky man shifted his hat back on his head. "Name's Lester Cowan." He motioned to his companions in turn. "That's Cliff Sherman and George Garrison, Foster. We got us a paper here that says Mr. Kiplinger's got legal right to toss your carcass off this tub.

"Guess all your fun 'n' games we've been readin' about in the newspapers, is about to come to an end," Lester snickered. "Mr. Kiplinger quit paying your docking fees, not to mention having your license to haul cargo in these waters revoked, Southerner. And, as of right now, we're repossessing Mr. Kiplinger's property."

"Yeah. Now," George seconded. He pushed his jacket back and exposed a gun strapped to his meaty

7

thigh. "You made a big mistake jilting that fancy Kiplinger girl. Her daddy's gonna see to it that you don't work again in these parts, he don't like you making his daughter a laughingstock in those high society circles you been running in."

George's gloating grin faded as he removed a paper from his vest pocket. "Mr. Kiplinger did say to give you one last chance to change your mind. Said if you make amends to his little girl, the presidency of his business empire and this boat can still be yours, and I'm to tear up this paper."

Nash's easy smile did not reach his eyes, as he took the legal document and tossed it aside. "Ya'll mind if I collect my gear from the wheelhouse first?"

"You're a fool, Foster." Lester, the tallest of the three, shrugged. "S'ppose there'd be no harm done if we let you take your personal things. But we're coming with you."

Nash finished closing the last three buttons on his shirt and sauntered into the wheelhouse, the men close on his heels. His face impassive, he grabbed a bottle from a cabinet. "Ya'll care to join me for a last drink on board ship?"

The three looked at each other and nodded. Cliff Sherman cocked a bushy red brow. "That's mighty amiable of you, Foster, considering why we come."

"No use arguing over a few rotting boards, I always say. Besides, I have invariably been of a mind to follow the wind, and the air has become rather stagnant around here lately."

Nash splashed amber liquid into four tin cups and watched the men guzzle down their drinks. Without touching his, Nash set it aside. "Since it may be some time before anyone moves this tub again, mind if I turn over the engines one last time? Just so they don't freeze up, of course."

George held out his cup for a refill. "Don't know why you should give a damn, since it ain't gonna be your business no more. But we got time. Go ahead."

"Thanks," Nash said amiably. "Ya'll pour yourselves another round."

"Don't mind if we do," Cliff said and took charge of the bottle.

Nash watched the men drink freely, then he went about firing up the steam engines.

The paddle wheeler gave a jerk.

"What's that?" Lester queried, and licked the spilled liquor off his thumb.

"The engines run a little rough. That is why they needed to be fired up. Blow the cobwebs out of them and ya'll get a better price, if Kiplinger decides to sell the paddle wheeler at auction," Nash announced, as if he hadn't a single care in the world.

Lulled into a false sense of security, Lester nodded his acceptance and returned his attention to the free booze. He'd heard Foster was a man to be reckoned with, so he'd brought along a couple of companions. He took a long swig of the liquor and gloated over how easy it had been to wrest the boat right out from under Foster, considering how everybody knew it was actually Kiplinger who was reneging on his deal with the man. Hell, Foster wasn't so tough or smart after all.

The door to the wheelhouse suddenly swung open, and a man about the same age as Nash's thirty years, with a slight build, and wavy auburn hair tied back at the nape of his neck, stuck his head in. "That . . . ah

9

. . . lady—Dolly Brooks—you sent below, said we got company," he offered with a confused grin.

"These men are here on Kiplinger's behalf to seize the *Yacht.*" The three snickered at such a misnomer, causing Nash to pause before continuing. "Seems the old man has decided to run true to his pledge to ruin me. At any rate, as I started to say, before we are forced to quit the ship, I thought I'd turn over the engines one last time, so they don't freeze up. I would not want Kiplinger to lose money on his investment."

Barth sucked back a sudden grin of enlightenment and nodded. "Freeze up. Right. I'll just go check the boiler. Wouldn't want Mr. Kiplinger to get stuck with a leaky boiler either."

Nash leaned against the wheel and patiently waited for the boiler to build a full head of steam, as the three guzzled down the liquor with abandon. His gaze went out the window and over the skyline of the city in the distance. It was a full moon, and despite the late hour New York was abustle with life. Lights illuminated faraway windows like stars against a glowing velvet night, and Nash grinned to himself.

Kiplinger owed him.

His attention shifted below and he noticed his first mate and old friend, aided by Dolly Brooks, toss off the mooring lines. With a mere nudge at the controls, Nash set the paddle wheel in motion. The gentle rocking motion of the boat barely changed, as he maneuvered the paddle wheeler from the dock and out into the middle of the harbor without arousing the lawmen's suspicions.

Once the boat was away from land, Nash casually stilled the great paddle wheel and pivoted toward the men, who had just polished off his last bottle. "Hope ya'll enjoyed the party, gentlemen," he said in a glib voice.

"You're not so bad after all, Foster. It was right social of you, seeing as how I heard Mr. Kiplinger'd promised you this tub, 'til you jilted his daughter. Now, we got to do our duty," announced Lester in a slurred voice.

"It is our duty," hiccupped Cliff, who set his cup down so hard that the last swig in the bottom splashed onto the floor. "Nothing personal."

"No, nothing," George added, mellowed from the alcohol.

"Glad to hear it," Nash returned. "Because then ya'll understand that it really is nothing personal that the party is over, and I am giving ya'll a choice."

Bushy red brows drew together. "A choice? What are you talkin' about?"

It was the first time the easygoing smile reached Nash's obsidian eyes. "I am talking about ya'll 'gentlemen' abandoning ship, before I am forced to toss your carcasses overboard."

Suddenly sober, Cliff fumbled with his holster. But his senses had been dulled by the liquor.

"I would not do that if I were you," Nash announced with an easy drawl, and pointed the gun he'd picked off the shelf at the man's chest. "I would hate to blow a hole through you before I tossed you overboard. Might have trouble floating ashore with a crater in your bow."

In helpless dismay, Lester Cowan observed Foster take Cliff's gun and toss it aside. Then he looked about and realized that they were no longer moored. "Mr. Kiplinger won't let you get away with this, Foster!"

11

Nash's easy smile never wavered. "Looks like ya'll may be wrong on that account."

"No one gets the best of Mr. Kiplinger without living to regret it!"

Nash ignored the man's warning and waved the gun toward the door. "If ya'll fine gentlemen will lead the way back toward the dinghy tied off the main deck, we shall conclude our unpleasant business, so we all can get on with the pleasures of living."

Daunted and feeling outfoxed by the Southerner, the men shuffled down the stairs to the main deck, missing sight of Dolly Brooks, who dashed behind a stack of kegs at the sound of voices.

"You aren't going to get away with this," Lester Cowan grumbled in a warning voice.

" 'Fraid I am about to prove ya'll mistaken."

"Where you gonna run to? Mr. Kiplinger'll have reinforcements all over your tail, the minute we reach the docks," George Garrison said in desperation.

"Then I guess I shall have to see to it that ya'll gentlemen have a nice long voyage back to the docks."

They reached the rail, where alongside a small dinghy bobbed in the black waters. Barth stood holding the rope to the tiny boat.

"I see you have read my mind again," Nash said with a chuckle to his childhood friend.

"Haven't I always? Besides, you said that Kiplinger was bound to try something sooner or later."

"Just one more thing before our guests depart. Climb down and remove the oars."

"You can't just leave us adrift!" sputtered Lester, as he watched the lithe man retrieve the oars.

Nash's grin widened. "Would ya'll prefer to swim?"

Lester's lips were tight when he shook his head, shooting his companions a silent plea for compliance. Hell, he couldn't swim!

"I did not think so," Nash drawled. "Although it's such a warm night, a swim might prove refreshing."

With sullen faces, filled with scowling hatred the three men crawled into the small boat, causing it to rock precariously. They grabbed the rickety wooden sides. "You'll pay for this. Mr. Kiplinger'll hound you to the ends of the world," Lester promised.

Nash laughed at that. "That is, unless ya'll fall off the edge first."

Dolly edged further back into the shadows, smiling to herself. Markus Kiplinger. One of the wealthiest men in all of New York! There was more than one way to get paid for the evening, she thought with sudden satisfaction and backed further into the shadows to wait.

Once the dinghy had quit rocking, Lester let go of the sides long enough to shake a fist at Nash. "You'll pay, you dumb Southern bastard! You could've had it all. But you tossed it all away. Now you'll pay."

His easy grin never leaving his lips, Nash moved to the edge of the paddle wheeler. With the toe of his boot, he gave the tiny boat a shove. "Bon voyage, 'gentlemen.' "

Nash waved at the helpless lawmen as the dinghy bobbed into the shadows and was finally enveloped by the darkness. Then he brushed his hands. "Think it is time we were underway," he said to Barth.

A look of concern flickered into the honey color of Barth's eyes. "But you have some unfinished business

13

first. And this paddle wheeler still does legally belong to Kiplinger."

The easy smile faded from Nash's full lips and was replaced with a bitter tightening. "The way I see it, Kiplinger owes me, and this paddle wheeler is payment as promised. Besides, it is common knowledge the old man handed this boat over to me."

"But he did not do it *legally*."

"And that is why those three came to kick us off the *Yacht*. Hell, I earned this tub, squiring Miss Jennifer Kiplinger around town at the old man's behest."

A troubled light flickered into Barth's eyes before he hooded them. "You could have married the lady, you know."

"Yeah. And I could have spent my life dancing at the end of Jennifer's daddy's purse strings, too. No thanks. Marriage was not part of the deal I made with Kiplinger. I kept my end of the bargain, and he is going to keep his."

"Jennifer and her daddy aren't going to let us steam out of their lives that easy. Not after you just made them both laughingstocks," Barth commented, not daring to give voice to his deepest thoughts about the beautiful debutante, or her father's need to control people. Catching himself before he divulged exactly what was on his mind, Barth paused.

"I can still picture the hatred in Kiplinger's face when you contradicted his announcement that you'd soon head his shipyard, right after you married his daughter. Why, I have never seen anyone's face turn as purple as Jennifer's. I think she could have killed you herself, if you had been within reach."

"She got caught in her daddy's trap. I told her I was

not going to be her daddy's puppet. Kiplinger thought he could corner me with that announcement. Well, he was wrong."

"So are you, if you think he'll be satisfied with just making sure your license was revoked and reneging on giving you ownership of this paddle wheeler. After tonight, Kiplinger'll not only want the boat back, he probably won't quit until he has your hide along with it."

"Well then, we had best quit standing here talking and get underway. We shall see how far Kiplinger's influence reaches. Do you remember hearing something at one of Kiplinger's parties about the growing steamship trade in Oregon Territory on the Columbia River?"

"Yeah," Barth said suspiciously.

Nash gave Barth's arm a friendly chuck. "Let's go check it out for ourselves. Bet there's plenty of money to be made out West for a couple of smart entrepreneurs like us."

Not waiting for a reply, Nash turned and headed back up the stairs toward the wheelhouse. Sidetracked by the subject of Jennifer and her father, Barth regained his senses and recalled his original question about unfinished business. Not to mention Nash's sudden decision to travel to the other ends of the country—on a paddle wheeler no less! Barth hailed back his friend.

"Nash, what about the woman you brought on board tonight?" he called out.

But Nash had already disappeared up the stairs.

Chapter Two

It seemed like an eternity since Nash had slept. His eyes felt as if they were filled with sand, and every bit of his six-foot-two-inch frame ached. Taking the paddle wheeler — as had been promised to him — seemed like the most expedient thing to do at the time, but now Nash felt as if an additional twenty years had been tacked onto his present thirty. He pinched the bridge of his straight nose and considered the last three days.

After they had steamed out of New York Harbor and south along the Atlantic Coast, they had been hit by a fierce spring storm. It had taken all the skill Nash possessed just to keep the paddle wheeler afloat. When the storm had abated, Nash thought he could relax and make plans for the trip around Cape Horn, but while they were put in at a tiny fishing hamlet, a frigate had spotted them and given chase.

As Nash leaned his forehead against the wheel, he still found it difficult to believe that he had managed to outwit the persistent navy vessel.

"Looks like you could use some rest," observed Barth, coming into the wheelhouse.

Nash's attention shot toward his bedraggled friend. "I'd say I'm not the only one who could use a break," Nash rubbed the stubble on his chin. "You don't look much better than I feel." His friend's hair was straggling over his ears, his white shirt was stained with grease, and his soiled trousers were ripped up his calves.

"Let's go kill the engines, so we both can grab a minute."

Nash tied off the wheel, tossed an arm around Barth's shoulders in companionable friendship, and together they left the wheelhouse. They had just reached the main deck, when Nash spied a vaguely familiar female form lounging near the rail.

"What the hell are you still doing on my ship?" Nash demanded, stalking toward her with his hands planted firmly on slim hips.

Dolly shrugged. "*Your* ship? That's not the way I heard it a few nights ago." She smiled to herself. Once Markus Kiplinger got the note she'd sent from that smelly fishing village, and caught up with the arrogant captain, she would collect a bundle of money.

Nash took a threatening step toward the buxom woman. "Did you know that while at sea the captain of a vessel has total authority? In case you didn't, that means I preside over life and death, and can legally order all under my command—and that includes you—tossed overboard."

"Like you did those three men?" she gulped.

Nash shrugged. "With or without a dinghy."

Dolly's green cat eyes rounded, and she reached out and grabbed the brightly painted life ring posted on

17

the wall. Then her eyes shifted to Barth. "Barth honey, you wouldn't allow him to do such a thing, would you?"

Barth stepped to her side, swallowing hard as he raised up to his full five-foot-eleven-inch height. "I invited Dolly to remain on board . . . with me."

"With you?"

"Uh . . . yes. She's going with me . . . ah, us, to Oregon Territory." Barth puffed out his chest. Despite the clenching of Nash's fists and murder in his eyes, he knew their friendship was firmly based on mutual respect of each other's decisions.

As the silence stretched taut between them, Barth hoped that Nash would not question his judgment, since he needed the woman's companionship to put Jennifer Kiplinger out of his mind.

To Barth's relief, Nash shook his head in disbelief and continued toward the engines.

"Then you aren't going to put me overboard, like you did those fellas back in New York Harbor?" Dolly called out.

Nash stopped but did not turn around.

"Nash?" Barth's voice was full of hope.

Nash combed a hand through his black waves as he pivoted around to face the couple. "Suppose we all could use an extra pair of hands, if the *lady* is willing to work for her passage."

"Thanks, Nash," Barth choked out, while Dolly threatened to squeeze the life from him with her exuberance.

"You better save the thanks. It is going to be a long, arduous journey." Nash looked Dolly up and down. "Everyone is going to have to carry their weight."

18

Despite his annoyance, he had a propensity for women with generous curves. But his bed was going to be cold and lonely; he would not go near her again, since Barth had apparently taken up with her. They had often competed for the same woman; it had become a friendly game, a tradition they shared since they had run away from the foundling home together as boys. But they had an unspoken agreement: They never knowingly bedded the same woman at the same time.

Continuing to ponder the sagacity of his decision, Nash turned and headed back toward the wheelhouse.

"Where are you going?" Barth asked. "I thought we were going to kill the engines and get some rest."

"There is going to be no resting until we reach Oregon Territory," Nash grumbled. Determined to make the best of an imperfect situation, he trudged back up the stairs.

WINTER 1859

The rugged shoreline of the Oregon coast was crowded with pines, jutting from craggy cliffs and marching down to the rocky shoreline, where the sky seemed to blend into the briny ocean blue. Nash guided the paddle wheeler north along the littoral, taking in the virgin coastline as he kept watch for the sea to change color at the mouth of the Columbia River.

Barth and Dolly strolled past the wheelhouse, catching Nash's attention. He uttered a string of oaths and hollered out the window, "Barth, I need you at the boiler. We are somewhere near the headland of the Co-

19

lumbia."

Barth made a big deal out of saluting. By the time he turned, he sighted the breakers and shoal water of a bar, signaling that they had indeed reached the entrance to the Great River of the West. On his left was Cape Disappointment, the headland named by Captain Mears, who in 1787 came close to finding the great river, but swung his ship seaward instead.

"Barth!" Nash hollered again. "Get going before we end up like a beached whale. Looks like we have arrived at the Columbia."

Barth snapped out of remembrances of the river's history and sped to the boiler, located on the main deck. Without further hesitation, he began tossing wood into the hungry flames, and the sturdy paddle wheeler managed to slip over the bar and up the four-mile-wide river toward the town of Astoria on the south shore. He recalled reading that Astoria was the first permanent settlement west of the Rockies, and excitement at actually reaching it filled him.

Nash worked the wheel with an able wrist. While the stacks belched smoke into a cloudless sky, he maneuvered the *Yacht* to dock at the shores of the town perched on verdant hills overlooking the mighty Columbia River.

Dolly let out a squeal and danced about the deck, relieved to finally reach this Oregon country that Barth and Nash had been constantly talking about. When she'd made the snap decision to remain on board until Markus Kiplinger caught up with Nash Foster, she'd never dreamed that she would end up traveling all the way to some remote outpost, so far from civilization. A sudden wave of worry washed over her relief, and she fretted over what she was going to do now.

In the next instant, the answer was delivered to her. More than one hundred men had converged on the docks, and were whistling and waving at her.

"You unattached, beautiful?"

"I got me trees full of bright green money," another hollered, and waved a fistful of dollars at her.

"Any more gals like you on board?"

Nash and Barth finished tying off the *Yacht* and joined Dolly. "Looks like you got a decision to make," Nash observed, and hooked his hands on the railing.

"Looks like," echoed Barth, and leaned against a post.

Dolly glanced from the crowd of hungry faces to the two men. During the last year she and Nash had made their peace. Now they were able to tolerate one another, and even enjoy each other's company on occasion.

Her relationship with Barth had evolved into one of friendship and respect. And Dolly had to admit to herself that she had developed a new respect for herself as well. So much so that as she returned to peruse all those hungry faces, she realized that she no longer wanted to return to the sporting life.

Dolly's attention snapped to Nash's profile. It was a fetching countenance, with black eyes set wide beneath straight, thick, black brows. His nose pointed straight downward toward firm, full lips and a strong jaw abbreviated with a deep cleft. She gazed at him a moment longer, almost wishing he were the marrying kind, then she blurted out without thinking, "I got a choice?"

The two men looked to each other, their faces unreadable. Then they turned silent eyes on her. To her chagrin neither man spoke.

"Aren't one of you going to answer?" she asked, when her patience could no longer be contained.

"You are the only one with the answer," Nash said.

"Me? You mean you aren't going to set me ashore amidst all those men to fend for myself?"

"I have not attempted to set you ashore in any of the other ports, have I?"

Dolly crinkled her brow, realization just dawning on her. "You mean, if I don't want to go back to the life I came from, I truly don't have to?"

"That's exactly what Nash means," Barth said.

"But I don't got no other way to make a go in life. And I haven't got no money."

Nash kept his face impassive. "I cannot say that you were one of my favorite people when we first started this adventure. But you have worked hard without complaining . . . much. And the way I figure it, any person who has toiled as hard as you have, deserves a chance for a fresh start."

For a moment a sharp edge of guilt threatened to slice her for writing that note to Markus Kiplinger. She breathed a sigh. Thank heaven nothing had come of it. A lightness filling her heart, she took a deep breath. "I'd truly like to take the chance to start over. Guess I'll wait until those men clear out, and then go look for honest work. I'd like to keep my room on board, 'til I got the money for a room somewhere, if you don't mind."

"You can stay on board as long as you like. After all, I owe you crew's wages."

"You do?" she said in a hoarse whisper, astounded at the man's generosity.

22

"Yes, I do. Unfortunately, I do not have the money to pay you right now. But as soon as I get a profitable hauling job, you will be paid for the work you did coming around the horn, as well as what I owe you for the night we left New York."

Dolly blushed at his reference to their one and only intimate encounter. It was then that she realized she had truly changed. She must have bedded fifty men and never blushed before now. She thrust out a hand. "It's a deal. Except I won't take nothing for that night back in New York. I'm not that kind of girl anymore."

Nash took her hand, calloused from the hard work coming around the Horn. It felt warm on that cold, blustery day, and reminded him that he hadn't had a woman for nearly six months. He dropped the hand and stepped back. "Ya'll remain on board, while I go round up somebody to unload the cargo we hauled up here from San Francisco. It is time we collect our money. The *Yacht* needs repairs and we are about out of supplies."

Before Nash could lower the gangplank, Dolly launched herself into his arms, and hugged him to a round of boos and hisses from the men at the docks.

Nash broke the hug and boomed out, "Sorry, fellows, this here little lady is off limits. The first man who is anything but respectful to my sister will answer to me!"

Dolly was astounded, but stood at least two inches taller as she watched Nash and Barth lower the gangplank, and Nash disembark and disappear among the throngs of disappointed men retreating toward town. She asked, "Does he truly mean it? About offering the likes of me his protection?"

"Nash is a man of his word. Furthermore, you heard him. You're family now. You've got two brothers. We'll both be looking out after you."

"Family? I've never had no family," she mumbled, and thought about how she had survived childhood on the streets of New York.

"Neither do Nash and me. We've been each other's family, since we were small children at an orphanage in Nashville. Nash doesn't like to talk about it, since he was left on the doorstep as a newborn. He adopted me when a bunch of bullies were beating up on me. He knocked the stuffing out of those boys, and we've been inseparable ever since."

"Oh." She nodded as a new understanding of the man Nash Foster materialized.

"Consider yourself lucky. Nash doesn't take easy to females. So telling those men you're his sister means he'll always be an invaluable ally."

Her eyes threatened to well up with emotion, and she placed a hand on his arm. "Thank you," she offered in a choked voice.

Barth blinked. "Don't think anymore about it. Come on, let's get those barrels unlashed and ready to be unloaded. Knowing Nash's salesmanship abilities, by tonight we'll be well on our way to becoming successful entrepreneurs. Why, by the time Nash gets through with the men who'll be taking delivery of these supplies, we'll probably end up with an exclusive contract."

With a new future, and dollar signs glistening a radiant silver before her eyes, Dolly hummed as she worked by Barth's side. She had a family now, and she intended to throw herself into her new role. And she vowed to protect her new brothers, as if they were truly blood kin.

Chapter Three

WINTER 1859
*Willamette River, Nearing the Wharves at Portland, Oregon
Territory*

Columbia Baranoff slid down the frayed rope that
dangled from the hurricane deck to the main deck,
landing on her backside with a thud in front of the
paddle wheeler's boiler. Not bothered in the least by
such an unladylike maneuver, she picked herself up
and proceeded to grab a screwdriver and tinker with
the testy boiler.

"Gracious, Mary Catherine, if I didn't know better,
I'd've sworn your ma birthed a boy, the way you
carry on," Titus Baranoff observed with a huff of exasperation from his comfy, warm position next to the
boiler.

Columbia's head snapped up at the sound of her
uncle's plagued voice. The man had fashioned a comfortable bed, sheltered from the misty cold wind that
blew off the river. A plump furry hat drawn down to
his eyes, scarf swung around a neck prickled with

25

gray stubble, and heavy coat peeking out from a mound of blankets covering his tall, thin frame, Uncle Titus looked like some homeless whistlepunk caught on the slopes of a logging camp in the dead of winter.

"Crissakes, Uncle Titus, don't know why you keep insistin' on callin' me Mary Catherine. You know I go by Columbia."

"Hmmph! Columbia indeed. It ain't natural, girl. It just ain't natural."

"Natural or not, I'm full-growed, and that's the handle I aim to use."

"Handle? Hmmph!"

Ignoring the disapproving trill in her uncle's voice, Columbia turned from him, tightened a final screw, then stuffed a curl back under her beat-up knit cap.

"Good thing you got hair the color of coal oil, or those locks of yours'd be streaked clear through with black greasy smudges, the way you keep working on this paddle wheeler's engines all the time."

"I'm workin' on the boiler, Uncle Titus," Columbia retorted, unconsciously stuffing a few more errant strands back under her cap. "And it's a good thing I can fix this boat's workin' parts, or we'd be out of business."

"Then maybe you'd learn how to be a proper lady and get busy and catch a husband, instead of piloting this paddle wheeler up and down the Columbia River like some man, Mary Catherine Baranoff."

Columbia bit her lip and silently prepared for a lengthy lecture from her dear uncle. She'd hoped that *this* time after their conversation over her given

26

name, he wouldn't launch into a sermon of how he had miserably broken his promise to his only brother to see her married off properlike. In a last-ditch effort to forestall the inevitable, Columbia kneeled down in front of the middle-aged man, set the screwdriver aside, and took his gnarled hands in her calloused ones.

"Uncle Titus, I love my life on the river. There's nothin' else on earth I'd rather be doin' than what I am. This river's my life, my home. I was born on this river—"

"How else do you think you got that durned fool nickname Columbia?" he moaned. "Your ma birthed you twenty years ago, in the very cabin you now inhabit. But your dear departed folks—the Lord bless and keep their souls—never intended for you to spend your entire life the way they did before the river claimed them so untimely, rarely setting foot on good honest dry soil. And if they'd wanted you to be called Columbia, they would have given you the blessed name themselves."

"And as I just told you, I like the name the other riverboat pilots pinned on me; it fits. Look at me." She leaned back on her haunches and held out her arms. "Mary Catherine is hardly a name that suits my likes."

"It would suit if you'd give up this dunderheaded dream of yours of becoming the first female licensed riverboat pilot on the Columbia River, and start living like a proper female should. We could buy a grand house on the bluffs overlooking your precious river, if you'd let me accept John Villamoore's generous offer to buy the *Columbia's Pride*. We could live like kings with what he's willing to pay! Maybe I'd get well, once I wasn't forced to hibernate under this mountain of blankets next to the boiler, just to try 'n' keep these ailing bones from freezing clear through on this blasted river."

He rolled his eyes and tucked a blanket up further around his neck. "But no. Oh, no. You insist on continuing with this silly pretense that I own and pilot this aging tub, and you merely help out where you can. Why, if you didn't work so hard, you'd probably fill out. Just look at you in those baggy overalls. You're barely more than skin and bones yourself. And why aren't you bundled up?"

" 'Cause I'm not cold," she answered in a mere whisper.

"Hmmph! Not cold indeed." He shook an index finger at her. "You aren't one of those polar bears up north. See that you get more clothes on you before you go back up top."

Columbia nodded dutifully just to pacify him, and got to her feet.

"Don't you try to walk away from your poor sickly old uncle when he's talking to you."

"I wouldn't think of it." Columbia hung her head to hide a smile. Despite his gruff demeanor and the way he constantly harped at her, she knew that he would forget all about his conjured-up illnesses and always come running to her rescue, as he had since he had taken over the responsibility to raise her when she was just nine years old.

He stared at her for a moment, then crinkled his

brows. "Let me see, where was I? Oh yes, I remember. And wipe that smile off your face, young woman. Anyway, as I was saying, you are going to come to regret the loss of the days that you didn't listen to me. I know what I'm talking about.

"I tell you, one of these days this little game of riverboat pilot that you're playing's going to come back to haunt you." He shook an index finger at her again. "You just mind my words. One of these days you'll rue the foolish decision you've made. One of these days you're going to wish that you had listened to your poor, ailing Uncle Titus, and had spent time learning how to be a proper lady who'd know how to attract a husband."

"I'll want to be a proper lady to attract a husband the day the Columbia River dries up and the fish start totin' cargo down the riverbed on their backs," she snorted, ignoring the old dear's reference to his imaginary ailments.

"I can see I'm wasting what little breath I've got left trying to save you from yourself."

Columbia bent down and embraced him, but he brushed her off. "Don't you go try 'n' soften me with one of those hugs of yours, 'cause it is not going to work."

"I wouldn't think of it, Uncle Titus," she said, and hugged him again for good measure despite his sputtering. "I love you."

"Rather you found some good man to love."

"Don't need no guldurned man under foot. I can do anything a man can do."

"Nonsense."

"What can't I do that a man can do?"

To rattle her, he answered, "You can't lean over the rail and piss into the wind, now can you?"

She glared at him. "You know as well as me that if you piss into the wind, it'll fly right back on you like a spray off the paddle wheel durin' a good gust."

"Mary Catherine Baranoff, the way you talk!"

"I didn't start it," she steadfastly defended herself.

"No, guess you didn't. But the fact still remains, that you can't piss *with* the wind neither."

"Oh, for heavensake."

He shrugged. "Well, can you?"

"No! But I don't have to beat out the competition. Furthermore, I already got myself a man in my life."

"If so, you sure been doing a mighty good job of keeping him a secret from me and the rest of the world. You mind telling your poor, sick uncle who this man is?"

"It's you. I got you and you're all I need," she insisted.

"I ain't going to live forever, you know. Then what are you going to do?"

"You taught me so well, that I'll manage just fine. But you're so darned ornery, you'll outlive us all."

"Aaagh, not with all that's ailing me." He waved her off. "Now, get on with you, girl, before you wear out this old ticker of mine arguing with me."

Columbia ignored his words and gave him a smacking kiss on the cheek. "I'll let you get some fortifyin' rest, so you'll be ready for the next round."

"Fortifying indeed. You do know some big words, despite refusing to attend school back East like your

30

ma wanted," he taunted. "Guess it's good you like to read."

"Guess so."

She sent him a frown, retrieved the screwdriver, and got to her feet, determined to put an end to her uncle's declamation before he got his second wind. She had work to do, if they were going to pick up a load and arrive at Lower Cascades before the competition could beat her out.

"You get below and put on a heavier jacket. We don't want GlennieLynn to be having to care for the both of us."

She saluted. "Yes sir."

Columbia hurried to her cramped cabin filled with all the belongings she possessed. The wall by her narrow bed was covered with precious likenesses of her beloved parents, and a wreath her mother had painstakingly woven out of her own dark hair. A tiny table stood in the corner heaped with papers that leaned against a small bureau which contained the few articles of clothing she needed. She grabbed her old battered jacket off the hook on the back of the door. Sliding her arms into the patched garment, Columbia headed back toward the wheelhouse, passing one of her six faithful crewmembers, who was feeding wood to the voracious fire.

The muscular man glanced up. "Your uncle's sleeping like a babe. Guess you wore him out, Miz Columbia."

Columbia smiled at the big, rough-hewn man. "Guess I did."

She had just passed Titus when the paddle wheeler

31

jerked, causing Titus to start. "Who the devil is piloting this boat, while you're down here watching me sleep?"

"Quit your worryin'. GlennieLynn's been watchin' over the crew at the wheel most the afternoon, while I've been workin' on the boiler."

He sputtered, "She doesn't know what she's doing, and neither does the rest of our green crew. Dear Lord, you'll send us all to a watery grave before it's our time, if you don't give up these outrageous notions of yours. If you hadn't made such a river rat out of GlennieLynn, she might've been my wife by now, and be taking care of a proper home, instead of working on this cursed river like she's doing."

Columbia opened her mouth to retort to his latest attempts to start another argument, but the belching of the ship's whistle drowned her out.

Two short blasts and one long one.

Trouble.

Columbia scrambled up the stairs to the top deck and raced to the wheelhouse. "What's wrong?" she demanded as she broke through the door.

A woman the size of a mountain looked up and handed an eyeglass to Columbia. "Have a looksee for yourself. Unless I miss my guess, that paddle wheeler up ahead of us is headed for the same dock."

"Is it one of Villamoore's?" Columbia hissed, setting the glass against her right eye.

"Don't rightly recognize it," came the gravelly female voice, filled with dread.

"Whether either one of us recognizes it or not, it couldn't be anyone but one of Villamoore's henchmen. Just look at him! He's tryin' to elbow us out of a rightly got contract to haul the freight waitin' for us. The dog's mother—"

"Columbia, your uncle don't like that kind of language." Then, in the next moment, as the boat ahead made a sharp turn in front of them, GlennieLynn snapped, "Why, the bastard!"

If Columbia hadn't been so mad, she would have laughed at the middle-aged woman's use of waterfront language. "I was right!" she spat. "Look at him! He's tryin' to edge us out of our rightful place at the dock."

In the blinking of an eye, Columbia nudged GlennieLynn out of the way, dismissed the young crewman, and took over the controls. Pulling hard on the whistle cord, in an attempt to ward off the persistent interloper, Columbia slitted her eyes. "If he thinks I'm goin' to easily give way, he's in for a big surprise!"

Columbia spun the wheel, causing the paddle wheeler to come around, and positioned it directly in the other boat's path.

"My God, Columbia, you're going to get us all killed!" GlennieLynn screamed and grabbed for the wheel.

Chapter Four

Columbia managed to hold her ground against GlennieLynn's efforts to dislodge her from her position. She clung to the big wheel and brought the paddle wheeler into a head-on collision course with the other paddle wheeler dead ahead, sending a churning, white-crested wave surging toward the other boat.

"No! You'll kill us all," GlennieLynn screeched, and gave Columbia another shove.

"Oof." Columbia hit her head as GlennieLynn's weight slammed Columbia against a small cabinet to the right of the wheel. She tried to get up, but lost her balance as GlennieLynn fought the wheel, forcing the big paddle wheeler out of the rapidly approaching boat's way just in the nick of time.

Columbia's Pride rocked precariously as the boats narrowly missed each other.

Columbia scrambled to her feet to fight the big wheel, and then stood helplessly by, watching as the other paddle wheeler glided past her and docked in her spot at the pier.

"Why, that son of a landlubber's dog!" she sputtered, and slammed her fist down on the cabinet. "Ouch!" She shook her throbbing hand.

GlennieLynn's shoulders slumped. "Sorry, Columbia, but that other boat wasn't going to give way."

"Neither was I!"

Out of breath and still shaking, Titus burst into the wheelhouse. "Didn't I tell you that that blasted stubborn streak of yours could get us all killed someday? That other boat nearly rammed us!"

Columbia jutted out her chin. "We're still standin' here breathin', ain't we?"

"No thanks to you," he puffed, clutching his chest. "Now, let's get this durned paddle wheeler into port, so we can get this run over with."

At the mention of the run, Columbia's gaze shot toward the docks and her dark mood deepened. "Looks like we've been skunked this time," she hissed. At Titus's bemused look, Columbia pointed toward the pier.

"Didn't I try to teach you that it isn't polite for a lady to point?"

"Hornswaggle that lady-stuff politeness! That devil's son John Villamoore has hired on another weasel to do his dirty work 'n' try to run us out of business."

Titus's line of vision followed Columbia's long, slender finger, and noted a paddle wheeler he'd never seen before, docked in their place. He scratched his head. "Well, if that don't set a record. There's actually somebody new who's crazier than

35

my niece on this river. I got to meet the man who managed to beat you out during a head-on competition."

"You're gonna meet the whoreson," she spat.

"You just quit that kind of talk, Mary Catherine, or one of these days, when I regain my health, I'm going to be forced to teach you the error of your ways."

"Hmmph!" Still mad as a badger over losing out at the dock, Columbia ignored her uncle's threat, spun the great wheel toward a nearby pier, and maneuvered the paddle wheeler toward the empty berth.

It was over two hours later by the time Columbia got the *Columbia's Pride* docked and secured. Stomping around the deck as she checked the lines, she grabbed a crowbar and stormed down the gangplank, Titus and GlennieLynn not far behind.

Titus surged forward through the snarl of dockworkers and ripped the rod from her hand. "You may have a wish to die, but I aim to keep you in one piece despite yourself."

Columbia stopped and glared at her uncle. "You can have the crowbar, but there's no way you're goin' to keep me from stoppin' Villamoore's latest henchman from stealin' cargo that's rightly ours!"

Ready to tear his graying hair out, Titus watched his determined niece fume toward the other paddle wheeler.

"What you going to do, Titus?" GlennieLynn asked, tugging on his coattails. "Columbia could get

36

hurt barging on to that boat alone."

"That durned fool girl! Go back and get the crew. Looks like we may have to save that child from herself again!"

GlennieLynn turned and hauled her bulk as fast as she could back toward the *Columbia's Pride,* to alert the men that Columbia was about to set herself adrift in the middle of a bunch of rapids again. As she reached the paddle wheeler, GlennieLynn glanced back over her shoulder in time to catch sight of Columbia stomping up the strange paddle wheeler's gangplank, past the dockworkers loading cargo.

Columbia stopped at the top of the gangplank, blocking the middle of the aisle, and stood with her legs apart, her arms crossed over her chest.

"Don't none of you bring another one of those crates on board this boat," she ordered.

"Now, Columbia," the leader of the dockworkers said. "You know Barkley's rule in this business: The first paddle wheeler here gets the job. You 'n' your uncle was beat out fair 'n' square."

Columbia stood her ground. "This is my . . . er . . . my uncle's cargo. Don't you budge another crate, Francis McGee, till I set this stranger straight!"

The men hid smirks at the little gal's nerve, calling big Frank McGee Francis, and they looked to him as the giant man nodded and directed them to set the crates down. The half-dozen men perched atop the cartons, crossed their arms, and waited for the sparks to fly. Despite the fierce competition on the docks among the riverboat pilots from the north and south sides of the river, and Mr. Villamoore's rapid takeover of much of the commerce on the river, Barkley's dockworkers had a soft spot in their hearts for the fiesty young girl and her uncle.

Her chin held proud, Columbia strode toward the hurricane deck. Two men stood talking with their backs toward her. Outside of Francis McGee, one was the tallest man she had seen in these parts. The other one was just a mite shorter, and the breadth of his shoulders was not near as wide. Her eyes shifted lower to the bigger man's backside and powerful thighs, and a strange quickening prodded the blood to heat her cheeks before she snapped her attention back to the task at hand.

It was obvious that the leaner-built man was deferring to the larger one. That was why her cheeks felt hot, she reasoned; she was going to have to take on the bigger of the two.

She took a deep breath to calm her pounding heart. She stepped forward, reached up, and tapped the mammoth man on the shoulder.

He pivoted around. "Yes? Aargh!"

Columbia's fist connected with the man's jaw, causing him to rock back on his heels.

"What the hell!" Nash howled at the throbbing pain. He grabbed the scrawny young boy by the collar and ripped the kid off his feet.

Barth grabbed Nash's arm. "He's only a lad, Nash."

38

"Lad or no, he is not going to come aboard my ship and punch me for no reason."

Dangling precariously, Columbia struggled, finally drawing back her heavy boot and laying the toe into the big man's knee.

"Yeow!" Nash yelped. As a reflex to this latest unprovoked onslaught, he shook off Barth's hand and drew back a fist.

When Columbia shook her head in a continuing effort to free herself, her cap slipped off her head and a snarl of long black waves tumbled freely down her back.

"My God, Nash, he's a she!" Barth hollered.

At that same moment Nash realized he had hold of a female, and immediately released his grip on her shirt front, sending her plummeting toward the deck.

Columbia landed with a thud at the man's feet. Leaning back on her palms, she glared up at the glowering man, whose expression instantly changed to contrition.

"Here, let me help you," Nash offered, and bent down to give the crazy female a hand.

"Not on your life!" She batted him away, scrambled to her feet, and brushed herself off. "How dare you try to hurt a lady?" she sputtered.

"Lady?"

"Yes. Lady. But *you!* You hire on with Villamoore and try to take the bread out of my poor uncle's mouth, you rotten river rat. You scurvy scrumbucket. You . . ."

Nash did a slow appraisal the length of the little hellion standing before him with her hands on her slim hips, as she proceeded to berate him. Without the cap covering her hair, there was no doubt that she was of the female persuasion, despite her scraggly appearance and loose-fitting coat. A thought flashed through his mind: If she were cleaned up to look like a proper female, she might not be half bad, although he personally liked his women with more meat on their bones. But what was coming out of that fetching, sensuous mouth negated any fleeting consideration he had given that she could be an attractive female. The female urchin in front of him had a mouth on her like a river wharf thug.

". . . vile rabble like you ain't gonna beat me and my uncle out of honest work. You ain't—"

"Your cap."

Columbia frowned, having been interrupted in mid-sentence. "What?"

"I believe this belongs to ya'll," he drawled, and held out the ragged knit cap.

Columbia sucked in her cheeks and ripped the cap out of the man's hand, plunking it on her head. "As I started to say, you ain't—"

"Look, darlin', I have not the foggiest notion what you are going on about. Ya'll come on board my ship, punch me in the jaw without so much as a how-do-you-do, and then proceed to kick me in the knee and lay into me. And as far as 'beating you and your uncle out of honest work,' I was here first, and the first man"—he cocked a brow and grinned at her attempts to impersonate a man with those clothes—"hauls the available cargo. So, ya'll had best get off my boat, before I have you tossed off, female or not."

Barth had been listening to the exchange and now stepped forward in an effort to intercede. "Nash, perhaps we might negotiate—"

"We were here first, and that is all there is to it," Nash hissed, daunting his friend and causing Barth to step back.

"Pity you ain't nothin' like him," she snapped, and sent the other man a grateful smile before slitting eyes on the big brute. "You ain't gonna get away with piratin' my rightful cargo!"

"Ya'll are lucky I am not going to have you arrested for assault, not to mention trespassing." In an effort to dismiss the thorny female, Nash stepped to the rail and called out to the dockworkers. "Ya'll can bring the rest of the freight aboard now."

"No!" Columbia screeched and darted past the man to the gangplank. Without ceremony she plunked down in the middle of the boards and crossed her arms and legs, effectively blocking the way.

At that moment GlennieLynn arrived with six crewmen from the *Columbia's Pride,* and Titus raised an arm. "Wait, fellows." To the men's looks of consternation, he added, "I think the Columbia River's just dropped a good sixty feet."

"Whatever you talkin' about?" GlennieLynn questioned, confused by it all as Frank McGee came to

41

stand awkwardly beside her.

Titus smirked, pleased with his own humor. "Just a little conversation about a dry riverbed Mary Catherine and I had a short time ago."

The men looked to GlennieLynn. She shrugged. "Don't look to me. I haven't got the slightest notion what he's mumbling on about."

"You men don't have to worry. Looks like everything is under control," Titus reassured them.

"You sure, boss?" the informal leader of the crew asked.

"I'm so sure, that you fellows can have shore leave for the rest of the day. We'll pick up the next available cargo. In the meantime, GlennieLynn and I will wait for Mary Catherine to rejoin us." He cast a quick glance in her direction. "I don't think she'll be long."

"Okay. If you say so," the man hesitantly agreed, and shot one last look at the altercation about to occur on board the foreign paddle wheeler, before he and the other men reluctantly headed in to Portland.

"I do think this is going to be mighty interesting, if not timely." Titus rubbed his hands together and leaned against one of the crates to enjoy the show. It was time that his niece encountered a man who was not going to be sidestepped by her double-fisted shenanigans!

"Think I'll join the boys," GlennieLynn said, glancing doubtfully at the *Yacht*. "You may find Columbia's antics amusing, Titus. But I don't want to be anywhere near when the fur starts flying."

"Suit yourself," Titus said, before his attention was drawn back to the newly arrived paddle wheeler and the drama unfolding aboard it.

"Nash," Barth called out. "What are you going to do about that female barricade?"

"Barricade? You mean barracuda, don't you?"

Barth swallowed back a grin at the accuracy of Nash's observation. Women had always fallen into Nash's arms, he had such a way with them. Barth couldn't help but get an inner chuckle from the girl sitting, as big as you please, on the gangplank. Unless he missed his guess, she wasn't going to swoon at Nash's feet like the others. "Maybe you ought to wait till she gets tired and leaves," he suggested, and decided to let Nash try his charm on her.

Stomping after the prickly female, Nash threw back over his shoulder, "I am not waiting for some pigheaded female who could not weigh much more than one hundred pounds with her pockets filled with river water. I aim to remove that stubborn creature, so we can get on with the business of earning a living."

Nash stopped just short of where the female sat, crossed-legged, her smudged face cherry red with rage, silently daring him to extract her from her position. A melting smile on his lips, he offered, "Darlin', why don't ya'll come on inside to the salon with me, and we shall discuss this unfortunate misunderstanding."

"Ain't no misunderstandin', and I ain't goin' no-

43

where with *ya'll*," she mocked. "And, I ain't your darlin' *neither*."

Nash's genial smile vanished with his patience. "In that case, are *you* going to go peaceably, or am I going to be forced to remove ya'll bodily?"

"Ain't gonna go peaceably, as you so rudely put it, until you tell those dockworkers to take that cargo to my uncle's boat where it rightly belongs! 'Til then, I aim to stay put right where I am . . . all day and all night if I got to."

"Troublesome female," Nash grumbled. In the wink of an eye, he swooped down and scooped Columbia up into his arms.

Arms and legs flailing, Columbia screeched, "You let go of me, you leech from a frog's back, before I'm forced to really hurt you!"

Nash couldn't help himself, the scrawny little firebrand had not fallen victim to his charm, and wasn't going to give up without a fight. But she was no match for his strength. With little effort he managed to pinion her arms to her sides, stride down the gangplank and over to the frail man bundled up and perched atop a crate laughing at them.

"Does this belong to ya'll?" Nash asked the man.

"I don't belong to no man," Columbia protested.

"She's right," agreed Titus, who was sizing up the man favorably. "No man'll have her."

"Uncle Titus!" Columbia choked out in disbelief. "I don't want no lazy, good-for-nothin' man."

"And no doubt your uncle's right. No man would want ya'll either," Nash announced, and plunked the

44

female down on the crate next to her uncle.

Titus bounded to his feet and thrust out a hand. "Titus Baranoff's the name, sir. And this is my niece Mary Catherine—"

"Columbia," she corrected glumly.

"Hmmph!" Titus sent Columbia a frown, then turned his attention back to the big man. "And who might you be?"

His anger beginning to turn to amusement, Nash took the man's hand. "Nash Foster."

Columbia surged to her feet ready to continue the fight, but before she could give the insufferable man a good tongue-lashing, Titus shushed her. "Hush now, girl, and let me find out where this young fellow hails from. Where you from, Nash?"

"Late of New York."

Titus was impressed by the man's mettle. "You brought that paddle wheeler all the way from New York?"

"Yes. And I plan to make my home here on the river now."

"Yeah, no doubt workin' for John Villamoore, the snake-bellied crook," Columbia grumbled.

"John Villamoore?" Nash questioned.

"He's one of the wealthiest—" Titus began.

"Most low-down, life's bloodsuckin' leeches on this here stretch of the river. And he hires men like you to try 'n' put good honest folk like us out of business, that's what!" Columbia interceded.

For no other reason than to rile the disagreeable female, Nash crinkled his forehead and asked,

45

"This John Villamoore have an office in town?"

"Yeah," Columbia answered with a note of suspicion in her voice.

"Two streets over from the riverfront," Titus supplied.

"Why you askin'?" Columbia demanded.

"Want to know where I might want to sign up."

Chapter Five

Columbia's ears burned, and it wasn't from the winter sun. She could not believe what she was hearing. She had just informed the newcomer about John Villamoore's character, and the man still had a notion to work for him! To make matters worse, her uncle seemed to be openly courting the friendship of the interloper, who had just stolen their cargo right out from under their very noses!

She opened her mouth to lambaste the man, but there was an unsettling presence about him that bothered her, and heated up her cheeks as she took in the handsome face shadowed with the hint of a beard. She glanced away to still such unbidden thoughts, and a sudden question popped into her mind.

"You married?" she blurted out.

The men ceased their conversation and gaped at her. Her uncle was grinning, and Nash Foster scowled at her as if she were some river pig who had just decided she would make a prize log.

"Mary Catherine!"

Columbia ignored her uncle's bellow of amused outrage over such an innocent question, and kept her eyes on the big man. "Well, are you?"

"If ya'll are wondering if I'm available, the answer is no."

"You can wipe that smirk off your face, Foster. I was just askin' 'cause that lady person standin' on deck over there"—she thumbed toward his boat's main deck—"is watchin' over you like some grizzly about to miss out on a coveted salmon spawnin' up-stream."

Nash glanced from Dolly to Titus. The older man had a strange look of disappointment on his face; it was the same look Nash had seen on Markus Kiplinger's face when he'd told the man he wasn't the marrying kind. Well, he'd dash any misplaced matchmaking ideas Titus Baranoff might be harboring!

Nash gave a shrug of nonchalance. "Ya'll giving the little woman cause?"

"Not unless your fancy wife's worried that I'm a high kicker, and aim to do a mite bit of voice-changin' on *ya'll*."

"Mary Catherine Baranoff!" Titus reproved again. "You owe our new friend an apology for such talk."

"Friend? Posh! I'll apologize *after* he unloads our cargo and gets his paddle wheeler out of our rightful spot."

"We are staying, so we might as well make our peace," Nash set in.

"Come on now, Mary Catherine, be reasonable.

48

Nash's new to these parts. It wasn't as if he edged us out, doing Villamoore's bidding. He's got to make a living just like us. We'll get another haul.

Nash listened patiently to the man plead with the pigheaded hellion, amused yet strangely intrigued by such an unconventional female. He was used to women trying to ply their wiles on him or resorting to tears. But the scrawny one before him had attempted to punch him out!

"Let's try this," Nash said in his easy Tennessee drawl. "I will forget that you tried to rearrange my jaw, you accept that I was here first this time, and we shall start all over. Fair enough?" he asked and held out a hand.

Columbia gazed down at the bronzed outstretched hand. It was calloused and rough. Subconsciously, she ran her fingers along her own palm, wondering what it would feel like to feel that rough hand on hers, before she snapped her hand to her side. Quickly dragging her mind back to what he was about, she had no intention of accepting such tactics, but she decided that she could keep a better watch over this latest threat if he thought she was congenial. Begrudgingly, she gave a curt nod and placed her small hand in his large one.

"Just don't go tryin' to steal no more of our business," she warned, and tried to snatch back her hand as the heat from his touch warmed up her innards all the way to her cheeks.

He held tight.

"I intend to compete for a fair share of the com-

49

merce on the river, nothing more," Nash said to re-assure her, and let her rip her hand from his.

The word "compete" caused Columbia to take an-other look at Nash Foster's wife. The woman was a bosomy showy piece, all gussied up in frilly female things peeking out from her fitted coat. Subcon-sciously Columbia ran a hand over her chest under-neath the heavy jacket she wore; it was nearly as flat as the river on a calm day. In comparison, the redhead had an overly well-endowed bosom, a tiny waist, and hips that rounded like GlennieLynn's over generous hourglass. An instant of female jeal-ousy grasped Columbia before she beat down such utter nonsense.

Columbia was still staring at the woman, when the man she'd seen with Nash earlier joined the woman at the rail. He had a pleasant face, not as hard as Nash Foster's. There was an openness about it that made Columbia silently wish he were the captain of the intruding riverboat, since she was sure he would be more pliable.

"Who's that good-lookin' man standin' next to your wife?"

"My first mate."

So the female tough, who was trying to act like a man, wasn't totally impervious to men, as she had sworn. Nash's expression hardened. He thought of all the women he and Barth had wagered on, and a few of the ones Barth had managed to stick him with. Despite a niggling doubt in the back of his mind about the wisdom of what he was about to do, and an instant of jealous annoyance, Nash hailed Barth over. To Nash's dismay, Dolly seemed to take his motion as an invitation, and she also was sauntering down the gangplank with Barth.

In order to stave off Dolly exposing his lie, Nash quickly stepped to her side and ringed an arm around her waist, pulling her against him.

Dolly opened her mouth in surprise at Nash's sudden intimate actions. Then, to add to her bafflement, Nash kissed her, silencing the question on the tip of her tongue.

Before anyone could comment or question, Nash smiled wolfishly and said, "My wife simply cannot get enough of me."

His eyes as round as Dolly's, Barth leaned forward. "Your wife?"

His grin never wavering, Nash offered to the Baranoffs, "Ya'll know we are newlyweds."

Barth and Dolly hid their surprise as Barth offered, "Suppose I'd know about as much about being a newlywed as some people I know."

"You married, too?" Columbia asked.

Barth's hands flew to his chest, and a smile brightened his face. "Not I."

Columbia noticed that his hands were not nearly as big as Foster's. His fingers were shorter and thicker, blunt, and did not elicit the strange sensations in her that Foster's had.

A strange light flickered into Titus's eyes. "Newlyweds. Well, I'll be damned and keel over if you aren't. Congratulations. Although it's too bad you

51

didn't wait for Mary Catherine. She's a mite thick-headed and impetuous at times, but with a little guidance, she'll make good wife material . . . at least I hope she will."

"Uncle Titus!" Columbia hissed, horrified.

Nash chuckled, but he did not like the sparkle in the older man's eyes. It was as if he knew that Nash was not married to Dolly and for some unknown reason it discomforted Nash. In an effort to still the uneasiness, Nash quickly made the rest of the introductions.

"Suppose I'd better let Mary Catherine here drag me off before I make her any madder," Titus announced. "She isn't a pretty sight when she really gets riled. Take my word for it. But you just keep in mind my words, Nash."

"In case I come across someone in need of an overbearing wife with an ill temper, I will."

Fuming inside her jacket, Columbia hauled her uncle away from the recently arrived competitors before Titus could embarrass her further.

Once they were out of earshot, Columbia turned on Titus. "How could you?" she demanded.

"How could I what?"

"How could you *what?* You know very well what. How could you offer me up like I was little more than a cargo barrel . . . and a right difficult one at that!"

"Somebody's got to look out for you, if you aren't going to take care of yourself. The way I figure it, Nash Foster'd make a fine addition to the family."

52

Columbia rolled her eyes as she fought to keep her temper under control. "In case you've lost your hearin', Nash Foster's married to that Dolly person."

Titus leaned forward. "And what if he weren't? Would he catch your fancy, if he were available?"

"Even if the man was the catch of the day, he wouldn't net *my* interest. Too egotistical and arrogant for my taste."

"There you go with those big words again, Mary Catherine," Titus said to further rile her.

"Well, he is. Furthermore, if I was forced to pick between those two strangers, I'd take the other one."

"Whatever for?" Titus asked, totally perplexed. While he found Barth a pleasant enough young man, Titus knew the moment he met the man that he was not strong enough to handle his niece. Mary Catherine would have the poor man doing her bidding inside of a week. The girl needed a man as strong-willed as she was, a man who could keep pace with her and outpace her if need be.

"That Barth seemed much nicer, that's what for. Let's head in to town and see if we can pick up another cargo, since you let Foster cheat us out of our rightly due."

Titus hesitated as a cold rain began to fall. "Why don't you go on without me? My bones are chilled clear through. You always manage better when I'm not along anyway."

"If you want," she returned, concern filling her eyes. "I'll meet you back at the boat as soon as I've found a cargo. When GlennieLynn returns, have her fix you something hot to warm your innards."

Titus leaned against a crate and watched the girl lope along the wharf. He let out a sigh of frustration. Despite all his efforts, there wasn't one thing feminine about Mary Catherine. She dressed like a man, she was too thin, and she had even developed a river rat's swagger in those heavy boots. Her hair was thick and long, and would surely draw a man with its rich luster, but she kept it stuffed under a cap. Titus shook his head and let his gaze drift back toward the paddle wheeler docked in their berth.

Titus scratched his chin as he watched Dolly Foster hurry down the gangplank in his direction. There was something funny about the way Nash Foster had claimed that woman as his bride, and Titus aimed to find out what.

"Mrs. Foster," Titus said as the woman neared him. "May I accompany you into town?"

"S'ppose it'd be all right," Dolly said hesitantly. "I'd be mighty obliged if you'd show me where the nearest mercantile is located."

Titus offered his arm. "My pleasure, ma'am."

As they strolled toward the nearest mercantile, Titus surveyed the woman out of the sides of his eyes. One thing Titus knew was women. And this one was not married. She didn't walk like a married lady, didn't talk like one. She held his arm more like she had just claimed him for the evening, and there was a huntress aura about her.

54

"How long have you been married?" he asked suddenly.

"I'm not married—" Dolly clamped a hand over her mouth.

"I thought as much."

"I mean, we've only been married a short time," she quickly amended in an effort to redeem herself.

A pleased grin swelling his face, Titus patted her arm. "You don't have to pretend with me. I didn't believe that line Nash threw out."

Dolly stopped and turned a serious face to Titus. "Please, you can't say nothing. Nash has treated me right; become like a brother. I can't let him down. If he says we're married, he's got a good reason, and I don't want to wreck nothing for him. Please," she pleaded.

Titus kept his face impassive, but he was smiling brightly inside. "Don't you worry none. I don't have any intention of causing your Nash Foster grief. Quite the contrary. I think that with your help, we could make him a very content and happy man."

"What about your niece?" Dolly asked, confused by all the falsehoods of the morning. She just didn't understand people. Folks never said or did what they meant.

"You can quit worrying. If everything works out the way it ought, my niece will be the first in line to thank us."

"Us?" she said weakly.

"I'll need your help."

"My help," she echoed, not certain she wanted to

hear what the man was about to say.

"With your help, I think that Mary Catherine and Nash will both be happy before either one knows what hit them."

Chapter Six

Through the lightly falling mist, Barth followed Nash back to the wheelhouse. There was a stiff cast to Nash's shoulders, and his strides had lengthened into those of a man who seemed determined to escape some fate he feared would claim him if he didn't move fast enough.

"What are you running from?" Barth called out.

Nash abruptly stopped. When he pivoted around, his face was a study in annoyed anger. His full lips were a mere slash, his eyes scant slits. His hands were balled into tight fists and perched onto his slim hips.

"What the hell are you talking about?" Nash demanded.

Barth recognized the leashed violence in Nash's voice, the tightly controlled temper, and sagely decided that now was not the time to pursue his line of thinking. Prudently, he decided to redirect the question that burned on his tongue. But when he opened his mouth, out came, "You just seem to be in such a hurry, as if you were being chased by someone with a shotgun, is all."

Nash stared at his friend. Barth was not very good at hiding what he was thinking. It reminded Nash of his situation with Kiplinger and his daughter. Nash frowned. Titus Baranoff and his niece were vaguely reminiscent of Kiplinger. Nash shook his head to shake off such an unthinkable parallel.

Nash had left New York to get away from men and their eligible daughters, and he didn't plan to get mixed up in a similar situation again.

Baranoff had something up his sleeve, Nash had seen that look on a man's face before — on Kiplinger's when he had decided to force Nash to marry his daughter.

"What are you getting at?" Nash asked Barth darkly.

Barth shrugged. "Nothing, really."

"Well then, why don't you let me be about my business, while you supervise the rest of the unloading and hire on enough men to make a full crew."

"But what do you plan to do?" Barth asked before he thought better of it. "The ship needs repairs."

"The repairs can wait. If you must know, I plan to change my clothes and go see a certain man about hauling cargo on a regular basis — that is our business, I believe."

"Villamoore?"

"What if it is?"

"He the kind of man you want to get mixed up with again?"

Barth had been listening to the conversation Nash had had with the girl and her uncle shortly before he had joined them. He silently wondered why Nash would seek out someone who sounded like Kiplinger's type of man. Just the little he'd heard made Barth think that Villamoore meant nothing but trouble. And trouble was the last thing they needed more of right now.

"I did not say I plan to get mixed up with him," Nash snapped.

"But you said you wanted to see Villamoore about hauling cargo."

"Hauling a few loads regularly, 'til we get on our feet, does not constitute getting mixed up, as you put it."

"Just be careful, my friend."

Nash threw back his head and laughed at the irony of it. "Aren't I always?"

Nash nodded and pivoted around, tucking his jacket collar further up around his neck as he started toward the dockworkers. "Hell, Nash," Barth mumbled to himself, "if you had been careful, we wouldn't be out here in no-man's-land right now."

"Where the hell is this no-man's-land?" Markus Kiplinger hissed.

"Oregon Territory," Lester Cowan reminded the distinguished older man.

"Yes, this damned Oregon Territory," Markus Kiplinger echoed, and let his eyes roam over the map of the United States that he kept on the wall in his richly appointed cabin. He knew his geography, but wanted to test Cowan.

Lester moved to the map and traced the route they were taking around the tip of South America. Silently he tried to figure out Kiplinger's motives. Markus Kiplinger was not the kind of man to go chasing around the world simply because his daughter had been jilted, regardless of the murky circumstances surrounding it.

Kiplinger had to have other reasons, and Lester was going to cut himself in on it, if at all possible. Getting even with Foster after the humiliation he had suffered at the big Southerner's hands made him firm his resolve to endure the infernal ocean voyage, just to see the look on Foster's face when "the little problem" he'd left behind caught up with him.

"You had better be correct that this is where Foster headed, or you'll come to regret it," Markus warned.

Lester's hand stretched around his thick neck and he unconsciously fingered the loose skin there. "That's where he was headed. The last time he was sighted by the navy, he was traveling south along the coast. Furthermore, that letter you got from some woman claiming to be traveling with Foster bears out my information."

"Well, you had better be correct." Markus rubbed his hands together, his eyes gleaming with the anticipation of one expecting to find the gold at the end of the rainbow. "When we catch up with Foster, I am—"

60

"You are *what*, Daddy?" Jennifer Kiplinger questioned and swished into the cabin, her pink satin skirts rustling at her ankles.

Lester let his eyes secretly rove over the young woman. What a fine piece she was, despite her pouty lips. His eyes settled on her full ripe breasts. His fingers itched to feel the lush velvety skin, and he understood why Foster had been unable to resist the rich young woman's charms. He chuckled to himself. He wouldn't have been able to resist her either. Only he would have been more careful.

Markus opened his arms and she walked into them. "Ah, Jennifer child." He stroked her silken blond tresses. "I am glad to see you are feeling better. Where is Ely?"

"He is sleeping," she said, and stepped out of her father's embrace to gaze out the porthole before she turned back to stare at her father. She had reasons of her own for consenting to come along. "Please do not be tiresome, Daddy dear, you still have not answered my question about what you plan to do with Nash Foster."

"You have only to consider what he did to you to know what I am planning for Foster. When I am done with that man, he will rue the day, or shall I say night, that he thought he could walk out on you and get away with it."

She heaved a plaintive sigh. "But it has been over a year."

"I don't give a damn if it takes ten years. Nash Foster is going to make you a contented and very happy wife, if I have to kill him to do it."

61

* * *

The thought of killing Nash Foster flashed into Columbia's mind as she watched the man swing open the door to John Villamoore's office and swagger inside. Swagger. There was no other word for it. The man had wasted no time heading directly to the competition the moment he thought she was out of sight.

Feeling strangely betrayed, Columbia took a buoying breath and stomped across the street toward the two-storied building housing Villamoore's plush office. She hadn't the foggiest notion what she was going to do. But she was not going to let Villamoore and his newest henchman get away with ruining her shipping business!

Columbia burst through the door, expecting to find Villamoore and Foster engaged in some kind of shenanigans. What she found was an elegantly furnished outer office filled with heavy mahogany furniture and nautical memorabilia. Determined to catch the two, she opened the door on the left. A closet. She went to the door on the right and creaked it open.

The room was empty.

Her gaze caught on an ornate desk cluttered with papers. Thinking she could come up with some evidence to put a stop to John Villamoore's quest to gain a monopoly on the river (by destroying competitors' boats or laying up the captains), Columbia did not give any thought to the possibility of his return, as she went right to his desk and began rummaging through the documents.

The door handle clicked, and Columbia froze at the sound of voices on the other side of the door.

"What do you think, Foster? We could be good for each other. I could make you a rich man, if you throw in with me," John Villamoore was saying as he let Nash Foster into his office.

The door creaked open and Columbia dropped to the floor. From her position under Villamoore's desk, Columbia's eyes rounded as she watched the meticulously cleaned boots which had to belong to Villamoore and the well-worn boots belonging to Foster head her way. Instead of remaining hidden and gaining the advantage of knowing what the two men were planning, Columbia impulsively sprang from her position, bumping her head in the process.

"Ouch!" she yelped as she popped up.

"What the hell!" Villamoore snarled, swirling around to catch sight of the annoying Baranoff female. Two strides and he was grabbing her arms, digging his manicured fingers into the bony flesh. "What are you doing in my office?"

He shook her until she thought her brain was going to be scrambled, but she refused to give him the courtesy of an answer.

"I said what are you do—"

Suddenly the shaking ceased, and Columbia's mouth dropped open as she watched, dumbfounded, while Foster yanked Villamoore back and gave the skinny man a shove.

"Don't believe in manhandling the fairer sex," Foster said in that Southern drawl.

Outraged, a waxy-faced Villamoore brushed off his monogrammed shirtfront and straightened his fine jacket. With barely contained hatred in his voice, he sneered, "She is the little problem I was telling you about. Just look at her. Dressed like a river ruffian. I'd hardly call her a member of the fairer sex."

"Does not matter."

Feeling more secure, Columbia self-consciously wiped her sweaty palms on her trousers and stepped forward. A triumphant smile on her lips, she picked a piece of lint off Villamoore's shoulder, examining it carefully. "I think he means it, Villamoore, you belly-low water snake. Better keep your hands off—"

The next thing she knew, before she could finish lambasting Villamoore, Columbia found herself being rudely escorted from the room. She flung her elbow back and braced herself to face down this latest attack.

"Just whose side are you on?" she demanded.

"I am not on anybody's side, as ya'll put it. I am here to see about getting a cargo to haul, and ya'll are interrupting our negotiations. So I suggest ya'll leave before I am forced to step back and allow Mr. Villamoore to toss you out of his private office," Nash said with a curve to his lips.

"Or get the sheriff to throw you in jail," Villamoore added.

"Or toss ya'll in jail," Nash reiterated to Columbia's scowl.

Columbia bit her lip to keep from letting out a string of expletives she'd picked up on the wharf.

She had been right in her first judgment of the big riverboat captain. He was one of Villamoore's henchman.

"No need to get the sheriff. I'll go. But you'd better not try to steal any more of my loads, Foster." She looked around Foster to glare at Villamoore. "And that goes for you and your other henchmen, too."

Her piece said, Columbia garnered all the dignity she had left and strolled from the offices.

"I was beginning to wonder about you for a moment, Foster. But I guess since you're new in town, you aren't aware of the way things work around here. Columbia and her uncle are troublemakers. They want things to remain the way they were years ago. They don't want to accept that I'm bringing progress to this area . . ."

Nash kept his face impassive as he listened to Villamoore drone on about the trouble Columbia Baranoff and her uncle were causing. Nash was sure that a portion of what the man was saying had some truth to it, but Nash didn't like the way the man had treated the girl. No gentleman roughed up a female the way Villamoore had done. Nash wouldn't allow that, regardless of who the man thought he was. But their problems weren't his fight. He'd had enough of getting involved in other folks' battles, and planned to stay out of this one.

Chapter Seven

For over an hour Columbia trudged from one office to the next, trying to round up a cargo to replace the one that that scoundrel Nash Foster had cheated her out of. Disgusted but not discouraged, she returned to the paddle wheeler without a haul.

Columbia went to her cabin and began stripping off her wet jacket.

"It's about time you returned, Mary Catherine," Titus said from his position lounging on her narrow bed. He drew himself up on an elbow. "I thought perhaps you met up with that good-looking young man, Nash Foster, and decided to mend your ways."

Columbia rolled her eyes. "Nash Foster. Posh! I ran into him all right. He was in John Villamoore's office, and they were plannin' to cheat us out of our rightful contracts."

His face paling, Titus came off the bed at the idea of Columbia nosing around Villamoore's, and a troubled light flickered into his eyes. "What were you doing in Villamoore's office? I thought I told you to stay away from that man."

"I saw that new friend of yours, Nash Foster, go into Villamoore's office." She snorted. "What else could I do? I followed him. I thought maybe I could catch those two cookin' up something illegal."

Titus threw up his hands. "And what if you *had* caught them? You could have been hurt or worse, girl."

"Villamoore tried to manhandle me, but Foster stopped him."

A small grin grew on Titus's face. "I know a good man when I see one."

"Not so fast. Foster ended up tossin' me out of Villamoore's office. Uncle Titus, the varmint has contracted to haul Villamoore's cargo after I told him what kind of lowdown, cheatin' snake Villamoore is. That is the kind of man Nash Foster is."

Titus listened to Mary Catherine criticize Foster. The more he heard, the more he liked the man and came to realize that Foster could be the one man in the territory who could indeed tame his niece's wild ways. Of course, Titus would have to force himself to spend more time with that good-looking Dolly, just to make sure that Foster would truly make the best choice. His cheeks warmed. It would be a sacrifice, but Mary Catherine was worth it.

"You look like your mind is faraway. And from the look of your flushed cheeks, it's someplace warm. What're you grinnin' for?" Columbia demanded, breaking into Titus's musings over the buxom Dolly.

He snapped his attention back to the stubborn girl. "I was just thinking that perhaps this Nash Foster bears watching, is all."

"I was thinkin' the same thing, Uncle Titus."

"Good. Good." Titus rejoiced. "Because I have a plan that will allow us to keep a close watch over the man."

Columbia perched on her bed and crossed her legs, leaning forward in anticipation of finally catching Villamoore. She had been disappointed in Foster, but no one was going to stand in her way. Especially not the handsome stranger.

"Don't keep me guessin'. What's this plan of yours?"

"You always were one to thrill to the hunt," Titus remarked. He wondered at the primitive huntress instinct the girl possessed.

"Then get to the tellin' and quit toyin' with me. What's your plan?"

A fleeting glimpse of disaster rolled before his eyes, before he managed to quell the foreboding vision in his mind. "Frank McGee came to see me after you left. Said that there was crew jobs open on Foster's paddle wheeler—"

"How could he!" she interrupted with a note of betrayal in her voice. "I thought Frank was our friend. He's showin' to be no better than a low-down—"

"Calm down, girl. Frank is our friend. That's why he came to warn me that Foster is offering top wages. Frank hoped that we could get underway before some of the men heard about the pay and we lost them. You know that some of the men have to think about their families. They've got mouths to feed."

"I know," she admitted with a tinge of unspoken defeat in her tone. She couldn't begrudge the men with families to feed the chance to earn more money.

"Well, as I started to say, Foster is hiring, so I've been thinking." He turned his head, but continued to watch her reactions from under the rim of his sparse lashes. "Since we don't have a cargo, why don't I hire on with Foster, so I can keep an eye on him? If he slips up, we'll have him dead to rights if I'm on board."

Titus turned to observe the mischievous gleam flicker into Columbia's eyes. He smiled to himself. She was undoubtedly thinking exactly what he had hoped she would. All he had to do now was set the hook he had been dangling in front of her nose.

"It's hard work, but catching Villamoore will be worth the sacrifice."

"It would, wouldn't it?" she mumbled, her mind working furiously.

He gave a nonchalant lift to his shoulders. "That's what I said."

"Then you agree?"

"Of course, I agree, it was my idea," Titus said. He had to be careful; he had given her enough line, now he hoped that she would jump into the net before she realized she had been baited.

Columbia got off the bed and paced back and forth across the threadbare throw rug. "It's a great idea—with one exception."

Titus cocked a brow, trying to present a troubled question on his thin face. "An exception?"

"Yes. I aim to be the one who's gonna become the crew member."

"No!" he protested with just the right amount of outrage in his voice.

"Don't be difficult, Uncle Titus. You know you ain't strong enough to do what needs doin'. Besides, you been under the weather lately. You'd never be able to keep up the charade long enough to get the evidence to stop Villamoore. And furthermore, you're needed here on board. We're sure to get another cargo soon, and you can keep our business goin', while I take care of Villamoore and his latest henchman."

Titus let Columbia work a little longer to convince him, before he relented with a sigh of defeat. "I suppose you are right, for once. My health isn't what it should be. All right, I'll allow you to be the one to go, but only if you promise to be very careful."

A triumphant smile lighting up her face, Columbia crossed her heart. "I promise. And don't you worry none. Nash Foster won't know what's hit him."

"Neither will you, if everything works out the way I've planned," Titus whispered to his feet.

"Beggin' your pardon?"

"I was just saying that I hope everything goes according to plan."

"It will. Now, I'd better get my gear together, if

I'm gonna get myself hired before Foster has a full crew."

Titus picked up her duffel bag and handed it to her. "I've already taken the liberty of packing for you."

Columbia quirked her lips, feeling that somehow she had just been manipulated by the old dear. But that was silly. She had been the one who had insisted on signing aboard Foster's boat. She changed her jacket and cap to help disguise herself. "I'll be back in less than a week. His first run for Villamoore shouldn't take longer than that. Keep an eye out for another haul while I'm gone. And stay out of trouble," she advised.

"You'd be wise to heed your own advice." He gave her a peck on the cheek and watched her leave, hoping that the spark he thought he'd seen flash between the girl and Foster would ignite. And he prayed that the girl wouldn't be burned by it.

Columbia breathed a sigh of relief as she stowed her bag in the crews' quarters on Foster's boat. Foster's first mate had been so harried, that he hadn't given her a second look when she swaggered on board and announced that big Frank McGee had sent her. He'd seemed so grateful to finish rounding out the crew that she had to smile at her ingenuity. A little grease, her hair hidden beneath an old cap, and her roomiest jacket padded here and there, had been all it took to disguise herself. It was going to be easier than she'd figured to fool Foster.

"What do you think you're doing down here?" boomed a loud voice from the portal.

Columbia's head snapped around. Nash Foster stood framed in the doorway, a big hand grasping each side of the doorjamb. He filled the space with his broad shoulders and long, muscular thighs, and his head nearly touched the top edge of the door frame.

"Just stowin' my gear." She turned and hurriedly stuffed her bag into her cramped corner, then shifted uneasily from one foot to the next under the big man's scrutiny.

"Well, what are ya'll waiting for? Get topside and start working for your pay, or I shall be forced to replace you."

No wonder he was offering top wages. He was a slave master! Just the type of man Villamoore would select, she thought, as she bit her tongue to keep from retorting, lowered her eyes, and scrambled past him.

Nash cocked a brow as he watched the youth clamber toward the deck. There was something strangely familiar about the lad. Nash dismissed the funny feeling. This was the first time that he'd had a full crew since leaving New York, and Nash did not intend to leave port shorthanded. Villamoore had offered a nice fat bonus if Nash could get the cargo to Lower Cascades and return with a cargo Villamoore was anxiously awaiting, and Nash intended to collect.

Thinking how he would finally be able to pay Dolly and the men the money he owed them, Nash followed the young boy.

Up on deck the hands were busy lashing down the additional crates they had loaded. Nash was watching the men when Barth joined him. "Villamoore sure jumped at the chance to hire you. Don't you think that's a little suspect, considering that we are new in town?"

"Actually, Columbia Baranoff showed up and cinched the deal for me. Villamoore was so impressed by the way I removed her from his office—that is after he calmed down—"

"Calmed down?"

"He tried to manhandle the girl." Nash thought how thin her arm had been. A sudden thought hit him, and his observant gaze shifted to the lad that he'd spied lagging in the crews' quarters.

"You never were one to stand idly by and allow that," Barth said, thinking how Nash had often taken bruises championing the other children at the foundling home.

"You know me too well, my friend."

"You've got a soft spot for underdogs."

Nash scratched his chin, realization dawning on him. "Columbia Baranoff could hardly be called an underdog. Hellion I think would be more appropriate for that scrapper." Mention of Columbia Baranoff caused him to scrutinize the lean young lad closer. "Where did you find that scrawny lad down there struggling with that barrel?"

Barth's eyes honed in on the boy, and he shrugged. "He found me actually. Said Frank McGee sent him."

"I just bet *he* did."

"If you're afraid he can't pull his weight, I'll let him go before he thinks his position is secure."

Barth started to leave the rail, but Nash placed a staying hand on his friend's arm. "No. I think I just might have the perfect position to use the boy's talents to the fullest. Go down and bring him to me."

Barth wondered at the calculating glimmer in Nash's eyes, but simply said, "Sure, Nash."

Nash watched Barth swing down the stairs and head toward his latest crew member. When the boy looked up in Nash's direction, any doubt he had about what he'd suspected vanished. He'd recognize those angry turquoise eyes anywhere.

His newest crew member was none other than Mary Catherine Columbia Baranoff.

Nash watched Columbia gesture as she was obviously arguing with Barth. A beleaguered Barth glanced up at Nash. So he was having a difficult time with her. Nash waved them up. He'd teach that darn fool girl to try and sneak aboard his paddle wheeler.

But as he watched her stomp up the stairs, Nash couldn't help but hold a grudging respect for the little fool. Although misplaced, her determination was admirable. And despite himself, Nash's opinion of the girl rose.

"You wanted to see me?" Columbia said in a dry gravelly voice, and kept her eyes glued to the floorboards. "I got work to do."

Nash kept his expression indifferent. "I have been watching you . . ."

Columbia's heart sank. She'd been found out.

". . . and I think I have a better position for the likes of you."

"I ain't seekin' no special treatment," Columbia said, anxious to get away from the big captain. He made a lump of trepidation form in the pit of her stomach, just being near him. "I'll just go back to work."

"You will go back to work. But not with the rest of the crew. I want you to serve as my personal cabin boy."

Chapter Eight

"Your personal cabin boy?" Columbia echoed in disbelief, as the lump of apprehension grew to massive portions in her stomach.

Nash puffed out his chest. He was secretly enjoying her discomfort, as he waited for her to unmask herself and leave his paddle wheeler in defeat. "I have always wanted a personal servant who will sleep in my cabin and tend to my every whim, regardless of the hour."

"Your every whim?" She said each word distinctly, considering what that could entail.

"Every whim I deem desirable." That should take care of Miss Mary Catherine Columbia Baranoff, Nash thought.

"You a whimsical man?"

"Ya'll have quite a vocabulary for a deckhand."

"My ma and pa taught me well. And I read a mite, too," Columbia said in her own defense.

Barth had remained silent in the background, but he now choked on the very thought that Nash suddenly wanted a cabin boy to coddle him. Nash was one of the most independent men Barth had ever known. Even during their years in the South, Nash had steadfastly refused to own slaves, saying that no man should be made to cater to the whims of another.

Barth glanced back and forth at the pair. For some unknown reason, there was a crackling tension in the air. At first he thought to question what was going on between the two. Then he consulted his better judgment and decided that the wise man made himself scarce at times such as these. Nash must have a reason for what he was doing. Barth decided it would be smart to remove himself. He'd find out later what motives drove his friend.

Columbia kept her stare directed at Foster, ignoring the retreat of his first mate. If Foster thought he was going to force her to leave so easily — when she was within days of finally getting something on John Villamoore — Foster was sorely mistaken.

"What about your wife? Will she want me sleepin' in the cabin with the two of you? It could be embarrassin' with the three of us cramped up in there."

"Or more interesting," he set out to taunt her, as her turquoise eyes turned more green in hue.

"I don't abide none of those types of shenanigans."

Nash had forgotten about the story he'd made up about Dolly and him, and he silently cursed such a tactical error. "Ya'll can quit worrying. I like my privacy when I make love to a woman," he announced in a husky voice, which caused two bright spots of color to rise on her cheeks and her eyes to darken further.

"Have you made love to a lot of women?"

Nash shrugged. "My share, I suppose."

She wasn't sure quite how to respond to the openness of his answer, so she shrugged and said, "Oh."

"Then it is settled?"

"You ain't said where your wife'll be layin' her head. I don't intend to come between a man and his wife, no matter where you want me to sleep."

He had to give her credit, she was inventive. "My wife will be sleeping in her own cabin. Seasickness, you know."

"I ain't gonna accept the job if I got to clean up after a sick female," Columbia stated flatly, keeping her voice low.

"Don't worry, the job is to fulfill my needs, not to take care of my wife's. It will just be you and me in my tiny little cabin," he added, to give her something else to think about.

"Just you and me?"

"That is what I said. It will just be us boys."

"Just us boys."

"You have a problem with that?"

"No, no, of course not."

Columbia took a deep breath and curled her fingers into her palms behind her back. She'd do what had to be done. After all, she had planned on sleeping in the crews' quarters. Sleeping in the same room with just one man ought to be easier than sleeping in a room with a dozen. And being a cabin boy should be a snap, shouldn't it?

"Where do I stow my gear?"

Nash's triumphant smirk faded. The little fool was

more obstinate . . . or more foolhardy than he'd thought.

"My cabin is the one on the end. You can start by shining my boots after ya'll settle in."

Columbia sucked back the rebuttal on the tip of her tongue, reminding herself that she would have the last laugh when she watched the sheriff arrest Villamoore and Foster. Columbia gave a curt nod and shuffled toward the crews' quarters, but that resonant baritone drawl stopped her in her tracks not more than two dozen steps from him.

What now? she wanted to cry out, but pivoted around in silence to await his command.

"What do they call ya'll?" Nash questioned. He wondered what ingenious answer she was going to come up with.

"Col . . . ah . . . Columbus," she blurted for wont of a better name.

"Columbus." Nash had to fight to keep from laughing at the girl's aptitude to think quickly on her feet.

Columbia sucked in her cheeks. "And what's wrong with it?"

"Nothing. It just seems that that is a mighty big name for such a runt. Maybe I out to call ya'll Collie instead. Suits your shaggy appearance."

Columbia stood fuming at the pleasure he seem to be deriving at her expense. But she managed to leash her tongue.

"What are ya'll standing there for? Get going. You've got lots of work to do," he said, and dismissed her with the turn of his back.

Columbia stood and glared at the broad shoulders

and thick neck for a moment, mentally measuring him for a noose. Then she made her way to the crews' quarters, reclaimed her duffel bag, and went to the captain's cabin.

She stowed her few possessions and then dragged all his boots out of the small wardrobe. She had just set about the disagreeable task when Foster's wife entered in all her frilly tan-colored finery.

"Nash, I—" Dolly drew up abruptly and stared at Columbia.

Columbia frowned at the buxom woman. For some unnamed reason, Columbia had taken an instant dislike to the woman and the way that Foster embraced and kissed her. Right now she resented the woman's presence.

"Who are you?" Dolly questioned, surprised to see someone in Nash's cabin. Her keen eyes studied the stranger sitting with knees bent to the side in the middle of the floor, surrounded by Nash's boots.

"I'm the new cabin boy," Columbia grumbled in her most masculine voice.

"That's absurd. How can you be the new cabin boy, when you are obviously of the female persuasion?"

Columbia crossed her arms and glowered at the observant woman. For all her apparent look of ignorance, the woman was a far sight too perceptive. Columbia squirmed on the floor, wrinkling her nose in disdain.

"You must've got your genders mixed up, lady. My name is Columbus and I'm the new cabin boy," Columbia said in an attempt to salvage her cover.

Dolly toyed with her full lips for a minute, as if she were experiencing a moment of uncertainty. "I may not be full of book learning, but I know men. And you aren't one of 'em," she insisted.

Dolly took a closer look, perusing the girl's fine features, her tiny hands, and the slight swell of her bosom outlined beneath her jacket. "Now I recognize you. You're the one from that other paddle wheeler, the one Nash nearly rammed, the girl he had to remove from his gangplank."

Columbia jumped to her feet, unsure whether she should knock the woman on the head and stash her in Nash's wardrobe, or toss her overboard before the woman went to Nash and unmasked her. But whatever she decided to do, one thing was certain: Columbia was no longer going to be able to convince the woman that she was a man. The woman must have known more than her share of men, if she could recognize Columbia as a female after barely more than one glance.

Her protective female instincts caught hold of Dolly and she took a threatening step toward the girl. "Just what are you up to?" she demanded.

Columbia had to think fast. She obviously could not carry through with her first inclinations. She had to come up with an explanation that would satisfy Nash's wife, so Dolly wouldn't unveil Columbia's masquerade before she succeeded in stopping Villamoore.

An idea popped into her head just as the woman was about to grab her arm. Columbia flung her arm out of reach and stepped back. "All right, I'll tell you,

81

if you promise to keep my secret."

The tension in Dolly eased and she relaxed her stance. "This had best be good, or I'm going directly to Nash and unmask you."

"All right. All right. Sit down and I'll let you in on what I'm up to."

Dolly settled next to where the girl had plunked down on the narrow bed and crossed her arms, impatiently drumming her fingers on her forearms as she waited for the girl to offer some kind of reasonable explanation that would satisfy her.

"I'm waiting," Dolly prodded with impatience.

"If you must know, I took the job on board so I could be near Barth. If I'm gonna catch his eye as a female, I figured I'd have a better shot at it if I got to know what he was truly like. You know, what he likes and dislikes."

"Barth?" Dolly said, incredulous. She had seen the way the girl had looked at Nash. Her uncle had mentioned the same thing and sought Dolly's help. Of course she had ultimately declined her assistance, although she had promised not to mention his request. "But if you wanted to be near Barth, why did you sign up as Nash's cabin boy?"

"This wasn't my idea."

Dolly looked unconvinced. "And just whose idea was it then, pray tell?"

"Foster's."

"Oh. I see." Dolly raised an eyebrow as she thoroughly digested what the girl had said. One thing Dolly understood was the crazy things women did when they were smitten with a man; she'd done a few silly things in her day, too. So, despite a promise to protect Nash and Barth with her life, she found herself sympathetic to a fellow sister's lovesick plight.

Dolly remembered all her partners. Barth hadn't been her first lover, but he had shown her the difference between merely using her body to satiate his lust, and concern for her as a woman. Nash had done the same, the one time she had been with him. So Dolly would have understood if it had been either man that the girl was enamored with.

"You prefer Barth over Nash?" she asked. She still had a difficult time accepting the girl's choice, after the way she had looked at Nash.

"Of course," Columbia said, confused that the woman could even consider that she would take an interest in a married man. Yet a funny sensation filled her gut at the question. "Foster is your man."

"Oh. Oh, yes. Nash is my husband, isn't he."

The two women stared at each other for long silent moments, as if they were contestants judging the other's mettle, until Columbia could no longer endure the suspense.

"You ain't gonna expose me, are you?"

"Can't say that I think what you're doing is wise, but one thing I understand is the outrageous things a woman'll do when she thinks she's in love. So, just as long as you don't cause no trouble, I won't say nothing."

Columbia was so overjoyed that she had managed to gain a cohort, she lurched over to Dolly, threw her arms around her neck, and hugged her. "Thank you. I assure you, you're doin' the right thing."

"I truly hope so."

Dolly pulled back and delved into the girl's bright turquoise eyes. They were clouded, as if she were hiding something. A moment ago when they had been discussing Nash, the girl's eyes had been more green. Dolly wondered if it was Nash that the girl truly was interested in deep down, and was afraid to acknowledge it since she thought Nash to be a married man. At that moment Dolly made a rash decision to spend time with the girl and ferret out the truth. It seemed the only thing to do after the talk she'd had with Titus Baranoff.

Dolly got up and straightened her sprigged skirt. "Guess I'd better leave you to your work. Nash can be a real perfectionist at times. Wouldn't want to cause you no trouble. But I'll come back later and give you a few pointers on how to catch Barth's interest, once you are yourself again."

"Thanks," Columbia said weakly, and returned to her work polishing Nash's scuffed boots.

Columbia hummed to herself, thinking that she had gained an accomplice, although an unwitting one at that.

A sudden twinge of guilt possessed her. She didn't like to use people. She'd always believed in honesty. Yet she figured that it was for a good cause. If she could rid the river of John Villamoore, it was worth doing what had to be done, even if it meant misusing her new friendship with Foster's wife.

But Columbia didn't have any female friends, and an unforeseen feeling of regret encapsulated her.

Chapter Nine

Columbia finished the last pair of Foster's boots and tucked them back in the wardrobe. She looked around the tidy room. To her surprise it was decorated very much like her own cabin. She stepped to the framed likenesses on the wall. It was a group picture of a dozen young boys, none of them smiling, and Columbia wondered if Nash were one of those unhappy little souls.

She moved about the room, fingering Nash's possessions. They told her about the man called Nash Foster. He was a meticulous man with few possessions, obviously used to traveling where the currents and his whims took him. Surprisingly, there were no feminine reminders of his wife. Only one daguerreotype of an attractive young blonde tucked in the bottom of a drawer. Her pa had kept many mementos of her ma. And Columbia wondered what kind of man didn't seem to cherish the small expressions of his life together with his wife.

After picking through his things a little longer, she

was drawn back to the picture of the young boys with haunted eyes staring out at her. She was running her fingers over the troubling likenesses, when she suddenly sensed a presence in the room with her.

"I see ya'll are living up to your name," Nash observed.

Columbia swung around, wondering how long he had been standing there leaning against the inside of the door. His face was closed, a dark mask. "Whaddya mean?"

"Just like your namesake, Christopher Columbus, ya'll have been exploring. Only I warn you, ol' Chris was lucky they found land when they did, or he would have been forced to deal with a serious insurrection."

"Then should I keep lookin' till I make a discovery, or perhaps find land?" Columbia laughed halfheartedly, trying to lighten the sudden dark mood stifling the atmosphere.

"I don't know what ya'll think you're looking for, but if you're not careful, land is exactly what ya'll will find, because I'll kick your scrawny backside off this paddle wheeler if I catch you *exploring* again."

Columbia frowned. She did not want to give him call to get suspicious. "Sorry. I just like to know who I'm workin' for, is all. Take that there likeness," she said, motioning to the group of forlorn children in the sepia-colored daguerreotype. "Looks like those boys weren't very happy gettin' their picture took."

Nash stepped to her side, and stared at the photo for a moment before he turned to Columbia. "No, they weren't," he said in a taut, low rumble.

She wanted to question him further, since it was apparent the photo held some hidden connection with the man who was Nash Foster. But she held her tongue. Her new position on board his paddle wheeler was tenuous at best, and she had a mission to accomplish.

"I got all your boots done," she said weakly.

Nash's mood seemed to lighten as the topic shifted away from his sorry childhood. He strode to the bed, plunked down, and crossed his ankles. "Maybe ya'll will prove useful after all. I'm ready for some food."

"Sounds good. I could down a whole salmon myself, my gut's so empty," she said.

"You? Who said anything about it being time for *ya'll* to eat?" Her eyes darkened, and Nash could tell she was upset with him. Those eyes were proving to be a good indicator of her inner feelings; they gave her away even when her face didn't. He decided goading her a little further would take her mind off whatever she was after. "Part of your job is to fetch my meals. Ya'll eat after I'm taken care of."

"Like a faithful dog waitin' for scraps from the table," she grumbled.

He smiled brightly, and for some reason Columbia's chest constricted.

"I never thought of it that way before. I've never owned a dog, but I must say this has possibilities."

Her chest relaxed at the implication and her nerves tightened. "Just remember, dogs bite."

"But not the hand that feeds them."

"Only if they get their bellies filled regularly and at the proper time."

"Well then, what are ya'll waiting for? Go fetch my meal, before you can no longer fight the urge to gnaw on something."

Columbia would have liked nothing better than to have bared her teeth at him at that moment, the arrogant man! But remembering why she'd come, Columbia nodded tightly and turned toward the door.

"Oh, and I want something hot and hearty."

"Hot and hearty," she echoed. It was a cold misty day, and thoughts of something hot and hearty caused her stomach to growl.

He sent her a wry, suggestive grin. "Just like I like my women."

Columbia slammed the door behind her so hard that it shook the hinges. She stomped off in search of his hot meal, giving free rein to her thoughts of how nice it would be to return with a scalding bowl of soup and proceed to dump it in his lap.

From a hidden distance, Dolly waited until she saw the girl head toward the galley before she hurried down the corridor and knocked at Nash's door. A gruff voice bade her enter and she slipped inside.

Nash's wily grin slid from his lips when he noted that it was Dolly instead of Columbia, and a pique of disappointment spread through his veins. "Oh, it's you," he said with a barely audible sigh.

"Who were you hoping for, your new cabin boy?" she asked, silently speculating at the displeasure she'd noted in his tone.

"Why would I be hoping it was my cabin boy? I just sent him to fetch my meal," he said gruffly.

"Why indeed."

He sat up, his back stiff. "What do ya'll want, Dolly?"

"Actually I came to ask about your new cabin boy," she said gingerly. She was on shaky ground and she knew it.

"What about him?"

She watched the hooded emotions fade to tempered annoyance. All the years she'd spent servicing men now served her well. Despite Nash's refusal to openly discuss the cabin boy with her, she could sense the bridled tension in him.

"I was just wondering why you hired a personal cabin boy. Barth told me that you plan to use the boy to fulfill your whims."

"So?"

She fidgeted with her fingernails. Just one frown from the formidable Nash Foster could be intimidating. It was evident that Nash had no intention of sharing his motivation with her. But Dolly had told the girl she would help her, and she had to manage to keep Nash from finding out the truth.

Despite her trepidation, she met his hooded gaze. "It doesn't seem like you, is all. In all the time I've knowed you, you've done for yourself. Now suddenly, you need some mere boy to do your errands."

The woman looked absolutely ill at ease, and Nash considered for a moment that she knew something she was not sharing with him. But, of course, that was foolish. He was the only one on board who knew the truth about his so-called cabin boy. "Maybe this is the first time I have had the luxury of being able to have someone else take care of the details of my

89

life. Ya'll need not worry about Columbus, I do not plan to beat him or anything."

"Columbus?"

"My new cabin boy."

"What about sleeping arrangements?" she blurted before thinking.

"What about them? He will sleep in here with me."

"With you?" Her voice broke.

Impatience was taking hold of Nash. "Oh, for heavensakes, he will be sleeping on the floor."

"Like some dog?"

Nash thought it a strange analogy, since he and Columbia had been discussing the canine population only a few moments ago. But he dismissed her strange concern as the result of having a soft heart. "Dolly, ya'll can quit worrying about the boy. He will be fine."

"I certainly hope so," she whispered.

She stood rooted to the flooring, trying to absorb what was really happening. But it was too confusing. She decided to continue to watch and wait, unless her interference was warranted.

"Is there anything else you wanted?" he asked, changing the subject.

"I — No, I — I suppose not."

She turned to leave, but as she grabbed the doorhandle it twisted. Dolly jumped back. Columbia entered, carrying a heavy tray ladened with an enormous meal.

For an instant their eyes met. Columbia's eyes darkened into an accusatory glare, before lightening to a vigilant turquoise. Dolly winked, which seemed to put the girl at ease.

"Welcome aboard, Columbus," Dolly said, cast a glance back at Nash, and was about to execute a quick exit when a silken male baritone stopped her.

"Why don't ya'll take your meal with me, wife? Looks like Columbus has brought enough for a whole fleet."

Columbia burned inside. She had indeed brought enough for a fleet. Uncle Titus had often been amazed at the amount of food she was able to pack away, and the fleet Columbia had in mind was her own stomach.

Again the two women's gazes caught. Columbia's eyes were filled with hunger, and Dolly wondered whether it was physical hunger or a hunger of another kind, a more potent craving.

"Well, if you're sure you'd like company?" Dolly finally said.

"Why would I not want my wife to dine with me, my little sea urchin?"

Your little sea urchin, indeed! "And I suppose you're her precious sea enemy," Columbia blurted before she could hold her tongue.

Nash forced back a smile and kept his face straight. "I believe it is sea *anemone*."

"I wouldn't be so sure," Columbia grumbled to herself, as she set the tray up for the pair. She stepped back, but Foster hailed her to the table and had the audacity to order her to cut bite-size pieces of the fish for him.

Columbia pretended she had the knife to Foster's throat as she sliced up the filet. "Are you sure you wouldn't like me to eat it for you, too, *sir*," she said much too sweetly.

Nash smiled just as sweetly. "No, I think I can manage that part. It smells delicious."

He turned his attention to his plate, and she was forced to watch in dismay as Nash and Dolly devoured the entire sturgeon and the potatoes she had lugged from the galley.

Nash looked up and caught the longing scowl on her face. "Oh dear, not a bone left on the plate," he observed, still quite pleased that he had the upper hand with the girl.

Columbia did not miss the underlying meaning of his observation, nor was she going to forget it, the exasperating man.

Dolly did not miss the silent message passing between the pair either. But she was unsure how to translate it. It was becoming more obvious that something was going on between them, but exactly what was anyone's guess.

"I think I should be getting back to my cabin now," Dolly announced and promptly stood. "Thank you for the delicious meal, Columbus."

"It was my pleasure, ma'am," Columbia said, and thought that it *was* her pleasure that the woman had just devoured.

Nash sauntered back to his bunk and plopped down. "Ya'll can clear away the dishes now," he announced with a flip of his wrist, folded his arms behind his head, and sank back to savour besting her.

"Thank you" came the icy reply.

Columbia started stacking the plates none too

gently, banging them back onto the tray when the first wave of dizziness washed over her. She was used to eating promptly, and her stomach growled in complaint. She grasped the table, leaning over it to steady herself as she started to sway on her feet again.

Nash, who had been enjoying this game of wits they had been playing, noticed the girl's legs begin to crumble from under her. His self-satisfied expression immediately changed to one of genuine concern, and he leaped off his bunk.

He was across the room in less than two strides and caught Columbia up in his arms just in time. Her head went limply against his shoulder and her arm dangled at her side. As he carried her to his bunk, his skin warmed beneath his shirt where he held her. She was small and delicately boned in comparison to his large frame, and the hint of no-nonsense soap scent which lingered at her neck heightened his senses as he laid her down.

He leaned over her and studied her face. Her eyes were closed, but thick black lashes curled out from the closed lids. Her windburned nose was gently turned up. His gaze shifted lower. Her lips were full, tempting him to kiss them.

Those lips were too much to resist.

His breathing growing ragged, Nash bent over slowly, and with a whispered touch pressed his lips to hers.

Chapter Ten

Columbia moaned, a deep throaty murmur filled with pleasure, which caused Nash to catch himself and sit back. What was he doing? he wondered. And he questioned why he'd had the overwhelming urge to kiss the female interloper. She was on his paddle wheeler to spy on him for some unknown reason, and he had better remember that!

As his own breathing returned to normal and his pulse slowed, Nash's fingers began working the buttons on her collar. Isn't that what you were supposed to do when someone lost consciousness? Touching the velvety flesh of her throat had the undesirable effect of causing his body to harden and a tension to build within him again. He shifted uncomfortably at the sensations being near her elicited from him.

Columbia's thick lashes flickered and her eyes opened slowly. Her eyes were a brilliant, mesmerizing shade of turquoise. A faint smile curved her lips. Her smile was drawing something from the depths of Nash, and he stroked her chin with the back of his hand while he finished working the button at her collar. As realization suddenly hit her, she batted his hand away.

"Whaddya think you're doin'?" she yelped in a cracking voice, and scooted up on the pillow until she was resting against the wall. With her palm she cradled her chin, where the heat from his touch remained. The sensation was foreign, and so exciting that it alarmed her.

A look of stark horror and confusion on her face, she grasped her jacket up around her neck and furiously reworked the buttons.

"You fainted," he said tonelessly.

Nash moved from the bunk and turned his back to her. It wouldn't do if she caught sight of his arousal, and it was difficult to hide at the moment. He busied himself stacking the empty plates.

"I did not! Females faint. Men pass out."

He hid a grin. She certainly was creative in her concoctions to make him believe she was a male. "Can't argue with you there."

"I got sick from hunger, is all," she grated.

Concern cooled his ardor and he turned to face her. "When did you eat last?"

Columbia had to stop and think. She'd been so busy lately that she had forgotten to eat. "Yesterday mornin', I think."

"No wonder ya'll were woozy," Nash said with tact, skirting the issue of her fainting.

She huffed out a breath. "I told you I had to eat regular."

"Didn't they feed ya'll on your last job? Ya'll probably worked for those Baranoffs," he added to goad her and watch her squirm for an answer.

"Actually I slaved for Villamoore," she said with a smirk. She watched his face fall and wondered if he had thought he was going to cause her to slip up and unmask herself. Of course, that was foolish. He didn't know who she was. His rude remark about her and her uncle troubled her. They had always taken care of their crew.

She crawled off the bed, took a plate out of his hand, and began clearing away the rest of Dolly's dishes in an attempt to set the troubling thoughts aside. Another wave of light-headedness caused the room to swirl before her eyes, and she grabbed at the edge of the table to keep her dizzy state hidden from detection.

"Sit down, young man," he said deliberately, to allay any suspicions that she might have that he had discovered her chicanery while she was unconscious.

Her brows spiked together and a line of misgiving ran down her forehead. "Why?"

"Because I am going to get ya'll something to fill that empty belly of yours."

"Why would you do that for me, a mere cabin boy?"

"It is simple. If ya'll are going to take good care of me, I cannot have you passing out on me," he said and left her staring after him, mouth agape.

Nash Foster's consideration took Columbia by surprise. She returned to the bunk, leaned back, and raised her knees, linking her arms around her calves.

She hadn't thought he had a generous bone in that immense muscled body of his.

The thought about his body caused hers to stir, and the sensitivity of his gentle touch induced troubling images to invade her mind. She settled her head on her knees and squeezed her eyes shut, fighting to erase such unwelcome inner reverie.

Jack Tarley stormed into John Villamoore's plush dining room and slammed the door behind him. Villamoore's blond head snapped up and his sparse mustache looked even sparser against his waxy pallor, as his thin lips stretched into a tight line of displeasure.

"What are you doing hiring a stranger to haul cargo?" Tarley demanded. "For someone who plans to control all commerce and portage along the river, hiring an outsider don't seem like the best thing to do."

Villamoore deliberately let his eyes roll over the tall man, whose big gut caused his belt to roll over his trousers. The man was a pig, totally vulgar and unskilled in any of the social niceties. Pity that the riverboat captain was a distasteful necessity.

Villamoore's fingers went up to the side of his head, and he quietly checked to make sure his toupee was on straight. His eyes caught on Tarley's thick curly head of hair. He detested tall men with full heads of hair, but he needed a man devoid of conscience to carry out his directives, and Tarley fit his present needs.

"Sit down, Tarley," Villamoore ordered in a voice that brooked no further dissent. With Tarley seated, they were the same height.

Villamoore returned his attention to the ledger spread out on the table, and finished making the entry he had been working on before he had been so rudely interrupted. Once done he closed the book and looked up again. Tarley was now sitting, properly subdued, on the edge of his seat.

"I'm glad you have calmed down." A gust of wind ruffled his papers and Villamoore left his chair. He crossed the room to shut the French doors. He glanced up at his treasured, life-sized portrait, then returned to his table, and leaned against the smooth mahogany surface.

"First of all," he stroked his thin lips, "do not ever burst into my home again, if you know what is good for you. Second, no one tells me how to run my affairs—"

"But, I just thought—"

"That is your trouble, Tarley. I do not pay you to think. I pay you to follow my instructions. If you cannot manage that, I am sure I can find someone who will."

Each word was delivered with cold deliberation and made Tarley's skin crawl.

"Sorry, boss."

It gave Villamoore a sense of self-satisfaction to make a big hairy man like Tarley kowtow to him. Back East Villamoore had been ridiculed because of his short skinny stature. He'd been overshadowed by taller men and made to feel less than a man most of his life. But now with wealth and power, and control of the stretch of river between Portland and the falls within reach, Villamoore felt like he was ten feet tall and could look down on all others.

"I am glad we finally seem to have come to understand each other, Tarley. As far as Foster is concerned, he is going to serve my purposes.

"Up until now we haven't been able to slow down that Baranoff girl and her uncle, let alone stop them. Hell, Foster did more to put a wrench in that one-boat operation a few hours ago, than all our, shall we say, artful tactics have done. Thanks to Foster, the Baranoffs are idle for the first time since I arrived in Portland three years ago."

Tarley's eyes brightened into a glitter. "You aim to use Foster to ruin the Baranoffs?"

"You are finally getting smart. What better way to put an end to the competition? Foster's new. It'll be easy to set him up to do the dirty work, while we keep our hands as clean as a newborn babe's."

"But a few of the men are grumblin' about you offering Foster their runs," Tarley said.

"Let them grumble. Foster will get a few token hauls that conflict with the Baranoff's schedule. Just enough to keep that girl's attention focused on her own problems and away from us. While they are all wrapped up in their own dilemmas, we shall snatch the final contract out from under the Baranoffs, before they know what hit them. Without any money coming in, they will be forced to sell, and I'll own this stretch of the river—lock, stock, and cargo crate. With them out of the way, the last few riverboat pilots still holding out will meekly accept what I offer."

"Gosh." Tarley bobbed his head. "You're real smart, boss."

"Exactly. That is precisely why I am the boss. Remember that, Tarley." Villamoore gave the stupid man an indulgent smile. He liked it when such underlings fed his ego, and for an instant he forgot that he was not the ultimate boss. Then the smile disappeared. "Now get back to work."

Tarley gave a quick nod and headed for the door, but stopped and turned a sheepish grin on Villamoore. "What should I tell the others?"

"Tell them that Foster's presence won't interfere with their work. If anything, he will make their jobs easier in the long run."

"What if Foster don't see eye to eye with the way things are going to be run?"

"He will either work for me like the rest of you, or he will find himself hauling cargo at the bottom of the river."

Villamoore let out one of his rare bursts of laughter. It was a cold calculating cackle that made Tarley shudder inside. Villamoore's mirth died and he glared at Tarley. "Don't you find that amusing, Tarley?"

Tarley broke into a wide grin. "Yes sir, Mr. Villamoore."

Villamoore waited until the door closed behind Tarley, then leaned back in his chair. He tented his fingers and glanced at the bust of himself he'd had commissioned. He liked the full head of hair the sculptor had given him. Then he gazed out the win-

100

dow. The view of the Columbia and Willamette rivers with their white caps chopping the waves was breathtaking, and soon he would be in complete control of all the shipping.

The paddle wheeler gave a jerk, and Columbia rushed out on deck in time to catch sight of the first white-capped wave churning the already choppy water. The giant paddle wheel at the stern had begun slapping the river as the boat edged away from the docks.

They were underway.

Columbia whistled a sigh of relief through her teeth. She had managed to outwit Foster. Now she'd be able to spy on him and find out what he and Villamoore were up to. Letting the tension drain from her body, she inhaled the fresh cold air, facing directly into the wind. She loved the feel of the cold wind on her face, and the roar of the engine beneath her feet.

Her attention was so transfixed on the towering pines reaching up the steep green hillsides dusted with snow, that she did not hear the pounding approach of one of the crew until he was almost upon her. It was Little John, a man the size of a riverboat who had worked for her and her uncle for over three years. She turned her collar up and pulled her cap down nearly over her eyes, in an effort to elude recognition. She couldn't be found out now. She just couldn't!

Columbia hunched over the rail and made a serious study of the white caps on the water bubbling beneath the boat as it cut through the current. She crossed her fingers and held her breath.

The man barreled past her and she exhaled. He hadn't seemed to notice that she was aboard. She made a quick turn and was about to hurry back to Foster's cabin when Little John's booming voice halted her progress.

"Columbia? Columbia Baranoff, that you?"

As Columbia pivoted back to face the giant man, she caught sight of two more crewmen heading their way. Without thinking, she grabbed Little John's arm and dragged him into Foster's cabin, slamming the door behind them.

Little John's ruddy face held shocked surprise. "I don't rightly understand. What you doing aboard the *Yacht*, Miz Columbia?"

"Please, Little John, Uncle Titus and I desperately need your help." She was still panting from the exertion it had taken to move the giant hulk of a man.

He shifted back and forth like an awkward schoolboy. "Golly, Miz Columbia, I'm mighty sorry for taking this here job, but I got four mouths to feed at home."

Her heart pounding with fear that Foster would return before she enlisted the man's aid, she put her hands up in front of her. "It's okay, Little John. Uncle Titus and I understand. But, please, we need your help."

"How can I be of help to you and your uncle, when I'm working for Nash Foster now?"

"I don't want Foster to know I'm aboard."

102

Little John scratched his head. "Then why you in his cabin? And why you aboard Foster's boat?"

"I can't explain fully right now, just help me, will you?"

"Golly, I don't know. Somehow it don't seem loyal of me to help you, if I'm taking somebody else's money."

"It's Villamoore's money you're takin'," she hissed, fighting to control her temper.

"No, it ain't. I'm working for Foster."

"And he's workin' for Villamoore. Trust me."

Columbia did not have time to offer any further account of her actions. The door was thrust open into her back, propelling her forward with such a force that she stumbled.

Little John spread his arms just in time to catch Columbia before she tumbled to the floor. Her head was knocked against his hard chest instead. He wrapped his arms around her in a protective reflex.

"Well, well, exactly what do we have here?"

Columbia's gaze shot up at Foster. He was standing with his hand curled tightly around the door handle. His face was an angry mask of questions, which she feared he was going to impose on her before she could finish coaching the giant of a man now tightly holding her in his arms.

Chapter Eleven

Columbia glanced up at Little John's stunned face, then back at the dark scowl on Foster's rugged features. She blinked, and for an instant she thought she saw a hint of jealousy spark across Foster's countenance before his mien became void of all expression and he raised an eyebrow. But, of course, that he could be envious was ridiculous. He certainly had no cause to be.

Columbia pushed herself out of Little John's arms and tugged on her jacket in a self-conscious gesture. She knew her cheeks flamed.

Columbia frowned at what could be implied from such an innocent occurrence. "I—I just tripped."

"Columbus, I never thought otherwise. Did ya'll?"

"Oh posh, of course not!" Columbia flashed Foster an angry look of surprise.

Little John scratched his head in confusion. "Col—?"

"Yeah, Columbus," Columbia interceded.

"Oh, yeah, Columbus," Little John responded, still befuddled.

"You met Little John?" Columbia offered. "Everybody calls him Little John as a joke to rile Villamoore, since John is also Villamoore's name, only Villamoore really is little."

Little John chuckled, but quickly ceased when he realized he was the only one who seemed to be enjoying the local humor. His gaze settled shyly on the captain, and Little John decided that whatever was going on between the pair, shouldn't involve him. "Well, I'd best be gettin' back to work now."

"Good idea," Nash answered dryly. Yet he did not take his eyes off the girl for a moment. He wondered why he had felt a stab of rivalry, seeing her in someone else's arms. Meanwhile the monster of a man withdrew like an awkward child.

Columbia tried to follow Little John from the cabin, but Foster blocked her exit. "Where do ya'll think you're going?"

"I got work to do," she mumbled, and made a second try to inch past Foster.

"Not so fast." He grabbed her jacket tails as she swung the door open. "Just go over there and sit down." He gestured to his desk.

Columbia scowled at the man and weighed her options. She didn't like the gleam in his eyes or the mischievous look on his face. He was up to something. Finally setting aside her fears, she settled tentatively on the edge of the chair and chewed on her lower lip.

She watched as he stepped outside the door and bent over. Even in his heavy jacket, Nash Foster cut a bold, exciting figure of a man. His body was big and solid, the bulges in his upper arms strained his

105

jacket sleeves, his thighs stretched his trousers. There was no doubt that this man possessed the strength to take what he wanted. Her thoughts had just shifted to dangerous ground when he unfolded his frame and swung toward her.

Her eyes saucered.

Foster was carrying a colossal tray of food. "You remembered," she whispered in disbelief.

"I told ya'll that was where I was going when I left you in my cabin . . . alone."

"Ah, Little John just came to say hello. He and I—"

Despite a burning desire to know what that man was doing in his cabin with the girl, Nash cut the chit off with, "It is none of my business how my crew chooses to spend their own time." He hesitated and took a breath. "But I will not have you privately entertaining your *friends,* when ya'll are supposed to be working or in my cabin."

The implication of what he said made Columbia's face burn with heat. "I don't know what you think I am, but I ain't!" she spat.

Nash suppressed a grin. "Of course not. Just do not do it on my time." He set the tray down in front of her. She reached for the fork, but his hands closed on the lapels of her jacket, skimming along her breasts as he withdrew the jacket from her.

Columbia was too stunned to protest his helping her off with her jacket. She could feel his feather-light touch heating her breasts through her rough workshirt, and her pulse beat in rapid succession.

She was trying to swallow the sensations that his

106

touch wrought when he broke the moment by taking a linen napkin out from under the plate, shaking it out, and tucking it at her throat.

"Just in case ya'll are as messy as you are clumsy." Columbia flashed him a scowl, but her stomach roared from the inviting aroma of the food, and she switched her attention from Foster and what his touch had done to her to her plate.

Nash settled back on his bed. Although she was not well endowed, he had felt the soft curve of her breasts when he'd helped her off with her jacket. He rubbed his fingertips together, and he silently longed to explore her secrets further. It had been a long time since he'd had a woman, he reminded himself. And he decided to rectify that the next port they put into.

Forcing his attention away from such nonsensical thoughts toward the girl, he watched her eat. She certainly wasn't one of those women who were afraid to put a bite down her throat, for fear of adding an extra pound or two.

Even forcing himself to focus on something as basic as eating brought his thoughts back to the girl's body, and what it would be like to nibble on her most sensitive spots, or have her gorge herself on his.

His most sensitive places awakened, and visions of what Columbia Baranoff would look like lying nude beneath him stirred him further. He could picture her face flushed, her breathing hard, her supple breasts pushing against his naked chest. He imagined setting her on fire until she begged for him to make love to her.

Ignoring his better judgment to put her ashore and

107

have nothing to do with the girl, Nash stood and stretched.

Columbia shoveled the last spoonful of fish into her mouth and nearly choked as she watched Foster shrug off his jacket, plunk it on the bed, and begin to toss off his socks and boots.

"What're you doin'?" She gagged as the fish clogged her throat.

Nash gave her a crooked grin. "Getting ready to bathe."

"But it's the middle of the day!"

"What better time? Barth is at the wheel and everything is under control."

"What better time?" she mumbled in mimicry. She yanked the napkin from her throat and swiped it across her mouth, to hide her shock as Foster peeled off his shirt.

His chest was an expansive mass of muscles dusted with thick curling black hair, narrowing as it led its way down to disappear behind his belt. She allowed her gaze to drift lower.

"What are ya'll staring at?"

Her gaze darted up to his lips. If she didn't know better, she could have almost sworn that he was trying to force back a grin.

"Me?"

"Ya'll are the only one in the cabin with me."

Columbia frowned. "I wasn't starin' at nothin'," she insisted.

"Well, what are ya'll waiting for then?"

Her frown dropped into confusion. "Waitin' for?"

"If ya'll do not get going and fetch my bathwater, I

am going to be standing before you naked, freezing to death."

The mention of male nakedness caused Columbia's gaze to shift again to the potent male portion of his anatomy. Outlined beneath his heavy trousers was hinted the mighty power of him.

"Ah, I guess I'd better get a move on," she said, her voice cracking.

Columbia was so flustered over such forbidden thoughts that she crashed into the closed door. Her hand flew to her nose. She glanced back at the smirking man as his remark about her clumsiness came to the fore.

"Ya'll okay?"

There it was again. Concern. His interest in her welfare disarmed her. She wiggled her nose to make sure she hadn't broken it, then removed her hand, and gave him a sheepish shrug. "Forgot to open the door."

Keeping his face impassive, he began to unbutton his pants. "It does help."

"Yeah." She skittered from the room.

Nash smiled to himself. He had gotten the response from the girl that he had hoped for. She was not experienced and merely amusing herself, while she was waiting to get whatever she was on board his paddle wheeler for. But if she thought she was going to remain comfortably ensconced on his riverboat until she was ready to make her move, she was sadly mistaken!

With that thought firmly entrenched in his mind, Nash began to strip off his remaining clothes.

Nash had barely settled into the tub—the one luxury he allowed himself on board the paddle wheeler—when the door swung open and Columbia entered. Her attention was focused on the two heavy buckets she was hauling.

For an instant he was sorely tempted to leap to his feet and help her with her steaming burden. But, of course, he couldn't let her think that he didn't expect his cabin boy to earn his pay, or she might get suspicious. Nash leaned back and rested the nape of his neck on the edge of the tub.

"It is about time ya'll returned. I have waited patiently long enough. Hurry up with that water."

Water sloshed over the edges of the buckets, as Columbia lugged the heavy wooden pails toward Foster. She was so engrossed in getting them to the tub, that she didn't glance up until she was standing at the edge.

"Oh, my!" she gasped and dropped both buckets on the floor. They teetered precariously before settling in an upright position.

Nash craned his neck in the girl's direction. She stood still, her tiny hands covering her mouth, her eyes as large as two life rings.

Her eyes were fastened on his private parts.

"What is the matter, Columbus? Ya'll act as if you have never seen a naked man before."

Foster's words startled her back to her senses, and Columbia swallowed hard. "Of course, I've seen a naked man. I'm a man, ain't I?"

"Of course, ya'll are," Nash said with a straight

110

face, making no effort to cover himself. "But ya'll are staring."

"It is just that I ain't never seen someone so b-big before, is all," she said lamely.

She snapped her eyes upward to meet his. He was watching her intently. His eyes penetrating, searching, smiling.

"What are ya'll waiting for?" he asked, breaking into the mesmerizing effects that his obsidian eyes had on her.

"Waitin' for?" she asked. She could feel the warm moisture build between her thighs, and she pressed them together as a sudden unexplainable sensation spread through that part of her body.

"The water. Pour the water in the tub before it gets cold. What did ya'll think I meant?"

"The water, of course." She smiled weakly.

She lifted one of the buckets and poured the water over him in a steady stream. The glistening drops slid over his naked body in a prism of colors, and she gasped when his maleness jerked in response to the warm liquid.

Columbia's gasp caused her to release the bucket, and it clattered to the floor. "It slipped out of my hand," she chirped in a cracking voice and quickly bent over to retrieve the other bucket. She never used to be this clumsy.

"Hurry up with that water," he said harshly, to mask his own rising ardor. He dropped a washcloth over himself and busied himself with sudsing another one.

He patiently waited until she had finished pouring

111

the rest of the water into the tub and had turned to leave him to his bath, before he said, "Where do ya'll think you're going?"

"I'm goin' to leave you to your bath," she returned in a small voice.

"What the devil do you think I am paying ya'll for? Come back here and get to scrubbing my back, before the water turns river cold."

"Scrub your back?" she asked, stunned and yet excited at the prospect of running her fingers over his naked flesh.

"Ya'll have a hearing problem? You keep repeating what I say."

"No problem," she managed in a rasp.

"Good. Then come here and get busy." He raised his hand and tossed the wet washcloth at her.

Columbia's reflexes were good and she picked the soggy cloth out of the air. With hesitant steps she moved to stand over Foster. The water was sudsy but she could still see the hint of him through the white film. Swallowing her reluctance, Columbia began to swab the cloth across his shoulders.

"Here," he plopped the soap in her hand, "rub this over my back and chest before ya'll scrub."

Columbia frowned at his strong back. It was bronzed from the sun and lightly dusted with hairs. And when she ran her hand over him, she held her breath. His skin was unexpectedly soft, the muscles beneath it hard and bunched. He was tense and she felt a sudden surge of power over him.

She scrubbed in circling motions, noticing his breathing deepen and quicken. Feeling emboldened, she tentatively moved to the side of the tub, and after lathering her hand, began to mop the front of his shoulders. When she moved down his chest, he shuddered.

She glanced at his face. His lips were pressed into a thin line, as if he were in pain. Surely her touch didn't pain him, did it? Tolerating questions in her mind was never easy for Columbia, and she blurted, "Am I painin' you?"

"I would venture it is safe to say that there are different kinds of pain. And ya'll are definitely causing me a great deal of it right now."

She immediately stopped washing him. But as quick as lightning, he grabbed her wrist and pulled her headlong into the tub with him.

Chapter Twelve

Surprised and overpowered, Columbia splashed into the tub. She came up sputtering and holding onto her cap, for fear the hair she had so carefully braided and stuffed inside the knit hat would expose her.

"What did you do that for?" she demanded in a squeaky voice, as she swiped the soapy water out of her stinging eyes.

"Me?" Nash said with an innocent face. "Ya'll are the one who seems to be so clumsy. Ya'll must have *tripped*."

Columbia glared at the man. How could she have tripped and fallen over the side of the high-top tub? Quite simply, she couldn't have. He was making fun of her being shoved into Little John's arms.

His body shifted, and she became all too aware that she was sitting on his lap. She felt something hard pressing against her bottom, heightening her senses. She scrambled to get out of the tub, but his hands held her.

"Let go," she yelped and squirmed in his lap. "I got

to get off you. You said I was painin' you a minute ago. I got to be painin' you now, sittin' atop you like I am."

A shadowed smile grew on his face. Her nicely rounded bottom was stirring him. "And as I already told ya'll, there are different kinds of pain."

"Pain's pain," she protested.

"Not true. The kind of pain ya'll are giving me is sweet torture," he rasped in a gravelly tone.

Columbia looked askance at him. "Captain Foster—"

"Nash."

"Ah, Nash, you ain't one of them funny fellows, are you?"

Nash wanted to laugh out loud. She was so delightfully naive. "I am being no more funny, as ya'll put it, than you were when I walked in on ya'll and one of my crew."

"That was an accident. I tripped. You sent me crashin' into Little John when you opened the door. But as I started to say, er, oh I don't know what I was gonna to say now. You got me all confused."

"I cannot say what ya'll are doing to me," he muttered under his breath.

She surged to her feet, but Nash held tight to her wrist, unfolding his unclothed frame to stand in the tub with her. Columbia fought to keep her gaze from roving over his muscular body. He was a perfect specimen, rough and angular and muscled, and she longed to touch him. She grasped her hands behind her back.

He pushed her down to a sitting position, putting

her at a rather precarious level with his jutting physique as he climbed from the tub. She swallowed hard to keep the gasp on the tip of her tongue from unveiling her, and made a study of her drowned shoes.

"Get those clothes stripped off and wash up," Nash ordered more harshly than he had intended.

Her color was high, and he almost felt guilty for enjoying her discomfort. In an effort to assuage his guilty conscience, he made himself stand back and recall her antics since he'd met her.

Columbia remained sitting, her soaked shirt clinging to her. "I don't need no bath," she insisted, refusing to look at him.

"Ya'll smell like you have been working on the ship's engines. And unless ya'll want to go back to working with the rest of the crew, instead of being in here with me, ya'll will get busy and get cleaned up."

A surge of anxiety rose in her throat. She couldn't leave now, despite the strange feelings he had elicited from her. Not when she was so close. Her glance shot to him.

He reached for a towel, turning his back as he bent to dry his legs, and Columbia hurriedly stripped off her shirt, pants, and shoes, and sunk up to her neck in the soapy water, covering her breasts with her arms.

He pulled his trousers on. Without bothering to button them, he returned to the edge of the tub. She was staring at him with wide eyes. He wasn't sure why he was goading her, but an overwhelming urge to glide his hand over her smooth flesh

116

overcame him, and he bent down behind her.

"What're you doin'?" she choked, craning her neck in an effort to see what he was up to.

"I am going to scrub your back for ya'll," he answered, and groped for the washrag.

"But you can't!" She grabbed the washrag, and plopped it into his hand before he came in contact with a part of her that would proclaim to him that she was not a he.

"Why not?"

"Well . . . because that's *my* job. I'm here to take care of you, not the other way around." She kept her arms crossed over her breasts, her heart doing a drum tattoo inside her chest.

"Hush up and quit arguing, before the water gets any colder." Nash lathered the rag into a bubbly foam and slathered it across her shoulders and down her back. Wanting to feel more of her velvety skin, to revel in its satiny smoothness, he dropped the rag into the water and replaced it with the palms of his hands.

Her skin was heated silk, soft and white once it dropped below the back of her windburned neck. The nerve endings in his fingers screamed as he descended below the water line and traced the indentation of her sides at her waist.

"My God, there is not a single muscle on you," he commented, in an effort to abate his growing hunger for her.

Columbia squirmed at the sensations that reached all the way to her secret core. "I don't look all ripply like you, but I'm strong nonetheless."

117

"No, ya'll certainly don't look like me," he muttered in a heated voice.

Unsettled and not totally understanding why, Columbia pushed his hands away from her, insisting, "I'll finish the rest."

"Nonsense. I have always believed in finishing what I begin."

His hand dipped into the water and redeemed the washrag. Then he strode around to face her. She was flushed with a glistening sheen of sweat across her upper lip. For an instant he wondered who was the most unsettled.

He swept the rag once across the base of her throat. "Move your arms. Ya'll are holding them so tightly across your chest, that one would think ya'll have got something to hide."

"Well, maybe I do," she rasped at the sensations his touch wrung from her.

He straightened and let the washrag slip from his fingers and splash into the tub. She was breaking . . . or was he? "Oh? And what could that be?"

She chewed on the tip of her index finger. She had never given up without a fight in her life. Her glance caught on his bare chest and she swallowed. "It's my chest. That's it. My chest."

"Your chest?" He had her. She was going to confess. Strangely, he felt no sense of triumph.

"Yeah, I ain't got no furred pelt on it like you got."

He nodded, fighting back a grin at the heights of her ingenuity. So their little game wasn't over. Excitement shot through him. "I would say that ya'll certainly don't. Ya'll do look a mite flabby under that

118

part of your chest ya'll are trying awfully hard to hide. Not enough hard work."

Nervous excitement blended into simmering rage. Not enough hard work indeed! And flabby! She didn't have an ounce of flab anywhere. She opened her mouth to discount such an assertion, but closed it. He wasn't going to rile her into making a hasty admission.

"I'm sure workin' for you will help with my flab."

He cocked a brow. "Among other things," he answered cryptically. "I am sure it will."

"So you can understand that until I shape up to be more like the rest of the crew, I don't like undressin' when the other fellas are around."

"When the *other* fellas are around," he echoed. She was quite a storyteller when she got started.

"Yeah, because I ain't got my full manhood yet."

He had to turn his head for a moment, so she wouldn't see the grin he could not keep from his face. "Ya'll haven't?"

She hung her head in shame, but kept a focus on him through the thick forest of her black lashes. "It ain't exactly something a young man likes to talk about."

Barely maintaining a dry expression, he said, "No, I am sure it is not."

"Then you can fathom why I'd just as soon finish up my bath by myself."

"Yes, I think I definitely fathom your problem. But now that I'm aware of your dilemma and understand it, it should not be so bothersome for ya'll to strip off your clothes around me anymore." He stooped and fished around in the tub to recover the washrag, glancing at her down-turned mouth.

Her face had filled with fright and stopped him cold. She was so alarmed, her lower lip trembling, the whites of her eyes so stark that he could not force her into a declaration of femininity. Furthermore, if truth were known, he wasn't sure he wanted to yet.

"Ya'll look as if you are about to turn blue." He sighed. He wondered why he was giving her such a graceful exit from her predicament.

"Ah, yeah. Yeah, I am. Since you insist on helpin' out, would you fetch more hot water? You certainly wouldn't want your cabin boy catchin' his death, now would you?"

Nash again had to give her credit. She had a quick mind. She was one of the most resourceful females he had ever known. He tossed her the wet rag and began shrugging into his shirt.

"Sit back and relax. I will only be a minute. And don't worry, your secret is safe with me."

Columbia nodded weakly. "Safe with you."

She watched him grab his jacket off a hook, sling it on, and head for the door. She rolled her eyes and let out a sigh, leaning her head against the edge of the tub as the door closed behind the man.

Nash waited outside the door, listening as he heard splashing, then the sound of sloshing footsteps stomping around inside his cabin. Chuckling to himself despite the unsetting feelings in his chest, Nash shook his head as he sauntered toward the wheelhouse to check on the paddle wheeler's progress.

Nash strolled along the deck, his hands in his

120

pockets, whistling. In spite of the fact that Miss Columbia Baranoff was on board his paddle wheeler disguised as one of the crew for some undisclosed purpose, Nash hadn't felt this lighthearted in years. And he had to wonder if it was all because of Columbia.

His sight caught on Dolly coming toward him. She was a voluptuous woman, soft and round. But somehow Nash no longer seemed to find such curves quite so enticing anymore.

"My, my, don't you look as if you just won a big pot at poker on board one of those fancy Mississippi gambling boats," Dolly observed.

Nash smiled down at her. "Not yet, but another card or two, and I may very well be holding a royal flush."

Dolly's knowing grin faded and was replaced by bemusement. She took his arm and strolled along with him as they headed toward the wheelhouse. "I hope you know what you're doing."

"I do not know what ya'll mean."

"You're gettin' mighty wrapped up with that girl from the other paddle wheeler. Don't try to deny it. Although I already guessed she was no male, Barth told me you told him that she is masquerading as your cabin boy, and we're all supposed to go along with it." She did not mention her little talk with the girl.

"Only until I find out what she's up to," Nash protested halfheartedly. He was annoyed he had made the mistake of confiding in Barth when he had asked Nash why he was carrying buckets of water for his cabin boy. And Nash was annoyed that Barth had told Dolly, but he made the decision not to do more than mention the matter to his friend.

Dolly scratched her ear. She couldn't understand why he just didn't unmask the girl, unless he had some reason for wanting to keep the girl on board. "What is it they say about the guilty party being the one who screams the loudest?"

"I think you mean the squeaky wheel gets the grease."

"Or the girl."

Nash stopped and glared at the woman. Icy winds whipped in off the river, yet his cheeks felt like two burning wheels of color. "Ya'll must be forgetting that I already have a wife I am quite satisfied with."

Dolly raised a gloved hand and stroked his cheek. "And as your *wife*, honey, I'll be waiting for the day you look to divorce me, so we can both get on with our lives . . . and loves. Just don't wait too long, or your own little trickery could come back to haunt you." She chuckled at the deepening red on his cheeks. "It's a mighty cold day for you to be so flushed, Nash honey."

Dolly winked, reached up on her tiptoes, and gave him a kiss before she hurried toward the paddle wheeler's salon to get out of the elements.

Nash glowered after the woman. She didn't know what the hell she was talking about. He had no intention of getting himself mixed up with love. He rubbed the back of his neck and stomped toward the wheelhouse, his mood no longer so light.

Columbia had rushed into dry clothes and slipped

from the cabin, despite her wet shoes, to get to Little John and explain before he spilled her secret, when she sighted Nash strolling along the deck with his wife. A surge of envy caught hold of her for a moment. She shook her head to do away with such ridiculous feelings. Yet she did not take her eyes off Foster, and when the woman kissed him, Columbia gasped.

She touched her fingers to her own lips. She could almost feel the pressure of his full, heated mouth on hers. And she continued her vigil of the man and his wife, unable to drag her eyes away from the pair. Regretting that she had not remained in his cabin and missed such a touching domestic scene, Columbia had to remind herself that Nash Foster was a happily married man.

Columbia forced herself to firm her resolution. The thoughts she had been having were foolish female notions, not those expected of a female with the goal to become the first licensed woman riverboat pilot on the river. She bit her lip and silently reaffirmed her original intention. No one was going to sway her from her target.

She was not going to let Nash Foster make a willing fool out of her!

Chapter Thirteen

A blast of cold air followed Nash into the wheelhouse, drawing Barth's attention to the door. "I was beginning to wonder whether you planned to spend the entire trip locked in your cabin with your *cabin boy*."

"Very amusing," Nash barked, then took over piloting the paddle wheeler through the swift current and past a mighty ice floe.

Barth leaned against a nearby cabinet and rubbed his jaw. "Well, your temper certainly hasn't improved. Obviously things aren't going quite as you had planned. Don't tell me you're beginning to lose your touch with the ladies?"

"Columbia Baranoff is no lady," Nash grunted, and shifted their course past a submerged reef that showed whitewater rapids above the surface.

"Oh? Does that mean the female has possibilities?" Barth laughed.

"I am not going to discuss the girl with ya'll. Particularly since ya'll have seen fit to share your knowledge of the situation with Dolly." Nash's words came out in a hiss.

Barth was startled and immediately sobered. It was the first time Nash had refused to discuss any of his exploits with the weaker sex. But Barth should have known better than to talk to Dolly about it. He studied Nash's proud profile. Nash's face looked as if it were set in granite river rock.

Barth's thoughts shifted to Columbia Baranoff. The girl was an unlikely candidate to capture Nash's attention, but she certainly had seemed to.

"What are ya'll staring at?" Nash growled.

Barth's attention immediately bounced back to his friend. "You know, we've been friends a long time, and you've never, shall we say, *barked* at me over a woman before."

"I would not exactly call Columbia Baranoff a woman," Nash said in a dry, controlled voice. Despite their close friendship, Nash was no mood to listen to Barth's prattle about Columbia.

Barth scratched his ear. "Let me see. Columbia isn't a cabin boy, that is certain. According to you, she isn't a lady. And neither is she a woman. Tell me, how exactly would you classify her?"

Nash's expression was cold as the snow-dusted hillsides climbing the steep banks of the Columbia River, as he transferred his stance from one foot to the next.

"That female is in a class all by herself."

Barth smiled brightly despite his friend's dark countenance. "That's precisely what I've been trying to tell you."

After finding Little John and gaining his assurances that the man would not spill his guts to Nash Foster,

Columbia felt relieved. She would not be unmasked before she could finish the job she'd set out to do.

Once back in Nash's cabin, Columbia busied herself rummaging through his papers. A packet of yellowed newspaper articles depicting Nash as the swain of a beautiful society debutante grabbed Columbia's attention. A stab of jealousy pricked her heart when she realized the articles went with that daguerreotype she had found among his possessions earlier. She dug the picture out and stared at it.

Columbia's hand subconsciously ran along her own baggy shirt and smudged pants. The woman smiling at Columbia was exquisite in her fashionable attire. Nash's taste in women ran toward the more generously curved, feminine feline-type.

She tucked the daguerreotype away and snapped the packet shut. What was wrong with her? Nash Foster was a married man. She shouldn't be having even a second thought over him. Then she had to wonder why a man who was happily married would keep such mementos, when he apparently did not possess any of his wife. If she were Nash's wife, Columbia would have disposed of any reminders of other women before she let him slip a ring on her finger. The thought of being his wife and all it entailed unnerved her.

A blast from the paddle wheeler's whistle signaled that the boat had reached its destination. In an effort to set aside such unbidden thoughts of Nash Foster, Columbia ran out on deck and watched as the crew worked the ropes to ease the paddle wheeler into place.

Her gaze shifted to the landing. The little town of Lower Cascades came to life early. It was a lively town, despite the icy blasts of wind that howled through the

126

gorge in winter. A stopping-off place to load and unload cargo, transported upriver by portage over a bad pack trail past the falls, and reloaded on paddle wheelers for transportation to towns further inland.

Any doubts she had harbored about the innocence of Nash's association with John Villamoore crashed when her gaze shifted and she caught sight of Nash as he disembarked and accompanied one of Villamoore's henchmen into a nearby warehouse.

Not about to miss out on the chance to listen in on the conversation between the two men, Columbia casually sauntered past a large cluster of dockworkers, busy unloading the cargo. So as not to look suspicious, and to get as close as possible without being detected, Columbia lifted a small crate onto her shoulder and entered the huge warehouse.

Inside the immense room, cartons were piled to near the top of the fifteen-foot ceiling, and Columbia wondered what could be stored in the containers. At the sound of raised voices from a small partitioned office near the back of the room, she crept closer to eavesdrop.

"Don't know why Villamoore hired another man," the burly man with hamhocks for hands was saying. "He's got enough men working for him already."

"Maybe he was looking for someone better suited for what he has in mind," Nash returned, unperturbed by the man's attempts to rile him.

The huge man glared at Nash, and Columbia could only speculate what evil Villamoore had conjured up now.

"I don't like your looks," the burly one sneered.

"Cannot say as yours particularly appeal to me

either. But why not keep our personal opinions to ourselves and conclude this transaction, so I can get my paddle wheeler loaded and return to Portland. I am sure that Villamoore would not appreciate learning that your personal dislikes held up his cargo."

The burly man's face purpled with suppressed rage. But he turned and scribbled something on a stack of papers on his desk, and thrust them into Nash's hand. When they started back toward her, Columbia scrambled for cover.

They had just exited the warehouse when ear-piercing shots ricocheted off the crates. All of a sudden chaos broke loose, and the men on the landing dove for cover. Columbia flattened herself against the floor and covered her ears, afraid to breathe.

A shower of bullets, followed by a wave of arrows and whoops, flooded the landing as a horde of Indians broke into the open. Grabbing a hapless dockworker, the Indians butchered the man, scalped him, and dumped his body into the river. The dockworkers tried to return the fire, but they were outmatched, and the marauding warriors swarmed over the landing killing everyone in their wake.

Nash hurled himself aboard the *Yacht* and helped six men scramble up the gangplank. Amidst the confusion, Nash hollered, "Chop off those lines, and let's get the hell out of here!"

An Indian, his raised arm holding a tomahawk dripping with blood, started up the gangplank. Nash grabbed a rifle from a stunned crewman and shot the savage. Another one let out a whoop and lunged at Nash. With the butt of the rifle, Nash sent a crushing blow to the man's jaw, knocking him into the river after his companion.

"My God, what's happening?" Barth yelled and rushed out to join Nash.

"We are under attack. Hurry, help me shove the gangplank out of the way, so we can get the hell out of here."

"But Columbia—she's on shore!" Barth cried.

In a panic at hearing that the girl was in danger, Nash grabbed Barth by the collar. "What do ya'll mean she is on shore?"

"I saw her follow you into the warehouse. She couldn't have gotten out."

"Dammit," Nash cursed, and launched himself on to the gangplank as the paddle wheeler drifted away from shore. "Go get help."

"Nash!" Dolly screamed, leaning over the rail on the top deck as the big wheel bit into the water and one of the crew guided the boat into the current. "Oh dear Lord, you'll be killed!"

"Barth, get her out of the way," Nash ordered as he disappeared around the corner of the warehouse while a half-dozen savages ran among the crates, breaking them open and collecting the booty inside. Others hunted down the hiding men and slaughtered them.

With the stealth of a thief, Nash drew his knife and crept among the overturned crates until he managed to slip inside the warehouse unnoticed. Despite the reining pandemonium outside, inside it was deathly still.

Not daring to call out Columbia's name, Nash searched the stacked crates. He was about to give up hope and make a dash for the river, when out of the corner of his eye he caught sight of a faint movement.

He crept around the corner. A loud thud clunked behind him and he swung around, brandishing his knife.

"Oof," he grunted and suddenly crumpled to the ground.

"Nash!" His name tumbled from Columbia's lips in horror.

She had just knocked Nash Foster out cold.

The board she held pitched out of her fingers, and she kneeled down to cradle his head in her lap. Her fingers stroked his cheek before they snaked into his thick black hair.

A bump rose on the back of his head.

He was going to be livid if he discovered his cabin boy was responsible. That is, if the Indians did not finish them off first.

Using all the strength years of working on her father's paddle wheeler had provided, Columbia managed to drag Nash's limp body next to an overturned empty crate. The huge crate lay on its side, and Columbia wasted no time tipping the crate until it crashed over Nash, shielding the unconscious man.

Columbia tried to lift the crate to crawl in next to Nash, but it wouldn't budge. More shots echoed outside and she grew panicky. Frantically searching, she grabbed the board she had struck Nash with and used it to lever the heavy wooden box high enough so she could clamber inside.

Through the cracks Columbia could see three Indians run into the building. She held her breath as they broke into the crates. She choked back a gasp when they pulled rifles out of the crates, giving them more

130

ammunition against the settlers. Villamoore had been shipping rifles upriver!

The haul seemed to satisfy them, and they ceased their searching.

Columbia scooted back as she watched legs adorned with leggings and rifles swinging at the Indians' sides, pass by their hiding place.

Nash moaned and her attention immediately switched back to him.

"You all right?" she asked in a strangled whisper.

His hand lifted to the great ache in his temples. He opened his eyes and tried to focus. "Chrissakes, where am I?" he mumbled and tried to sit up.

"You're okay. Just lie still for a while, you'll be fine. We're inside a crate in the warehouse." She smoothed an escaped curl from his forehead.

He reached up and caressed the inside of her wrist with the pad of his thumb. "And do I have ya'll to thank for saving my life?"

"In a roundabout way," she said sheepishly. She hoped he would not question her further. The roughness of his fingers heated the blood in her veins.

"How roundabout?" he questioned. His fingers smoothed their way up her arm to the collar at her neck. With the backs of his fingers, he nuzzled the smooth column of her neck before dipping beneath her shirt collar.

Her skin was on fire despite the cold, damp warehouse. Her breathing quickened, as he traced an index finger down the front of her shirt and slipped his hand inside the shirt opening.

All conscious thought that she was masquerading as his cabin boy fled her mind. They became what they truly were: two people, a man and a woman, thrown together by dire circumstances beyond their control.

"What're you doin'?" she choked and brought her hand up to stop his arousing quest, in a frantic effort to reestablish conscious thought.

Nash's hand covered hers. She was trembling. His fingers slipped around her wrist. Her pulse was erratic, pounding against the insides of his fingers.

He searched her face in the dim illumination. Streams of light bathed her countenance, and gave her a radiance that he found difficult to resist. Her pupils were dilated, leaving a mere slender ring of turquoise, and she was blinking rapidly. He let his gaze rove down to her mouth. It was slightly parted, her tongue running along the sensuous full curve of her upper lip.

He gently laid her hand on his chest to show her how she was affecting him. Then he reached up and traced the outline of her lips. He moved to run the back of his hand along her jawline. She did nothing further to stop him.

If he wanted to take her, she was his.

Chapter Fourteen

Off in the distance the sounds of the Indians could still be heard, as they broke open the remaining crates and probed their contents. But for Nash, the main danger that existed wasn't from the Indians. It was from the slim female cradling his head in her lap.

"Guess we oughta stay put for a spell." Columbia's observation broke into Nash's troubling thoughts.

He continued to stroke the silken satin of her chin. "If ya'll think that is the wisest thing to do." His voice was whisper soft.

Her fiery fingers dipped inside the opening of his shirt, and his breath caught when her touch came into intimate contact with his bare skin.

"I ain't sure what's the wisest thing"—*with you*—"under the circumstances, but if we aim to hang on to our scalps, it's the smartest."

"The smartest, hmm?" He did not ask what the danger of the circumstances were for her, but for him, it was the increasing intimacy of her touch.

"I'd expect so," she answered in a raspy voice.

Suddenly conscious of the path she'd traced with her

fingers, she tried to pull her hand away, but he held it there, against his pounding chest.

"Can ya'll feel what you are doing to me?"

"Yeah."

Every breath she took seemed to heighten the tension burgeoning inside her. Despite the warning bells clanging in her head—this man was trouble in more ways than one—she was having a difficult time heeding her own mind. He had awakened something that was totally foreign to her: a wild, raw craving deep within her heart that was demanding to be fulfilled.

She bit her lip, hoping the pain would bring her back to her senses. She broke the sensitive skin on the inside of her lower lip and tasted blood.

Nash could sense that she had withdrawn from him, and he acted quickly to maintain the advantage he felt was slipping. He snapped his hand back and sat up. Holding his head at his temples, he fastened his gaze on her. "My God, what is going on?"

"Whaddya mean?"

"I think I must have been knocked on the head harder than I realized."

"You were?" she asked and crashed back to the reality of their situation. "I mean, you *were!*"

"For a short time, I thought ya'll were somebody else."

"Somebody else?" Disappointment grasped her. "Your wife, you mean?"

"Wife?"

"Dolly." The name fell cold between them, and Columbia shuddered. She had almost forgotten herself.

"No, not Dolly. I must have been temporarily stunned, because I thought ya'll were that female from that other paddle wheeler. The one that nearly collided with mine back at Portland."

Nash raised himself up on his elbow and pretended to make a study of her face. She shifted uncomfortably. Yet this time Nash did not feel a sense of gratification at making her squirm. He felt a strange sense of loss.

"Ya'll do resemble the girl, Columbus."

The disappointment of a moment ago fled, and Columbia's hand flew to her cheek. She could still feel his touch, warm and caressing against her skin. "I suppose I do look a mite like her . . . in a manly sort of way, of course."

"Of course."

"But why would that make any difference? You got a mighty handsome wife on board your paddle wheeler waitin' for you."

He looked directly into her questioning eyes. "Yes, I suppose I do," he said, with just the slightest hint of regret in his voice.

"Then why were you doin' what you were doin' to *me*, even if you thought I was that river girl?"

Nash sighed. "I wish I could tell ya'll. Can't though. I cannot say why I reacted the way I did. Other than it must have had something to do with the bump I got on my head." He rubbed the knot, suddenly aware of its throbbing. "By the way, how *did* I get this bump?"

"You really want to know?" she questioned. She was stalling for time, hoping that she could come up with a reasonable explanation without having to tell him that the bump was courtesy of her own hand.

"Something tells me I would be better off not knowing." She couldn't help but smile in relief. "But I am going to ask anyway, just the same."

Columbia's face fell. She hadn't come up with a

135

very good story. "Would you believe Indians?"

"Since my scalp is still intact, I would say no."

She pinched her lips. "If you must know, I did it. I heard a noise and thought you were one of them Indians. I grabbed a board and hit you on the head, before I realized it was you." She shrugged. "I was only protectin' myself. And after all, I did save your hide by draggin' you over to this crate and usin' it to hide us out."

He mulled over her explanation and decided not to make her squirm any longer. "I guess ya'll did at that."

She breathed a sigh of relief and relaxed against the side of the crate. "You think it's safe to get out of here now?"

Nash didn't want to leave their cozy position. He liked the closeness and did not want it to end. "Perhaps we ought to wait awhile longer. Just to make sure that those Indians have truly left."

Columbia nodded. "Good idea."

He shifted his position and pillowed his head back in her lap. Columbia's hand automatically started for his forehead, to stroke her fingers through the coarse texture of his hair.

She stopped herself in midair.

"What're you doin', layin' back down?" she rasped.

"It's my head," he offered easily. He looked up at her with those inviting obsidian eyes. "Terrible headache. It helps to set my head down on something soft. It does not bother ya'll, does it?"

Bother me? she thought uneasily. *Of course, I'm bothered.* "No. Guess there's no harm in it."

"Good. Because keeping my head down makes me feel so much better."

"I'm sure it does," she answered feebly, all too aware

136

that his head rested against the apex of her thighs.

"While we are waiting, ya'll might fill me in on what's going on around here."

He didn't know, did he? "What's going on?" she echoed.

"With the Indian problem."

She let out a sigh. A feeling of frustration circled her. "Oh."

She made herself relax and leaned back on her hands, forcing herself to think of something other than Nash Foster, and what being so close to him was doing to her. "I'm not sayin' that the Indians ain't to blame for what's happenin' here today, but the whites ain't been very nice to them, considerin' they were here first. The whites started killin' the Indians several years back, because they were in their way." She shrugged. "So the Indians stole guns and started shootin' back . . ."

As Nash listened, he was drawn by her big heart. She seemed to have a good understanding of the situation. She was unselfish and sympathetic in her assessment, which made him rate Columbia very favorably against Jennifer Kiplinger and her self-seeking, spoiled heart.

". . . things really got out of hand when a group of volunteers broke a truce flag with *Peo-peo-mox-mox*."

"*Peo-peo-mox-mox?*"

"A local Indian."

He nodded his understanding.

"Instead of talkin' like they should've done, they caged him up, then shot him. Afterwards they cut off his ears and scalped him. And that ain't the worst of it. They pickled them and sold them as souvenirs. Ever since—"

More shots rang out, breaking into Columbia's tale. She shot a glance at Nash, and was silently thankful that

137

they were safely tucked away from all the carnage that must still be occurring outside.

"Anyway, as I was sayin', as more 'n' more folks moved into the area, the problems just seem to grow. Don't know where it's goin' to end. But Indians is just one of the things a body's got to contend with haulin' cargo up from Portland."

"Guess I'm learning to contend with Indians first-hand."

Nash detected the subtle hint, she was trying to warn him off hauling cargo between Portland and Lower Cascades. He knew she could not come right out with what she was thinking, since she was masquerading as his cabin boy.

"How long have you been on the river?" he asked.

"All my life."

"Then ya'll know Columbia Baranoff?"

Columbia blinked at the unexpected question, but quickly hooded her eyes. "Guess I'm a mite familiar with her."

"Tell me about her."

"Why?" He was looking up at her with those incredible black eyes that reflected a hidden fire. She felt the fire in her own eyes begin to simmer, and she had to turn before she gave herself away.

"Just curious, is all."

"Not a lot to tell, really. She grew up on that paddle wheeler, her ma and pa ran it then. She got her love of the river from them."

"What happened to them?"

"The boiler blew, and the river claimed them when she was nine," she said with a sadness in her voice. "Folks figured she'd leave the river and go back East to school, like

138

her uncle wanted. But she proved them all wrong. She grew up here, managed to get that old boat pieced together, and kept it runnin'. She was doin' pretty well, too, until 'bout three years ago, when John Villamoore showed up in Portland with his pockets full of money and big plans to take over all the haulin' on the river."

"I thought her uncle was captain of that boat."

"Unc . . . ah . . . Titus is," she said too quickly, in an effort to cover the mistake she had almost made. "And what about you?" she asked hurriedly, in order to shift the direction of his probing questions.

He had made her uncomfortable. Despite the desire to learn more about her, he decided not to push her. "I was an orphan. Grew up in Nashville in the same orphanage as Barth."

"Nashville?"

"In answer to the question on your face, yes, I was named after Tennessee's capital city. Guess the people at the orphanage ran out of boys' names before they got to me," he added bitterly.

"I like the name. Why, think about the girl we were just talking about."

"Columbia?"

"Sure. She took the name of the river she loves. So why shouldn't you have the name of the town where you were born and spent your formative years?"

He had to smile at the analogy. "Guess that gives Columbia and me a common bond," he said, and gazed directly into her eyes again.

A strange twinge squeezed her chest at the way he mentioned that they shared a common bond. His voice had been soft and full of innuendo. The similarities of their situations in life, both not having parents, also

139

caught her. They had more in common than she had realized.

"Was livin' at the orphanage so bad?" she questioned. Concern for the sorry childhood he must have had and remembrances of the picture in his cabin filled her, and she found herself wanting to reach out to him, to stroke away the tension she felt invade his body.

"As soon as Barth and I were old enough, we set out on our own. Managed to scrape enough together to buy the *Yacht.* The rest is history," he offered, skirting the sordid details of what brought him to the Columbia River.

"What brought you to Oregon country?"

"Fortune."

The mention of money—coupled with Nash's working for Villamoore—caused her sympathy to fade.

"If you're after quick easy money, workin' for a snake like Villamoore ain't so smart."

"Oh, I don't know. I think that it has worked out pretty good so far," he said. He should thank Villamoore. If it hadn't been for the man, Nash wouldn't be lying with his head in Columbia's lap right now.

"You got brains enough, you don't need to work for the likes of Villamoore."

"Thanks for the vote of confidence." He flashed her a bright smile. Quietly he firmed an earlier resolution to find out exactly what Villamoore was up to. "Ya'll not only look like Columbia Baranoff, ya'll are starting to sound like her as well."

She thought fast. "That's probably 'cause most folks in these parts feel the same way about Villamoore. Given a choice, the good people around here would rather see Villamoore and his kind run off the river. But folks got families to feed."

140

"Is that Columbia's choice? Would she truly like to see Villamoore run out of Oregon?"

"More'n anybody."

"Ya'll seem to know more about the girl than most."

Columbia pinched her lips. She had let the subject of Villamoore loosen her tongue too much. "No more than any of the others who've lived in these parts all their lives. It's just that most is afraid to talk about the man."

Nash nodded. She had not answered his inquiry, but he decided not to press the girl further. She was getting jumpy, and he did not want to frighten her.

More sounds of gunfire broke into the silence that had fallen between them.

"Sounds as if we are going to be here for a while. Better get some sleep."

"Why?"

"We shall need rest, then we can escape under cover of dark."

"Good idea," she said with a nod. But the warmth that continued to assail her body from where his head rested made sleep an impossibility.

Columbia leaned her shoulder against the rough wall of the crate and closed her eyes, but sleep did not come. For hours she listened to Nash's gentle snoring. She inhaled the fragrance of leather and manly scent that mixed with the smell of the wood that sheltered them; it only served to heighten her senses.

In an effort to put him out of her mind, she shifted positions, but his arms snaked around her waist, his face burrowed at the base of her lap. Her feminine core heated and she held her breath.

It was going to be a very, very long afternoon.

Chapter Fifteen

The light inside the warehouse was beginning to wane, but distant sounds of sporadic gunfire still issued around the town. Columbia's leg was starting to go to sleep. When she tried to shift positions without awakening Nash, she was suddenly grasped by a cramp in her hip. She jerked at the unanticipated spasm.

"What is wrong?" Nash started, abruptly wrenched awake.

She rubbed furiously at the pain. "Cramp."

"Here, stretch out and I shall rub it for ya'll."

She shook her head in protest, but he pushed her down on her side and began to knead her hip joint. "Relax, Columbus, ya'll will be feeling better before you know it."

Better wasn't the word she would have used to describe how she was feeling. His fingers were magical fire through her trousers, and she squirmed.

"Lie still." He kneaded for a while longer. "How does that feel?"

Her throat was as dry as a ship's boiler fully loaded. "Feel?" Her voice cracked.

"The cramp?"

"Oh. Fine. You can stop now." Another spasm grabbed her and she flinched.

"Maybe ya'll ought to pull those trousers down, so I can rub the skin directly," he advised.

At that Columbia scooted as far away from him as possible, and stared at him. "I ain't takin' my pants down for you or nobody."

He had taunted her without meaning to, but the thought of running his fingers along that soft sensitive skin was nearly overwhelming, and he found it difficult to control the urge. Although patience had never been one of his better qualities, he had the distinct feeling that it was a virtue he was going to be forced to acquire with this female.

"For a young man, ya'll sure got some funny notions about modesty. I was just trying to help work out that cramp, but if ya'll would rather suffer with it—"

"It's fine now," she shot back.

Two loud blasts from an approaching paddle wheeler filled the air, saving Columbia from having to continue with her weak excuses. Moments later the sounds of gunfire and shouts of men routing the remaining Indians closed in on the warehouse.

"Sounds as if the *Yacht* has returned with reinforcements," Nash offered, trying to keep the disappointment from his voice. While he was relieved that the Indian threat was over, he regretted having to leave the intimacy of their hiding place.

The cramp gone, Columbia struggled with the weight of the crate and scrambled out into the open.

Nash followed the girl toward the paddle wheeler.

Soldiers roamed over the landing, tending the wounded and restoring order and confidence in the shaken populace now milling around in frightened clusters.

"Nash! Nash!" Barth yelled and ran to meet them. "My God, I was afraid when I left with the boat to get help, that I'd return to find you dead." His eyes trailed to the girl. "I see you found what you went looking for."

Columbia's hand flew to her chest in disbelief. "Me?" She swung on Nash. "You left the safety of your paddle wheeler to come lookin' for *me?*"

Nash merely shrugged. "I would do the same for any member of my crew."

"Sure you would," Barth mumbled.

"Nash!" Dolly cried and rushed into his arms, effectively making Columbia feel as if the woman were stabbing her in the heart.

The curvaceous woman slid her arm around Nash's waist and led him back on board the paddle wheeler, leaving Columbia no other choice than to trail behind them. At the top of the gangplank stood a young captain who Columbia recognized as Phillip Youngston, a sly weasel of a man she had glimpsed hanging around the docks. She was sure he was out to make a name for himself. Thankfully she hadn't had many personal dealings with him since his arrival at Fort Vancouver.

"Captain Phillip Youngston at your service, sir." Youngston stretched out his hand. "I'm glad we were able to reach you in time. Luckily, my men and I were on our way here, and your friend was able to hail us and offer us transport so we could rout the enemy."

Nash assessed the beanpole of a man with the limp

144

handshake as a glory-hogging Yankee climber. "My cabin boy and I were lucky. But I cannot say the same about the cargo we were to haul downriver for Villa-moore. And from the looks of the warehouse, I would say that the Indians managed to clean the place out."

For an instant a strange glint sparked into the man's gray eyes, and Columbia wondered about it until a sergeant's shout intruded into her thoughts.

"Captain Youngston, looks like the rest of them red-skins got away. The men are waiting for further orders."

"If you'll excuse me, Captain Foster, a soldier's work is never done. Duty calls. I do hope we'll have another opportunity to meet again. Maybe in Portland for the celebration at Mr. Villamoore's."

"Celebration?" Columbia rasped, without thinking that her question would draw attention to her. All eyes turned in her direction, and she immediately lowered her head.

"Got the news on the way up here. Oregon has become the thirty-third state. Mr. Villamoore is planning to host a ball in honor of statehood. Heard he has invited the governor and other important people. As one of Mr. Villamoore's latest business associates, Captain Foster, I have no doubt you'll be included . . ."

Columbia listened to the soldier drone on with his own overstuffed self-importance. But her ears perked up when he talked about Villamoore. There had been speculation among the riverboat pilots that Villamoore had bought the protection of the army, and Youngston seemed to be very informed on Villamoore's latest dealings.

When their voices dropped, Columbia edged closer

145

to see if she could glean any more information from the self-absorbed man, but Nash grabbed her arm.

"Columbus, go get yourself cleaned up and get me a hot supper. And then I shall be ready for a bath."

"Another bath?" Columbia cast him a frown and did not move.

"What are ya'll waiting for? Get moving."

"You're a Southerner, sir?" she heard the captain ask Nash, as she grudgingly shuffled along the deck. She'd get him a meal all right, but it wouldn't be hot or to his liking if she could help it.

Columbia stopped to eavesdrop once she rounded the corner.

"Col—Columbus, why don't you come with me?" Dolly amended her near mistake of referring to the girl as Columbia within earshot of others on board, as she came up behind her.

Columbia swung around and stopped short. She had not expected to see the concern written across Nash Foster's wife's face. Columbia secretly wanted to dislike the woman, but how could she when the woman was smiling so warmly?

"You need something?" Columbia finally managed to get out.

"No, but I think that you do."

Dolly swung around and headed toward a small cabin not far from Nash's. Columbia wistfully glanced back toward the men, still engaged in a conversation she would not be able to overhear now.

"You coming?" Dolly asked.

Columbia's head swivelled back toward the woman. What choice did she have? "Yes, ma'am."

Columbia followed the woman into her tidy cabin.

146

Dolly shut the door, turned the key in the lock, and dropped it down the front of her ruffled shirt front, causing Columbia disbelieving discomfort.

What could the woman be up to?

Columbia blinked and stood up straighter as she edged out of reach.

Furrowing her brows, Columbia said, "I don't know what you got in mind, but I think I'd better get your husband's supper before he comes lookin' for me. Can't afford to lose my job. I need the money, and as I told you, I got a hankerin' for Barth."

Dolly threw back her head and laughed. The poor girl obviously thought she could continue to fool Dolly into thinking it was Barth the girl was after. Despite the obvious spark between Miss Columbia Baranoff and Nash, the girl hadn't fallen total victim to his easy-going charm, as most females did.

Dolly feared the game the pair seemed to be playing with each other, and wanted to unmask Columbia before Nash got hurt. But Dolly had taken a liking to the young girl, and privately admired her pluck.

Ignoring her better judgment, Dolly sat down on the bed and patted the place next to her. "If you need money, I can think of a real exciting, not to mention most amusing, way to earn a little extra," she said in a velvety purr, and wrapped a red curl around her index finger.

Columbia pointed to the door. "But what about your husband? What if he comes in? He—"

"I locked the door, remember? This is just between us girls."

Not knowing what else to do, Columbia shuffled over to the bed and eased on to a far corner. She did not take her eyes off the well-endowed woman, while she waited for Nash's wife to make some dreadful suggestion.

Dolly inched over to Columbia and put her hand on the girl's shoulder. The girl cringed. With the crook of her finger, Dolly raised the girl's face and studied it.

Columbia Baranoff had a fresh young face with large turquoise eyes, fringed with a thick forest of lashes. Her nose was curved up, and her full lips were set in a defiant slash.

"You are a pretty young woman," Dolly observed.

Columbia jerked her head away from the cloying woman. "I ain't pretty," she muttered. "I got to go."

Columbia scooted off the bed, determined to keep her distance from the woman, but Dolly grabbed her arm.

"Not much meat on those bones."

Columbia flung her arm away. "I got enough. I don't know what you got in mind, so you'd better let me out of here before I'm forced to tell your husband that you might've been up to no good."

Again Dolly had to throw back her head and laugh. The girl was spirited, direct, and irrepressible, despite her apparent unease. "I like you."

Columbia frowned. "I was afraid you did and that's the problem, ma'am."

Dolly continued to chuckle. "No, no, you don't know at all."

"I got a feelin' I might know what you got on your mind, and I ain't gonna be a party to none of it. You hear me?"

"Yes, yes, honey, I hear you. Now come back and sit beside me. I promise not to make you uncomfortable again. I don't know what came over me, but I just couldn't help myself. It is just that you looked so sure I was up to no good."

Columbia gingerly perched on the edge of the bed and glared at the woman who was grinning back at her. "And I suppose now you're tryin' to tell me that you weren't tryin' to get me to do something for you that might let you go against your marriage vows?"

"I'm not that kind of woman, I assure you. But I do like my men, yes."

"What?"

"I said that I'm partial to the male species." The girl gasped, but made no further effort to learn what Dolly was talking about. Dolly waited a short time longer, but still the girl remained silent, staring at her with wary eyes.

"Look, honey, you may be able to fool a man with that act, but you can't fool another female. So you might as well quit trying."

Columbia narrowed her eyes. "I don't rightly know what you're talkin' about."

"You can quit acting. I know you're not interested in Barth."

Not giving the girl a chance at further denial, Dolly's hand swooped over and scooped off Columbia's cherished knit cap.

Columbia let out a squeal and grabbed for the cap, but the hair she had so carefully hidden tumbled over her shoulders and down her back, long and shiny black. "So what did you do that for? You already know I'm female. I suppose now you're gonna run right to your husband and tell him."

Dolly picked a lint ball off the well-worn hat. "I'm

not goin' to tell Nash a thing as long . . ."

"As long as what?" Columbia asked suspiciously.

Dolly got up and wandered around the little cabin. "As long as you tell me exactly what you are up to."

"I ain't up to nothin'," Columbia' insisted.

"I know you said you dressed like a boy to catch Barth's attention. But that isn't the only reason you're dressed like a boy and working on board Nash's boat, is it?"

"I can't tell you."

"Can't or won't?"

Columbia remained silent, glaring at the woman as she frantically tried to figure out how to salvage her scheme. The woman was standing in front of her, tapping her foot, her fingernails drumming along her crossed arms.

Columbia sighed. "All right, if I let you in on my secret, will you promise not to say nothin' to Nash?"

"Depends on what you're hiding. If you're on board to hurt him in any way, I'll personally toss you overboard."

The woman's vehemence took Columbia by surprise, but then she had to remember Dolly was Nash's wife, so her response was only natural. Columbia took a deep breath, crossed her fingers behind her back, and hoped that the woman would accept the story she was about to spin.

Columbia slumped her shoulders and hung her head in order to give credence to her explanation. "You ain't goin' to like it none."

"Try me."

"Okay. From the first moment I set eyes on Nash, I got a hankerin' for him. Just couldn't help myself. And

150

my pa taught me to go after what I wanted." Columbia paused and set her expression into one of guilt-ridden conscience.

Dolly cocked a brow and said, "So you thought you could get closer to Nash and edge me out, by sneaking on board and working for him?"

"Bein' his cabin boy was his idea, not mine. I just wanted to be near Nash, and maybe find out if you two were truly happily married. If you wasn't . . . well, then . . ."

"Then you thought you could steal Nash for yourself?"

"Yeah, if you must know." Columbia pressed her lips together and waited for Dolly's response.

Dolly threw back her head and laughed. "Let me get this straight. You let me think you were pining for Barth, because you hoped to snatch Nash out from under me, if his marriage wasn't in your opinion what it should be?" She paused and her faced turned serious. "And that is truly the only reason you are on board?"

Columbia took a buoying breath. "What other reason could there be?"

Chapter Sixteen

From the look on Dolly's face, it was evident that she was beginning to believe that Columbia had a hankering for her man and that was the only reason she was on board. Well, if the woman wanted to accept that she had a secret yearning for her husband, and if that would satisfy her, that was what Columbia would confess to.

"Okay. Yeah. That is the only reason I sneaked on board . . . because I got a hankerin' for your man." Columbia hung her head as if ashamed, but she watched the woman from beneath her thick lashes.

Dolly clasped her hands together. "I knew it!"

Surprise at the woman's exuberance overwhelmed Columbia. Her eyes rounded and her head bobbed up. "You ain't riled?"

The girl looked suspicious, and Dolly suddenly realized that she had better be careful, or the girl would find out that Nash and she weren't truly married. She had taken it upon herself to confront the girl, and she did not want to upset or anger Nash.

Dolly took a deep breath.

"Well, I'm not going to say that a wife would readily welcome it. But . . . well . . . Nash and me, we aren't exactly ah, jealous. That's it! We aren't jealous of each other."

Columbia nodded and pretended to understand. But fact was, she didn't understand at all. If she were married to Nash Foster, she wouldn't allow another woman anywhere near him without one hell of a fight. The thought of marriage popping up again—and especially to Nash Foster of all people—totally unsettled Columbia, and her hand unconsciously went to her rapidly thundering heart.

"I can see from your expression that you're a little puzzled by our arrangement."

"Can't say that I conceive it," Columbia admitted and dropped her hand.

Dolly leaned forward and squeezed the girl's work-roughened hand; it was trembling. The girl's reaction to her announcement only served to reinforce Dolly's suspicions that she truly did have feelings for Nash. "If you promise not to let on to a soul, I'll let you in on a secret."

Columbia wanted to trust the woman, but a lingering doubt made her pull her hand back and place it in the other one in an effort to still the shaking. "I'm not sure that's a thing you should—"

"Nonsense." Dolly rolled her eyes. She was trying to help the little chit, and here she was having to force it on her! After all, it wasn't as if she were breaking a promise; Nash hadn't actually sworn her to silence. "The simple truth is that I don't love Nash."

Columbia's brows shot up. "Ain't he no good?"

"Honey, Nash is the best, believe you me. Nash was

153

kind enough to marry me to help me out of trouble. You see, I needed a protector."

Columbia kept her face impassive, despite the increased furious thudding of her heart. "Then you truly don't love him?"

"Oh, I do. I do," Dolly amended the tale she had just conjured up.

A surge of disappointment filled Columbia, and she said, "Oh."

"I do love him, but not the way you think. More like the love of a sister for a brother." Columbia's face slid into an expression of hopeful confusion. "I can see that you don't understand. You see, he married me and took me away from New York to save me from a lowdown snake that was after me."

"That why you have separate cabins?"

"Yes."

"No matter. He's still your man, all legal before God," Columbia reasoned, having forgotten her supposed intention for being on board.

Dolly pressed her lips together. If the pair were meant to be together, she was not going to be the one to stand in the way of the scheme of things, even if a few more innocent falsehoods were necessary. "We aim to get divorced just as soon as it can be arranged." Dolly smiled overly bright, then mumbled, "Yes, that's it. We'll be getting a divorce just as soon as it can be arranged."

An idea suddenly sprinted into Dolly's mind: a way she could repay Nash for giving her the opportunity to change her life. She clasped her hands together in glee and moved to the edge of her seat. "If you'd allow me, I can still be of service to you in the meantime."

154

Columbia did not like the dancing gleam in Dolly's eyes. The woman had something up those fancy satin sleeves of hers, and Columbia fretted that whatever it was, she was not going to like it.

"I can see you're a mite wary. But if you'd allow me, I can help you land Nash instead of Barth like we agreed before. I know Nash better'n anybody in these parts, I reckon, 'cept of course for Barth, I suppose, and I can help make you into the kind of woman he can't resist."

Lines furrowed across Columbia's forehead. "I ain't never wanted to change none. What makes you think he wouldn't have a hankerin' for me the way I am?" she blurted out, before suddenly realizing that she had been caught up in Dolly's enthusiasm and forgotten why she was aboard Nash Foster's paddle wheeler.

"Oh, he would. He would, I'm sure. It is only that I might be able to move things along a little faster, is all."

"Move things along a little faster?" Columbia echoed. But her thoughts of moving things along a little faster had shifted to a different vein, and she ran an index finger along her lower lip.

"Yes. If you dressed up like a finely attired young lady, Nash immediately would be so smitten, that he would not be able to think about anything else but you . . ."

Dolly gushed forth with a myriad of suggestions for making Columbia over, but Columbia's mind was awhirl with the possibilities of using Nash Foster's attentions to finally get something on Villamoore.

Cutting Dolly off, Columbia asked, "You sure that Nash wouldn't be able to think of nothin' else but me, if I let you gussy me all up like some frilly female?"

"I can guarantee it!" Dolly jumped to her feet and grabbed Columbia's hand. "You just come with me. I've the perfect outfit stored in my trunk downstairs, it'll have Nash's heartstrings all tied in knots before he knows what did it."

Dolly was dragging Columbia down a corridor, chattering like a schoolgirl, when Nash rounded the corner. "What do ya'll think you are doing with my cabin boy?"

The seriousness of his tone caused Columbia to yank her hand back and stop in her tracks. "She was lookin' for me to help her with—"

Nash's black eyes flashed. "Thought I told ya'll that your job was to care for me . . . only for me."

His choice of words was unsettling. "You did but—"

"No. No buts." His steady gaze shifted to Dolly, who had remained silent under his censoring stance. "If ya'll need anything, wife dear, have one of the crew help you. Columbus only takes orders from me. Is that understood?"

Columbia's first impulse was to inform him that she did not take orders from any man, but thought better of it. Instead she realized she could use this time on board his paddle wheeler to learn more about Foster's habits, which might come in handy later.

Dolly opened her mouth to protest, but shut it at Columbia's silently beseeching gestures from behind Nash.

"You don't have to worry none, for the rest of the trip I'll be the best cabin *boy* you ever had," Columbia announced, to reinforce the silent message she had been trying to convey to Dolly.

If he discovered now that she had been masquerad-

156

ing as his cabin boy, she would never be able to use him to trap Villamoore. And he certainly would not become very smitten with someone who had practiced such a deception on him.

Nash cocked a brow. Something told him to beware. Females putting their heads together generally meant only one thing: Trouble. "Wife dear, I want to see ya'll in my cabin. Now."

He took hold of Dolly's arm and began to usher her toward his cabin. The sound of softly padding footsteps echoed after them. He stopped and swung around to come face to face with Columbia. "What do ya'll think you are doing?"

"I'm your cabin boy. I'm goin' to your cabin. What else would I be doin'?"

He took hold of her shoulders and swung her around. "And since ya'll plan to be the best cabin boy I have ever had, you will be taking yourself to the wheelhouse to fetch me one of my special cigars. I need a smoke."

Columbia sucked in her cheeks. He was using her own words to defeat her. "Thought you wanted food and a bath?"

"Later. I have changed my mind. Now I need one of my special cigars."

Despite her annoyance she smiled brightly. "Special it'll be."

"I am looking forward to it."

"I'll just bet you are," she groused.

Columbia hid her disappointment behind a big salute and headed toward the wheelhouse, grumbling to herself on the merits of being one's own boss.

"What'd you do that for?" Dolly whined once she

was left standing alone with Nash.

"Because you and I need to have a private little talk" — he swung the door to his cabin open and nudged her inside — "alone." Nash closed the door. "Sit down, Dolly."

With apprehension filling her breast, Dolly settled gingerly on the straight-back chair at his desk. "I'm sitting."

"Good." He stood over the woman with his fists on his hips. "Now ya'll can let me in on what you were cooking up with that river girl."

"What makes you think we were cooking anything up?"

"Do not try that innocent routine on me. What are ya'll up to?"

"Up to?" she gulped out. She felt like a trapped animal frantically groping for an escape. None came to her.

"Yes, up to. And I want the truth," Nash said with conviction.

Dolly swallowed the uneasiness clogging her throat. "We were merely having a little girl talk, is all," she offered with a meek shrug.

His brow cocked up. "What kind of little girl talk?"

"You know. The kind when one female asks another in the know about a certain gentleman what takes her fancy," she hedged. "So you don't have to worry anymore about getting mixed up with her yourself," she added for good measure, remembering a talk they'd had earlier.

A twinge of jealousy speared Nash, although he certainly could not understand why he felt envious of one of the crew. Actually the man should be pitied. Mary

158

Catherine Columbia Baranoff was a mere green cattail of a female, barely recognizable as female on her best behavior. Yet, as he pondered such an outrageous notion for her sneaking on board his paddle wheeler, he concluded it was conceivable. The very thought of her with another man irked Nash though.

"What certain gentlemen?" Nash heard himself ask.

The tiniest smile materialized at the corners of Dolly's lips, and the method of escape she had worried about came to her. Nash was not as oblivious to the girl as he thought he was. "You jealous?"

"*Annoyed* with her presence on board would be a more appropriate word."

For an instant Dolly's plans for Nash and Columbia crumbled. But Nash had started to pace. It was a sign she had seen in other men when something weighed heavily on their minds. Obviously Columbia was weighing heavily on Nash's. He suddenly stopped and swung on her.

"Which one?"

"Would you believe Barth?" she said in a small choked voice, meant to make him think that he had forced it out of her. She didn't want to lie to Nash, but after all it was for Nash's own good. Some men didn't know what was best for them, until all the details were arranged and events set in motion. In Dolly's mind Nash was one of them. "Yes. It's Barth. The girl said that she took an instant liking to him back in Portland, and sneaked on board so she could get closer to him . . ."

Dolly prattled on about the girl's request for help with Barth, but Nash was no longer listening. His mind was busy replaying the time he had spent with

159

Columbia. In the short period he had known her, she had made an impression on him like no other female ever had, and if anyone was going to lay claim to Mary Catherine Columbia Baranoff, it was going to be him and no other.

But before Nash could proceed with a deeper exploration of his awakening feelings for Columbia, he had to find out what Villamoore was up to. The scoundrel was out to ruin Columbia and her uncle, not to mention what else he might have in store for them. And Columbia thought Nash was mixed up with Villamoore. Nash had to put a stop to it, in order to prove to her that he was not part of whatever scheme Villamoore was planning, or she would never believe that his intentions toward her were without ulterior motives.

". . . I've got a feeling from the way Barth has been secretly sneaking glances at Columbia when he thinks no one is noticing, that he just might have an interest in her as well," Dolly was saying when Nash returned his attention to her.

He scowled. The realization that his friend Barth might be harboring the same powerful desire for Columbia only served to further complicate things. Even though Barth hadn't said anything to him, if he truly was preparing to stake out a claim to Columbia, Nash was going to be forced to change his owns plans for her, regardless of his personal desire to possess the girl. Barth was the closest thing Nash had to family; he was like a brother. He could not compete with his brother over a woman . . . or could he?

Nash's scowl deepened, causing Dolly to pause. Her plan to arouse Nash's jealousy and encourage him to take an active interest in pursuing Columbia before Barth snatched her up for himself did not seem to be working in the manner she had hoped. Simply put, it was not having the desired effect.

"What's the matter, Nash honey? You look as if you have just been jilted."

"In a sense, maybe I just have." Nash gave a bitter laugh at the sudden irony of it all.

Chapter Seventeen

Dolly scratched her head and stared at Nash. His comment about being jilted did not make any sense. She thought about it for a moment longer, then decided that he must have been referring to that woman back in New York that she had overheard Nash and Barth talking about.

Thinking about Barth, she rose to her feet. She had to get to him and beg him to go along with her plan. "Now that you know what we were talking about, mind if I get back to my cabin? I've got a lot to do."

"I think I have heard more than enough. Go ahead." Nash turned his back to her, effectively dismissing Dolly from his mind.

He plunked onto his bunk, feeling strangely weighted down by a problem he had never encountered before: the first inkling of something much more powerful and consuming than he had ever experienced. He rubbed his aching temples. Women had always been a game with him and Barth, a friendly competition, a temporary diversion. But this was different. Although he could not quite fathom such crazy feelings, he did not want to make Columbia an amusement. Did Barth—or did Barth's secret intentions—run along the same lines as his? And did his own intentions include more than possession?

Although he was not exactly sure what it was, Nash knew he wanted more from Columbia than he had from the other women he had bedded. If he had merely wanted to bed the feisty female, he could have accomplished that back in the warehouse. But with great difficulty he had controlled himself. He shook his head. That certainly was another first in his life.

"Damn!" Nash surged to his feet and stomped to the hook where his heavy jacket hung. "Is what I feel for her supposed to be grand, or some such nonsense like that?" Nash grunted to himself, feeling anything but grand.

He had overcome the rotten deal that life dealt him with each turn of the cards, and he would overcome this, too. If Barth and Columbia wanted each other, Nash was going to put her out of his mind . . . wasn't he?

He shrugged into his heavy jacket and left his cabin. A cold gust of wind slapped at him as he trudged along the deck. Columbia was heading toward him. The sight of her caused Nash a momentary instant of regret, and his mood darkened.

"What are ya'll doing up on deck?" he asked harshly upon reaching her.

Annoyed by his tone, Columbia thrust out her hand; her fingers curled around three of his smelly cigars. "I was doin' your errands. Here." She stabbed them at him. "I'll go get your meal next," she announced in a tight voice.

"Forget the meal. Instead, report to Barth. Ya'll will be joining the rest of the crew for the trip back to Portland."

Columbia felt like she had just been kicked in the gut. "Ain't I doin' my job?"

Nash gritted his teeth. She had done her job all right. Too well. "I just do not need ya'll any longer."

He started to walk away from her, but Columbia grabbed his arm. "You ain't gonna hire me on to be your cabin boy for the trip, and then in the middle of it, just up and send me packin' to bunk with the crew. No sirree. We got a deal and I aim to hold you to it. You're stuck with me 'til we get back to Portland. Then I quit!"

Her piece said, Columbia swung around and, despite the shaking in her knees, managed to return to his cabin and slam the door behind her. She threw the bolt and slid to the floor. She was on board to trap Villamoore through Nash, she reminded herself. But a strange empty feeling had settled in the depths of her heart.

Nash did not want her. Columbia decided that he had been merely funning with his cabin boy back at the warehouse. It shouldn't make any difference how he felt toward her, since he didn't know his cabin boy was Columbia, but the simple fact was, it did.

Columbia forced herself to get to her feet and started to strip off her jacket. She caught sight of herself in the mirror on the table. She really was a sight, she admitted. No man would want somebody who looked like she did — greasy strands of hair sticking out of her cap, dirty men's clothes, streaked face.

She leaned over and smoothed her palms over her smudged cheeks. "Maybe Uncle Titus's right. You're a sight, Columbia," she said to her reflection. "No matter. With Dolly's help, you're gonna set that man's head to spinnin'. Then when he's got a hankerin' for you, you'll be able to use him to stop Villamoore."

The paddle wheeler's whistle blasted, catching her attention. They would be starting back to Portland shortly, and then Nash Foster would be sorry. If — once she was all gussied up in female frillies — he thought he could treat her like some fancy loose woman for his own pleasure, discard her, and expect her to go away meekly, like he was doing to his cabin boy, he would discover he had picked on the wrong female!

Columbia grabbed her heavy jacket and ran out on deck. Standing at the edge of the gangplank, Captain Youngston was bidding farewell to Nash. She watched them shake hands, then the soldier departed just before the gangplank was swung into place and the paddle wheeler edged away from the shore.

"Psst. Psst. Columbia," came a high-pitched hiss.

Columbia swung from the rail. Dolly was frantically waving. "Hurry. Over here."

Columbia followed Dolly to her cabin. Once they were safely inside the cabin out of earshot, Dolly let out a squeal and clasped Columbia by the shoulders. "Everything is proceeding as planned."

"Everything?" Columbia questioned at the woman's

165

exuberance.

"Yes. I spoke to Barth, and he's agreed to help out." She shrugged. "Or at least not to run and tell Nash."

"Why? I thought he was Nash's friend," Columbia said, bemused.

Dolly gave the girl a conspiratorial grin. "He didn't want no part of it at first. But when we talked about how Nash wanted you as his personal cabin boy, and protected you like you were a fine jewel, Barth finally agreed. Let's face it, even if Nash don't realize it himself yet, you two are the perfect pair."

"Yeah. The perfect pair," Columbia muttered. Only what Dolly didn't know was that Nash had already made other arrangements. Then she realized she shouldn't be so all-fired stirred up. He was getting rid of his cabin boy, not *her*.

"What's the matter, honey? You got a change of heart?"

Columbia thought about her beloved paddle wheeler and her plans for the future. Nothing or no one was going to get in her way of obtaining that goal.

"No. No change of heart. Nash Foster is the one I want."

"Good. Let's get a better look at the hair you keep hidden. I want a better look at what I got to work with."

Before Columbia could stop the woman, she had snatched her cap off and Columbia's wavy mass of black hair plunged over her shoulders and down her back. Dolly smoothed a hand down the length of heavy tresses.

"You shouldn't try to hide your hair; it's lovely."

"No, it ain't. It's grease black." Columbia grabbed her cap back and hurriedly stuffed the unruly strands back inside the cap. "It just keeps gettin' in the way all the time. Why, it's so long that it almost got caught up in the engine one time, when I was workin' on it. Then there was the time it got singed, 'cause I was workin' on the boiler. Almost cut it off once, but Uncle Titus stopped me."

Dolly took in a deep breath. She had her work cut out for her. Columbia was not going to be a willing student.

The paddle wheeler jerked, nearly knocking Dolly off her feet. She grabbed for the edge of the bed. "My God, we must have hit something in the river! We're going to sink! We'll all be sent to the bottom."

"Ain't nothin' to worry about. We got a pretty late start from Lower Cascades. I suspect we just put in for the night. Night ain't no time to be navigatin' the river."

Dolly sank onto the bed and breathed a sigh of relief. "We weren't out on the river very long."

Columbia merely shrugged and decided that now was not the time to make the effort to explain the ways of riverboating.

Patting her pounding chest, Dolly glanced up in time to see Columbia open the door. "Where you going? We got a lot still to do before you'll be ready to make a grand entrance for Nash."

"Maybe so. But right now I got to tend to my duties as cabin boy."

Columbia shut the door behind her and headed toward Nash's cabin. Her mind was filled with dread over spending the night in the same cabin with Nash after what had already transpired between them. She could still feel the way he'd touched her and set her skin on fire while they were inside the crate, and she wondered what the night would bring.

It was way past midnight by the time Nash returned to his cabin. He had spent hours carefully prying open the crates the crew had managed to load before the Indian attack. He closely examined the contents of the containers he was carrying for Villamoore. The only thing that Nash had learned was that Villamoore was a very careful man. The crates had contained nothing more than cargo that might have been expected of any ordinary citizen. Nash was running a simple haul of supplies and goods sent from upriver.

Nash had to smile to himself as he closed the door, Villamoore was apparently testing him. Nash wondered about the rifles the Indians had found in the warehouse.

He put the man out of his mind and glanced around his cabin.

A dim light flickered in the gently swaying lamp, sending shapeless patterns around the walls. A tower of cold food rested on a table next to a bath of obviously cold water. Clean clothes rested neatly on his bed. The girl had done all the things a wife might have done. "That's the last thing I need," he breathed, caught unprepared by such an outrageous thought.

His gaze snagged on Columbia.

She lay huddled beneath a blanket on the floor next to his bed . . . fast asleep.

Nash let his eyes rove over her slender form, hinted at beneath the cover. Despite her thinness, Columbia was not entirely lacking for curves. Her waist dipped, then the blanket rose over the gentle swell of her hips and draped seductively along the length of thighs, that promised to be able to wrap a man within a lovemaking embrace.

It was tempting to slip beneath the cover and envelop her with his body, shield her from the cold, protect her as if she were his own. But she thought that he was unaware of who she really was. So instead, Nash lit the lamp next to the bed, and turned out the hanging one. He kneeled down and scooped her up in his arms.

"Umm." Columbia moaned in her sleep and wrapped her arms around his neck, nestling her face against his chest. Her actions were at once erotic and innocent. And Nash had to fight an inner battle to restrain himself.

He leaned over, and with one hand threw back the blankets. Settling the sleeping girl down, he tried to straighten up. But her hands were clasped tightly around his neck.

"Come on, my sleeping darlin', relax your hold," he crooned in a rich whisper.

She groaned no in displeasure when he worked her fingers free. And in her sleep, with her pert, windburned face turned up toward him, she reached out to him as if expecting to be kissed.

It was more than he could withstand.

Originally Nash had planned to tuck the girl into bed and then join Barth. But even in her sleep she was beckoning him. Against his better judgement, Nash quickly tossed off his clothing and slid between the covers.

To his further amazement, Columbia cuddled along the length of ·him and entwined her legs around his, setting him on fire. Her arms snaked over his chest, and soon her head was cradled in the crook of his arm.

"If ya'll only knew what a temptress you truly are," Nash murmured against her temple, before he leaned over and snuffed out the light. He then gently dropped a kiss on her forehead, marveling at how soundly she slept, and knowing that being so close to her meant that he was not going to get any sleep.

Staring up at the dark ceiling, Nash futilely tried to direct his burning senses to somewhere else.

Columbia's senses were also burning. She had not been fully asleep when Nash returned; she had been just drifting off. She had feared that he would order her from the cabin, and she had no intention of going, so she had feigned deep sleep. At first when he'd lifted her into his arms, she groggily had thought to protest, but then a sweet lethargy overcame her.

Yet once she had curved her arms around his neck and leaned her head against his hard chest, a strange warmth tingled through her. It was the same feeling she had experienced before when he had touched her.

When he had laid her down on the bed and seemed poised to leave, she could not bear it. She wanted to lie next to him. And in Columbia's sleepy mind, it was a perfectly natural thing to do.

Only she hadn't counted on the burgeoning excitement that coursed through her entire being, bringing her to full awareness when he joined her on the bed. Something was driving her, an urge as old as time itself that she could not control, that she did not want to control. She pressed her hips tightly against his, and rubbed her inner thigh up and down his leg.

Her hands had just begun their descent over his hardened nipples, past his belly, and were drifting lower, when suddenly she found herself thrust backwards from the sudden shift of weight off the bed.

"Damn it all to a watery hell," Nash cursed in a soft, pained voice and leapt from the mattress.

He relit the lamp, turning it up until he could just barely make out her features. "If I did not know better, I would swear ya'll were not asleep," he whispered to her slumbering form.

He nudged a pillow into his vacated spot, and she promptly cosseted it to her as she had him. Disappointment filled Nash. "So it was not me ya'll wanted," he said aloud without meaning to.

Columbia kept her eyes closed, although she longed to respond. She longed to inform him that she wasn't asleep, and to open her arms to him. She longed to tell him that it was he who she wanted.

For some reason, while she had lain in his arms, she felt she could trust this man who should be her enemy. With his displays of kindness, his consider-

171

ation, and manly gentleness, he was awakening the woman within her. He could have taken advantage of her, yet he hadn't.

And for the first time in her life, she wanted to learn what mating with a man was all about.

Chapter Eighteen

Columbia stood at the railing and watched the city of Portland come into view through the icy pelting winds. The entire town seemed to be all decked out. American flags and streamers fluttered from buildings, proclaiming Oregon's statehood. The paddle wheeler eased into the dock draped with red, white, and blue.

She was excited that Oregon now had statehood, but a certain disappointment filled her that the voyage was about to end. She had not accomplished what she'd set out to do. She was no closer to trapping Villamoore. And Nash had left the cabin last night and had avoided her since, barking at anyone who had the misfortune to come within earshot.

Columbia jammed her hands into her pockets and walked down the gangplank. Masquerading as Foster's cabin boy had only served to throw her together with the man and nearly addle her brain, although a nagging in the back of her mind kept coming back to the guns the Indians had pulled from the crates in the warehouse in Lower Cascades.

"Columbus, where do ya'll think you are going?" Nash shouted from the hurricane deck. "Ya'll have not finished serving as my cabin boy yet."

Columbia pivoted around. "And I ain't gonna either," she shouted back. "I already told you—I quit."

Nash did not want her to leave, despite his resolve to stay away from her. "If ya'll do not return now and finish the job you were hired for, ya'll will not get paid."

Despite a secret urge to remain, she ignored him and kept walking. He could keep his money, although she had to admit money was hard to come by, and it would come in mighty handy to keep their creditors away a little longer. She put such gloomy thoughts from her mind. She had to locate Uncle Titus.

Nash watched the girl jauntily continue to stroll away from him. It was the first time a female had left before he was done with her. "Just as well," he muttered. She was the object of Barth's attentions, and Nash did not need complications in his life right now.

He was still glowering after Columbia when Barth joined him at the rail.

"Are you just going to stand here and let Columbia walk out of our lives?"

Nash turned a black scowl on his friend. "I do not know what ya'll are talking about—*our* lives. As far as I am concerned, she is nothing but a prickly thorn in my side, sneaking on board for some reason."

"Definitely a thorn of a different breed, I'd say."

"Humph! I'm glad she is gone. Now I can get on with the business of making a living."

"Well, maybe *you* feel that way. But I for one found her delightfully refreshing. And who knows, she may have possibilities," Barth said deliberately. "There aren't a lot of females out here with Columbia's character . . ."

"Character, yes," Nash mumbled.

As Nash listened to his friend espouse Columbia's virtues, he was growing more and more irritable by the moment. Unable to endure his friend's prattle any longer, Nash said, "If ya'll are so interested in that wild female, why don't you go after her?"

Barth stared at his friend. It wasn't like Nash to get so annoyed over a female. Perhaps Dolly was right after all. Nash was smitten with the river girl, but had not admitted it to himself yet.

"Since you don't seem to need me here to supervise the rest of the unloading, I think I will. Of course, I'll have to wait in the background out of sight until she's no longer dressed as your cabin boy."

Nash had just watched Columbia stroll from the paddle wheeler, and now he was watching Barth trail after her. Nash had never run after a female in his life. And he wasn't going to do so now.

"Nash, honey," Dolly said as she joined him, "I'm headed into town. Anything I can get for you?"

Dolly was decked out in pink muslin, sporting a bag large enough to hold the wardrobe-filled trunk she had acquired since leaving New York.

"Yeah. A woman."

"I'd say you just missed your chance at a rather good one." At his dark frown, she added, "I'm sure you'll find another at the ball Mr. Villamoore's throwing. By the way, how long do I have to prepare for it?"

"Youngston did not say." Nash's gaze caught on the skinny, bundled-up man weaving his way through the crates toward the paddle wheeler. "But if ya'll care to stick around, it looks like Villamoore will be able to tell you himself. He is about to join us."

Dolly glimpsed the blond man laboring up the gangplank. His hair sat bunched on his head at an awkward angle, and his lithe, slithery appearance didn't appeal to her at all. Men who dressed like dandies and carried fancy carved canes when they did not need them could not be trusted. "No thanks. But from the air of him, I think you'd be smart to watch your back when dealing with that one."

Nash kept his face impassive. He watched her saunter past Villamoore, and the man's head swivel around to leer at her before he turned and finished boarding the paddle wheeler.

Villamoore offered a gloved hand. "Ah, Foster, who was that delightfully lovely lady who just disembarked from your paddle wheeler? I certainly have not seen her around these parts before."

The self-important, understuffed snake. Nash ignored the outstretched hand. "My wife."

Villamoore startled back and dropped his hand. "No offense meant."

"None taken. Men often find Dolly attractive."

Once Foster had outlived his usefulness, Villamoore decided that he would more than admire Foster's wife from a distance. She was a scrumptious tart from the looks of her, and Villamoore intended to savor those strawberry-sweet lips.

"What can I do for ya'll, Villamoore? Ya'll obviously did not come down to the docks to discuss my wife's appearance."

Villamoore's lips quirked into a smirk, and he

176

flicked his cane over his shoulder. "You are direct. I like that about you, Foster. Actually, I am here because I heard that you handled yourself well at Lower Cascades yesterday. Indians aside, most men are intimidated by my man there. But not you. There's a place in my organization for you, if you're interested."

"Might be. What are ya'll offering?" Nash leaned against a post. Villamoore must have quite a spy network for news to travel so fast.

"Before we discuss the details, why don't you and your lovely wife join me Saturday evening at my home to celebrate Oregon's statehood. You'll have an opportunity to meet Oregon's leading citizenry. And it will give you the chance to see the kind of people who are going to follow me in leading this state into the future."

Although Nash had no desire to mingle socially with the likes of Villamoore and his kind, it was the perfect opportunity to learn who the man's accomplices were. "We shall be there."

"I knew you would," Villamoore said with cocksure arrogance. "Dinner's at eight."

Villamoore took a pouch of money from his pocket and tossed it to Nash. "The first installment in our new association. There's enough there so you won't have to take on another cargo until after the celebration. By then I'll have plenty of work to keep you busy. In the meantime, outfit yourself and that lovely wife of yours."

Nash easily caught the hefty poke, his lips thinning ever so slightly. "Thanks," he forced himself to say.

"That's only the beginning. There will be a lot more where that came from. And I've arranged for you to have a line of credit." Villamoore turned away, paused, and turned back to Foster. "Oh, and bring along that first mate of yours. Could be I might have a position for him in my organization as well. It will be formal wear Saturday evening."

Nash nodded. "Saturday."

"Saturday? What do you mean Uncle Titus won't be back 'til after Saturday?" Columbia asked GlennieLynn. "Where'd he go? Who hired him? What's he haulin'? Why ain't you with him?"

GlennieLynn leaned back on the straight-back chair in her cramped parlor. She was feeling every one of her nearly forty years. She longed to settle down, and had gotten mighty tired of waiting for Titus to marry off the girl, although she loved Columbia dearly. "You sure are chockful of questions, Columbia."

"You know the trouble we've been havin' gettin' hauls. It just don't make sense that Uncle Titus got a job so fast, is all."

"You don't give him enough credit sometimes." Columbia continued to stare at her. GlennieLynn sighed. "Oh, all right, Frank McGee got Titus the haul down to Astoria. Don't know what, but what he'll get for makin' the trip ought to keep you two goin' awhile longer."

A knock at the door interrupted their strained conversation.

GlennieLynn glanced nervously at the door. "Ain't you gonna go to the door?" Columbia asked, craning her neck toward the portal.

" 'Course I am." GlennieLynn pushed her bulk out of the chair and picked at her short fingernails as she shuffled to the door. She slowly creaked it open.

"Glennie darlin'," Frank McGee crooned, and gave her a big bear hug before she could warn him that she was not alone. She stood stiff, hoping he would temper his usual exuberance. "Give your lovin' man a smacking kiss before I—"

Frank broke off when he noticed someone move in the background.

"Frank, Columbia's here visitin'. Come on in and say hello." GlennieLynn awkwardly stepped aside so Frank could enter.

"Hello, Columbia. Didn't expect to see you here," he blurted out.

Columbia got to her feet. "Guess not. I'd best be goin'."

GlennieLynn put a staying hand on Columbia's arm. "No. Please. I want you to understand about me and Frank."

Despite an urge to leave, Columbia felt she owed GlennieLynn something after all the years the woman had spent mothering her. "Don't you think you oughta tell it to Uncle Titus?"

"Columbia, we didn't plan nothing, it just sorta happened. You got to understand. I'm getting no younger. Frank and me're going to have a real home. We're fixing to up 'n' get wed."

Shock reverberated through Columbia. "What about Uncle Titus?" Columbia turned on Frank. "Is that why you got him the haul to Astoria, Francis McGee? To get him out of the way?"

"It isn't like that, girl," GlennieLynn insisted. "Frank went to Titus like a man should and laid out his heart. Your uncle fathomed it all and said he was pleased for

179

us. Further, I'm not no loose woman that'd dangle two men."

Columbia was immediately contrite and ashamed of herself, for thinking that GlennieLynn would sneak behind Uncle Titus's back. "I'm awful sorry, GlennieLynn." She took their hands. "I wish you both all the happiness in the world. But I got to get goin' now."

Her cap in hand, hair flying free, Columbia ambled through the streets of Portland, feeling a deep sense of guilt that she had been responsible for her uncle losing the big-hearted GlennieLynn. If she had sold the *Columbia's Pride* to John Villamoore like her uncle had wanted, perhaps he would have been the one with GlennieLynn now instead of Frank McGee.

Columbia stopped in front of a shop window and gazed at the fancy dress hanging there. She just did not fit in with the rest of the female population, because none of those frilly things appealed to her in the slightest.

She had just turned away from the shop when Dolly came rushing out. "Thank goodness I finally found you. I've been looking all over town for you."

"What for?" questioned Columbia, who was in no mood for Dolly's dress-up nonsense.

Dolly narrowed her eyes at the girl. "Something the matter? You don't seem yourself."

"Just a case of misery, is all," Columbia responded.

"What put that pining look on your face?"

Columbia did not usually discuss family business with others, but right now she needed another female to talk to. "If you must know, my uncle's ladyfriend just told me she is gonna up and wed somebody else. And it's all my fault."

"Titus?" Dolly asked, remembering the very favorable impression the man had made on her when they'd first met.

"Yes, Uncle Titus. Now he ain't got no one, because he's been havin' to spend all his time lookin' after the likes of me and the paddle wheeler."

"Nonsense. If your uncle and that woman were meant, there wouldn't of been nothing that would've stood in their way. So quit your worrying about it. Your uncle'll get another ladyfriend to keep company with before you even know it."

"Hope you're right," Columbia muttered, not completely convinced. She started to step off the boardwalk.

"Wait. Aren't you interested in why I came looking for you?"

"Not particular. No."

Dolly let out a huff. She intended to help the girl, whether she wanted it or not. "I haven't been lugging this bag filled with lady's things all around town for nothing."

Dolly took Columbia by the arm and began ushering her into the shop. "You're coming back inside with me. And you're going to let me show you what you'll look like as a fancy dressed lady."

"I ain't no lady. And nothin' you can do to me on the outside is gonna make me one on the inside," Columbia protested.

Columbia was prepared to resist Dolly's efforts to take her into the dress shop, until Columbia noticed Nash Foster and John Villamoore heading toward them on the other side of the street. Columbia's hand went to her bare head. Her hair billowed around her shoulders and down her back.

If Nash caught sight of her still dressed in her cabin boy's outfit, but without her cap, her masquerade would be exposed, and she'd never be able to trap Villamoore through Nash. And in the back of her mind, a wee voice warned her that if Nash found out she had tricked him, he would never forgive her.

Columbia grabbed Dolly's arm. To Dolly's surprise Columbia dragged her into the shop. "You certainly don't waste no time when you change your mind, do you?" Dolly said, out of breath.

"This was your idea, after all. Let's get to it. I ain't got all day."

Chapter Nineteen

Barth stood south of the dress shop, his collar turned up against the cold wind, and watched the gusts whip Columbia's lustrous black hair about her face. He was just about to abandon his vigil when Dolly rushed out. The two women spoke briefly, and Columbia hauled Dolly inside the store.

The girl did not appear to be up to anything unusual to him. Perhaps the only reason she was on board Nash's paddle wheeler was because she had an interest in him.

He stepped off the boardwalk. "Barth," he heard a familiar voice call. He swung around. It was Nash.

"Barth, I would like ya'll to meet John Villamoore. Looks like we may be doing business together, in the future."

The men exchanged pleasantries and Villamoore excused himself, leaving Barth and Nash standing alone together.

"What are ya'll doing in this part of town? I thought you were going to catch up with Columbia," Nash said.

Barth motioned toward the dress shop situated

among a line of stores. "Columbia's in there with Dolly. I was going to wait until she came out, but that might appear as if I've been following her. So I thought I would head back to the *Yacht*."

Barth took a few steps toward the docks but Nash did not join him. He stopped and pivoted around. "You coming?"

Nash shot a furtive glance in the direction of the dress shop. An idea flashed into his mind. "No, I shall join ya'll later."

A slight grin lifted the corners of Barth's mouth and he stepped back and chucked Nash on the arm. "Business, huh? Sure. See you back on board."

Nash scowled at Barth's back as his first mate stuffed his hands in his jacket pockets and strolled back toward the paddle wheeler whistling. Nash waited five minutes then crossed the street and entered the shop.

"May I be of assistance, sir?" the frail aging modiste asked, her gnarled fingers woven tightly together in front of her.

The woman appeared spinisterly in her dowdy dress, spectacles and severe hairstyle. Not the kind to meekly fade into the scenery. "I noticed my wife come in here earlier and since I have finished my business, I thought I would join her. Otherwise she might spend hours shopping."

The woman raised her chin and stood her ground. "Your wife?"

"Her name is Dolly Foster. Tell her I am here," Nash advised, with enough authority in his voice to daunt the woman.

"Very well." The woman stiffly motioned to a tufted chair in a far corner of the shop. "Please be seated.

184

I shall inform the ladies of your presence."

Columbia's heart nearly stopped at the deep baritone syllables of Nash Foster's voice drifting from the front of the shop. She hugged the dress Dolly was insisting she try on to her chest and hissed, "What am I gonna do now?"

Dolly shrugged, then took the garment from Columbia. She gathered it in her arms and slipped it over Columbia's head, fussing with the ruffles. "Why should you do anything different than what you're already doing?"

"Your husband's out front," Columbia cried. "What's he doin' here? He must've followed us."

Dolly threw up her hands. "Nonsense. You heard him say that he saw me come in."

"But I can't let him see me like this." Columbia held out the full skirt. "What if he recognizes me as his cabin boy?"

Dolly stepped back and gave the girl a lengthy perusal, before she answered. "I'd say that Nash is going to be so taken with you as a female, that his cabin boy will be the last thing to enter his mind."

The modiste entered the room. "Mrs. Foster?"

Dolly smiled sweetly at the prune-faced woman. "Yes?"

"Your husband is out front. Would you care to go over your charges with him?"

Columbia watched a wicked glint stream into Dolly's eyes. "No. Let him wait."

"But, ma'am, he was quite insistent that I inform you he is here."

"And you have. Thank you." Dolly dismissed the woman with a flip of her wrist. "Wait." She hailed the woman back. "Bring in that red satin that's on that dressmaker's form. My friend has decided to try it on."

The woman gazed at Columbia in disbelief. Everyone in town knew that the girl did all her shopping at the general mercantile in the boys' section. Trousers and shirts, wool socks and work boots and long johns.

"Is there a problem with the red satin?" Dolly inserted into the woman's reverie.

Her head snapped up. "No. No problem. I shall get it directly."

"Whaddya think you're doin'?" Columbia wheezed.

Her face an innocent mask, Dolly moved over to Columbia. "Just followin' the plan. Now raise your arms."

Nash was impatiently drumming his fingers on his arm when the modiste came out from behind the curtain and headed for the gown in the window. He watched her unpin the brilliant frothy creation.

His thoughts drifted to Columbia, and how exquisite she would look in red with her jet black hair in curls, her cherry cheeks and full red lips . . . her arm linked with his attending Villamoore's statehood celebration.

The woman draped the gown over her arm and hurried back to the dressing room, ignoring his patent stare.

Columbia was standing in the back room in her ragged long johns when the woman entered. She handed the gown to Dolly. "Might I suggest the latest lace under-fashions recently arrived from Paris to accompany the gown?" she said tactfully.

"You sure might," Dolly wholeheartedly agreed.

"I don't need no different drawers." Columbia

smoothed the worn, sturdy cotton down her stomach. "These serve just fine."

"Yes, to repair an engine perhaps," the modiste observed with a condescending smirk.

Columbia drew herself up, prepared to give the woman a good piece of her mind. There was nothing wrong with good serviceable drawers. "You don't know nothin' about engines, do you?"

The woman was taken aback by the vehemence in the river girl's tone. "Well, no. But—"

"Columbia," Dolly interceded before the entire shopping expedition got out of hand and they were forced to leave before outfitting Columbia. "What the lady is trying to say, is that your underwear is fine during the day. But at night when you are dressed up, lace suits better."

"Yes, yes. That is what I meant. No offense, of course," the woman amended, fearing the loss of a sale. "Shall I select several undergarments to choose from?"

"No."

"Yes." Dolly overrode Columbia's adamant objections and sent the woman back out to the main part of the shop, with orders to return with the shop's finest.

Growing increasingly impatient, Nash had gotten up and wondered about the tidy shop, decorated in tasteful lavender-striped wallpaper. There were several gowns he could visualize Columbia wearing. But his attention was grabbed at the skimpy lace underdrawers marked "the latest fashion from Paris."

He picked up a chemise, conjured up an image of Columbia attired in the daring lace just for him, and the thought made him smile. The silk drawers were smooth and cool to the touch, and Nash could imagine

187

Columbia slowly peeling the garment down her long, slender thighs, until she stood before him naked and ready.

"Ah-hem." The modiste's clearing her throat snapped Nash from his heated preoccupation, and he found himself red-faced, holding a woman's unmentionables. She stuck out her hand, her face a haughty facade. "May I?"

Sheepishly, Nash placed the bits of silk and lace in the woman's hand. "Just admiring your wares," he said lamely.

She raised her heavy brows. "Yes, I can see that."

She took them from him and returned them to their proper place. Then she picked through the rest of the neatly folded undergarments and selected two of the plainest sets.

"Are those for my wife?" he asked.

The big stranger had a lot of gall! she thought. But she refrained from speaking her mind, since he obviously was the one who would be paying the enormous bill. She gave him a benign smile. "Your wife sent me to select several garments for the young *lady* with her."

Nash's interest was immediately heightened, and he lost all the embarrassment of a moment ago. Stepping forward, he took the plain underdrawers from her hand. "In that case" — he rummaged through the entire pile until he came up with the sheerest, most alluring garments — "these are perfect."

The woman inspected the sheer garments with raised brows. "But, sir, the garments are for the young lady. These are hardly the type she would select, I am certain."

"So am I. But take them to her nonetheless," he said,

in a voice which brooked no further argument.

"Yes, sir."

Nash settled back in the chair, crossed his legs, and tented his fingers, watching the bewildered modiste gingerly carry the undergarments to the back. A surge of anticipation filled his chest, and he deemed to be the one who Columbia wore those frilly things for, despite his earlier decision.

When Columbia caught sight of what the woman had selected, her mouth dropped open. "I ain't gonna wear those. Why, that stuff is downright indecent."

Dolly squealed with glee. "That is the idea, honey."

Columbia snatched the lingerie from the woman's hand and shook them. "These wouldn't hold up in a mild breeze, not to mention a sou'wester. No. They just won't do."

Dolly gave the frazzled modiste a sympathetic look. And the woman said, "They weren't what I had chosen. Your husband personally selected these for the young lady —"

"You mean Nash is the one who picked this flimsy stuff out?" Columbia wailed, aghast.

Dolly clasped her hands together. "We'll take them. You can leave us be for now," she added and dismissed the bemused woman.

"Get out of your drawers and put these on," Dolly ordered. "And don't give me no backtalk."

"But how did he even know we were here?" Columbia questioned again, as she grudgingly complied with Dolly's directives. The silk felt cool and decadent against her skin.

"We already went over that. Furthermore, what difference does it make? All that's important is that you've

189

caught his attention. Now all you have to do is keep it."
She picked up the gown. "Raise your arms and let's see
what this looks like on you."

Columbia slipped into the gown. Secretly, she felt
feminine for the first time in her entire life in the frilly
attire, and she gaped at her reflection in the full-length
mirror. Then her attention caught on her bosom and
she plucked at the loose fabric. "I ain't got nothin' to fill
this part of the dress out with."

Dolly heaved an exasperated sigh, her own ample
chest rising and falling. The girl was an expert's challenge. "Then we'll make do."

Dolly dug in her reticule and pulled out two hand-
kerchiefs. Columbia shook her head in horror when
Dolly wadded the linen into two balls and started stuffing the hankies down the front of Columbia's gown.

"Dolly, I can't—"

"Nonsense." Dolly batted Columbia's hands away.
"God helps them that help themselves. All we're doing
is improving on what God didn't have time to get done
with." She shrugged, pleased with her handiwork. "Nobody can fault us for giving the Maker a hand." She
adjusted the mounds until she was satisfied. "In other
words, we're just helping Him out with His work a
little."

Columbia gazed down at her protruding chest. "A
little?"

"You look magnificent," Dolly concluded, and gave
Columbia a shove through the curtain before the girl
could mount another round of protests.

One minute Columbia was arguing with Dolly, and
the next she found herself awkwardly standing in plain
view of Nash Foster. Frantic, Columbia swung around

and tried to slip back behind the curtains, but Dolly was standing on the other side holding them closed.

"Dolly, let go," Columbia hissed. If she could have gotten her hands around the woman's neck, she would have squeezed her well-meaning breath out of her.

"Miss Baranoff?" came the dulcet, deep notes of Nash's voice.

She was caught. There was no escape.

In an effort to make the best of a horrific situation, Columbia took a deep breath, forced a bright smile, and pivoted around. "Fancy runnin' in to you here."

She was not prepared for the expression on Nash Foster's face.

"You hungry?" she blurted out.

He unfolded his large frame and joined her, his eyes roving over her. "Hungry? Why would ya'll think I might be hungry?"

" 'Cause you looked like you were about to lick your chops."

Nash forced back a burst of laughter at her wonderful naivete. "I suppose one might be able to say I am experiencing a sudden surge of hunger." He scratched his head. "But I cannot say that it is for food."

"What for then?" she asked.

He wisely avoided her question at the humph of disapproval he heard echo from the modiste, who was trying to appear as unobtrusive as possible, while still listening to everything being said.

"I almost did not recognize ya'll."

Columbia's hands flew to her stuffed bosom before she caught herself and dropped them to her sides. "I don't usually wear this kind of getup."

"Ya'll should more often."

Columbia crinkled her nose. "Oh, posh. Whatever for?"

"Ya'll are a beautiful woman."

His compliment caught her totally off guard, and her cheeks flamed until she was sure they were the same crimson as the gown. A denial of his compliment perched on the edge of her tongue. She knew she wasn't beautiful. She was plain and skinny. But for the first time in her life, she swallowed the retort.

"Thank you."

Nash was so mesmerized by the vision that stood before him, and so caught up with thoughts of what she was wearing underneath the stunning gown, that before he thought about what he was doing, he said, "I would be honored if ya'll would accompany me to the statehood celebration Villamoore is throwing Saturday night."

"But what about your wife?"

4 FREE BOOKS

TO GET YOUR 4 FREE BOOKS WORTH $18.00 — MAIL IN THE FREE BOOK CERTIFICATE T O D A Y

Fill in the Free Book Certificate below, and we'll send your FREE BOOKS to you as soon as we receive it.

If the certificate is missing below, write to: Zebra Home Subscription Service, Inc., P.O. Box 5214, 120 Brighton Road, Clifton, New Jersey 07015-5214.

FREE BOOK CERTIFICATE

4 FREE BOOKS

ZEBRA HOME SUBSCRIPTION SERVICE, INC.

YES! Please start my subscription to Zebra Historical Romances and send me my first 4 books absolutely FREE. I understand that each month I may preview four new Zebra Historical Romances free for 10 days. If I'm not satisfied with them, I may return the four books within 10 days and owe nothing. Otherwise, I will pay the low preferred subscriber's price of just $3.75 each; a total of $15.00, *a savings off the publisher's price of $3.00.* I may return any shipment and I may cancel this subscription at any time. There is no obligation to buy any shipment and there are no shipping, handling or other hidden charges. Regardless of what I decide, the four free books are mine to keep.

NAME _____

ADDRESS _____ APT _____

CITY _____ STATE ____ ZIP _____

TELEPHONE ( ) _____

SIGNATURE _____ (if under 18, parent or guardian must sign)

Terms, offer and prices subject to change without notice. Subscription subject to acceptance by Zebra Books. Zebra Books reserves the right to reject any order or cancel any subscription.

Chapter Twenty

Long awkward moments passed once Columbia had reminded Nash that he was supposed to be married. Silently he cursed himself for coming up with that bald-faced lie. There was no one he wanted more to escort to the celebration than Columbia. Hell, there was no one he wanted more than Columbia—dressed in fancy clothes or overalls . . . or better yet, nothing at all.

In an effort to salvage the situation and stave off the modiste's gossip, Dolly fluttered through the curtains. "Nash dear, isn't it just a wonderful coincidence that we ran into Columbia here? Since her uncle is out on a haul, I've invited her to stay on the *Yacht* with us. And how simply grand of you to suggest that Columbia accompany us to Mr. Villamoore's celebration. A wife couldn't ask for a more thoughtful husband. Don't you think so, Columbia?"

At the moment Columbia was not thinking anything of the kind. Her mind was still reeling over staying on his paddle wheeler as herself, and her shock when

Nash had said she was beautiful. She shifted her feet, heightening her senses at the touch of the rich fabric against her bare skin.

When Columbia did not answer, Dolly linked her arm with Nash's. "I know you want to be near me, honey, but we girls've got a lot more shopping to do."

The modiste stepped forward. She was not going to continue to wait on those two without being paid. "Do you wish to settle their account before you depart, sir?"

Hell, he hadn't had the money Villamoore paid him for even a day. Then his gaze shifted to Columbia. The instant of annoyance he'd felt faded. He would give her anything. He dug into his pocket, pulled out the pouch, and dumped an ample portion of the coins into Dolly's eager hands.

"That should be enough to cover all your purchases . . . dear."

Dolly sent the arrogant modiste a haughty grin. "Bring out the rest of your wares. And we'll need a hoop skirt for the red satin."

Saturday morning dawned icy cold. Storm clouds lurked to the west, hinting at an impending storm. Wind already chopped the mighty river, rocking the paddle wheeler as Columbia stood at the rail, tossing bits of her leftover breakfast to the screeching gulls. She watched the big white birds soar overhead, diving to snatch the food in midair. It was one of life's simple pleasures that she had delighted in since childhood.

Staying on board Nash's paddle wheeler made her feel like the gulls—relying on handouts. She hadn't spent a single night away from the *Columbia's Pride* since she was born. Even during repairs she had remained on board. She pitched another scrap to the squawking birds. Other than GlennieLynn's place, which was no longer an option, she had nowhere else to go.

"I like a woman who cares about animals," Barth said as he joined her. He leaned an elbow on the railing, took a corner of bread from her, and flung it to the hungry birds.

"How about Nash? What kinda woman catches his eye?" she blurted out, and immediately dropped her eyes.

Barth lifted her chin with the crook of his index finger and gazed deeply into those exquisite turquoise eyes. "It would take someone uniquely different from the rest of the women he has known."

"You think I'm u-uniquely different?"

She had asked a serious question, and Barth had to fight to keep a smile off his lips. He took her by the shoulders and gave her a peck on the forehead. "There is no doubt that you are the most uniquely different young woman Nash and I have ever encountered."

Nash had just rounded the corner and drew up short. Barth was holding Columbia in his arms, kissing her. Jealousy stabbed him. At first he thought of turning around and leaving them alone, but something inside him drove him forward, despite the unspoken agreement the two men had always adhered to regarding women. "Morning."

Barth dropped his hands. "Ah, Nash, we were just feeding the seagulls."

"I saw for myself exactly what ya'll were doing," Nash grunted.

Barth gave Nash a snappy grin. "You care to try your hand at it?"

Nash did not miss the double-edged meaning to Barth's words. If Barth had meant kissing Columbia, the answer would be an unequivocal yes. Nash did not bother to reply, he was so annoyed. He secretly considered warning his friend to back off, but they'd been friends too long, and that was out of the question at this point. "We have work to do before attending Villamoore's celebration tonight."

"I can help," Columbia offered. "I can do just about anything that needs doin' on board one of these paddle wheelers. Want to earn my keep, you know."

"You will," Nash answered cryptically. But working on board the paddle wheeler was not what he had on his mind. "Dolly was looking for you earlier. Ya'll had best go see what she wants," Nash suggested. He had something to say to Barth and didn't want the girl to overhear their conversation.

Nash watched Columbia toss the rest of her bread to the gulls, then prance along the deck until she disappeared from sight. Once he and Barth stood alone on deck, Nash leaned over the rail, keeping his gaze averted from his best friend. "I see ya'll are finding Columbia irresistible."

Barth's head snapped up. In all the years they'd been together, they'd never had this type of strained conversation over a woman before. Friendly competitions, wagers, even trying to outdo the other. If one of them were truly interested in a woman, the other automatically kept his distance. This definitely was a first for Nash Foster, and Barth wondered what it was costing such a proud man to broach the subject.

196

"And what about you? Are you finding her irresistible as well?"

"What makes ya'll think I have any interest in the girl?" Nash said harshly.

A question answered with a question.

Barth smirked. "I suppose because we've never had this type of discussion before."

Nash's lips thinned. He was in no mood for his friend's flippancy. "Well, we are having it now."

"Don't go getting hot under the collar. I find Columbia a refreshing change from the women we have both known. As far as what I do or don't intend, I can't say."

Nash was losing patience. "Can't or won't?"

Barth could not help himself, he was enjoying Nash's discomfort. Heaven knew, it was about time Nash got a sample of what he had dished out. An idea to help Dolly's strategy along a mite flashed into Barth's mind. "I guess that depends on you, my friend."

"On me?" Suspicion emanated from Nash.

"Of course. Whether you are game for a little friendly competition or not."

Nash narrowed his eyes. Unlike earlier competitions the men had enjoyed, this was different. Columbia was not worldly-wise like the others; it was not just a contest to Nash. "What do ya'll mean *competition?*"

"Simple. We'll both court her. We'll let her make the decision. It will be Columbia's choice. The loser does the gentlemanly thing and steps aside."

Nash stared at his friend long and hard before he thrust out his hand. "All right, Barth, ya'll are on."

The burden weighing heavily on Nash's mind was

suddenly lifted. He no longer had to restrain himself. Columbia was now fair game, and Nash considered himself an expert hunter.

They had competed before, but this time was different. This time Nash was not playing games. This time Nash did not intend to lose, and he had no intention of "doing the gentlemanly thing" should Columbia make the wrong choice.

Nash had always held to the belief that all was fair in love and war, and he saw the weeks ahead as a combination of both.

"Can't I wear a combination of both?" Columbia complained bitterly, as Dolly finished tossing aside all her comfortable clothing. "Nobody's gonna know if I got silk stockin's or wool socks on underneath this dress. And I'm much more comfortable in my own shoes and socks than tryin' to maneuver in those high heels." Columbia motioned to the new pair of shoes near the bed. "Why, I'll probably fall flat on my rear in those things. I ain't never worn their like — "

"Well, it's about time you did," Dolly advised. "Sit down and put on the stockings, so I can finish your hair. It's almost time to leave."

Columbia grudgingly complied and Dolly chattered as she fashioned Columbia's thick waves into the latest style, swept high on her head and tied with a red satin ribbon. "Wasn't it just grand of Barth to offer to be your escort?"

Columbia rolled her eyes. "Just grand. But I got to say that if I had my way, I would toss this enormous silk dress with your hankies stuffed in the top to make my bosom bigger, this horrible corset that won't let a body breathe, and this hideous beehive-shaped contraption made of steel wires held together with tape that makes it hard just to get through a door, let alone sit down—"

"It is a hoopskirt, Columbia," Dolly advised. "Those hankies will get you many an admiring glance. And besides, it is the latest fashion."

"Fashion or no, I'd dump it, and all the flimsy underthings that go with it, and spend the evening playin' poker with the crew with my own chest, just the way God gived it to me. This dressin' up and squeezin' my toes into uncomfortable shoes just to impress a man— a married one at that—is for the birds!"

The mention of birds brought the seagulls to mind, and Columbia wished she could fly back to *Columbia's Pride* and forget she'd ever encountered Nash Foster.

"You'll adjust, honey. And tonight at the celebration, once you get the chance to try your wings, you'll be the talk of the town," Dolly said, and hummed as she put the finishing touches on Columbia's hair.

By the time they arrived at Villamoore's palatial estate, atop a hill overlooking both the Columbia and Willamette rivers, Columbia's sides itched from the corset that Dolly had drawn so tightly.

At Dolly's insistence Columbia was sandwiched in between Barth and Nash, and she had to fight to keep that infernal hoopskirt apparatus from flipping up into her face. Both finely dressed men were being so attentive that she hadn't had an opportunity to scratch.

They alighted from the hired carriage, and both men offered Columbia a staying arm when she stumbled, leaving Dolly standing alone in all her blue crinoline finery.

"Thank you," Columbia said to her rescuers. "Guess I ain't used to these tall shoes yet."

"Until you are feeling confident, I shan't leave your side," Barth announced.

"Neither will I," Nash seconded, feeling like an awkward schoolboy competing for his first girlfriend, and not very happy about it.

"What about your wife, old man?" Barth questioned with a sly grin on his face. "You can't leave her standing all alone, or have you forgotten about *your wife?*"

"Yes, my wife." Barth was pleased at Nash's black scowl. Nash was mired in a trap of his own doing, and Barth wondered what ingenious scheme his friend would come up with to extricate himself from it.

Nash had been bested during the first round, but even as he offered Dolly his arm and strolled to the entrance of the immense house, he was planning his next move.

Nash got a strange sense of déjà vu as they entered the mansion and the butler took their wraps. It bore a striking, uncanny resemblance to a home he felt he had seen or been inside before. But he could not recall where or when. Potted plants lined the foyer and immense winding staircase. Crystal chandeliers glistened a prism of colors on the heavy brocade furniture, as they were ushered through the milling crowds to the frescoed ballroom draped in red, white, and blue, reserved for entertaining vast numbers of people. An orchestra provided over two hundred revelers with patriotic tunes, and long tables ladened with delicacies were decked out in the country's colors. Two fireplaces crackled at each end of the room, providing warmth on the cold night.

"Gosh, nearly everyone's wearing red, white or blue," Columbia commented, in disgusted awe at such wasteful opulence when the men on the river were barely eking out a living.

"The most fitting colors, don't you agree?" John Villamoore said as he joined them attired in a midnight blue coat. "Columbia, my dear, you look stunning this evening. I am glad you could join us." His eyes fastened on her false breasts, and he kissed her hand. She wanted to rip the hankies from her chest and wipe her hand with them. Then he turned to Dolly. "And Mrs. Foster, your beauty puts my humble home to shame."

After all the years that Dolly had lived on the streets, she recognized a line when she heard one. But she was up to her part. "Please, do call me Dolly." She then turned to Nash. "It is all right with you, dear, isn't it?"

Nash nodded and, after exchanging banal pleasantries, watched with relief as Villamoore claimed Dolly for a dance. That left him free to concentrate on Columbia.

Nash turned around to petition Columbia's hand for the first dance, but while Nash had been forced to pay court to Villamoore and Dolly, Barth had whisked Columbia onto the dance floor. Nash watched the pair weave through the crowded floor until they were at a far corner.

Barth had taken the advantage again, Nash thought darkly, as he stood glaring at his friend, enjoying the company of the first woman who had captured Nash's genuine interest. In all the years he had squired some of the most beautiful woman around, he had to go and find a scrawny river girl fascinating! And due to his own tongue, making her think he was a married man, he could not openly pursue her.

Nash made his way over to the refreshment table and ordered a good stiff drink from the attending servant. He tossed it down and ordered another.

As Nash watched Columbia whirl about the floor, he thought her body seemed more womanly tonight for some reason. Must be the manner in which she was dressed, he concluded. The evening was still young, and growing emboldened, Nash decided not to stand idly by and allow Barth to monopolize Columbia's attention the entire night!

Chapter Twenty-one

Much to his dismay, Nash spent the next hour at the celebration being introduced to Villamoore's inner circle. And when he was invited to join the men in the library away from the revelers, Nash cast a longing glance toward Columbia and Barth sitting on the other side of the great room.

"You don't have to worry, Foster," Villamoore said with a sly grin. "We aren't going to keep you all evening. You'll have plenty of time to pursue the ladies."

"With so many lovely ladies in attendance this evening, it is difficult to concentrate on matters of business," Nash drawled.

A distinguished white-haired man raised his glass. "Spoken like a true Southern gentleman, Foster. I think you are going to make a fine addition to our group."

While they sipped from the fine crystal, Captain Youngston and General Shallcross joined them, attired in full-dress uniforms. Nash was introduced to the tall, distinguished commander from Fort Vancouver. After pleasantries were exchanged and the men drifted toward other revelers, Villamoore and the others warned Nash away from Shallcross, a staunch Union supporter, and suggested they talk where there would be more privacy.

Six men adjourned to Villamoore's library. The thickset man poured brandy, and Nash listened while the men spoke of their allegiance to the South. There was war coming between the North and South, and they intended to provide an invaluable supply line to the Confederacy, and to sabotage the army's efforts to secure the valuable Columbia River and the frontier for the Union.

And while Villamoore espoused noble justifications for wanting to control all the shipping on the Columbia River out of Portland, Nash had no doubt that the man's true rationale was pure and simple greed.

"And so you see, Foster, with your help and the help of our Southern sympathizers here and in the army, we shall be able to make a valuable contribution to a most noble and just cause." Villamoore raised his glass in toast, followed by the others. "To the South, gentlemen."

"And to our thirty-third state, Oregon," Nash put in, closely watching the others.

Nash noted that the men exchange furtive glances, and then the eldest added, "For as long as it remains as such."

As Nash sipped from his snifter, it became clear that Villamoore and his cronies had insurrection plans in mind more grandiose than just supporting the South. That unsettling thought brought to mind the guns stored in that warehouse in Lower Cascades, as well as

Captain Youngston's cryptic comments. While Nash had grown up in the South, he did not hold the same loyalties as the fanatics surrounding him, nor did he like what he suspected were Villamoore's more sinister motives.

With the distinct, uneasy knowledge that he was getting deeply involved in something much more treacherous than Villamoore's desire to ruin Columbia's business, and the man's plans to support the South should war break out, Nash excused himself and returned to the celebration.

Nash scanned the faces in the crowd, not knowing who could be trusted. When his gaze came to rest on Columbia, standing alone before one of the fireplaces, he decided to put Villamoore out of his thoughts. Rashly, he decided that tonight he was going to make her his. With that in mind, he took advantage of Barth's preoccupation with Dolly on the dance floor and went straight over to Columbia.

"Are ya'll enjoying yourself?" he asked Columbia. Looking down at the lovely young woman, she seemed to have shrunk in height by inches.

"Can't say that this is the way I'd choose to spend my time." She paused. "What about you? I suppose you like these fancy shindigs."

Nash smiled at her honesty, and a craving for her swelled in his loins. "I can honestly say there are other pursuits I would rather be engaged in right now."

"Me, too," she seconded. "There's nothin' I'd rather do than get out of this corset before it squeezes the breath out of me."

"Sounds like an excellent idea to me." There was nothing he'd rather do than help her out of the corset, he longed to add. He held out a hand. "If ya'll will grant me the honor of this dance, we can waltz over toward the door and escape without anyone being the wiser."

"What about your wife?"

There it was again, that damn lie coming back to haunt him. He took a buoying breath. "Columbia, there is something I must tell ya'll about Dolly and me."

"You don't got to. Dolly told me you only married her to protect her, and you two'll be gettin' a divorce soon."

Nash nodded, feeling an inner relief that he was not going to have to bare his falsehood and take the chance of her never speaking to him again.

"Since Dolly and Barth are obviously enjoying themselves, and since ya'll know that my marriage is about to end, shall we go?"

He had expected her to place her hand in his, but instead she bent over, lifted her enormous hoopskirt into a most unladylike pose, and forced her feet back into her high-heeled shoes. Nash almost laughed at the raised eyebrows of the people whispering behind their hands about Columbia's antics. But he found her genuineness more and more endearing, rather than disgraceful as several of the women had commented.

"Shoulda just tossed the things in the fire and marched out barefoot," she announced loudly, unabashed, and made the scandalized women turn away. "Guess I'm ready for some slow foot-stompin' now."

Columbia took an unsteady step but her ankle twisted, and she teetered backward before Nash caught her up in his arms and whisked her out onto the dance floor. She was unsure of herself, but in Nash's arms, she knew she could show them all up.

They were making steady progress toward the patio doors, when all of a sudden a woman screeched, "Fire! Fire! That girl's on fire!"

Columbia glanced around and realized that it was her voluminous skirt that was flaming up behind her. "Oh my God, Hades has come up to claim me!" she screamed and tried to beat at the devouring flames.

Everyone in the room stopped what they were doing and stood back to watch in horror. Only Nash seemed to have presence of mind. He tackled Columbia, threw her to the floor, and quickly used a nearby Persian rug to wrap her up and smother the flames.

"Are ya'll all right? Ya'll are not hurt, are you?" If Nash had expected Columbia to be meekly sobbing when he unwrapped the rug, he was mistaken. Her breath was labored and she was choking. And mad as a beaver whose dam had just busted.

"This preposterous barrel of torture!" she ranted, and stood up to rip off what was left of the smoldering skirt. "Why anyone in their right mind would let themselves get bound up in such a contraption is beyond me, unless they were intent on bein' a one-woman blockade runner and needed a place to stash stuff."

She stepped out of the bent metal hoopskirt and leaned over to survey her stinging legs, covered only with what was left of her tattered petticoat, silk stockings, and garters. When she had ripped the skirt off, she loosened the top of her bodice, and the two hankies Dolly had insisted she use to enhance her breasts tumbled to the floor.

Nash fought back a grin. Now he knew what had made her seem more womanly tonight. With casual chivalry he bent down, retrieved the hankies, and offered them to Columbia. "I believe these bosoms belong to ya'll."

In angry embarrassment over all the smirking eyes on her, Columbia snatched up the stuffing. "What're all you starin' at? I bet more'n half of you done the same dumb thing. Why I let myself get talked into doin' it, I can't rightly fathom. Don't need such silly things." She tossed the hankies into the fire, proclaiming, "There ain't nothin' wrong with the way nature done by me. Don't know why havin' a big bosom is so important anyway."

The ladies blushed, furiously fanning themselves. They cast clandestine glances at each other, and insisted their smirking husbands turn away.

Again Nash had to hide a smile. More than once he had undressed a well-endowed woman, only to find that he had been tricked. Those women had been overly apologetic, but not Columbia. She was proud of herself just as she was. And he found that he was proud of her as well. In an effort to salvage what was left of Columbia's rapidly dissipating reputation, Nash stripped off his coat and covered her with it.

"What're you doin' that for? Oh!" she gasped as Nash scooped her up into his arms and made a quick exit through the patio doors. "What'd you do that for?" she demanded again once they were outside.

He strode purposefully back to the awaiting carriage through the snow that had begun to fall. "I am taking ya'll back to the boat, so I can tend to those burns."

"I don't need no tendin'. I take care of myself," she

protested. But the fact was, being held in his strong arms, against his hard chest, feeling his heart drum against her ear, made her forget the stinging burns, and a stinging of a different kind invaded her entire body.

Recently Columbia had been thinking a lot about the mating ritual, and tonight she had the overwhelming desire to discover for herself what it was all about.

Nash's body was experiencing an awakening all its own. They would be alone on the paddle wheeler, since he had given the crew the night off to celebrate Oregon's statehood, and Nash's mind was astir with what he intended to have happen once they boarded.

He set her in the carriage, directed the driver, and settled in next to her, circling an arm around her shoulders and drawing her to him. To his gladdened surprise she did not object. But she did flinch.

"Do ya'll hurt?" he asked out of genuine concern.

"A little," she admitted in a weak moment.

"It will be all right. As soon as we get ya'll back to the paddle wheeler, I will put salve on those burns." Nash leaned out the window and ordered the driver to hurry.

Once settled back inside, he turned her face up to his. It was dark inside the coach, and he could just barely make out the outline of her lips. They were partially open, as if she were waiting for him to kiss her. Unable to help himself, Nash brought his lips down and tasted hers.

Nash's kiss was probing, demanding, coaxing, and Columbia found herself drifting with the most glorious sensations she had ever known. She moaned at the pleasure, and snuggled closer to the source of the heat

209

pressed against her chest. Her breasts came alive and her nipples hardened into peaks. Her other senses awakened, crying out until her arms slipped around his neck and she deepened their kiss.

The carriage drew to a stop, and the driver jumped down and opened the door. "Ah-hem. We're here, sir," the embarrassed man announced.

Columbia and Nash broke apart. "Ya'll made excellent time." Nash paid the driver and included a handsome tip. Snow continued to fall in a flurry of white against the black night, as he lifted Columbia from the carriage and carried her up the gangplank through the silently falling flakes.

The paddle wheeler gently swayed underneath his feet as he strode purposefully to his cabin. He tenderly settled her onto his bed and sat down beside her. She rose up on her elbows, but he pushed her back down.

"Let me take care of ya'll."

Columbia had always taken care of others, but allowing Nash to care for her just seemed natural somehow. He propped her up on his thick pillows and began to peel away the remnants of her tattered petticoat and stockings. She was amazed at how gentle his touch was as he examined her thighs.

"Is it bad?" she asked.

"Looks to be very minor," he pronounced, his voice tinged with relief.

"Are they ugly?"

His head snapped up; there was heated passion in his eyes. "They are lovely," he murmured. Her brows drew together in confusion, so he amended, "Your legs. Long, slender, soft, white."

She swallowed back the question about the burns as

his fingers rode higher up her thigh. The sensations delighted and pleasured her, and she forgot all about the burns until he slipped his fingers underneath the lace of her drawers. "Ouch."

Nash immediately stopped his exploration and headed for the door.

"Where you goin'?" she puzzled.

"I shall be right back. Just relax. And do not worry. I shall take care of everything."

Feeling an exhilaration he had never encountered with a woman before, Nash hurried down the gang-plank, gathered up a handful of freshly fallen snow, and rushed back. Columbia was lying in a most seductive pose when he reentered his cabin. One arm was resting behind her head, her knee was bent, showing off a delicate bit of ankle and thigh.

"What're you doin' with that snow?"

"It will soothe the burning," he said, and applied the cold flakes to the red blotches on her thigh.

"Will it also soothe the burnin' I got in the pit of my heart for you?" she questioned openly.

Nash thought he was going to explode right then and there, he was so pleasantly startled by her candor. He began rubbing the melting snow along her thigh, rivulets of water running down her heated flesh to pool on the blanket.

"The snow's runnin' off my leg," she squealed.

It was too much to resist. Nash leaned over and slowly ran his tongue along the cool stream, reveling in her smooth, satiny flesh and the downy hair dusting her thigh. Then he looked directly into her darkened turquoise eyes.

"Is that better?" came the dulcet tones that mesmerized Columbia.

"Hmm. Much." His heated gaze was hypnotic, and she felt herself drawn into it, claimed by it. "Don't stop."

Nash needed no further encouragement. He leaned over her, one hand resting on each side of her body. "I want you, Mary Catherine."

He had used her given name, and on his lips, it fit. She smiled sweetly up at him. "Even with my small bosom?"

Nash stroked the soft swell of the nubs of her breasts with the pads of his thumbs. "Your bosom is perfect to me. And I want ya'll more than ever."

"I've been wantin' you for some time, too."

She took a breath to offer a simple litany of how he made her all quivery inside, but he silenced her with his hungry mouth. Their kiss was almost savage in its intensity, each one starved for the other. Columbia followed Nash's lead, using her tongue and teeth in response to his.

She started to tremble when his fingers flowed over her breast again, and her nipple rose hard against the silk top to meet his questing touch.

"I am going to undress ya'll now," he murmured against her mouth. Then he sat back and helped her remove the remains of her gown and lace chemise. With a reverence before unknown to him, Nash caressed her small, firm breasts, suckling at the nipples as he kneaded the soft flesh.

"Your breasts are perfection."

Columbia was speechless with impassioned anticipation as he gently took her by the shoulders and turned her back to him. With deft fingers he unworked the laces on her corset and tossed the restricting garment aside, leaving her dressed in nothing more than the French lace drawers.

He ran his hands down the sides of her waist and over her hips, delighting in the texture of lace, silk, and milk-white skin. Then he turned her around to face him and pulled her hips tight against his, rocking back and forth in a preview of what was to come.

"Ain't you gonna take off my drawers?" she asked in a breathy whisper. She may be inexperienced, but she had heard the dockworkers talk among themselves and knew what to expect—looked forward to it.

"All in due time, my beautiful river princess. All in due time."

Making her heart race out of control, he kneeled before her, dropping exquisite torturing kisses down her belly, which caused her muscles to contract in response. His fingers hooked the string holding her drawers up, and slowly pulled them over her hips and carefully down her thighs until they draped over the tops of her feet.

Columbia tried to step out of the restricting lace, but he grabbed her bottom with gentle hands, and pulled her to him, kissing the furred mound at the apex of her thighs. She squirmed at the heated liquid sensations that coursed through her, and pressed herself against him harder as he continued to nearly drive her wild.

"When am I gonna get to undress you?" she panted from the exquisite torment he was subjecting her to.

Nash looked up at her flushed face, grinned, and got

to his feet. His arms akimbo, he said, "I am all yours. Do with me as ya'll please."

Columbia did not take the time that Nash had when she undressed him. She practically ripped the shirt off his back, causing him to chuckle. "Ya'll are a wild one."

She had his trousers half-unbuttoned, but stopped. "Ain't it okay?"

Nash thought of the society ladies he had made love to. Most of them had been more like stiff boards, letting him do all the work. "Mary Catherine, it is more than okay."

There it was again, her given name. She smiled at him, then promptly tore the two remaining buttons from his trousers.

Once they stood before one another nude, Nash pulled her into his embrace, kissed her long and hard, gyrating his hips against her. Then he laid her back on the bed. Together they explored and delighted in the sensual pleasures of the flesh and the scents of love-making, Nash taking care not to allow the burns to cause her discomfort.

When Nash thought he was about to explode if he didn't get inside her, he carefully parted her legs, mindful of her burns, and kneeled between them. He took hold of himself to guide himself into her, but she placed her hand over his.

"Please, let me do it," she rasped, her voice thick with passion.

He was hard and hot, his shaft velvety smooth as it throbbed in her hand. She took delight in its response when she squeezed it, as she slowly guided him to the entrance of her woman's core. Nash assisted by parting her woman's lips, and she stroked the engorged length of him as he entered her.

She was a tight fit, a virgin, and Nash hesitated, not wanting to hurt her. He took her mouth instead, imitating a lover's rhythm with his tongue.

Columbia had other ideas. She lifted her hips, grasped his buttocks, and plunged him deep within her, crying out with pleasure once he was fully absorbed into her body.

His restraint snapped, and they broke into a frenzied rhythm, their bodies pounding against one another, capturing, claiming, branding, until a mind-shattering climax claimed Columbia. Unable to hold back any longer, Nash exploded, releasing his seed into the woman he knew now for certain he had to possess totally.

Spent and completely exhausted, Columbia fell asleep in Nash's arms to the gentle rocking of the paddle wheeler. But Nash lay wide-awake, staring up toward the black ceiling and wondering how Columbia would react when she discovered that he had lied to her.

Chapter Twenty-two

Columbia awoke hugging one of Nash's plump pillows to her breast. She had overslept. She smiled to herself. She was a woman now. Reliving what she had shared with Nash, she couldn't understand why women she had overheard talking in the mercantile proclaimed that mating was simply something a woman must *endure* as part of the marriage contract. If that kind of mating occurred every night, she decided that maybe marriage wouldn't be so bad after all!

A warm glow still surrounding her, she sat up and glanced around the cabin; Nash was nowhere in sight. But on his desk in the corner, a tray piled with rolls, butter, jam, and a pot of coffee, and decorated with a fragrant sprig of greenery from a pine tree, awaited her.

She slipped into Nash's shirt hanging on the back of the chair and began to devour the breakfast he had so thoughtfully provided for her.

Columbia was licking the excess raspberry jam off her fingers when Nash entered the cabin.

"Morning, sleepyhead. How is the injured one this morning?"

"I'd forgotten all about it." Without giving thought to the view she was presenting to Nash, she brought her foot up to the table and examined the cluster of blisters adorning her thigh. "A couple of days and I'll never remember it happened."

Concern filled his eyes even as they heatedly roved up her shapely legs. "Ya'll sure?"

Columbia nodded, rose, and walked toward him. She had not bothered to button his shirt. It hung open, revealing her womanly charms, and making Nash's body hard and ready for her again. "I must say, my shirt never looked better."

"I know how it'd look even better," she announced with a girlish giggle.

Without the shame so rampant in so-called civilized society, she let the shirt slip off her shoulders and drift to the floor.

"Ya'll are right, my shirt looks much better where it is."

He opened his arms and she stepped into them. With the tip of his tongue, Nash licked the raspberry jam smudging the corners of her mouth. "Umm, and the jam never tasted better either."

"Guess I ain't always so proper when I eat, like those city women you know."

He held her from him. "My dear young lady, there is not one thing I would change about ya'll. But what about me? I am one of those city-slickers late of New York that most riverboat folks from these parts want nothing to do with."

217

She found a glimpse of insecurity in one who seemed so self-assured, endearing. Then her lips tightened ever so slightly, and she stiffened. "That could be remedied if you'd stay away from Villamoore."

When Nash did not respond, Columbia felt a moment of disappointment before she set it aside and said, "The only other thing I'd change about you is your marital status. I still don't feel right about Dolly 'n' all. She's been a good friend to me. I don't want to hurt her none, if deep down she's got feelin's for you and is just puttin' on a brave front."

She stepped out of his embrace and crossed her arms over her chest. "I don't think we should be here like this again, until you and Dolly's got the proper papers."

There it was again, that damned lie haunting him like a persistent ghost. At least he'd already sent Dolly into town on an errand that would finally put it to rest. "Believe me, Dolly is not just putting on a brave front. As a matter of fact, she has already gone into town to find an attorney. She wants to be free as badly as I do."

"True? You ain't funnin' or nothin'?"

He crossed his heart. "Cross my heart."

She stepped forward, threw her arms around his neck, and began pressing a multitude of kisses across his face. His hands rode up and down her sides, coming to rest on her firm buttocks. She was so trusting that Nash felt a stab of guilt. But as he touched the wild and uninhibited girl, all he wanted to do was devour her.

He was just about to take her back to bed, when a horrendous explosion erupted not far off shore, shaking the walls of his cabin and rocking the paddle wheeler.

"What the hell!"

They broke apart and rushed to the porthole. Black smoke billowed and whipped against a cloudy windy sky three hundred feet from the docks. Wooden planks and shattered bits of cargo had blasted a hundred feet into the air and were raining into the river.

"Oh my God, a paddle wheeler's blown!" Columbia cried and rushed to the door.

"Wait! Ya'll cannot go out on deck like that." Nash grabbed his long coat from the hook on the door, and Columbia flung it on, along with a pair of shoes.

Through a light icy rain melting the snow from last night, Nash followed her up to the hurricane deck. She went to the railing, while he rushed into the wheelhouse to retrieve his spyglass. She stood still in horror, watching the disaster.

The deadly tragedy brought back to mind memories of her own folks' deaths in the same manner. If they hadn't insisted that she visit her Uncle Titus that fateful day, she would have been on the paddle wheeler with them. Her heart filled with sadness, and she wiped at the tears of memory as Nash joined her.

A confused concern filled his face. "Are ya'll okay?"

She took a deep breath. "My folks died that same way."

"It is one of the dangers of these damn riverboats.

I am sorry, Columbia."

"Enough about me. What's goin' on onboard that paddle wheeler?"

He peered through the spyglass. At the far bank across the river, he noticed two men row to shore. He swung the glass back to the chaos aboard the disabled paddle wheeler. When he took it from his eye, Columbia noticed a strange, troubled expression on his face.

"What is it? What's wrong?" She made a grab for the spyglass, but Nash held it away from her.

Worry over how she would react when she got a closer look at the paddle wheeler, which was now listing precariously to the left, filled Nash's heart. In a low, calming voice he advised, "Columbia, ya'll do not want to see it. Take my word for it."

Panic gripped her. She swung around, leaned over the rail, and squinted her eyes toward the unfolding disaster. "Oh no! No! It's the *Columbia's Pride*, ain't it?" she cried, hysterical. "Uncle Titus! No! I got to get to him. I got to!"

Nash caught her. "Go get some clothes on, ya'll will need to warm if you are going to be of help. Meanwhile, I shall head the *Yacht* out there, and we will see what we can do to help."

Columbia stood still, trembling with the haunting memories that suddenly were bombarding her again. Images of her beloved folks lying side by side in their caskets rose before her eyes. She remembered taking her mother's stiff hand and kissing her cold lips goodbye. She had kissed her father also, before Uncle Titus had dragged the nine-year-old she had been away.

Her shaking increased. Now Uncle Titus, her only living kin, may have just suffered the same tragic fate.

Nash grabbed her shoulders and shook her. "Columbia, get hold of yourself. Ya'll are a strong young woman."

Barth ran past Nash and Nash ordered, "Get the paddle wheeler underway. We have got to get out there and see if we can help."

"What's wrong with Columbia?" Barth questioned.

"Just get a move on. I shall see to Columbia and join ya'll in a minute," Nash snarled.

Barth started shouting orders, as Nash lifted Columbia in his arms and carried her back to his cabin. They passed a frantic Dolly returning from the turmoil in town, and Nash ordered her to accompany them and take care of Columbia, so he could get back up on deck and render aid, should anyone be left alive.

Nash deposited Columbia on his bed and rushed back to the wheelhouse. Dolly moistened a rag and laid it on Columbia's forehead. Columbia was staring at the ceiling, her trembling hands covering her mouth, fighting back the tears which were welling up in her eyes.

"Come on, girl. Don't keep it bottled up inside you. Talk to me," Dolly urged. "It'll help to get it off your chest."

Columbia felt a dam burst inside her and she cried out, hugging Dolly. "Oh Dolly, that's my uncle's paddle wheeler out there. He's all I got left. He just can't be dead. He just can't be," she sobbed uncontrollably.

Shock hit Dolly full force, but she hid it for the girl's sake. Instead she held the girl in her arms, rocking, and crooning to her. "Your uncle's too tough not to survive."

"But my folks." Columbia hiccupped and sniffled. "I lost them the same way."

"Oh, you poor child." The *Yacht* jerked and began to rock on the swells of the river, as the mighty paddle wheel thrashed the water. "We're on our way there right now. You can stop your worrying. Nash is a wonderful, incredible hunk of man. He'll find your uncle if anybody can."

Through the haze of her tears, Columbia gazed at Dolly. "You still love him, don't you?"

Now hardly seemed the best time to have this conversation, but Dolly took out a hankie and dabbed at Columbia's tears. "Child, I just got back from looking for an attorney to release Nash. As I told you, I do love him, but not the way I can see that you do. Your kind of love is special, and I want to be free to find that same kind of love for myself. So quit worrying about Nash and me. We're as good as divorced already.

"And as for your folks, they lived the kind of life they loved. And although their deaths were tragic and untimely, they were lucky enough to pass on from this world together, while they were doing what they loved doing. And I'm sure they're looking down right now on the child their love created to carry on for them. So you see, in you there will always be a part of them that will live on. Further, I know they would not want you grieving over the past."

Columbia sniffled and wiped her nose with the back of her hand. "How'd you get so smart?"

"Life gives us all struggles and sadness we got to overcome. Some of us learn from our struggles and sadness, and become better because of it. Others just keep making the same dunderheaded mistakes over and over again. Until Nash offered me a chance to change my life, I was one of them who kept making the same stupid mistakes over and over again. I thought life owed me. Now I realize that I got inside me what it takes to make a go in life.

"Honey, you're one of them who's got what it takes. So keep your folks alive in your heart, but don't let what happened to them keep you down from getting on with what's got to be done."

The paddle wheeler hit something, causing it to lurch. They must have reached the exploded boat. Columbia hugged Dolly. "Thanks. You sure do know how to pull a body out of self-pity."

Columbia leaped from the bed, threw on Nash's pants and shirt, and tied the baggy outfit with his belt. Donning his heavy slicker, she ran out on deck, plunking her cap on her head.

The river was littered with debris, bodies floated facedown, others were still alive, frantically waving and screaming for help. Nash had already lowered a dinghy, and his crew was on their way to pull the survivors from the icy river. Columbia did not see her uncle among them. The entire top deck of *Columbia's Pride* had been blown completely off, leaving a ravaged shell, with the paddle wheel badly mangled and dangling from the back.

Columbia raced to Nash, who was busy directing the rescue efforts. "I got to get on board that boat," she cried.

"It is too dangerous. From the look of it, it could sink at any moment."

"I don't care. If I'd been on board seein' to the boiler, it wouldn't've blown. Uncle Titus could still be alive on board. He's my only kin. I got to try."

"I am sorry, Columbia. No. Now, do not blame yourself."

Columbia narrowed her eyes at him, but deigned not to argue. She had found that males always thought they knew best and expected their word to be as final as law. Well, she hadn't managed to keep her business going for years by deferring to the pigheaded male species. She swung around and headed toward the main deck.

"Where ya'll going?" Nash hollered.

"Can't tolerate watchin' my paddle wheeler sink outa sight, if it's gonna. I'm goin' below."

"Smart girl." He seemed to accept her explanation, and returned to direct the rescue efforts so they could get out of the way of the beleaguered paddle wheeler as soon as possible.

Columbia slid down the stair rail. In all the confusion, no one paid any mind to her as she made her way to one of the two remaining dinghies. With the expertise of years of practice, she lowered the small boat into the choppy water and climbed down before anyone realized what she was about.

Columbia set the oars and pushed off from the *Yacht*. With furious strokes, she dragged the oars through the water, putting all her strength into it. If Uncle Titus was still alive, she was going to find him.

"Miz Columbia," Little John yelled. "You come back here before somethin' bad happens to you."

Columbia ignored the giant man and continue to row, ploughing the oars through the current in a frantic effort to reach the *Columbia's Pride* before it carried Uncle Titus to an unknown watery grave. She had to know his fate.

Nash watched the damaged paddle wheeler list in the current. He caught sight of a dinghy heading directly into the maelstrom, which could swallow up the small boat if the paddle wheeler shifted on its side and sank. Then he recognized the person manning the tiny dinghy.

"My God, Columbia, you little fool! Ya'll are going to get yourself killed!" he shouted into the increasing storm.

Chapter Twenty-three

The storm was intensifying as Nash made a dash for the last dinghy. Wind and rain, turning to ice on deck, whipped at his face.

"It's Miz Columbia, boss," Little John hollered to Nash. "She's taken one of the boats."

"Why didn't ya'll stop her?" Nash accused as his fingers worked the ropes securing the small boat. If Columbia had been within reach at the moment, he would have tied her ankle to the rope.

"She snuck past me." Little John hung his head.

"Ya'll shouldn't feel guilty. Ya'll could not have stopped that pigheaded hellion once she had made up her mind, unless ya'll would have sat on her. Help me lower this boat, I am going after her. And heaven help her when I catch up."

"Let me go, too. Maybe I can help," Little John offered, partly out of guilt and partly out of fear about what the captain might do to Columbia when he did catch up with her.

Nash jumped into the boat and set the oars. "No. Ya'll stay here and help with the survivors. I am personally going to deal with that little hellion."

Little John shoved Nash's boat off, and Nash rowed as if a demon were chasing him. He passed the last boat with survivors heading back to his paddle wheeler. The men's cut and bleeding faces were grim.

He pushed himself past his normal endurance. He had to get to Columbia before the foolish girl got herself killed, and denied him the pleasure of wringing her neck. As he neared the crippled paddle wheeler, he could see her scrambling on board. In her rush to look for her uncle, she had forgotten to tie off the dinghy and it drifted downriver. Hell, if he hadn't come after her, she would have been trapped.

"Uncle Titus!" Columbia screamed as she searched through the debris, fearing he might be trapped below. *Columbia's Pride* listed precariously to the right, and the girl had to grab onto a post to keep from being tossed into the angry river. Regaining her footing, she fought the sheeting rain and slipped down what was left of the stairs leading to the lower deck.

Rubble lay scattered everywhere, and she hardly recognized what had once been her most prized possession. She tore at the fallen planks, refusing to abandon her search.

"Columbia, you little fool, where are ya'll?" She heard Nash's angry voice topside.

Nash heard the thunderous sound of a beam crashing below on the weakened hull, coupled with an agonized scream. His heart racing with fear, he practically flew down what was left of the stairs. There at the bottom, Columbia's leg lay pinned beneath the fallen support beam. She was frantically trying to shove the heavy wood from her person, but to no avail.

Nash rushed to her side and tried unsuccessfully to slide her out from under the wood, which held tight to its victim.

"Looks like I got myself stuck," she said, with a calmness she did not feel. She could not let him see the panic she felt. She'd spent her life proving that she was every bit as strong as the best of men, and she could not revert to sniveling ways now.

"Looks like. Don't worry, I shall have ya'll out from under there in a minute."

"I'm not worried," she snapped.

Nash ignored the bravado she was trying to present him. Hell, if *he* were stuck on a sinking riverboat, *he'd* be scared. He tried to lift the beam, but it would not give way. Putting his shoulder to it, he shoved with all his might. The damn thing would not budge.

He was panting from the exertion and leaned over, resting his palms on his knees to catch his breath.

"What're you just standin' there for?" Columbia questioned. "Grab that board over there" — she pointed to a board pitched against the wall — "and use it to lever this dadblamed beam off me."

As Nash worked the board, he had to smile. She just might have gotten herself out from under the beam without his help! She had used the same ingenuity to hide the two of them in that crate at Lower Cascades. She certainly would never be a clinging vine. She was a resourceful and daring young woman. She would undoubtedly insist on equal status, would accept nothing less. He managed to raise the beam just enough for Columbia to crawl free.

She stood up and rubbed her leg. "Looks like nothin's broken."

He swallowed a retort about her foolhardy behavior and reached for her hand. "Come on, let's get off this tub before we end up going down with it."

She ripped her hand out of his. "No. I ain't leavin' 'til I find Uncle Titus."

The paddle wheeler turned on its side, sending them flying against a wall. Nash recovered first and grabbed Columbia, tossing her over his shoulder. "I am sorry about your uncle. But I am *not* going to let ya'll drown while making some futile search for a man who is probably already dead."

"No!" she screamed and kicked. "I can't leave him here."

"Ya'll have got no choice."

Nash stomped up the splintered stairs. A blast of wind and rain hit them when they emerged on deck. It took great effort to dump the struggling girl into the dinghy, and keep her pinned there while he took his boot and pushed off from the remains of the *Columbia's Pride*. Columbia continued to struggle and fight as the dinghy drifted away from the paddle wheeler.

She stopped grappling with him and watched in heart-wrenching dismay, as the paddle wheeler turned belly up and sank just beneath the surface.

"If I'd been on board for the haul, this never would've happened," she cried in self-reproach.

"Ya'll have got to quit blaming yourself," Nash

soothed and cradled her head against his chest.

"But I was on board your paddle wheeler dressed up as your cabin boy, tryin' to find out what you were doin' workin' for Villamoore," she blurted out, not caring if he found out.

"I know. Ya'll were the best cabin boy I ever had," he said, in an effort to take her mind off her uncle.

Columbia leaned back from him and searched his face. "You knew all along? And you let me continue the masquerade? You even had me wash your back, knowing that *I* was *me?*"

Nash wiped the rain out of his eyes. "Guilty. But ya'll have to admit, you enjoyed your bath a little, didn't you?"

He had made a fool out of her. He had let her think she had him hoodwinked, when all along he was playing a game with her. A game that had cost her uncle his life. She edged away from him. "You been funnin' me all along, ain't you?"

"No."

"Was takin' my virginity a game, too?" she cried. "Or did Villamoore put you up to it, to turn my attention aside from what you two are plannin'?

"I'll bet you all had quite a laugh, when I let you talk me into goin' to Villamoore's shindig."

He grabbed her by her trembling shoulders. "No. Stop it, dammit. Ya'll are just upset over your uncle. Ya'll do not really mean those things."

"In a shark's tooth I don't," she screamed to be heard over the howling wind. "But I admit when I'm wrong. You didn't take my virginity. I foolishly gave it to you."

She was too distraught. There was no use arguing with her now. Later he would straighten out her twisted notions.

A wave washed over the small dinghy, and the oars broke from their oarlocks. Nash made a grab for them, but they had gotten caught by a swell and were well out of reach.

"Looks like it's just you and me, until someone on the *Yacht* realizes we are in trouble and comes to fetch us."

Columbia bobbed to her feet and frantically started waving to the paddle wheeler in the misty distance. Nash grabbed her back down. "What are ya'll trying to do? Dump us both in the river?"

"If it means gettin' away from you—yes!" She crossed her arms over her chest and turned her head away from him, refusing to look at him. All she could see were tremendous waves and floating debris of what once had been her whole life.

All of a sudden her eyes fastened on a floating beam off to the west, and her distress of a moment ago over Nash vanished from her mind. Something was moving on it. "Nash! Look!" she pointed excitedly.

He tried to follow her line of vision. "What am I supposed to be looking for?" he questioned.

"Out there on that beam. It looks like an arm waving. I'm sure of it."

Nash strained his eyes. Something was flapping up from the beam. But it could just be some torn canvas.

"Please. Help me paddle in its direction. Hurry!"

He did not want to disappoint her, especially since she had accused him of using her while she had been masquerading as his cabin boy. A fact he was not very proud of, since she was nearer the truth than he cared to admit.

Together they managed to maneuver the small dinghy through the icy water toward the beam. As they neared it, it became obvious that a half-drowned man was desperately clinging to the floating wood.

Columbia stood up and nearly capsized the boat. "Uncle Titus!"

With the last of his strength, Titus reached for Columbia. As their fingers touched, his eyes rolled back in his head. His grasp on the beam slipped away, causing his unconscious body to slide beneath the surface of the icy river.

"No!" Columbia screamed and tried to dive in after her uncle.

Nash grabbed her, threw her to the bottom of the dinghy, and dived over the side. It seemed an eternity as Columbia watched the surging rings spread out from where Nash had hit the water.

She was motionless, not daring to breathe as she counted the time that Nash could be under the water before he would have to return to the surface for air—if he did return to the surface.

And she prayed.

Columbia had counted to one hundred and three before she thought her lungs were going to burst, and she gasped for breath.

Still no Nash or Titus.

She stood up, about to dive in after them, when

Nash finally broke the surface of the water, his arm wrapped around Titus's neck. "Quick." He fought to fill his lungs with air. "Help me get him on board."

With great effort Columbia held onto Titus's arms, while Nash hoisted himself into the dinghy. Between them they managed to drag Titus on board.

"He's not breathin'," she cried.

Feeling that he was losing consciousness himself from the cold, Nash fought to remain alert while he frantically worked on Titus. Nash pumped on Titus's midsection until the unconscious man coughed up a bucket full of water, choking.

The exertion sapped the last of Nash's strength, and he collapsed next to Titus.

The rain was coming down even harder now. Frigid, bone-chilling drops. Titus's lips were blue and his face was cast in hollow gray. Nash had an arctic white pallor on his usually bronze face. In an effort to warm the men and keep the rain off them, Columbia stripped off her slicker, tented it over them, and climbed inside, so her body warmth would help to provide some much-needed heat while they waited to be rescued.

From the north shore Jack Tarley sloshed back and forth in the gooey mud, mad as a bear with its nose caught in a honey hive of angry stinging bees. He punched his meaty hands together in frustration. Everyone on board was supposed to have died in that explosion.

"Come on, Jack. I got the boat ready to go out

again and finish the job, before that interfering Foster's paddle wheeler reaches them," his coconspirator suggested.

Jack grabbed the puny little man by his jacket collar and hauled him off his feet. "You damned fool, Barney. If you had done a better job of jamming that boiler, it would have blown that entire riverboat and everyone on board to kingdom come."

Jack knocked Barney into the mud facedown and proceeded to hold his face submerged with his boot, while Barney fought desperately to free himself. But he was no match for Jack's mammoth size. Satisfied that he had given Barney a sample of what would happen to him if he screwed up again, Jack removed his boot.

Gasping for breath, Barney crawled to his knees and wiped the mud off his face. "What'd you do that for?"

"That's only a sample of what Villamoore'll do to both of us, if that Columbia bitch and that bastard of an uncle of hers manage to salvage their riverboat."

"Well then, let's get a move on," Barney whined.

"Forget it. There is no way we could get to them before Foster's paddle wheeler. Furthermore, I don't intend to get caught. We blew the boat. Let's get out of this rain and wait until they're out of the way. Then we'll come back and make sure that there's no way they'll be able to salvage the *Columbia's Pride*."

The two men tied off their small boat and made their way to a lean-to they had set up earlier. Jack sat down, picked up his spyglass, and put it to his eye. From his dry perch he watched Foster's paddle wheeler bearing down on the dinghy, bobbing in the current in the middle of the river.

"Villamoore is goin' to be real interested when he learns that it was Foster who was responsible for saving Titus Baranoff's life."

A calculating grin spread Jack's heavy lips. "You know, Barney, Villamoore just might not think Foster is such hot stuff anymore. Maybe Villamoore'll come to realize that he needs my likes more than the likes of Foster." Jack puffed out his barrel chest, absorbed in his own self-importance.

"Yeah," Barney agreed. "You was more important before Foster came to town and made you just another one of Villamoore's boys."

Jack backhanded Barney. "I'm still important, you ignorant jackass. And who knows, maybe I'll be the one to take control of all the shipping out of Portland, instead of Villamoore."

Jack turned his attention back toward the river, and with grandiose visions of ousting Villamoore, Jack's interest heightened as he watched the paddle wheeler come alongside the small dinghy.

Chapter Twenty-four

By the time Nash regained consciousness, his head was lying in Columbia's lap. He shifted positions and she squirmed, making him smile. She was not impervious to him. They were under some sort of covering the girl had fashioned; at closer inspection, Nash realized it was his heavy rain slicker. She certainly was resourceful.

Titus lay deathly still next to him, but Nash could see the man's chest move up and down. At least he was still alive. Columbia's fingers were absently stroking Nash's cheek, and she was crooning his virtues. Nash decided to continue to play possum and take advantage of his position until the *Yacht* came for them.

"Nash? Columbia?" came Barth's beleaguered cry. Nash experienced a moment of disappointment; he had been enjoying her magical fingers and hearing what she thought of him. But Titus needed help. Nash sat up and threw off the slicker.

"Thank God! I was afraid you went down with the boat," Barth said.

Nash glanced at Columbia. "We were lucky Columbia did not get us both killed with such a dumb stunt."

She glared at him. "Too bad you still ain't out cold."

"Yeah, pity. But fact was, I felt those fiery little fingers of yours in my hair, not to mention your words of praise to my manhood." Her cheeks flamed red and she clenched her teeth.

"I was thinkin' about somebody else, so don't go lookin' so smug."

Nash cocked a brow, then turned his attention to Titus. "Help get Titus on board. He is in pretty bad shape."

Columbia released a sigh of relief. At least he didn't make any further comment about what she had been saying. "If it weren't for me, Uncle Titus'd be a goner."

Nash's smirk faded. What she'd said was true. She was responsible for saving Titus's life . . . if he lived. There was a tenacity about the girl that wouldn't allow her to accept anything less than what she went after. She was irrepressible, and he admired her spirit . . . although he considered it misdirected at times. Hell, he couldn't think of much that he didn't prize in the untamed river hellion.

Nash grasped Titus's limp body under the arms. With Columbia's help, he lifted the old man up and handed him over to Barth and Little John.

"Take him to my cabin," Dolly, who had been hovering nearby, directed Little John.

Barth helped Columbia on board, his hands lingering on her waist a little longer than Nash approved.

"Columbia has got her feet squarely on board now," Nash grunted.

"So she does," Barth grinned and released her.

For Nash's benefit, Columbia gave Barth a wide smile. "Thank you. You're a true gentleman in comparison to some I've met lately." She glanced back at Nash, then trailed after her uncle, watching Dolly fuss over the unconscious man. Strange, she thought, Dolly had paid little attention to Nash. But, of course, on second thought it made sense, they were divorcing after all.

Barth watched the trio disappear through the door to the salon, then turned to Nash, a grin on his face. "Do you plan to remain in that dinghy, or are you going to come on board? Looks like you could use a change of clothes."

Nash glowered at his friend. "At the moment, I could use more than just a change of clothes," Nash grunted, as he laboriously climbed over the railing.

"That bump on your head and your stiff muscles massaged by a certain river girl, perhaps?" Barth chuckled as he followed Nash sloshing toward the wheelhouse.

Nash stopped and threw back over his shoulder, "Careful, Barth. Ya'll are straining our friendship."

"How can you say such a thing to such a *true gentleman?*"

Nash's face darkened, and his black eyes sparked angry fires. It was evident that he was fighting to restrain his temper.

Undaunted, Barth held up his hands, palms out. "What's the matter? Can't you take the competition?"

"Competition, humph!" His friend may not realize

238

it, but he had already branded Columbia as his. And nobody was going to change that. And although nothing had been spoken between them, he had already made the decision for both of them.

Nash entered the wheelhouse and took over the wheel from the crewmember who had been manning it. Nash spun the huge wheel and headed the *Yacht* toward Portland.

"Why don't you get out of those wet clothes? I'll take over the wheel," Barth offered.

And let you take credit for getting Columbia's uncle to a doctor? Nash thought darkly. *Not on your life.* "Just go feed the fire, so we can make better time," he ordered.

"Order the crew to toss more wood into the fire. We need to make better time, or my daughter will be an old lady by the time we catch up with Foster," Markus Kiplinger ordered the harried captain of the steamer.

"Oh, Daddy, I do not know why we could not have remained in San Francisco a little longer. It is such a fascinating city," Jennifer whined, as she watched the magnificent city crowded on the hillsides fade into the distance.

"It just does not make sense to make such a tiresome voyage and not stop and rest awhile, especially when we had the perfect opportunity," she added, thinking how important it was that she look her best when they finally did reach their destination.

"You know very well why time is of the essence." Markus ran a hand through his snowy hair. If Foster

239

hadn't committed such a cardinal offense, he could almost understand the man not wanting his daughter. She had been acting like a shrew. Being cooped up on board ship with her was almost more than even he could endure, but the trip presented an opportunity he could not pass up.

Jennifer glanced at the nosy captain, then let out a huff. "Just because you learned that Nash picked up a cargo to take to some place called Astoria." She shrugged her indifference. "I still do not understand what difference another week or two would have made."

Markus narrowed his eyes. "It would be a week or two longer than I intend to let that man get away without doing his duty by you."

Markus's gaze clashed with the captain's, and the captain immediately redirected his attention to the rolling waves in front of the steamer. If Kiplinger had not paid him so extraordinarily well, he would have been more than happy to set the troublesome pair adrift, even though the ship did belong to the man. He pitied that poor bastard Foster when Kiplinger caught up with him. With his money, Markus Kiplinger could wield enough power to force Foster to do anything he wanted.

Once Columbia was assured that Titus was being cared for and that Dolly intended to remain at his side, she stormed out of the doctor's office, wishing she could have Nash Foster drawn and quartered for telling the doctor that she had pulled a stupid stunt which nearly got them all killed. Nash was hot on her

240

heels. She stepped off the wooden boards into the street, where he grabbed her arm.

He swung her around easily to face him. "Exactly where do ya'll think you are going?"

His features were set in hard lines. Well, she didn't have to answer to anybody. She glared back. "Since when did I have to start answerin' to you as to where I go and what I do?"

"Since I made ya'll mine last night," he shot back. She could manage to make him lose control!

Columbia's eyes rounded. His? She pondered the sound of it for a moment. She scratched her ear. "*You* made *me yours?*"

"That is right."

Her balled fists on her hips, she stepped up closer to him until they were nose to nose. Or almost, considering that he was much taller than she. "Let me get this straight. Just because we mated, you think that I belong to you, and that gives you the right to order me about like some slave?"

A crowd was starting to gather about them, intently listening to the quarrel. This was hard enough as it was, without forcing him to say what he had to say in front of an audience. His temper threatening to take over, he grabbed her by the upper arm and dragged her off toward his paddle wheeler.

"Where do you think you're takin' me?" she howled and tried to dig her heels in.

"Someplace where we can have this discussion in private," he spat back, and kept right on marching at a pace that forced her to trot to keep up.

Nash marched down the center of the street in order to avoid the pedestrians who had stopped to gawk at the scene of him towing an uncooperative Columbia, screeching at him like some wild-eyed banshee.

Unable to endure such shrieking any longer, Nash stopped and yanked her into the doorway of a vacant storefront. Her back was to the door, his massive body blocking her escape.

"Before we continue to the boat, I want your promise that ya'll are going to make some sort of effort to conduct yourself like a respectable, civilized female, instead of some bellowing fishwife."

Bellowing fishwife indeed! In a last-ditch effort to escape the furious man, Columbia swung her back to him and grabbed the doorknob. She tugged on it. The damn door was locked. When she swung back around to face him, he was smirking.

"Since ya'll have no way to escape me, why don't you do us both a favor and come along willingly, so we can get this little matter settled?"

She glared at him. He had stated that she belonged to him. He hadn't even bothered to ask her what *her* feelings were. And to top it off, he then calmly referred to it as "this little matter" without the least bit of emotion in his voice. Why, the arrogant, overconfident male specimen.

She thought fast to come up with an excuse to avoid such a discussion.

The simple fact was that she didn't want to *belong* to any man. Yet she had to admit to herself that she had been thinking a lot about him, and she couldn't deny that she'd like to mate with him every night. Of course, that wasn't the same thing as belonging. She tried to convince herself that it was lust, pure and simple. Nothing more. Yet an unnamed feeling deep down kept niggling at her.

"Are ya'll going to stand there glaring at me, or have you made up your mind to come quietly?" he questioned, breaking into her musings.

She glanced past him, over his shoulder. Of course, they had to be standing across the street from John Villamoore's office. She noticed the curtains part ever so slightly, then close.

"Well?" he prodded again. "What is it going to be? Are ya'll going to come along under your own power willingly, or do I gag and hogtie you?"

"I'll come. But only if you agree to take your paddle wheeler out and try to raise *Columbia's Pride*."

"Fair enough."

Again they headed toward his paddle wheeler, but he held her arm as if he didn't trust her to keep to her word. She glanced in the direction of Villamoore's office again, but the curtains were closed. She thought of mentioning it to Nash, than decided to let it drop. They had been creating such a stir, that no doubt whoever had been in the man's office must have heard the commotion and just peered out to see what was going on.

By the time they reached Nash's paddle wheeler and were settled in the empty salon, Columbia was panting. She felt as if she had just run a foot race, and was out of breath. She grabbed at the stitch in her side.

"I agreed to come along," she puffed. "But you didn't have to make a race out of it. And you didn't have to tell that damned doctor that I pulled a dumb stunt tryin' to save my only kin."

"So that is what has got your dander up."

She crossed her arms over her chest. "That and you thinkin' that I belong to you without givin' *me* a say in it."

Nash smiled at that. "I should have known better than to think ya'll would docilely accept the fact."

If he thought he would pacify her with such talk, he was sorely mistaken. *"Docilely accept the fact!* The fact! Posh! It ain't no fact," she said in a raised voice.

Nash was very calm when he said, "But it is."

She jabbed him in the chest with her index finger as she said, "I ain't but never had one goal in life. And that is to be the first licensed female riverboat pilot on the Columbia River."

"Goals change, Mary Catherine," he said calmly.

Columbia surged to her feet. "Mine don't. And quit callin' me Mary Catherine. That's a woman's name."

"And ya'll are a woman now, whether you care to admit it or not. I made ya'll a woman last night. And ya'll are going to be *my* woman."

She was steaming now. But despite her anger, she settled back into a chair across from him. "That's a mighty interestin' notion, since to my way of addin', that gives you one woman too many."

Nash tented his fingers over his mouth and squeezed his eyes shut. He should have been horse-whipped for that damned lie. It was like a monstrous phantom; it just kept returning time and time again to haunt him. He opened his eyes to gaze into those incredible turquoise pools of hers.

"I have already told ya'll, that Dolly was in town earlier taking care of that. As soon as we sign the papers, I shall be free. And from what I could see of Dolly when we brought Titus on board, I would say she has already set her sights on another man."

"Well, that don't matter. I still got my dream. And while I won't deny that I enjoy matin' with you"—he grinned at that—"I don't aim to give up something I've wanted since I was knee-high to a lifeboat, just to become some drudge for a man I only lust after." His grin faded at that. "My ma taught me to keep to my dreams, and I aim to do just that."

Nash hid his exasperation. "Nothing more than lust, huh?"

She raised her chin. "That's what I said. And a little lust ain't gonna get in the way of my dream."

For a long moment he stared at her in disbelief. He was used to women falling at his feet. Pursuing him. Kiplinger had even tried to trap Nash into marriage with his daughter, and he had managed to escape. And now here he was, for the first time in his life, practically outright declaring his overwhelming desire to possess one of the strangest females he had ever met, and she was turning him down flat.

"Tell me, how do ya'll propose to fulfill this fantasy of yours of becoming the first licensed female riverboat pilot on the Columbia River, when your dream presently is lying at the bottom of the river?"

Chapter Twenty-five

Columbia saw red, stiffened, then her heart dropped. He was no different than any of the other riverboat men, who thought her dream was nothing more than pure fantasy, to be laughed at and to chide her about. Deep down, in that special secret place in her heart, she had held out the hope that Nash Foster was not like the rest. Well, she was not going to give up as long as there was still a chance.

She stiffened her back. "When I agreed to come here with you and hear you out, you agreed to help me raise *Columbia's Pride*. I've held to my part of the bargain, and I expect you to hold to yours."

"I keep my bargains," he snapped, irritated that his honor was in question. Hell, he had never had to work this hard for a woman in his life. "I shall try to raise your precious riverboat. But ya'll know as well as I do, that she sunk so far off shore that it may be next to impossible to bring her up. And even if we do, it is no more than a splintered pile of wood."

"Fair enough. All I expect is for you to *try* to

bring up my 'splintered pile of wood.' " Sarcasm dripped off her honey-sweet voice.

For me to try, he thought with dismay. *You are the most trying female I've ever encountered.* But Nash had never turned down a challenge in his life. And Columbia was proving to be the most formidable one yet. One that he did not intend to lose.

"Hurry up, Barney. If you give the boat a good shove, we can get out to that wreck and finish the job before they come back with help," Jack Tarley snapped at his coconspirator, who was trying with all his might to push their small boat away from shore. "Put more shoulder into it, you lazy fool. Mr. Villamoore does not intend to lose any more shipping contracts to that darned river girl and her uncle."

Barney strained so hard that the veins stood out bright blue in his scrawny neck. He stepped back and took a running start, pounding himself against the hull. Finally the boat broke free of the bottom, and he fell flat on his face in the river mud.

"Just like you to sit down before a job's done," Jack said in disgust. "Get off your ass and get in the boat. We got work to do." Jack sneered and set the oars.

It did not take them long to locate the wreck and make short work of the hull, caught just beneath the surface. They remained in the area long enough to make sure that all traces of *Columbia's Pride* had completely disappeared.

247

"She won't be usin' that wreck as a thorn in Mr. Villamoore's side anymore," Jack boasted, through the low clouds pouring down a heavy drizzle. "Come on, let's get out of here and report to Mr. Villamoore."

"But don't you think we ought to hang around a little longer?" Barney suggested. "Just to make sure?"

"We've done our job, you fool. Now row!"

As they docked they noticed Foster's paddle wheeler leaving the wharf, the girl pacing back and forth on the hurricane deck. "Don't you think it's kinda funny that every time we see Foster, that Baranoff girl is with him?" Barney mentioned.

Jack's toothless grin widened. "Maybe he's pokin' her."

"That scrawny splinter of a female?" Barney choked. "Can't imagine there's much there to even hold on to."

"It's all the same in the dark," Jack bragged.

"Guess with your experience, you oughta know," Barney said with envy.

Jack puffed out his chest in manly pride. "So true. But I bet that fiesty little girl would give a man one hell of a ride."

"Mr. Villamoore might be real interested to hear about them two."

Jack rubbed his jaw. "You just keep your puss shut. I'll decide if we oughta tell him or not."

They trudged directly toward Villamoore's office. "Thought we was goin' to get dry first," Barney complained.

"Shut up. Money in a wet pocket's as good as in a dry one."

They sloshed into Villamoore's plush office, their muddy footprints tracking across his fine Persian rug. Villamoore stepped out from his inner office. His thin face immediately turned an angry purple.

"What do you two think you are doing, coming in here like that"—he waved to the tracks on his fine rug—"ruining my carpet. That is the second one that's been destroyed this month," he whined. "Get off it, you two imbeciles."

The two men jumped to the edge of the room, wringing their hands in awkward nervousness. "We ain't ruint any other rugs," Barney squeaked out, and knelt down with his handkerchief in an effort to rub off the mud.

"No. That damned Baranoff girl managed to catch her skirt on fire at the celebration I was giving, and Foster wrapped her up in it."

"We wasn't invited," Barney commented.

Villamoore was getting impatient with their prattle. "It was not for the likes of you. Now, what did you come here for?"

Jack relaxed his tense stance, and a smile took over the worried line of his lips, despite Mr. Villamoore's disparaging comment about their persons. "You should be happy to hear that that river girl and her uncle aren't goin' to be causin' you no more trouble with that boat of theirs. We took care of it. It made a magnificent explosion when the boiler blew. Why, you should've seen the planks fly. A hundred feet or more."

Villamoore had been glaring at the man on the floor, making a bigger mess out of his prized rug. But he forgot all about the rug as he listened to Tarley. "Did you make sure it couldn't be salvaged?"

"After Foster pulled Baranoff out of the river and headed back to Portland, we went back and sent the wreckage to the bottom. There won't be any salvaging." Jack paused. "About that river girl, boss. Foster seems to be spending a lot of time with her. You sure you can trust him?"

Villamoore recalled the episode with Foster and the girl in the doorway across the street a short while ago, as well as the time he had spent with her at the celebration. Foster did indeed seem to possess more than just a passing interest in that trouble-making girl.

"Saw them take Titus Baranoff to Doctor Barker's office," Villamoore said absently.

"Foster and the girl pulled him out of the river," Jack reiterated, to get his point across about Foster's loyalties. "From where we sat, Baranoff looked more dead than alive. If he isn't a goner, he should be out of commission for a long, long time."

Columbia shoved the man working the winch aside. Using all the strength in her arms, she worked one of the cables Nash had managed to attach to the edge of the paddle wheel that was bobbing above the surface.

Nash secured his cable and joined Columbia. "Here. Let me," he offered.

She stepped aside and watched him wind the winch tight and secure it. Once he had directed his men to finish securing her precious paddle wheeler, she said, "I could've done it."

"Yes, I know. Ya'll do not need a man for anything. Ya'll can manage your life just fine without anybody. So ya'll need not bother thanking me. I am sure ya'll could have raised the boat without me."

"Uncle Titus and me got on fine before you came."

Columbia looked at Nash and the bunched muscles across his back as he furiously worked. He was very angry with her. And while she *had* managed just fine before he so rudely came into her life, she secretly had to admit that if it weren't for him, she never would have been able to raise what was left of her paddle wheeler. She had never seen the like before, the way he had worked those big hooks and cables.

When he finally straightened up, she said awkwardly, "I do want to thank you for helpin' raise my paddle wheeler."

"So ya'll are willing to admit that without me you probably would not have been able to raise her?"

Columbia pressed her lips together. He was right and he knew it. "Guess that's one instance where you came in mighty handy," she conceded.

"There is another instance, as ya'll put it, where you need a man."

She cocked her head. "Oh? And when would that

be?" The moment the words left her tongue she was sorry, for she could see the devils dancing in his black eyes.

"When ya'll get the urge to mate," he said, using her term for their lovemaking.

She slapped an index finger to her lips. "Shh! Somebody might overhear you!" she cried, scandalized.

He took a step toward her. "Not if we went to my cabin," he said, with a come-hither grin on his face. Then the amusement left his face. "Ya'll regret the time we spent together?"

She frowned. Of course, she didn't regret it. She gazed straight into his eyes. "No. But I'm gonna be very busy for some time, gettin' my boat pieced back together in runnin' order. So if you get one of those overwhelmin' urges, I suggest you look elsewhere to slack it."

"Lady, if I get an overwhelming urge to slack my need—as ya'll so eloquently put it—ya'll are going to be the first to know." He winked at her. "And just to let ya'll know, if you get any similar urges, I shall always make myself available. So, do not even think of looking elsewhere. Ya'll are still mine, even if you refuse to admit it to yourself yet."

Columbia ignored his stubborn declaration. He seemed intent on holding to something that was not going to be. "Let's get the *Columbia's Pride* into the docks. I got to get busy and start collectin' parts to patch her back together again."

Nash shook his head. "Ya'll will never get that wreck running again."

252

"Uncle Titus and me put it back together after my folks were killed in a like explosion."

"Ya'll do not have your Uncle Titus behind you this time," he reminded her. "From the shape he was in by the time we got him to the doctor's, he is going to be laid up in bed for a long time."

"Well, then I guess I'll just have to manage all by myself, won't I?" she answered stubbornly.

Barth had been listening from around the corner and decided to join them. A big grin on his face, he said, "A true gentleman would never allow a lady to struggle by herself." He glanced from Columbia to Nash. Nash's expression was as black as midnight on a moonless night. He knew he shouldn't, but he was secretly enjoying Nash's anger immensely.

"I'm sure Nash could spare me long enough to give you a helping hand. I've had experience patching paddle wheelers back together, and with the help of some of the other riverboat pilots, I'll bet we'll have her back in action in no time."

Columbia glanced from man to man. Normally she would have declined Barth's offer. She didn't like to be beholden to any man. But there seemed to be some sort of strange contest going on between them. If she accepted Barth's assistance, it would send a crystal-clear message to Nash that she was her own person.

Without giving further thought to the repercussions, she said, "I'd be most honored to accept your help, Barth."

Barth offered his arm. "Shall we go into the salon, and discuss your plans to refurbish the paddle wheeler?"

Columbia took the proffered arm. "I'd be delighted," she answered. But she looked back at Nash. He looked as if he could kill, although he said not a word.

A strange feeling of disappointment encircled her. Barth was every bit a gentlemen — kind, caring, and reasonably attractive, not to mention attentive. But his touch did not set her innards to tingling like Nash's did.

Lust, Columbia, that's all it is. Lust. She kept repeating the sentence in her mind over and over, even while Nash's repeated declaration that she belonged to him continued to play haunting chords on the strings of her heart.

She looked up at Barth again, trying to force herself to see him in a different light. He was a handsome man. It shouldn't take more than that to get Nash out of her mind, she tried to convince herself. He simply did not arouse her the way that being near Nash did. Maybe if she worked at it, perhaps she could use him to put Nash out of her mind once and for all.

She'd never know if she didn't try, she pondered. Experimenting with Barth certainly would be a good way to find out if it was just her body that was betraying her and nothing more.

She smiled at the idea. "I'll do it."

Barth gazed down at the girl. "You'll do what?" he questioned.

She was startled from her preoccupation with Nash. "Huh?"

"You said, 'I'll do it,'" he repeated her words.

"And I will, too." She smiled innocently up at him, ignoring the heavy mist forming droplets on her thick lashes.

"What?" Bemusement framed his face.

She tucked herself in closer to him. "You'll find out soon enough, I guess."

"I can hardly wait." He flashed her a sunny smile. "I have the distinct feeling that I am going to enjoy whatever it is you have in mind."

As he opened the door for her, Barth glanced back to make sure that Nash was still watching. Pleased that his friend had not shifted his black glare, Barth winked, just to infuriate Nash further, then turned his attention back to Columbia.

They settled by a window, where Columbia could keep an eye on her precious paddle wheeler as they steamed toward the docks in Portland with the mangled vessel in tow.

"I think if we start by making the hull seaworthy first, then we can—"

"I don't want to talk about that right now," she broke in.

Barth smiled, and took her hand when he noticed Nash pass by the window. He sent her one of his most seductive smiles, grinning inside as he heard Nash stomp off down the deck. He knew Nash would like nothing more than to pound him. But they had made a bargain. Shook on it. So Nash's honor demanded that he adhere to their agreement.

"I am completely at your disposal. We can discuss any topic your sweet heart desires."

Columbia looked askance at the man. He had the strangest look of anticipation on his face that she'd ever seen. Crissakes, he must have read her mind. "How did you know that I wanted to talk about matters of the heart and that crazy desire stuff?"

Chapter Twenty-six

If Barth hadn't been firmly planted in his chair, he would have fallen on the floor, he was so taken back by Columbia's straightforward comment. "Let me get this straight. You want to talk about matters of the heart and that crazy desire stuff?"

"Yes, that's exactly what I said. I need some advice about lust."

He nodded slowly, as he fought to come up with a reason why the girl would ask such a question. Perhaps he was misinterpreting something in their conversation. "You want to talk about lust?"

"You got a hearin' problem?"

Barth suppressed a grin. "No, I evidently heard you correctly." He scratched his earlobe. "I suppose now all I need to do is try to figure out a tactful way to explain what it is."

"I don't need no explanation of its meanin'. I know what it means."

"You do?"

"Sure. It is when a body gets an overwhelmin' cravin' to mate. You see, that's my problem."

Barth nodded as she spoke, keeping his face impassive. Her expression denoted a dead seriousness, which he had a most difficult time understanding, considering she wasn't exactly a role model for woman of the world. "Your problem."

"Yes. I got this overwhelmin' cravin', only I don't know what to do about it."

Barth had been enjoying Nash's discomfort over the girl, because he knew that she was something special to him. And he had to admit to himself that he found making Nash jealous gave him a bit of satisfaction. But he had not been prepared for this topic of conversation at all!

Nash paced past the window again, and suddenly Barth realized what the girl's dilemma was all about. They were both hooked. But neither one was about to admit it. Pride and cussed stubbornness sure made life interesting and difficult.

Barth was still pondering over his part in all this, when he heard the creak of the door. Without glancing back, Barth knew that Nash had entered the room and was standing in the background. An idea flashed into Barth's mind.

"If I can be of service to help alleviate this sexual craving, this lust you are experiencing, I shall be more than happy to oblige at any hour of the day or night."

Columbia had not noticed Nash come in. "No. No. It's not just a cravin' for *any* male body, at least I don't think so. It seems to be wrapped up with the funny way my heart pounds when—"

"I am around," Nash announced dryly and joined them.

Nash's face was blacker than she'd ever seen it before. Suddenly the tension in the room became so thick that Columbia tried to edge out of her seat. "Think I'll go back on deck and keep watch over my boat. We're almost to Portland."

To her shock, Nash clamped a hurting hand around her wrist. "Ya'll are not going anywhere."

Barth cleared his throat and rose. "I suppose this is my cue to exit."

"Very wise of you, old friend," Nash said in a serious voice filled with barely restrained anger.

"Yes, well, remember, Columbia, if I can be of assistance, let me know," Barth could not help adding and wisely left.

"Thank you, I will," she called out to his back, partly to irritate Nash for breaking into her conversation with Barth. Nash deserved to be kept off balance. Nobody was going to take it for granted that she belonged to him. A taunting smile curving her lips, she returned her attention to the angry demon restraining her in the chair.

"Ya'll . . . will . . . not," Nash said with deadly deliberation. "If ya'll are craving a male body so bad that you could not wait to discuss this need of yours with my first mate, I will be more than happy to satiate this urgent craving of yours."

"You're hurtin' my wrist."

Nash loosened his grip, but not enough for her to effect an escape. "If you'll let go of me, I can go direct the dockin' of my paddle wheeler," she said indignantly.

"Not so fast. First there is the little matter of taking care of this craving of yours."

She tried to jerk free. He held fast. She glared at him for a moment while she collected her thoughts. "You'll forgive me if I decline your more than generous offer."

Nash stared at her, a brow quirked. "How eloquent ya'll can be when it serves your purpose. But the fact is, I have no intention of being so remiss as to have ya'll running around Portland with this rampant craving lust ya'll are experiencing gnawing at you. Why, who knows what insanity it could drive ya'll to."

Livid, she managed to rip her wrist out of his grasp and lurch to her feet, retorting, "It's *my* lustful cravin', and I'll do with it what I damn well please."

She swung her back to him and began to stalk out on deck, but he caught her up in his arms before she realized what he was all about. She screeched at him to set her back on her feet. He ignored her as if he hadn't heard a word she was screaming at him.

Little John was walking toward them and she swung out her arm. "Please, help me, Little John. This devil's tryin' to kidnap me."

"Remember who ya'll work for," Nash warned and kept stomping toward his cabin.

"Little John, ain't you gonna help me?"

"Sorry, Miz Columbia," he mumbled, then put his head down, and hurried out of the way. That pair together was like getting caught out in a raging sou'wester. And he wanted no part of it.

"Barth!" Columbia cried, as she sighted him standing topside above them.

He glanced over the rail. "Don't worry, Columbia, I shall see that your paddle wheeler is taken care of,

260

while you are otherwise engaged." He grinned at Nash. "Deference is mine."

"Oh! All you men stick together," she groaned and quit struggling. She crossed her arms over her chest and deemed not to rise to any further bait he tormented her with, as they entered his cabin and he tossed her down on his bed.

To her chagrin, he swung a chair in front of the door and straddled it, leaning his chin on the straight back and staring at her without saying a single word.

It seemed like an eternity as she sat, cross-legged on his bed staring back at him. She had expected him to try something, or at least say something scathing, then she could offer a stinging rebuke. But the exasperating man was not cooperating at all.

The longer she sat there, the more she thought that perhaps he was merely trying to frighten her. Although the very thought of his hands touching her body in those intimate places admittedly excited her, surely he was only bluffing. The entire crew must know by now that he had brought her to his cabin against her will. Well, sort of against her will. She actually hadn't fought that hard.

The longer she mulled it over, the more she realized that the first move was hers. He was the stalking predator waiting to see whether she would make the fatal mistake. *Fatal mistake.* An interesting choice of words, considering the direction her mind was going.

The paddle wheeler bumped against something. They had obviously reached the docks at Portland. She could not outwait him any longer. She really should be out directing the drydocking of her beloved riverboat. Then she needed to check on her Uncle Titus.

She lifted her chin in a display of bravado, and decided to test the waters, so to speak. "Now that we've sat here long enough for my ardor to cool markedly — frozen solid as a cake of ice as a matter of fact — you can remove your person from the door and let me get on with what needs doin'."

She cautiously rose and moved within a foot of him. His body language did not give anything away when he rose in concert and moved the chair between them aside. Now she found herself face to face with the man who was at the root of her problem of lustful craving.

Everything about him was sensual. The breadth of his shoulders, the way his chest hairs peeked out at the open collar of his workshirt, the narrowing of his waist, and those strong muscular thighs and arms. She swallowed the tingling in the back of her throat, rapidly spreading down throughout her, and let her gaze drift up to his face. His full lips were slightly parted as if he were preparing to kiss her. His eyes held a black hunger, which mirrored the longing she knew she was not very successfully hiding in her own face.

"It appears that against our own wills, our lives have become irretrievably entangled," he murmured, in a voice heavy with the unhidden promise of passion. "Yours with mine; mine with yours," he added in a husky whisper.

"So it appears," she managed past the furious pounding of her heart between her ears. Her earlier determination was abandoning her, leaving her with that recognizable craving she had thought she could ignore. She *could* not ignore the man in front of her.

Slowly, his hand came out and lifted her chin. He dipped his head and brushed her lips with his. Gazing into her turquoise eyes with an untamed intensity, he breathed, "What do ya'll think we should do about it?"

"What we *should* do?" she echoed, struggling to keep her wits about her.

Poor choice of words. "Forget all the *shoulds* in this world, Mary Catherine. Want. What do ya'll *want* to do about it?"

This time both hands came up and inched her jacket from her shoulders, letting it slip down her arms. His fingers stroked up and down her arms, while his eyes beckoned her not to hold back.

He was seducing her. And she had to admit he certainly was an expert at it. Her senses were aflame with desire, overriding all her earlier boastful comments that her ardor was as frozen as a cake of ice. The obvious truth as she melted against him was that she was having a difficult time restraining her own fervor toward the man.

He bent his head again. This time he nibbled at the long column of her neck. The sensations were exquisite torture, meant to give her no option to resist.

She no longer wanted an option. Her eyelashes fluttered closed. She was trembling with anticipation. Gone were the arguments that she was her own person. Gone was her control. Gone was all rational thought.

"That is right, Mary Catherine, close your eyes and just let yourself feel," he said softly. "Feel what I am doing to ya'll."

She groaned from deep within her throat, as he lifted her from her feet and set her next to his bed. She opened her eyes to watch him shrugging out of his jacket. He tossed it aside. Before he worked the buttons on his shirt, the back of his hand stroked her downy cheek and his lips caressed hers. His shirt joined his jacket, and then he stripped off his remaining clothing.

The soft light coming into the cabin through the porthole seemed to spotlight his furred chest, flat belly, and that potent manly portion of him.

"Touch me, Mary Catherine," he said in a commanding plea. "Feel how much I want ya'll."

She let her fingers trace the path of his chest hairs. When she reached his stomach and lower during the intimate foray, his muscles tensed and he hardened. "Can ya'll feel what you are doing to me?"

She lifted her gaze to fasten on the heated coals of his eyes. "Yeah," came the breathy answer. "I want to feel the same way when you touch me in those same places."

Nash smiled at the wonderful, open young woman. "I shall do my best."

With lingering torture, he took his time undressing her, when she would have gladly ripped off her clothing and consummated her overwhelming desire for his body without any more delays.

First the shirt was slid from her. His calloused hands cupped her breasts and he suckled at the hardened nipples, wrenching an unintelligible cry from her throat at the sweet agony he was inflicting upon her.

"That is right, Mary Catherine, *feel!*"

While she remained standing, he slid the work-pants down her slender thighs. A pleased smile spread his lips. "Ya'll are wearing a pair of those fancy lace underwear."

Columbia blushed. "Don't know why I put them on this mornin'."

"I'm glad ya'll did," he crooned. He let his palms rub over the sheer black lace, until he cupped the mound hidden beneath the dainty garment. She pressed herself against his hand as an insistent tingling began at that place at the top of her thighs. "It is almost a pity to remove them."

"No, it ain't," she said and stepped out of the garment.

"Ya'll are right." His appreciative eyes drank in her every curve, every valley. "Ya'll are much more beautiful the way you are now."

"So are you."

All restraint snapped. Nash grabbed her buttocks and lifted her up onto him. She wrapped her legs around him and finished guiding his arousal deep inside her.

Columbia wasn't sure—didn't care—how Nash managed to stride the last steps to the bed and end up on top of her without withdrawing from her. He held still, his entire length buried in her, his eyes gazing down into hers.

"What is it?" he questioned, dropping nipping kisses on her eyes, the tip of her nose, her lips, her chin.

"What is what?" she managed between returning his kisses with her own voracious mouth.

265

"The question I see in those beautiful turquoise eyes of yours."

She hesitated a moment, then a wicked grin captured her lips. "You really want to know?"

"I want to know everything ya'll desire," he murmured.

"Then I was wonderin' if the man is always on top?"

Nash threw back his head and laughed. "Ya'll are priceless."

In the next instant Nash grasped his arms around her and rolled over, Columbia ending up in the pinnacled position. She giggled in delight and ran her short fingernails down his chest.

"Take me, I am all yours," he announced and grabbed her to him.

What had been playful delicate kisses and sweet caresses vanished into a frenzied rhythm. Each suddenly in a mad rush, in response to the driving urgency of their bodies, until first Columbia, then Nash reached that ultimate wild, vibrating, and shattering climax.

Columbia collapsed on top of Nash, panting and thoroughly drenched from their mating. Nash brought his hands up and smoothed the wet strands of her hair back behind her ears.

She raised up just enough to look into his contented face, beaded with perspiration. He kissed her lips, then said against her mouth, "I think we just managed to take care of satiating that urgent lustful craving ya'll were talking about earlier."

Chapter Twenty-seven

Columbia gasped at the cavalier way in which he had just spoken of their mating. She propelled herself off him, feeling as if that frozen cake of ice had just been strapped to her back. She stomped over to her clothes and tossed them on, not bothering with those damn black underdrawers.

Baffled by her sudden odd behavior — after they had just made the most delicious love he had ever experienced — Nash raised himself up on his elbows.

"Why are ya'll in such an all-fired rush all of a sudden? I was not any way near finished yet." He grinned, fully expecting to be able to talk her out of leaving, for his plans ran along the lines of remaining ensconced in the cabin together the entire day.

Steaming that all he had thought about what they had just shared was that he had done his duty and satiated her lustful cravings, Columbia narrowed her eyes, speechless, she was so put out. In a sudden fit of rage, she snatched up those damned underdrawers and lobbed them at him.

A direct hit. They landed in his face. He took

them in his hand and swung them around on his index finger, a seductive smirk on his lips. "A gift to remember this time together, no doubt?" he quipped.

The man was waving those damned underdrawers around like a victory flag!

"For ya'll maybe," she spat in a mocking voice, unable to hold in the gnawing at her gut any longer. "As for me, I fully intend to forget I ever let Dolly talk me into buyin' those ridiculous things."

"I was the one who paid for them, if ya'll will recall," he reminded her gently.

"So you did."

Her smile was so uncharacteristically sweet that Nash finally realized something was very much more amiss than he originally thought. He set the undergarment aside and got up to go to her. Her hand thrust forward, palm out.

"Don't you dare come another step closer."

He furrowed his brows in question. A few moments ago she had been the sweetest, wildest, most creative creature. "What has gotten into ya'll all of a sudden?"

She kept her gaze on his face, away from that gorgeous body of his, for fear she would weaken. "Nothin's got into me," she snapped. "You simply served your intended purpose real well. As you said, or should I say, *boasted* once it was over, you took care of my urgent lustful cravin'. Now I won't have a need to be anywhere near you again. And should I get such a cravin' again, I'll make it a point not to mention it to anyone while you're anywhere within earshot," she spat, next she swung open the door and slammed it behind her.

If Nash hadn't been naked, he would have rushed after her. As it was, he cracked open the door and hollered at her swiftly disappearing back. "Little fool, I was trying to tell you that I want ya'll here by my side, dammit!"

At that moment Dolly emerged from her cabin, her arms ladened with blankets. She glanced in the direction he was bellowing. "My, oh, my, such finesse you have, Nash. Pity she didn't seem to hear you declare your *honorable* intentions so eloquently, or I'm sure she would have swooned in her tracks from such poetic verse. Or do all your women display the same intent to run away from you, while you are declaring you want to make them your mistress?"

"Don't be ridiculous," Nash grunted. "I have never before told any female I wanted her to live with me."

"At least not in that manner, I truly hope."

"Not in any manner. Furthermore, how and when I choose to do what I do is none of your business," he snapped.

"Don't tell me you've truly taken the fall? And now that you have, you've finally come up against a female you can't easily conquer." Her dancing cat eyes caught a glimpse of his male torso. "And you cut such a dashing figure, too."

"Mind your own damned business, Dolly!" Nash snarled and slammed the door. He sent his fist crashing against the door in exasperation at the sound of Dolly's laughter.

That little fool Columbia had misunderstood what he had meant, and before she had made such an untimely exit, had twisted his words to use against him. His lips set in a firm line, determined to set the record straight as he jammed his legs into his trousers.

Once he was dressed, he headed up on deck. Barth was finishing up directing the hoisting of the wreck of the *Columbia's Pride* onto dry dock, where damage could be assessed and repairs begun.

"Where is Columbia?" Nash snapped out, galled that he had to ask Barth about her whereabouts.

Barth grinned up at his obviously nettled friend. Columbia had been as cranky as a wounded elk when she'd emerged to inquire after her paddle wheeler. And now Nash appeared to be the same, only doubly so. "She stopped for only a minute to make sure everything was proceeding on schedule with her boat, then headed into Portland. To check on her uncle, I'd guess."

Dolly waved a gloved hand up at Nash from her waiting carriage. "You're welcome to ride with me. I'm headed in that direction. Unless, of course, you plan to continue to be your disagreeable self. In that case, you can find your own transportation."

Barth smirked and several of the dockworkers chuckled, giving Nash the inclination to strangle Dolly had she been within reach at that moment. But since Titus had been moved, Dolly could save him precious time locating the man . . . and Columbia, who was the true cause of his ill temper.

"I shall be right there," he called down. "Hold the carriage."

Barth finished directing the docking of the *Columbia's Pride* and stopped Nash just before he reached the awaiting carriage. He put a hand on Nash's arm.

"Go easy on Columbia. She's not like the women we've known."

Nash glared at his friend, and the words "the women *we've* known" stood out in his mind like a festering sore. He scowled at Barth, which caused the man to remove his hand.

"When you refer to 'the women *we've* known,' ya'll better not have meant that in the Biblical sense where Columbia is concerned," Nash said darkly.

"I thought we were having a friendly little competition over the girl. But from the looks of you, there is nothing friendly about it. You really have lost your heart this time, haven't you?" Barth observed under Nash's black frown.

Nash glared at Barth for a moment before he spoke. "My heart is right where it should be. Just be sure that ya'll keep a tight rein on yours where Columbia is concerned." He paused. "And as far as any of those lustful cravings she was speaking to you about—"

Barth brought his palms up to ward off Nash's building wrath. "You don't have to concern yourself about that. I fully intend to leave that entirely up to you—"

Nash's facial features relaxed and he swung around to join Dolly until Barth's parting volley hit him square between the shoulder blades.

"—unless she comes to me directly."

Nash pivoted around and returned to Barth. "If she comes to ya'll directly, I want to know about it. Do I make myself clear?"

Barth had never seen Nash act so possessively before. They had always been friends, regardless of the circumstances. For the first time Barth feared that something, or more precisely, *someone* could easily come between their lifelong friendship. "Nash, I like Columbia, truly I do. But I love you as a brother. If the girl means that much to you, I shall gladly back off."

Nash was about to say good, but an idea materialized in his mind. All he had to do was say the word, and Barth would keep his distance, which at first sounded like the best way to solve his problem with Columbia. But the more Nash thought about it, the more he realized, that if Barth continued to see Columbia, and she in the end chose Nash, then he had truly won her, not merely just intimidated anyone else who might have had an interest in the girl, thereby winning by default. Knowing that Columbia would select him over all other suitors suddenly became very important to Nash, and he recognized that he had to be Columbia's free choice if they were going to have an amicable relationship.

"Did you hear what I said?" Barth questioned Nash, who seemed to be miles away. "I said if you want, I'll back off."

Nash's head snapped up. He might be about to do the dumbest thing he had ever done in his life, but he said, "No. I mean yes, I heard what ya'll said. And no, I do not want ya'll to back off. She is fair game. As a matter of fact, I want ya'll to come along."

As they headed to join Dolly in the carriage, Barth was beginning to wonder if the bump Nash had sustained on the head while he had been rescuing Titus Baranoff had suddenly affected his brain.

* * *

Columbia rushed to the doctor's office to see her uncle, only to learn that Titus had been moved, at Dolly's request, to a room over the Dockside Saloon. At Columbia's questioning over Titus's injuries, the doctor shrugged.

"It didn't worsen his condition to move him. And Miss Brooks said that the music would help him heal faster."

"You mean Mrs. Foster?"

Doctor Barker looked askance, then amended. "Yes, of course, Mrs. Foster."

"Has Uncle Titus regained consciousness then?" Columbia asked hopefully.

"Well, not yet. His injuries are pretty serious. Broken bones, some pretty bad burns, and a concussion. Mrs. Foster said that even an unconscious person can feel the vibrations from music, and it is a healing balm. And whether that is scientifically true or not is debatable, but it certainly can't do him any harm, Columbia."

Columbia nodded her reluctant acceptance. "About your bill, Doctor—"

"There is no need to concern yourself with that. It has been all taken care of. Mrs. Foster said that Captain Foster has assumed responsibility, and she has offered to stay at Mr. Baranoff's side. So you run along now and go visit that uncle of yours. And try not to worry, Columbia. Although I cannot make any promises that he will pull through, your Uncle Titus is a tough old bird—not at all as weak as he has been complaining all these years—or he would have died already. I shall look in on him from time to time, to see how he is progressing."

Columbia smiled weakly, although not completely relieved over her uncle's condition and Nash's assumed responsibility for the bills. She thanked the doctor, holding back her irritation over his "Mrs. Foster said," and hurried over to the Dockside.

Titus lay deathly still on a narrow bed in the small tidy room over the boisterous saloon. The floor vibrated from the loud music below.

"I hope Dolly is right. If anything can revive the dead, that music can," she mumbled to herself as she crossed the bare floor and sat on the edge of the bed. She took Titus's bandaged, limp hand in hers, and closed her fingers around it.

"We managed to raise the *Columbia's Pride*, Uncle Titus. And I'll have it rebuilt in no time, so you got to quit lyin' in that bed and get well real soon, so we can get back in business," she chattered as if he were fully aware. "After all, I got to have a licensed man at the helm, so we can keep takin' hauls away from Villamoore."

She felt tears spring to her eyes when she perused his battered and burned face. Self-recriminations filled her clear through to her soul, and Columbia spent some time baring her heart to the unconscious man. He squeezed her hand ever so weakly, and she focused her attention on him. He was coming around.

"Uncle Titus?"

His eyes slowly fluttered open and he tried to smile. He winced with the effort. "Columbia," he said with a laborious rasp.

"Thank God I didn't kill you," she cried, tears now flooding down her cheeks. "I'm so sorry. I should've been with you instead of paradin' as Foster's cabin boy, then this never would've happened."

"Not your fault. Villamoore's men," he said with great difficulty, "blew boiler. Saw them."

"I'm gonna kill him."

"No. Best revenge is for you to get *Columbia's Pride* back on the river."

"I'm already workin' on it. All I need to do is find a riverboat pilot to work for me," she announced with more optimism than she felt. Finding someone to work against Villamoore was no easy task, since he either hired or frightened away all the good pilots.

"Not someone to work for you. No good," he struggled past the pain to get out what needed to be said before he lost consciousness again. "Villamoore hire or scare away." Her thoughts exactly.

"Then I'll find a partner 'til you're well again."

"No. Partner could sell out before well enough to return. Won't do. Only one solution." He groaned at the pain in his side.

Worry wrinkled her brow and she shot to her feet. "I'll get the doctor."

With arduous effort he reached out to her. "No. Come. Sit."

Columbia settled back down, but was acutely aware of his labored breathing and the pain he valiantly tried to hide. She stroked his forearm. "What can I do for you?"

"Not me. Business."

"I'll do anything, Uncle Titus," she said to humor the pain-riddled man. "Anything."

He coughed and groaned at the pain caused by the spasms. "Husband."

She wasn't sure she had heard him correctly, his voice had faded to a mere whisper. "What do you want me to do?"

His mouth opened and she leaned over him, putting her ear near his lips, so she could make out what he was trying to say. "You choose husband. Protect you from Villamoore should I die." His last words were said with a gasp for breath.

She wanted to leap to her feet and shout *No!* She did not need a husband! She would exact revenge against Villamoore personally for what he had done to her uncle. Instead, she sat still, stunned, at odds with her loyalty and devotion to her beloved uncle, and her own aversion to having some man control her life.

Chapter Twenty-eight

As if a cruel fate had stepped in to work against Columbia retaining her freedom, Dolly, followed by Nash and Barth, walked through the door. Her attention snapped to them before she heard her uncle's straining voice. Her head swung around in time to see him struggle to point.

"Choose. Good choices."

"He's awake!" Dolly squealed and rushed to his side. She took his shaking bandaged fingers in hers. "What is it you're trying to tell us, Titus honey?"

Nash and Barth set the blankets they had brought aside, and moved closer until they were all crowded around the injured man. All leaned forward to hear what Titus was trying to say. All, that is, except Columbia. She stepped back, for she knew exactly what he meant.

Uncle Titus expected her to make a choice—to choose a husband of all things—between Nash and Barth.

Her gaze left her uncle's quivering lips and scanned the two men. Barth's attention was focused on her uncle. But while Nash had also moved closer out of concern for the injured man, his eyes bored into hers.

Dolly's high-pitched voice broke in between Columbia and Nash. "Oh, Columbia, the poor man's lapsed back into unconsciousness again." Dolly looked directly at Columbia now, her eyes probing. "He must've had a real urgent need to manage to get out those couple of words in his pitiful condition."

A real urgent need.

Columbia's and Nash's gazes locked again. Both recognizing the strange coincidence of the close parody of Dolly's statement. Barth noticed it, too. But to him it was obvious he was the third party, aware but excluded from their private moment of shared comprehension.

"Do you have any idea what he was trying to say?" Dolly's question broke the building tension in the small room.

All three shook their heads, but Dolly was staring directly at Columbia. "Are you sure, Columbia, that he didn't say anything before we got here?"

Columbia swallowed hard. She could not make a confession in front of Nash and Barth, or in front of Dolly, for that matter. She had some hard thinking to do. But she couldn't just come right out and lie either. Telling tall tales wasn't her way. Her eyes wide with feigned innocence, Columbia answered, "I think he must've been delirious, because he made no sense at all."

That seemed to satisfy Dolly, who returned her full attention to Titus. And truth be known, what Columbia had said was true. Uncle Titus had to have been demented to suggest such an outrageous scheme.

If Columbia thought she had gotten herself off the hook and bought herself more time to thoroughly digest such an extreme solution, she was mistaken, for Dolly suddenly turned back to her.

"I hope those weren't his dying words," Dolly said remorsefully. "If so, we'll never know what his wishes were."

"That would be a crime," Columbia managed to force herself to agree.

"Truly it would. I've always believed that a dying man's wishes should be honored if at all possible," Dolly announced in earnest.

"Dolly," Nash said in a chastising voice. "Ya'll do not know that Titus is dying."

"True enough." Dolly hung her head, but kept watch for Columbia's reactions. "But his injuries are serious enough that only the Lord in heaven knows whether Titus'll make it for sure or not."

"No more of such talk," Nash warned. "Ya'll should not upset Columbia further by even bringing up such a remote possibility."

But the possibility did upset Columbia, and continued to plague her long after she had excused herself from Nash and Barth and left her uncle in Dolly's care. That, and the fact that Villamoore had been responsible for nearly killing Uncle Titus and sinking the *Columbia's Pride*.

Her mind suddenly fired on a course of action which would make it unnecessary for her to consider Uncle Titus's desire that she choose a husband between the two men, Columbia marched through the rain puddles accumulating in the potholes on the road. She pulled her knit cap down on her forehead, and snugged her jacket collar up around her neck.

Columbia had come up with her own solution to keep Villamoore from causing her or anyone else any more grief, and at the same time a way to avenge her uncle. She stomped onto the boardwalk in front of the general mercantile and barged through the door. The bell echoed wildly. Heads snapped up at her bold entrance, and three women browsing through the bolts of fabric cast her disparaging glances. Columbia pulled a face at the old crows, and they immediately looked away. Frank McGee and GlennieLynn nodded in greeting, then went about their business.

"What can I do for you, Miss Columbia?" The store clerk, standing at the potbelly stove, rubbed his hands. The girl hadn't even bothered to wipe the mud off her boots before entering. Now he would have to clean up after her. "Come on over to the counter, and we can go over your account while I fill your order."

Columbia hesitated and thought to tell GlennieLynn about Uncle Titus. But she was with Frank McGee now. Furthermore, Columbia had pressing business. As she advanced to the glass counter where Harold Tucker kept what she'd come after, Columbia tried to come up with a plausible excuse to put the storekeeper off from demanding another payment on her growing bill.

She put her hands on the glass counter and peered at the array of weapons arranged in a neat row. She grabbed her hands back when Harold Tucker approached. A stern look of disgust on his face, he immediately grabbed the bottom edge of the white bib apron he wore, and wiped the glass clean of smudges where she had set her fingers.

"I'm not dirtyin' the place up," Columbia protested. "I came in to make an important purchase."

Harold wrinkled his brow. "And what about your bill? Did you come in to put something toward that, too?"

Columbia's fingers slipped into her pockets; they were bare, except for a hankie. She twirled the greasy bit of cotton around her fingers. With any luck Tucker may not have heard about the *Columbia's Pride* yet. "You'll get your money just as soon as Uncle Titus's last haul from Astoria is delivered."

Harold's face softened. "Heard he had gone out." He paused and rubbed his jaw. "All right. I'll add your purchases to your bill. But just this one last time. There'll be no more credit until your account is settled; Titus being a longtime friend or not."

Columbia kept her glee subdued at managing to pull it off; Tucker had not heard the news yet. She tapped an index finger on the glass case, pointing to what she wanted. "That one will do nicely, I think."

Harold's mouth dropped, but he pulled the item from the case and set it on the counter. "What'll you be needing a gun for, Miss Columbia?"

Columbia picked up the pistol. It felt cold and smooth and deadly in her hands. "It's personal. I'll be needin' some load, too. A small bag'll suit."

"You sure you aren't going to start trouble with that gun if I sell it to you?" he demanded, knowing the river girl's reputation.

281

"You don't got to worry none about that, Mr. Tucker. You know me," she said with an innocent smile.

He lifted his brows. "That's why I'm asking."

Columbia forced a smile, sidestepping an answer to his question. "When I was growin' up, I never could get nothin' past you."

She had hold of the gun she needed now, and the only way Tucker was going to get it away from her, was if he fought her for it.

His ego stroked, Harold let the question fade despite a nagging concern. He placed the bag of load on the counter and watched it rapidly disappear into the girl's jacket. "Don't you want me to show you how to load it?"

"No. I'll manage fine when the time comes."

Growing increasingly uncomfortable, he questioned, "What are you aiming to shoot with that gun?"

Columbia stuck the gun in her waistband and headed for the door, before tossing over her shoulder, "I'm merely aimin' to lessen the varmint population in Portland a mite, is all."

He scratched his head, wondering if the girl had just put one over on him. "With a pistol?"

Just outside the mercantile, Columbia literally bumped into Nash and Barth striding along the boardwalk. Nash closed his arms around her. "Where are ya'll going in such a rush?"

Columbia wiggled out of his embrace. Her heart was pounding for fear that he would discover what she was about, not to mention what being in his arms did to her. "I got business," she answered in

282

clipped tones, pushed past them, and kept walking. She did not dare to glimpse behind her, afraid that Nash might have decided to follow her. She heard the bell over the door of the mercantile and dared a peek. She let out a sigh.

Nash and Barth had disappeared inside the store.

Columbia stopped in an alley down the street from the mercantile long enough to load the gun. She was about to step back onto the boardwalk, when a strong hand clamped on her arm.

"Dresses like a man, swaggers like a man, but feels like a woman hiding her charms in a man's breeches. Ready for some fun? How 'bout it, Miz Col-um-bi-a?"

Columbia whirled to face the stranger who knew who she was, the gun in her hand pointed at his heart. The evil smirk on the stranger's face dropped, and the color drained from him as his eyes fastened on the gun.

"How about *what?*" she said with menace in her voice.

He swallowed hard. "Nothing. No harm meant." With one hand raised over his head, he bent down real slow, picked up some of the shot she had dropped, and offered it to her, palm out. "I just didn't want you to forget this."

"Keep it. There's still plenty left for the likes of Villamoore," she announced without a second thought. "And don't let me see that ugly face of yours anywhere near me again, or I might be inclined to shoot first next time."

"Yes, ma'am," he said, and scrambled away before she could interrogate him and learn how he knew who she was.

Shrugging off the fact that he knew her on sight, since she was known by many on the river, Columbia tucked the loaded gun back into her pants. She was pleased with the way she had handled herself, and decided to let the incident serve as a prelude for her showdown with John Villamoore.

Feeling more confident than ever, Columbia wasted no time heading to Villamoore's office. She pulled her gun out and barged through the door. The outer office was empty, as was the inner office. Disgruntled that her quarry wasn't cooperating, Columbia borrowed a horse tethered out front and headed directly to Villamoore's home.

She found Villamoore seated at an immense table in his opulent dining room, sipping tea. She had expected him to shake in his boots when she barged into his home with her gun drawn.

Instead, he threw her off balance by lifting the cup in toast. "I have been expecting you for some time now, my dear. I am delighted that you did not disappoint me. Please. Won't you join me? There is nothing like a hot cup of tea on a cold, rainy day, don't you agree?"

"Why ain't you scared?" she asked suspiciously and held her ground.

"Quite simply, because I have nothing to be concerned about, my dear."

"I ain't your dear. I come to settle a score. Your men sank my . . . ah . . . my uncle's paddle wheeler and nearly killed him in the process. We was lucky to raise what was left of it."

His eyes flashed ever so slightly upon hearing that the paddle wheeler was not at the bottom of the river, and that Titus Baranoff still lived. "How truly sorry I am to hear about the unfortunate mishap. But you know that riverboats are notorious for exploding from time to time."

"Especially when your men see to it that the boiler overheats," she spat.

"Every one of my men have been here with me, and I can personally vouch for them," he said with a smirk. "So you must be mistaken." The amusement left his long face and he toyed with his thin mustache. "Your uncle is getting old and sloppy. I would say it is time you sold what is left of your old riverboat for scrap. I might even find it in my heart to make you a generous offer, the kind man that I am. Now put that gun away, before you accidentally harm someone with it."

"This is the kind of man I think you are." Columbia was holding the gun with both hands. His comment about her uncle so enraged her, that she swung toward an enormous Ming vase showcased in the corner of the room and blasted it.

It shattered into thousands of flying fragments.

Villamoore flinched and gritted his teeth. "That was very foolish of you, Columbia. That vase was priceless."

"I'd say it's still priceless, 'cause nobody's gonna give a price for it now. And unless you 'fess up to sinkin' the *Columbia's Pride,* I'm gonna pull the trigger on you next. You got three minutes before you look like that broken jar of yours."

Tense minutes passed as the pair attempted to stare each other down. Villamoore was staring down the barrel of a loaded gun. Sweating, he was now sorry he had dismissed the staff and the informant who had spotted the girl, then came directly to alert his boss that the Baranoff girl was heading his way with a loaded gun. Villamoore had thought he could handle the girl alone.

Columbia had never shot a man before, but she had put herself into a corner with her boastful threats. Her mind whirled with the consequences of shooting the bastard through his black heart. Despite the urge to just go ahead and fill him with lead, she settled on winging him, just to make sure that he knew she meant business.

"Your time's up, Villamoore. You prepared to write out a full confession, or you prepared to die?"

Villamoore got up from his chair slowly, palms out as if to ward her off. His knees were shaking so bad that he thought he was going to crumble back into the chair. "You'll hang if you shoot me!"

"I think I'll more 'n' likely be thanked and win a medal for riddin' the river of your likes."

Columbia shifted her stance so her feet were planted securely apart. Still holding the gun with both hands, she squeezed one eye shut, slowly took careful aim, and squeezed the trigger.

Chapter Twenty-nine

Nash burst through the door and grabbed Columbia's arm, just as the gun went off. The shot harmlessly slammed through the heart of the lifesize portrait of Villamoore, hung high on the wall behind the trembling coward of a man.

Columbia struggled to regain control of the gun, managing to get off another blast. But she was no match for Nash, who now ripped it out of her hand from behind her and tossed it aside. Livid at being thwarted and the gun snatched from her possession, she managed to swing around and slap the man square in the face.

"You bast—" She paused, startled to see Nash, a red handprint outlining his cheek. She gasped as he pinned her arms. "You! How could you stop me? That crook's responsible for nearly killin' Uncle Titus and sinkin' the *Columbia's Pride*," she cried.

Nash continued to hold her, although he pivoted her around. In an amused voice, he said against her ear, "If ya'll will look on the wall behind Villamoore, you will see that ya'll accomplished your mission with uncanny precision."

Columbia's angry gaze shifted from that unharmed skunk Villamoore upward. Villamoore, too, who had collapsed in his chair and was dabbing the nervous perspiration from his brow, swiveled around to follow his savior's directions. He grabbed his heart with one hand, his crotch with the other, aghast that the girl had put two holes through his most treasured self-image.

Despite her anger, Columbia had to chuckle at Villamoore's gasp of shock.

Villamoore climbed on a chair, his fingers twisting in the gaping perforations in his portrait. "She shot me clean through the heart!" he choked.

"You forgot to mention that I shot you in your private parts, too," Columbia blurted out with a chuckle. "Must be a better shot than I thought, to hit something so small." She laughed outright at the glower now on Villamoore's face. "Pity it was only your ugly picture.

"If I could've got off another shot, I would've rearranged the hair in the picture to match that lopsided thatch sittin' cattywampus on your bald head." She tried to get free so she could kick the chair out from under the red-faced little skunk, now desperately trying to right his toupee.

"Shut up. And stop struggling. Ya'll have caused enough trouble for one morning," Nash hissed and tightened his hold on her.

"And what did you do, follow me? Or were you comin' here to get your workin' orders from that stinkin' skunk, like the rest of his henchmen?" she accused.

Nash frowned at the troublesome girl. "Barth, get her out of here," he ordered his first mate, who was standing silently at the door with his arms crossed and trying to keep the amusement off his face. "Take her out of here."

Barth stepped forward to take control of the hellion.

"Wait!" called out Villamoore, whose face was purpled with rage as he came off the chair. He checked his image in a nearby mirror, to ascertain that his hairpiece was now properly secured in place. "I want her arrested for destroying my priceless property, not to mention attempted murder."

"You mean of that moth-eaten, dead animal skin crouched on your head that you try to pass off as your own?" she taunted, knowing full well she'd get to his pride if nothing else. "I should've used my pistol to part it down the middle for you. Would've looked more natural that way."

In a menacing voice, Nash growled, "I thought I told ya'll to shut up?"

Columbia shrugged.

Nash's black eyes flashed. He was furious, and Columbia wasn't sure who was going to be the recipient of his wrath. Although she had a sneaking hunch it was going to be her. Well, she had a few choice things to say to that interfering interloper herself.

"Get her outside, before she puts her foot in her mouth far enough to choke herself. I want to talk to Mr. Villamoore alone."

As Barth was dragging her from the room, a livid Columbia shouted, "I got a right to hear what you're gonna say, since it obviously has to do with me."

Nash waited patiently until Barth had managed to remove Columbia from the scene, then motioned for Villamoore to sit down.

"I don't want to be seated." Villamoore swung out an arm. "Look at all the havoc that river girl has wrought on my beautiful home, not to mention threatening my person. No. I want her arrested. And I want it done now!"

Nash ignored the hysterical man's outburst, pulled out a chair, dusted off the broken bits of vase, and settled down. "I think I might have a better idea as what to do with the girl, rather than having her arrested."

Regaining his composure, Villamoore straightened the lapels on his finely tailored jacket and narrowed his eyes at Foster. "Before we discuss your idea for her disposition, how did you just happen to appear at my home at precisely the right moment?"

"I did not just happen to appear here, as ya'll put it. I saw the girl go into the mercantile. When she came out, she was headed toward your office with a determined look on her face. Lucky for ya'll I was suspicious and checked with the clerk in the store and learned she bought a gun. The rest was simple deduction."

Columbia was standing right outside the doorway, as far as Barth could force her considering her threat to raise his voice an octave higher with a well-placed kick from her boot. Her sour gaze spun on her captor. "You two followed me!" she spat in a whispered hiss.

"Hush, if you want to remain here and listen."

Columbia glowered at Barth, but gave a curt nod and craned her ear to overhear what that devil Foster was going to propose to keep her out of jail.

"I knew she was headed in my direction," Villamoore boasted in an effort to redeem his ego. "She pulled a gun on one of my men, and knowing how she blames me for everything that befalls her and that uncle of hers, the man came directly here and warned me. So I was prepared to handle her."

"Yes, I noticed how well ya'll were *handling* the girl when I came in."

Villamoore frowned. "So you made a timely entrance. Get to the point. Why shouldn't I let her rot in jail?"

It was over an hour before Nash emerged from Villamoore's estate. Barth had convinced Columbia that it would benefit her if Nash found her outside the house as he had directed, since he was bound to be rather upset with her.

Rather upset was an understatement when Nash spied her sitting in the shelter of a pine tree, twirling a twig between her fingers, as if she hadn't a care in the world. The fire in his face spoke for him when he stalked over to her, grabbed her by the arm, and forced her to her feet.

"That's no way to treat a lady," she snapped.

"Lady? After the dumb stunt ya'll just pulled, not

to mention taunting the man about the size of his private parts and his hairpiece? He is not likely to ever forgive ya'll for that," Nash warned.

"Suits me just fine. Furthermore, I did no more than speak the truth, his privates are probably as scrawny as the few true strands of hair he's got left. I thought lettin' him know how good I am at shootin' at small targets would be good for him."

Nash ignored the enjoyment she seemed to derive out of the havoc she had created. "If I had not been able to convince Villamoore that his image would suffer more with ya'll jailed, right after your uncle was nearly killed in a suspect sinking of that damned paddle wheeler of yours, ya'll would be spending your time behind bars . . . instead of locked in my cabin."

"Locked in your cabin!" She jerked free and stood glaring at him. "I'm not gonna stay locked in your cabin," she snorted, and raced for her horse.

Nash caught up with her, circled his arms around her waist, and swung her foot out of the stirrup as she was trying to mount. "Not so fast. And where did ya'll get that horse?"

She was glowering more than ever now. "I borrowed it, since you're so interested."

"Jesus Christ! What did ya'll plan to do? Add horse stealing to your other crimes? Where did ya'll get the damn horse?"

"From in front of that stinkin' skunk's office, if you must know. For heavensakes, I didn't commit a crime; I just borrowed it. I was gonna return it."

"Once ya'll had used it to make your getaway after you shot Villamoore, I presume."

"Yeah," she spat out, furious.

The rage in his voice disguising the fear he'd felt since discovering what she was up to, he swung toward Barth. "Get this horse back to where it came from, before whoever owns it discovers it's missing."

Barth sauntered past the pair, a smirk on his face. "I shall be happy to." He chuckled. "That is, if you think you can handle Columbia by yourself."

"I shall handle her, if I have to hogtie and gag her."

Columbia had been silently preparing to attempt another escape, but the fear that Nash would indeed carry out such a threat, and had the overpowering strength to follow through with it, forced her to stay calm. "That won't be necessary. But I warn you, you're not gonna get away with kidnappin' me and makin' me a prisoner on that paddle wheeler of yours."

Barth mounted with the quip, "Ah, they say the road to love is often uphill. But for you two, it seems to be more on the scale of a mountain."

She felt Nash tense. She watched Barth ride off down the hillside, then hissed, "You can quit worryin' about what Barth just said about love, because I could never love you now, even if I had a mind to earlier, which I didn't. As a matter of fact, I think that I hate you for stoppin' me from takin' care of Villamoore."

For an instant Columbia thought she had truly wounded Nash with what she had said, and she was sorry. But the instant of regret she had felt for saying such awful hateful things came to an abrupt end, as he tightened his grip on her and roughly escorted her to a waiting wagon.

"And what makes you think I have any particular affinity for ya'll either at this moment?" he snorted, plopping her on the wagon box.

Despite his angry response to her statement, the fact was that Nash did indeed have a particular affinity, so to speak, for the crazy hellion. He just had to figure out a way to overcome all the mounting obstacles standing in their way, before he could move her permanently on board the *Yacht*. Including this latest additional one involving Villamoore that Columbia had just managed to stir up.

All the way back to the docks through the light mist that continued to fall, Columbia refused to talk or even look at Nash. She had so many feelings all jumbled up inside her chest, she was afraid she'd explode.

She had given him her virginity, even mated with him a second time, and could not deny that her hankering for him was so strong sometimes that she ached clear through. But then there was the fact that he was married, although Dolly had been in search of one of those lawyer fellows and had explained that Nash had only married her to do her a favor. He saved Columbia's life when her skirt caught fire. Nash had gone to rescue her Uncle Titus, and even risked his life to come after her. He had managed to raise her beloved paddle wheeler against all odds, and was seeing to its restoration. He was even paying for Uncle Titus's medical bills.

The thought of Uncle Titus and what may have been a deathbed request flooded into her mind. Her attempts to seek an answer to their problems had not ended with particular success. She squeezed her eyes shut. Actually, it had been a dismal failure. But that brought another question to mind: Were Nash Foster and his first mate really working for Villamoore, and only helping her and her uncle for some sinister reason?

At the docks Frank McGee approached them as Nash jumped from the wagon and handed Columbia down, despite her continuing refusal to speak to him.

"See you found her."

"Yes," was all that Nash offered, although from McGee's expression it was obvious the man was dying to ask about Columbia's latest misadventure. "Thanks for the loan of your wagon."

"GlennieLynn was worried that something awful might happen to Columbia . . . ah . . . she'll want to know."

"Tell GlennieLynn that Columbia is just fine." Nash's lips tight, he clamped a hand around Columbia's arm and guided her up the gangplank, leaving Frank McGee shaking his head.

Little John tried to pretend that he did not see the angry couple about to stomp past him. But he could not help but wonder what Columbia had done this time.

"Little John," Nash barked out.

Little John jumped to attention. "Sir?"

"Inform the crew that we shall be in port until the crates that Villamoore has coming upriver from Astoria arrive. Once the crew finishes up their duties on board, they can either take shore leave or earn some extra money working on the *Columbia's Pride*."

Columbia kept to her silence. If he expected her to thank him after he had mentioned her paddle wheeler in the same breath with working for Villamoore, he was sorely mistaken. And if he did get her boat back in working order, would she be forced to take a husband to pilot it?

Titus sat up, keeping his bandaged hands raised while Dolly plumped his pillows. "Oh, Titus, I wonder if we done the right thing trying to make Columbia think you're on your death bed, so she'll choose a husband to pilot her boat after it's put back together?"

She finished with his pillows and he lay back, a grin on his face despite the pain he felt. "I explained the first time we met and talked about Mary Catherine and Nash, that I've been trying to get her to marry and settle down for years. She has pulled some pretty underhanded stunts on me over the years, trying to keep me from selling that paddle wheeler out from under her.

"And just think about the underhanded stunt Nash Foster pulled, telling the girl that you two are married. What I did, sending her on board to work for him, was nothing. And don't you ever tell a living soul I was behind it."

"I won't. But—"

"But nothing." He cut her off. "The two of them have both shown how underhanded they can be when it suits them." He shrugged. "What better match can there be than two devious young people who are obviously attracted to each other? Let's face it, they deserve each other."

Dolly picked up the cup of broth she had gotten from the Dockside downstairs and began to spoon-feed Titus. "I'm not saying that they aren't attracted to each other, because they are. And I'm not saying that they don't deserve each other, because they do." She stopped speaking for a moment to wipe the corners of his mouth. "And I'm certainly not saying that either one of them isn't devious in getting their own way, because they'd both qualify for that award, if one was being handed out."

"Then exactly what is it you're trying to say?" Titus questioned between spoonfuls of broth.

Dolly set the empty bowl aside, troubled lines furrowing her forehead. "I guess what I'm truly worried about, is that you said you told the girl to choose between Nash and Barth. If Columbia pays heed to your wishes that she make a choice, what if she ups and makes the wrong one?"

"Worse yet, what if the chosen one refuses to cooperate with what you got in mind?"

Chapter Thirty

Jack Tarley crunched across the shattered pieces of glass strewn over the floor of Villamoore's dining room. He stopped abruptly when he sighted Villamoore seated with his back to him staring up at his portrait.

"Excuse me, Mr. Villamoore. Sorry for interruptin'. No one was at the door, so I just came in." Tarley's eyes surveyed Villamoore's portrait, and he had to fight to suppress the urge to laugh at the sight. "I'll be damned. That fancy picture of yours has got a hole shot right clean through your heart, not to mention the hole where your private parts ought to be."

Villamoore swung around in his chair and glowered purple rage at the big man with the full head of hair. God, how he hated men of normal height with hair. "What do you want?" Villamoore questioned with disgust, and rose to lean his fists against the fine linen tablecloth.

Tarley shifted uneasily, his boots crunching more fragments of glass. "Just came to tell you that Barney and me are keeping watch over the *Columbia's Pride* like you wanted." He beamed. "That river girl ain't going to be no more bother to you."

"You dumb bastard!" Villamoore picked up the heavy silver teapot in front of him and threw it at Tarley.

Tarley ducked just in time, and the pot struck a bust of Villamoore atop a pedestal, sending both crashing to the floor.

Feeling awkward, and unsure what had brought on Villamoore's latest fit of temper, Tarley bent over to retrieve the fallen statue. When he replaced it atop the marble pedestal, he gulped, "Looks like a chunk of the hair got broke off."

Barely able to contain his rage, Villamoore's hand automatically went to his own head for the second time that morning. He quickly realized he had touched the same place broken on his plaster likeness. He quickly withdrew his fingers when Tarley turned back to him.

"I don't rightly understand. I thought you'd be pleased to hear that we are on the job, keeping on top of things."

"Moron, I would be if Titus Baranoff were dead, and that damned riverboat of his was at the bottom of the river. But it isn't. And Baranoff's still alive. You idiots botched the whole damned thing." Tarley opened his mouth, but Villamoore silenced him with a wave of his wrist. "Foster just left with that river girl, who nearly killed me. She is the one responsible for the damage you see before you. While he was here, Foster informed me that he raised the boat and it's in dry dock being repaired right now."

"I told you Foster couldn't be trusted," Tarley boasted, feeling a little more confident that he had been right about the newest man Villamoore had hired. He relaxed, relieved that he did not have to be the one to inform Villamoore that the riverboat had been raised.

"If it weren't for Foster—" Villamoore broke off. It was too damaging to his male pride to recount in detail the humiliating incident with the Baranoff girl. "Well, let's just say that he took the girl off my hands, before I was forced to personally deal with her."

"Then he took her off to jail?"

"With her uncle nearly killed and that boat sunk? How do you think that would look if I had her jailed now, you stupid jackass?"

"But if Foster's working for you, why'd he raise the boat?"

Villamoore knitted his fingers together and slowly twirled his thumbs. "Said it would keep her attention focused on the lengthy repairs he's planned, and her nose out of my business."

"You believe that?" Tarley ventured.

"The notion had merit. But just to test Foster's loyalty to the cause, I am going to have him take the next special haul when it arrives."

"That one's supposed to be mine," Tarley sniveled. He didn't give a damn about noble causes or the South. He had plans for that extra money, and losing out to the likes of Foster did not set at all well with

Tarley. An idea sparked into his mind. "What if Foster opens the crates and discovers what he's haulin' isn't what's marked on the outside? Don't you think it's a mite too risky, considerin' how Foster always seems to come to that girl and her uncle's rescue?"

Villamoore threw back his head and laughed. "You idiot! Although Foster already has been introduced to some of the others who support our cause and they accept him, do you really think I would completely trust that Southerner before he has proved himself to me? I have already devised a little test. If he passes it, he's in. If not?" Villamoore's evil grin spread the width of his long face. "Well, I shall simply have to set Foster up for a big fall."

"What about the girl? You know that river girl would run right to Shallcross at Fort Vancouver if she got her hands on any evidence."

Villamoore subconsciously touched the edge of his toupee at the top of his ear, as his vision lifted to the humiliating ruination of his portrait, then shifted to the damaged bust. Perhaps he would prove to her personally that his anatomy was more than male enough for the likes of her. One way or another, she was going to pay for the trouble and the now public embarrassment she had caused him. "Then I suppose I shall just have to fix it so the pesky girl takes the fall with Foster."

Nash flipped the lock on his cabin door. He expected an angry confrontation with Columbia and

301

did not intend to be disturbed. When he turned to face her, he tripped over the muddy boot she had stuck out. He let out a string of invectives and grabbed her as he fell. If he was going to fall, the little hellion was going with him.

They landed with a thud on the floor, Nash on top of Columbia. To maintain the advantage he quickly pinned her hands over her head.

He should be furious and fed up with her antics, but he could not help himself. She was the most irrepressible young woman he had ever met, and, heaven help him, that was one of the things he found adorable about her. He smiled down into her angry turquoise eyes. "Don't you ever give up?"

"You must have tripped, like you said *I* did, when I fell into your tub that time you forced me to bathe you while I was pretendin' to be your cabin boy."

Nash chuckled. "My God woman, don't ya'll ever forget anything either?"

"Not stuff that leaves an impression on me."

"I am glad that I have managed to make such a lasting impression. Now, after I saved ya'll from yourself again this morning, you finally have to admit that ya'll are meant to be mine, so I can move you in with me. Who else would continuously chase after ya'll and still want you?"

Columbia tried to remain angry, but the fire in his black eyes was already smoldering, which threatened to torch her heart. "Look, I got to admit that you got a certain drawin' power."

He leaned over and kissed her lips. His tongue

302

laved the outline of her mouth until her lips parted. To his pleasure she eagerly thrust her tongue against his, simulating the mating ritual. He released her hands, pulled the knit cap from her head, and buried his fingers in the thick mass of her hair, spreading it out around her like a wake from a boat.

For her part, once her hands were freed, Columbia furiously began unworking the buttons at his throat. They became two wild, untamed animals possessed with a raw hunger for each other.

Nash broke the kiss, and with labored breathing, murmured as he nibbled on her ear, "Try to deny ya'll are mine."

The feelings in her innards were so strong, so powerful, so potent, that she was sorely tempted to mate with him right where she lay without further preface. But there was something that had been gnawing at her all day since they'd left Villamoore's house; something that refused to relinquish its hold on her; something that suddenly held her back and brought her to her senses. She pushed at his chest. "You got to let me up."

"I was not done. As a matter of fact, I had barely begun," he said in a thick voice full of passion, which implied he had no intention of moving. At least not moving, so to speak, in accordance with her request.

"Nash, please. We got to talk."

He stared down at her; the fire blending with question and disappointment in his eyes. "Ya'll sound serious."

"I am. Please."

303

"Very well." Frustrated, his body still aching for her, he eased himself off her and helped her to her feet. "Can whatever it is be said sitting, or would ya'll prefer to stand?"

"We can sit." She plopped down on the narrow bed and patted the space next to her.

Nash took the chair at the desk and propped his boots up, crossing his ankles. He leaned back and folded his arms behind his head. "All right, I am comfortable. What are we going to argue over now?"

He was distancing himself from her, beginning to close his inner self off with a cavalier posture she was coming to recognize. She wondered if he had learned to do that as a child in the orphanage when he hurt, just as she had tried to withdraw her feelings after her folks died. But she'd had her beloved uncle to help her over life's huddles. Nash hadn't had any blood relatives. Never depended on another. Never really shared his deep inner self with anyone.

"I don't aim to argue."

He dropped his hands to the arms of the chair with a sigh. "What then?"

She took a deep breath. She had to get it out, before she burst and gave in to that infernal lustful craving she got each time she was anywhere near him. "What I want to talk about is belongin' to you."

Now she had his full attention! The lustful craving would have to wait. He took his feet off the desk and leaned forward, his face a blank slate. She wasn't sure whether he was preparing to launch himself on the bed, or leave her alone in the cabin. But however he reacted, it was now or never, and she had to get it out.

"I know you're as good as divorced, and Dolly seems to've taken to Uncle Titus, so that ain't a problem no more. And I can no longer deny that you're the one that sets my blood to boilin'. I already said as much." She let out a belabored sigh. "If only it hadn't been for Uncle Titus's deathbed request —"

Nash was definitely getting suspicious, for his brows drew into a straight line. "Deathbed request?"

"Before you all got to his room earlier, he said I should choose between you and Barth, because if he dies, I'll need a h-husband to pilot the *Columbia's Pride,* although someday I intend to be the first woman to get a license."

In a sudden rush of emotion, she burst out, "Oh, Nash, Uncle Titus had to fight just to get the words out, he's in such a bad way."

Nash's left brow lifted and he seemed to tense. "I see."

"No, you don't. You see, although I still got serious questions about your connection with Villamoore, before Uncle Titus said I got to make a choice from a purely practical way of lookin' at things, there wasn't one to make. I hadn't given a marriage paper much thought. I'd been thinkin' that I would want you to belong to me — not the other way around."

His right brow went up to join the left. "Other way around?"

"Yes, me belongin' to you, like you keep insistin'."

305

Nash almost wanted to laugh at the outlandish vein their conversation seemed to be taking. Almost. Until marriage had entered the conversation. In an effort to settle the issue, so they could get down to some serious lovemaking, he said, "Ya'll can have it either way you want: I shall belong to you, you will belong to me, or we shall belong to each other if ya'll would prefer, and we will not worry about a marriage certificate."

"But no. I mean wait. It ain't that simple no more."

Nash took a deep breath. Why did he know there was going to be a *but* involved? "But?"

"But it's like I just said. That was before Uncle Titus said I got to make a choice of a husband. Since Uncle Titus could very well die, I got to honor what could be his last wishes—like Dolly said, remember?

"Yes, Dolly. How well I remember," Nash grunted. At the moment he wished he had never picked up that red-head.

"So in keepin' with Uncle Titus's wishes, I got to at least take the time to do some serious thinkin' about Barth as a choice for mate material." She shrugged. "I never really took his attentions to heart before, because you were all that truly ever interested me, I got to say. As a matter of fact, even from the first moment I laid eyes on you after you stole my spot at the docks in Portland, I noticed you above all others . . ."

Nash managed to patiently listen to her sum up in detail all the interactions they'd had from the first moment they'd met, the time they had spent in the crate, the time they'd spent together while she masqueraded as his cabin boy, the statehood celebration, her paddle wheeler sinking, Villamoore, and every other detail — some he'd rather have forgotten — involving the two of them.

By the time she got to, "You do understand why I got to make a real serious effort to find out if Barth can stir up the same kind of feelin's in my innards as you do, don't you?" Nash had heard enough.

As Nash stared at her in disbelief, he was secretly wishing that he had left Titus Baranoff clinging to that beam after the paddle wheeler exploded, and that the current had swept him and the sunken boat out to sea, instead of Nash risking his life to rescue the interfering old river rat and raise that damn wreck.

Chapter Thirty-one

Nash knew better than to argue with her this time. Columbia was stubborn, pigheaded, and determined to honor what she seemed to view as a sacred family commitment. He beat down the urge to inform her flatly that it did not matter what *practical* conclusion she reached, he had already made the final decision. Although, there definitely were times he was left wondering what insanity drove him to desire such a troublesome, impossible woman.

And despite the level of his pique, he could not ignore his earlier feelings on the importance that he be her choice. Nor could he ignore what he now considered a mistake, encouraging Barth to pursue Columbia after Barth had offered to step aside.

If he really stopped to consider it, nothing had truly changed. Only, thanks to Titus Baranoff, Nash's venture to make the first woman he had ever truly desired his had just become considerably more complicated—especially since marriage had not been included as part of his original intention.

Columbia snapped her fingers twice. "Nash? You do understand, don't you?"

"Huh?"

"You seemed to be miles away. You did take in what I was tryin' to tell you, didn't you?"

Nash got up and went to the door. "Oh, I think one can say that I have taken in the whole picture."

He opened the door and Columbia got to her feet. "Good. Then I'll just wait up on deck for Barth to return."

"Think again." Nash slipped through the door and locked it in her face.

Columbia pounded on the solid door. "You ain't bein' fair. I can't do what's got to be done locked in here, you river polecat!"

"Maybe ya'll can't, but I can." Nash smiled to himself. "Besides, all is fair in love and war, and I would say this is a combination of both."

His last comment made him stop and ponder what he had just said as he went up on deck. It seemed vaguely familiar, and he wondered if he had used it before in reference to Columbia. Knowing her as he did, it certainly would make sense — except for the word love. Desire, lust, craving to possess . . . yes. But love in the true sense of the word . . .

Not more than half an hour had passed when Nash caught sight of Barth sauntering up the gangplank, and he recalled when he had made the comment plaguing his mind — right after they both had agreed to court her and shook on it. The loser was supposed to do the gentlemanly thing and step aside.

"I managed to get the horse back without anyone

309

being any the wiser," Barth said as he joined Nash. "Do you have the young lady in question safely ensconced in your cabin?"

"Securely locked away."

"Isn't it a simply grand sunset? It always is after a storm," Columbia said and joined them on deck.

Barth smirked at Nash's deep scowl. "Most secure, I see."

Nash ignored Barth's sarcasm. Nash had noticed the change in her speech. Now his eyes were busy surveying the physical change in Columbia's appearance as well. She was standing at the rail in a most fetching ice blue dress. It was ruffled at her shoulders; a dark blue sash formed a bow at her tiny waist, the full skirt lying flat against her legs from the wind, which perfectly outlined a slender feminine figure usually hidden by the baggy trousers she wore. Her hair, normally hidden under a cap, flowed freely down her back in long black curls tied with a blue ribbon he recognized as belonging to Dolly.

"You look absolutely lovely, Columbia," Barth said.

"Please. Do call me Mary Catherine, won't you?" She offered her hand to Barth.

Barth started to reach out, but Nash was quicker. He took her hand in his. "It has been during my greatest pleasures to call ya'll Mary Catherine."

"Yes, and some of us derive pleasure from such insignificant things." She smirked at Nash, for she knew exactly what he was eluding to. He had called her by her given name when they had mated. She tried to pulled her hand back at his frown, but he held tight.

Columbia sucked in her cheeks and glanced past Nash to Barth, gritting her teeth into a smile despite the tight squeezing sensation threatening to crush her fingers. "You will dine with me tonight, I hope."

"My pleasure to dine with you will be anything but insignificant."

Nash narrowed his eyes, knowing what the girl had in mind. "No doubt it will be monumental."

Barth merrily overlooked Nash's sour comment. What could be earthshaking about having dinner with the girl? "Just give me time to go clean up and change."

"I shall be waiting in the salon."

Forcing herself to continue to ignore the crushing hold Nash had on her hand, Columbia smiled sweetly at Barth and watched him head toward his cabin.

The moment they were alone, Nash swung her to face him. "Don't ya'll think your little scheme is just a trifle transparent, *Mary Catherine?*"

"Not any more so than your jealousy. You should have known a simple lock would not stop me." She put on her most practiced smile and managed to snatch her aching hand back. Although she was not about to admit it, it did her heart good to know that Nash was jealous.

"Jealousy. Ha! I was merely trying to spare Barth from your uncle's silly notions. I should have bolted and barred your door, then hammered the bar with nails. Of course, that was when I thought ya'll were genuine. Where did that delightful river girl-talk go?" he accused.

His remark about her uncle and her genuineness took her back for an instant. But that was not going to deter her. "I am genuine, as you put it. I am merely cutting corners by putting my know-how to use, if you must know."

She stared at him, expecting a retort. When he did not say anything, she said, "You do not have to look so baffled. I have always known how to speak properly, like the snobby society matrons up on the hill. I do read a lot. It simply has never fit the way I choose to live."

"Then why are ya'll suddenly changing *now?*" he demanded.

"I just told you. If I am going to conclude this experiment for Uncle Titus's sake in a timely fashion, I thought that Barth would respond to me quicker, if I were dressed and acted like a lady."

"Oh, he has already *responded* to ya'll, and it has nothing to do with the way you talk or dress," Nash grunted.

Columbia disregarded the telling comment. "Are you going to offer your arm and escort me into the salon, like a gentleman would a lady? Or don't you plan to join us this evening?"

"I would not miss this for anything, Mary Catherine."

His lips were a mere straight line when he offered his arm and she linked hers around it. As he escorted her into the paddle wheeler's salon, her mind was busy attempting to interpret what he had meant. Did he think she would fall flat on her face during dinner, and he wanted to be

312

there to see it? Or did he plan to undermine her?

"My, but ya'll have not wasted a single moment," he commented dryly. "The table is quite elegant."

"One of my many talents," she said with a self-satisfied grin, not mentioning that she had run into Little John and ordered him to hurriedly throw something together for dinner.

White linen draped the round table. Gold-rimmed china graced the place settings, around an interesting arrangement of pine and bark.

He even pulled out her chair and seated her, like a gentleman would for a lady friend. Columbia had just dropped the fancy linen napkin into her lap, when Dolly stuck her head in the door.

"There you two are. Mind if I join you?" She was already crossing the room and claiming a chair before either one could respond. She shrugged out of her wrap and put a hand on Columbia's arm, leaning over to whisper, "I see you have taken Titus's advice. Good girl."

Columbia thought the comment odd, since she and her uncle had been alone when he told her to make a choice. "What advice?"

Dolly colored and appeared flustered. "Why, Columbia—"

"It is Mary Catherine now, Dolly," Nash interrupted with a wicked grin. "And do tell us what advice ya'll are talking about. We are both waiting to hear with bated breath."

She did not miss his heavy sarcasm. She scrambled to redeem her near faux pas. "Your uncle is still hanging on." Columbia nodded her gratitude for the update on his condition. "After you left, Titus came around long enough Col—Mary Catherine, and managed, with great difficulty, to tell me about your need to choose a husband."

Barth had entered the salon just in time to overhear Dolly's remark. "What is this about Columbia—"

"Mary Catherine," all at the table chorused.

"Yes, Mary Catherine," he corrected himself and took a seat. "Well, what is this about Mary Catherine needing to choose a husband?"

"I guess ya'll have not heard yet," Nash supplied with amusement in his voice. "It seems that Titus's deathbed wish is for Col—Mary Catherine to choose between us. Ya'll see, she needs a husband to pilot her paddle wheeler once it is restored, since Titus may not live long enough to offer her cover any more. And we have been selected as perfect husband material."

Even as Nash spoke in a witty voice, he was thinking that if he could get his hands on Titus right now, it was most doubtful that the man would live through the night.

Barth shook out his napkin and placed it in his lap. With a big smile hiding his trepidation at the notion, he announced, "How gratifying to know that I am in the running for such an honor."

Columbia fought to keep her face void of expression, despite the deep red she knew stained her cheeks. Nash was scowling and Dolly looked to be in a stupefying shock as the soup arrived.

"We shall require two more place settings," Columbia advised Little John. "It appears there will be two more for dinner tonight."

"Yes, miss," the man said, and scrambled back to the galley to fulfill the girl's orders. He glanced back over his shoulder at the girl, all decked out in lady stuff. He shook his head. Columbia sure had been acting crazy since he first saw her dressed like a man and posing as a cabin boy. From one extreme to the other. It was one for the record books.

"Ah chowder, one of my favorites," Barth proclaimed. "How thoughtful of Mary Catherine to provide a special meal for me! I hope you don't mind if I don't wait for you to be served." The others nodded, and he proceeded to lift his soup spoon and dip it into the bowl. He did not look up until the other two bowls of soup and place settings arrived. "Aren't you all going to enjoy your soup? It is truly delicious." He took another spoonful, then added, "You know, I have always wanted to be captain of my own paddle wheeler."

Columbia choked. Nash popped up and patted her on the back, none too gently. She wiped her mouth and turned around to glare at him, while he retook his seat.

"Ya'll will make a fine captain," Nash declared. He gave an astonished Columbia a bland smile, and then began to enjoy his dinner.

It had suddenly dawned on him that he had been going after her in the wrong way. She either ignored or did just the opposite of what he wanted and expected. Despite Barth's pleased posture, there was no doubt in Nash's mind that Barth's view of marriage and its obligations were no different from Nash's. Barth knew Nash wanted Columbia, and Nash realized that Barth had been baiting him, and enjoying it, the joker.

It was Dolly's response that puzzled him. Nash intended to pay Titus Baranoff a little visit and clarify a few things for himself.

All through the salad, vegetables, fish, and dessert that Little John served in silent bemusement, Nash praised Barth's abilities and accomplishments. Dolly squirmed in her seat, and Columbia seemed filled with annoyed contemplation.

Nash refolded his napkin and placed it beside his emptied plate. He stood up and, to Dolly's surprise, pulled her chair back.

"Come along, Dolly." He took her arm and drew her to her feet.

"But I haven't finished my dessert yet," she whined. She bent over, grabbed a fork, and scraped up one last bite.

"Col—Mary Catherine needs to be alone with Barth. Come along, you and I need to talk about your excursion to locate an attorney this morning."

"My excursion?" She grabbed her heart. "Oh, yes, my trip to find an attorney." Her smile was brittle. "Everything is all taken care of."

"I shall need to see the papers," Columbia said. There was something suspicious about the way Dolly had been acting all evening.

Dolly swallowed hard. "The papers?"

"Do not worry, as soon as they are ready, I shall personally see that they are delivered to ya'll," Nash

316

interceded. Now all he had to do was locate some damn attorney who would be willing to go along and make out some legal-looking documents to satisfy the girl.

"Say good night, Dolly," Nash instructed, tossing her wrap around her shoulders.

Dolly gave a weak nod and found herself being escorted from the salon at a rapid pace. Outside she announced, "I had better get back to Titus. He might regain consciousness, and I should be there."

"I'll tell ya'll what, we shall both be there."

"What about the attorney? And aren't you going to stay here and protect your interest in the girl?" she argued.

"Oh, I do not think that my interests will suffer too much from my absence. Especially since I am going to check on Titus. The attorney will have to wait until tomorrow. So bundle up. It is going to be a cold, dark walk." He held her arm and directed her down the gangplank.

"Are you sure?" Dolly chirped.

"Are you sure, Mary Catherine?" Barth questioned, wondering why Nash had left them alone.

"Of course, I'm sure. I want to walk in the moonlight. Oh, and you can call me Columbia again." She rose from her chair and strode to the door, before Barth could do the gentlemanly thing and assist her.

Barth tossed his napkin on the table and chased after her. He had found the whole thing amusing at first, frankly enjoying Nash's unusual discomfort. But somewhere between the time when he had first accepted her invitation to dine and have dessert, the situation had changed.

The notion of marriage had been laid on the table. Yet it hadn't seemed to cool Nash's ardor for the girl. The air virtually crackled with electric tension when the pair was together, and Barth did not intend to get struck by those two wild lightning bolts.

Columbia and Barth stepped outside and were hit by a cold wind from off the water. "Are you sure you want to walk in the moonlight? You don't even have a jacket on."

Columbia took his arm. She had to find out whether those lustful cravings were for Nash alone while she satisfied her uncle's request. She wasn't practiced in acting coy, but she'd give it a jolly good try. She smiled up at him and fluttered her lashes. He was now gazing intensely into her eyes. It must be working. She batted her lashes at him again just for added measure.

"If you have something in your eye, perhaps I can be of assistance."

She sighed. This coy routine was not nearly as easy as it looked when she had seen other women do it. Well, she would try a sultry voice. "There is nothing in my eye."

"Oh. Then aren't you getting rather cold? Your voice sounds like it is getting hoarse."

So much for the come-hither, vocal chord routine. She decided to try a seductive pose. She leaned into him and put her palm against his heart. "You could keep me warm."

"Until Nash tosses me out into the cold," he muttered and stepped back.

"Pardon?" Surely she had misunderstood.

"I said, I could never be so bold," he improvised. He was standing as stiff as a dock piling!

This coy business wasn't working worth a damn. It was taking too much time and energy on her part, and the fool man was not cooperating at all. Maybe he was not as quick-witted as Nash. She might just as well get this over with, before she froze to death, while trying to get him to take the hint.

"Well, I can." She linked her arm with his and started dragging him along the deck.

"Where are you taking me?" he choked.

"I'm takin' you to your cabin, so you can seduce me."

If Nash hadn't already staked a claim on the girl, and he wasn't like a brother, Barth would be the one doing the dragging about now, she was making him so hot. The simple hell of it was, brother or not, Barth was not sure how long he could continue to resist her. The threat of marriage hanging over his head or not.

Chapter Thirty-two

As she dragged Barth along the deck, Columbia noticed Little John clearing away the dinner dishes. She stopped and stuck her head in the door. "Little John, bring two bottles of—" She broke off and redirected her attention to Barth, who had a rather befuddled expression on his face. "Whaddya like to drink?"

"Me? Better make it whiskey. Straight."

Columbia said to Little John, "You heard the man. Deliver two bottles of the finest whiskey on board to Barth's cabin. Oh, and two glasses. We won't be drinking straight from the bottle tonight."

"Miz Columbia, you sure I shouldn't fetch Doc Barker? You've been actin' a mite peculiar lately," Little John ventured to say.

"There's nothin' peculiar about a woman like myself conductin' a good honest comparison before pickin' out a husband. So just bring the whiskey. And don't be long."

She was slipping back into her river girl self, which Barth had to admit he found almost as fetching as

Nash did. There could be worse things than being shackled to the girl, not to mention being captain of his own paddle wheeler. Why the hell had he agreed to help Dolly make Nash jealous of Columbia when the girl was masquerading as Nash's cabin boy?

They closed the rest of the distance to Barth's cabin without another delay. Barth hesitated outside. "Are you sure you want to do this?"

She frowned up at him. "This is the way you begin all your seductions?"

"Well, not exactly. But—"

She thrust open the door. "Then let's get inside, so you can quit bein' so tightened up and get down to business."

Columbia had barely walked into his cabin and plunked down on his narrow bed, followed by Barth, when Little John arrived and set two bottles of whiskey and two glasses down on a small table by the bedside.

"Would you like me to pour, or stay with you, or something?" Little John questioned, ill at ease.

"No. But if you can find a Do Not Disturb sign, like some of those fancy hotels got, you can hang it on the door."

A startled Little John looked to Barth. Barth merely lifted his shoulders. "You heard the lady."

"Yes. I'll do my best." His eyes were as big as cannon balls as he nodded and backed out of the room.

Barth splattered two big slugs of the amber liquid right to the top of the glasses. When he glanced up to hand one to Columbia, the girl was lying along the length of his bed, one arm resting provocatively behind her head. Her hair was strewn out around her like alluring black silk stockings piled on a bed. Her lips were slightly parted, as if waiting to be kissed. His gaze slid lower. She had kicked off her shoes and was running one foot up past her ankle.

He belted down both drinks. Then poured two more and polished those off, too. He was streaming more whiskey into the glasses, when Columbia said, "Shouldn't your seduction efforts be focused more directly on me?"

He glanced at the lovely vision and smiled through the warm glow of the liquor.

"Don't look now, but the whiskey is overflowin' the glass and runnin' onto the floor."

Barth jumped and righted the bottle. "Damn waste." He filled the other glass, then joined her on the edge of the bed, finishing off his before he finally handed one to Columbia. Columbia sat up to sip the fiery liquid, but Barth grabbed it out of her hand and gulped it down.

Just as well. She didn't care for the taste of liquor anyway. And she was starting to get impatient. "Well, shall we get to it? I want to get this comparison over with."

Barth delved deeply into those turquoise eyes. There was no fire there, no overpowering desire, only cool determination. But he was heated enough for them both now. "Don't worry. There will be no further delays."

He gathered Columbia up into his arms, and slowly bent his head. His heart thrashed against the inside of his chest with the first taste of her full, lus-

322

cious lips. Although the girl was a mite stiff, he pulled her in closer, deepening the kiss.

Columbia allowed herself to be encircled within Barth's embrace, fighting back a yawn. She waited for that special feeling to grasp her innards.

Nothing.

She snaked her arms around his neck and let her fingers wind in amongst his auburn hair, fresh with the smell of soap.

Nothing.

She opened her eyes. His were closed, and his face was bathed in the agony of unspent passion. What the hell? She put her all into it, pressing herself against him, in an effort to satisfy any doubt.

But just as she had made the extra effort, Barth's arms slid away, his lips left hers, and he lay back against the pillow.

Surprised at the effect she must have had on him, Columbia twisted toward the man. His eyes were shut and there was a serene smile on his lips. "You certainly got a very different way of seducin' a woman, I must say."

She suppressed another yawn, shrugged, and cuddled into the crook of his arm.

Dolly held fast to Nash's arm, hesitating to climb the stairs to Titus's room. "Maybe we both shouldn't disturb him? Why don't I go up first and see how he's faring?"

"If that loud music from below in the saloon has not disturbed him, nothing will. We shall both go."

He started up the stairs, holding tight to Dolly's arm.

Nash thrust the door open and stepped inside. He had expected to see the man quite conscious. But Titus lay against the pillows, his breathing labored.

Dolly breathed a sigh and rushed to his side. A look of relief brightened her face when she turned back to Nash, and announced, "Doesn't look like there is any reason for you to remain, since he's still out cold."

Nash moved to stand over the man. "Maybe we should call the doctor, it looks as if he is having trouble getting air into his lungs."

"No!" Then she quickly amended, "I mean . . . I can care for him." She was wringing her hands.

"No doubt ya'll already have been," Nash drawled. As he leaned over the prone man, Nash casually palmed his pocketknife.

"Yeoww!" Titus roared and must have come off the mattress a good two feet. "Oah," he groaned. "What did you go and poke me in the side with that sharp thing for?"

Nash tucked the small knife back into his pocket. "Works just as good as smelling salts when warranted." The amusement faded from his face and was replaced with a colder look. "Ya'll had best come up with an explanation real fast, or I am going to rip you out of that bed and bodily haul ya'll to Columbia to explain yourself, you faking marriage broker."

"Wish you'd remember that I am an injured man, even though I've been conscious."

Nash pulled up a chair, obviously unmoved by Titus's declaration of his weakened condition.

"How'd you know? I thought I was putting on a pretty good act."

Nash rolled his eyes. "Ya'll are Columbia's uncle, aren't you?" At Titus's astonished look, Nash added, "Ya'll were breathing more like a man who had just run a race when we entered."

"Thought I had managed to get settled back in bed and looking quite natural myself."

Nash just shook his head. "Besides, Dolly was awfully nervous tonight at dinner. So I had my suspicions before we even arrived."

"Sorry." Dolly quietly stepped into the background.

"Don't go blaming Dolly. I talked her into helping me." Nash's brow lifted ever so slightly, and he crossed his arms over his chest. "I didn't mean any harm. I will do anything to make amends."

"Ya'll can start by recommending a lawyer who might not object to a little fancy footwork."

Titus gave the slightest smile of understanding. "Dolly told me about your *marriage*. Go see Sam Parks. He's a longtime friend. He'll fix you right up with what you need, so you can be free to claim my niece."

When Nash did not immediately respond with gratitude, or his intention to claim Mary Catherine, he burst forth with, "Hell, man, anybody can see that you and my girl are crazy about each other. I knew it from the first time you two met." His gaze shot to Dolly, standing quietly across the room. "Didn't I, Dolly?"

"He did mention it to me at the time, Nash," she offered in no more than a bare whisper.

"So you see, I had to do something. I just couldn't allow her to let you get away 'cause of all her crazy shenanigans. She's got a real big heart, although she doesn't always exercise real good sense."

"Like some others I know," Nash commented dryly.

Titus's eyes turned downcast. "I just figured if she thought I was dying, and for a while *I* truly thought I was, she would finally agree to take a husband, since she'd need one once the paddle wheeler's back in running order. Oh hell, she told me you had your eye on her, and her eyes have been on you, too." He shrugged. " 'Course, when she was baring the secrets of her heart to me, she did think I was unconscious at the time."

Nash rolled his eyes. "Of course."

"Then you can see a little humor in it, can't you?" Titus ventured.

Nash did not appear amused. "And am I to presume that the little humor ya'll are talking about was suggesting that she choose between Barth and me?"

"That was just to make her think she had made up her own mind. You know how stubborn and headstrong the girl is. One of the fellows from downstairs was up a little while ago, and told me all about the commotion the girl caused at Villamoore's. She's been told time and time again to stay away from the man."

"True enough. And at this very moment your precious niece is trying to make me jealous by courting Barth's attentions."

Dolly stepped forward at the shadow of doubt across Titus's face. "It's true, Titus. You should have seen her tonight. All gussied up and speaking like a real cultured lady. Even having everybody call her Mary Catherine instead of Columbia."

"My God, this is serious." Titus was obviously jolted.

"I got a lot of experience in this area, and I tell you, that girl had her mind set on Barth tonight." Dolly shook her finger at Titus. "Why, I've never seen anything like it, the change in her, I mean. I mean that she—"

"That is enough, Dolly. We all get the picture," Nash said tightly.

"Then what are you doing here checking on me?" Titus gasped and struggled to get out of bed. "That girl is so impetuous, she is just likely to up and do something foolish before she realizes the trouble it'll bring her."

"It certainly would not be the first time," Nash quipped.

Titus threw up his bandaged hands. "How can you be so unfeeling? We've got to stop her before she goes too far! She could give herself to the man before she realizes what he's taking—what should be saved for her marriage bed!"

Deadpan, Nash said, "The one that either Barth or I am to provide?"

"Of course," Titus practically shouted, and totally missed the sarcasm in Nash's dry voice. "Now, let's get a move on."

"Settle down and relax, Titus," Nash counseled. He kept his face straight, for he had already claimed Columbia's virginity, and her luscious little body was

327

going to belong to him alone—not that marriage had to have anything to do with it. "I would not have left her with Barth, if I thought there was the slightest chance that things would go too far."

Titus just kept shaking his head. "Then you don't know the girl as well as I thought. She'll cut her nose off to spite her own face, before she'll back down, even if she realizes that she's wrong. Once she starts something, there's no stopping her, although she understands there will be dire consequences.

"Why, I remember once when one of Villamoore's paddle wheelers was on a head-on collision course with us, expecting us to give way. Well, the girl didn't. She wouldn't. She held that wheel, and we only missed getting rammed 'cause the other boat gave way at the very last moment. The same thing happened with you. If GlennieLynn hadn't pushed her out of the way, you two might very well have collided, she's so pigheaded. And then there was the time—"

Nash let out a string of oaths, shot to his feet, and sped from the room.

"Wait! I'll go with you," Titus offered to a slamming door.

Dolly went to Titus and stroked his cheek. "Titus honey, you aren't in any shape to be running after Nash. Besides, I think we'd all be better off if we stayed out of the way, and let nature take her course."

As he stomped up the gangplank, all Nash could think about was Columbia, and the course she had set for the evening. His breath came out in puffs of white from the cold night. But he was anything but cold. He was hot, not to mention furious. He could see that the salon was dark and no one was out strolling on the decks.

"Captain," Little John said in surprise, coming out on deck. "Why don't you come to the galley with me and let me get you some more dessert? There's still some left."

There was no mistaking the look in the mountain of a man's eyes. He was aware of something that was going to make Nash even more furious, if that were possible.

"Where is she?" he demanded.

"Well . . ." Little John broke off and dropped his eyes. Nash stormed past the man, and in Columbia's defense, Little John called out, "I'm sure she's not in his cabin anymore."

Nash did not have to ask whose cabin. Nash stomped to Barth's door and, without hesitating, thrust it open. The door made a thunderous crash against the wall.

Columbia and Barth were lying on the bed together, a blanket haphazardly draped over part of them. She was in the crook of his arm, her hand resting on his chest, one leg partially covering his.

"What?" Columbia mumbled and looked up, squinting in an effort to focus her eyes.

Nash stood framed in the door, his black eyes flaming fires of rage. His hands were clenched into fists. And he looked like a dam about to burst in a storm.

She noticed that he was glaring at the generous

329

amount of thigh which was exposed. She sat up, careful not to awaken a gently snoring Barth, and pulled her skirt down. "What time is it?"

"Three o'clock in the morning." It was the second time tonight that he had to fight the urge to yank someone out of a bed. Only this time he could barely control himself, he wanted to wrench her out of that bed so bad, and then flatten Barth against it. And he would have, too, except that he still had hold of one last bit of reason. He was the one who had left her alone with Barth. And then there was the matter of the agreement he had made with Barth.

He scanned the room in an attempt to calm himself down before he gave in to his male territorial urges. Two near-empty whiskey bottles adorned the table near the bed. Two glasses rolled on the floor. Hellfire, the bastard must have gotten her drunk first!

Nash's restraint snapped.

To Nash's utter amazement, Columbia met him halfway across the room, her hands on her hips, the anger on her face a mirror of his own.

"What the hell're you doin' just gettin' back at this late hour?" she demanded.

Chapter Thirty-three

Nash stared in amazement at the nerve of the hellion! Her appearance was disheveled. The left side of the ruffle at the top of her wrinkled dress had ridden lower than modesty should allow in Nash's mind. At least she wasn't standing before him naked—only barefooted!

"After what ya'll have done, what the hell gives you the right to stand in front of me demanding that I explain what *I* am doing here at this hour? What are *ya'll* doing in Barth's cabin at this hour?" he demanded none too quietly.

After what she'd done! But she hadn't done—as he put it—anything. Well, she was not going to give him the satisfaction of telling him that she had not followed through with her plan.

"Why shouldn't I be in Barth's cabin at this hour? I told you exactly what I'd planned," she hissed. "The question is, what're *you* doin' here?"

He grabbed her arm. His face was an angry mask. Columbia could tell he was fighting for control, and a part of her found pleasure in his reaction. Of

course, there was that other part of her that wasn'
going to submit to any man.

Columbia was sure he could have frozen ice, hi
glare was so cold. She decided to push him a littl
further. "Well? You gonna explain your reasons fo
disturbin' us or not?"

She thought he was going to choke on his anger
His fingers dug into her arms. Then suddenly he re
leased her, and his expression became hooded. "Sinc
it seems that I have disturbed ya'll, it seems only nat
ural that I should awaken Barth, so he can join ir
this informative conversation."

"No!" She tried to stand her ground. She did no
want Barth informing Nash that nothing had hap
pened.

He easily picked her up and set her aside.

She certainly did not have to hang around and be
humiliated while they had a good laugh at her ex
pense, when Nash discovered that Barth had done n
more than pass out. Columbia made a dash for the
door, but he easily swung around, clamped a stee
hand on her arm, and dragged her over to Bartl
with him. She held her breath as he shook Barth.

"What the devil?" Barth started. He sat up and fo
cused on the pair standing over him. "What time i
it?"

"Three o'clock."

"What're you doing here at this hour?"

Columbia's gaze shot between the two men. Bartl
appeared to be quite confused, as could be expected
But Nash almost seemed bored now by the whol
thing.

"Well, since ya'll have seen fit to romance the lady . . . and ya'll have, haven't you?"

Barth glanced at Columbia, but remained silent, ignoring the question delivered with silken finesse.

"Ah, the unspoken rule. Never discuss one's intimate encounters with a lady. How gentlemanly of ya'll, my dear old friend. But, as I started to say, since we both seem to be in the, shall we say, *enviable* position to be knowledgeable grooms now, how do ya'll propose to decide which one of us marries her?"

"Propose. Interesting choice of words."

Nash did not respond. He stood still, waiting.

Barth rubbed his eyes in an effort to clear his head. He sent a finger into his ear in an attempt to clear his hearing as well. "Now that we are both in a position to marry her," he finally echoed.

"We could flip a coin. Toss the dice. Or perhaps cut the cards," Nash suggested.

Barth sat up straight. Standing up might not be the wisest course of action at the moment, considering the black hot coals burning in Nash's eyes, despite his ever-so cool demeanor.

Then an awakening, realization suddenly hit Barth. Nash actually thought that he had gone all the way and slept with Columbia. Columbia was standing mute, and Barth was unable to tell whether she was enjoying this or as mad as hell.

"Well?" Nash prodded at Barth's hesitation.

Barth shrugged and made a snap decision to play along. He wasn't sure why. "I was considering the options. I was thinking. I don't think that cards would offer us both a sporting chance, considering your expertise in the practical use of slight of hand with cards, when the situation warrants, of course."

"Of course," Nash said dryly. He removed a coin from his pocket and began tossing the shiny piece in the air. "The coin?"

Columbia watched the spinning money shoot skyward three times, then grabbed it out of the air. She shook her head. "Not the coin," she said in a calm voice, hoping to put a crack in what she was praying was merely a calm veneer covering Nash's anger.

"Oh? Well, I suppose, despite the late hour, I could round up a pair of dice from one of the crew. Would that be your preference, Barth?" Nash deliberately ignored Columbia, leaving her out of the conversation. He was much too angry underneath his devil-may-care attitude, and feared he would lose his temper altogether.

Barth shrugged. "Can't say that tossing dice would be the most infallible method of selection."

To everyone's surprise, Nash plunked down next to Barth and cupped his chin, resting his elbow on his knee. "Then I suppose we shall both be forced to put our thinking caps on, and come up with the most equitable solution agreeable to all."

Columbia was flabbergasted, to say the least. If nothing else, she had expected to break up a fight, and then be able to gloat over Nash's misplaced jealousy. But no. This sudden platonic lunacy was driving her crazy. The exasperating men sat in front of her like identical duplications of two damned statues lost in thought.

Columbia slapped her hands on her hips. Patience was not her forte, and hers was cracking. "Equitable solution agreeable to all? What the hell do you two think you're doin', bargainin' for a prime boat or cargo or something?"

Nash let his eyes rove over the woman. Hell, he had made her one, and the thought that Barth had also come to know her in the most intimate manner was driving Nash toward the edge. But he was determined not to exhibit his murderous feelings, at least not in front of Columbia. "Umm, I would say prime is a most appropriate term. What do ya'll think, Barth?"

"I think that it is rather late, and I don't know about you two, but I need my beauty sleep."

To Columbia's further chagrin, Nash jumped to his feet. "Guess we shall have to settle this temporary impasse in the morning." He took her arm. "Come on, little bride-to-be, Bartholomew needs his rest."

Barth watched the pair depart, then breathed a sigh of relief. He was glad that was over, for now at least. But one thing was sure: Despite Nash's unperturbed bearing, the man was past livid. He only referred to Barth by his given name when he was truly furious.

Barth laid his head on his pillow, berating himself for not simply putting an end to the jumbled muddle by denying that he had bedded Columbia. But the girl had not denied it. And now he wondered, if he *did* repudiate his participation, whether it be too late to be believed?

Even if his conscience would allow him to rest, rest

was not to be, for Barth could close his eyes, but he could not close his ears to the loud, angry voices suddenly spiking through the door.

"What the hell was *that* all about?" Columbia lobbed the first volley.

No longer able to mask the ferocity of his feelings, Nash raised his voice in concert with hers. "Ya'll mean to tell me you do not know what ya'll did in there, or was it not memorable enough for you?"

"What *I* did in there! What about what *you* just did? Unless you're the one with the short memory, I told you long before dinner exactly what my intentions were."

"And I locked ya'll in my cabin."

"For heavensakes, you didn't think I'd stay locked away like some pliable female, did you?"

"Whatever would give me the idea that a lock would stop ya'll?"

"Oh hell, you sat all through dinner, and then went off with Dolly. Where the devil were *you* all evenin'?" she demanded.

"I have not accounted to anyone since childhood."

"And I won't be accountable to any man now," she shot back.

"Then can I assume mankind is saved, because ya'll have changed your mind and plan to remain an unfettered river rat?" Although he was still furious, Nash fought to enlighten Columbia before he did something totally irrational. "Let me spell it out for ya'll. Ya'll no longer aspire to be the *blushing* bride?"

Her hands flew to her hot cheeks. My God, she must look as if she were blushing. "In name only!"

she blurted out. "So I can continue with my same life as a river rat, as you so eloquently put it, once my boat is runnin' again."

"It is a little late to want a marriage in name only now, don't ya'll think? Ya'll not only are no longer the innocent young girl you once were, but after tonight, ya'll could become a mother and no one would know who the father was!"

At that Columbia's hand flew out, and she slapped him as hard as her strength would allow. "You bastard!"

She tried to turn away from him, but he grabbed her arm. "That is right, darlin'," he snarled sarcastically. "I am a bastard, if ya'll will recall."

Columbia was breathing hard, but the hurt she denoted through the harsh contempt in his voice was plain. It brought her back to her senses. This crazy scheme had gone too far.

"Only when you accuse me of something like sleepin' with another man, when all Barth did was kiss me!"

Nash narrowed his eyes. God, how he wanted to believe her. "But ya'll were lying in his arms!"

"He had one too many and fell asleep. His kiss didn't do much for me; it left me sleepy. If you must know, I also fell asleep. Oh, hell, I never planned to go through with it anyway."

Barth cracked his door and peeked out. "If you need corroboration, it is true, old man. Although I have to admit that it does nothing for my masculinity to know that my kiss nearly put her to sleep," Barth said, and judiciously closed his door. He opened it

337

again. "If you two plan to continue your loud *discussion,* would you mind taking it elsewhere? If my kissing is so bad, it is obvious that I need my sleep, so I can find a willing woman and start practicing."

Columbia waited until the door closed again. "Good night," she said, her anger spent.

Suddenly she found herself swung up into Nash's arms. "Oh no, ya'll are not going to drop that insignificant bit of information you just happened to neglect to mention earlier, and then walk away. We have some more talking to do, and we are going to do it in my cabin."

Columbia had never had a doubt in her mind as to who would be her first choice, if she were to ever take a husband. Now that that time had become imminent—due to circumstances out of her control, she tried to convince herself—she kept her tongue.

She was dropped none too lightly on his bed. She waited as he kicked the door shut. Then she said, "Is it true?"

"Shouldn't I be the one asking that very question?"

She waved off the lift of his brow and tone in his voice, which should have warned her he was most serious. "You'll get your turn. Is it true?"

He pinched his lips. This girl was more stubborn than a paddle wheeler stuck high and dry on a sandbar. "Is what true?"

"Me about to be the bride-to-be? Is that where you two went tonight?"

Columbia watched every nuance of Nash's stance. He shifted feet, dragged his fingers through those thick black waves, and his lips thinned, as he turned a chair around and straddled it. She knew he wanted her; he'd demonstrated that. But marriage. That was something entirely different. Marriage meant that you each belonged to the other. It was, after all, a rather time consuming responsibility.

"I went to see your uncle," he said, which intruded into her thoughts.

She tried to hide her disappointment. He did not intend to discuss her original question about marriage.

"Aren't ya'll going to ask me how I found him?"

"I've no doubt Dolly has been doin' a perfectly splendid job carin' for Uncle Titus. She does seem to have a real knack for takin' care of a man's needs," she said, in a bitchy voice that she immediately regretted.

"Dolly does not deserve that, Columbia."

"No, she don't. But the simple fact is, I don't want to talk about her or my uncle. I know he's gettin' on okay. He's a tough old bird under that helpless, meek front he sets out. It may be a long recovery, but he'll pull through," she announced with a bravado she hoped she could believe herself.

"No doubt he will," Nash answered.

Then the long silence began.

Nash rested his chin on the back of the chair and seemed to be assessing her, as if she were being measured. She could almost picture him with a sextant in his hand, studying her for direction. For her part, Columbia held their eye contact. She would show him just how strong she could be. She was not going to look away first . . . despite her suddenly churning stomach.

"Ya'll really did not sleep with Barth, did you?" He suddenly got up and sat next to her.

For an instant the thought of being angry crossed her mind. But Nash phrased his question so quietly, so earnestly, his eyes delving, probing into hers with such intensity, that she swallowed the retort.

"You're the only one I have mated with."

As if fate had decided to take over, Uncle Titus burst through the door, a shotgun gripped firmly in his bandaged hands.

"I had a sneaking suspicion after you left that you had already made up your mind to have my niece. But, my soon-to-be nephew, I didn't think you meant it so literally. You certainly didn't waste a moment after leaving, did you?" He struggled with the bandages and pain to cock the gun. Nash could have ripped it away a hundred times in the interim, but hadn't. Finally, Titus pointed it at Nash. "Shall we set the date?"

Unperturbed, Nash said to a shocked Columbia, "What was that ya'll were just saying about your uncle being meek?"

Chapter Thirty-four

Columbia took in the entire scene, not sure whether she should be horrified, gratified, or mortified. Uncle Titus stood on wobbly legs, the gun held in unsteady burned hands, wrapped too tightly to allow him any control over the weapon. Dolly clung to the doorjamb, her cat eyes as round as a pilot's wheel. Nash had an undecipherable expression shadowing his face.

"Put the gun down, Uncle Titus, before you shoot yourself in the foot."

"This here gun's going to be a part of me until that deflowering sonofa—"

Her nerves nearly unraveled, Columbia cried, "Uncle Titus, please!"

"—until *he* marries you, girl," he finished after ignoring her plea. "You don't deserve less."

"No, she does not," Nash said quietly.

"I don't?" Columbia choked.

While Titus's attention was momentarily focused on Columbia, Nash grew impatient and disarmed the man with no more effort than reaching out and taking hold of the barrel. Nash tossed the gun aside, and helped Titus to the chair Nash had vacated earlier before he collapsed.

Dolly moved to Titus's side. "Don't what? You all are speaking so low, I think I missed something."

Nash did not look at Dolly, instead his heated gaze remained directly on Columbia, when he answered, "Columbia does not deserve less."

"What are you saying?" Titus demanded.

"Isn't it obvious?" Nash offered.

Columbia crinkled her brows. "Not to everyone."

Titus, still determined to control the situation, even without a trusty gun in his hands, suggested, "Why don't you spell it out nice 'n' clear."

"I will marry Columbia."

Columbia felt as if she had been kicked in the gut, instead of being proposed to. Her entire private life had just been laid bare, forcing Nash to wed her. That is not what she had envisioned a marriage proposal to be.

"Are you going to just sit there, girl?" Titus questioned.

"Why ain't you dead?" Columbia demanded of Titus, causing brows to lift around the room.

"Dead? Aren't you going to at least thank your uncle for seeing that the man does right by you?"

"She has a valid question, *Uncle* Titus," Nash put in to ruffle the interfering old man.

"I am not your uncle yet, Foster." Titus swung his attention to Mary Catherine. "I made a sudden recovery, thanks to Dolly."

342

"Miraculous. The moment you awoke, you must've hopped out of bed and come runnin' to save me from bein' branded a fallen woman, you faker."

He held up his hands, submitting them as evidence. "I was hurt, girl, just not as bad as you thought. Although I got to admit, it scared me more'n I can tell you. So much so, that I'm never going to go back out and live on that dadblamed paddle wheeler again. Ah gawd, I just want to see you marry and be happy, is all," he confessed.

"I tried to keep him at the Dockside, and let you two settle things without his help, but he wouldn't hear of it," Dolly announced with a shrug of guilt.

"Were you *all* a part of this scheme to get me married off?" Columbia's gaze made a swing around the room.

Titus hung his head. Dolly blinked and looked away. But Nash. Nash merely kept his unreadable gaze steady. Columbia got to her feet. "Well, I have news for all of you. I'll stay on the river with my paddle wheeler with or without a husband. Once I get the goods on Villamoore, I won't need no man to pretend to stand at the wheel for me."

"Then am I to assume ya'll have just declined my offer to marry you?" Nash inquired tonelessly.

Her anger sparked, threatening to ignite, and before Columbia could stop herself, she snapped, "No. I accept!"

In triumph Titus clasped his bandaged hands together. "Ouch."

"You can quit lookin' so pleased, Uncle Titus.

343

There ain't gonna be no nuptials anytime soon," she actually smiled now, "since Nash is still legally wed."

"Maybe ya'll have forgotten, but I already told you, ya'll will have the papers in your eager little fingers tomorrow morning," Nash proclaimed.

The triumphant smile withered on Columbia's lips. "Tomorrow morning?"

"Tomorrow afternoon would be a great day for a wedding," Dolly suggested. "I simply love weddings, don't you, Titus?"

Titus looked into her eyes. There was an eagerness there, and he felt the noose tighten around his own neck. Yet it felt pretty good. "Yes, Dolly my dear, I sure do."

"We really should have one day to prepare," Dolly amended, envisioning arrangements for a dress, the preacher, a cake.

"Than it is settled. Day after tomorrow in the afternoon it is," Nash declared.

Columbia swallowed any further objections. This was her doing, after all, wasn't it? Underneath the strange niggling of foreboding, she was secretly happy, wasn't she? Well, one thing was certain: The day after tomorrow, her life was going to be changed forever.

"By the day after tomorrow, your life is going to be changed forever. So you can quit fretting about the length of the voyage, Jennifer. We will arrive in Portland tomorrow, locate Foster, and I'll see you two

344

married without further delay," Markus boasted to his pouting daughter.

Jennifer leaned her blond head against the porthole in her finely furnished stateroom. "Delay. I detest that word. Delay." She swung on her father, perched on the edge of her bed like a king. "That is all my life has been since you got it in your head that we had to follow Nash Foster to Oregon Territory—"

"It is a state now, Jennifer," Markus said gently.

"State? Territory? Who cares? I could still be in New York enjoying the social life, if you had not insisted that we follow after Nash Foster. Why, I do not even recall what he looks like any longer." What she had said was not entirely true, but she was not going to discuss it with her father.

Markus kept his face impassive. "Do not even say such a thing, after that bastard left us both with a little reminder."

"He did not leave you with any reminder, as you so eloquently put it, Daddy. I am surprised you even batted an eyelash when you had found out he left, you have always been so busy making money."

"Money you have always enjoyed spending." He got up and headed for the door. He had instructions to give to Cowan before they reached their destination. "Furthermore, if you had not used those long lashes of yours in Foster's direction, I would have left you in New York."

He swung open the door, but she was across the small space and put her body between the door and her father before he could leave. "What did you mean, you would have left me in New York?"

His eyes flashed before his business face that she so detested dropped into place, and he set her aside. "Don't be tiresome, Jennifer. I shall look in on Ely before I join Cowan."

"Why have you been spending so much time with that man, Daddy? I do not like him. He is a no-class lowlife. Certainly not the type one would want to be seen in public with."

"Don't concern yourself with the likes of Lester Cowan. The man has been useful in the past; he'll serve his purpose."

"What purpose?" she pressed.

"It is merely business. Don't trouble that pretty little head of yours."

"Business?"

Markus rolled his eyes. "Why God bothered to give females a brain at all I shall never comprehend. Jennifer child, it was merely a slip. You know how business has controlled my life until this little incident with you. We are here for only one purpose: Foster is going to do right by you tomorrow, or I shall see him dead. Now, get plenty of rest. We'll be docking in Portland in the morning, and I want you in top form."

"If you want me in top form, would you mind finally allowing me access to my trunks in storage? At your orders the storage area has been kept under lock and key, since the beginning of the voyage."

She noticed Markus's lips tighten ever so slightly. "No need for you to go down to such a dark, dank

346

place filled with rats, no doubt. Just tell Cowan which trunk you require, and I'll see that he fetches it for you."

Jennifer settled on the bed and spread out her fine, checked woolen skirt. "One would think you are hiding something down there, Daddy," she said coyly.

His fingers clamped on the edge of the door so hard his knuckles stood out white. "Don't be silly, daughter. The hold merely contains the ship's stores for the voyage. It simply is no place for a lady of your station. Now, get that rest. I shall send Cowan to you when we are done with our business."

Jennifer lay back on the plump pillows and studied her long fingernails. "I suppose I would hate to break a nail rummaging through those trunks. Inform Lester that I shall require the dark green velvet dress and matching shoes, gloves, and coat."

"Which trunk do you want him to look in?"

She gave her father a cute sigh. "I truly do not recall which of the six trunks the maid packed the things in. He will just have to search until he locates everything I require."

"You will have the dress before you join me in the salon to dine this evening."

He started to close the door behind him, but she hailed him back in her most petulant voice. "Daddy, inform the chef that I shall be dining in my cabin this evening." At the flicker of annoyance on his face, she added, "You would not want me to tax myself, would you? After all, I do intend to be as vibrant as a blushing bride tomorrow,

347

once you have located Nash."

"Have not a care, everything will be taken care of as soon as we locate Foster, Jennifer child."

"Thank you, Daddy," she said in that whiny voice of hers.

Markus shut the door, checked in on Ely, then sauntered out on deck to join Cowan. The late afternoon was cold and rainy, and Markus turned up his collar against such inclement weather.

Lester shivered, sure he must be ice blue by now. "Mr. Kiplinger, I've been waiting for you."

"You can quit now, I'm here." Markus opened his mouth, but shut it again as one of the men who had paid passage from Astoria to Portland walked by. Markus did not like the way the man carried himself. Too cocksure. And Markus Kiplinger prided himself on being an astute judge of character. He had made only one mistake—Nash Foster with his refusal to marry Jennifer, when he would have received financial rewards beyond his wildest dreams—and Markus did not intend to make any more.

"Let's go into the salon. There should not be anyone in there at this hour, so I can give you instructions on what I want you to do when we dock in Portland tomorrow morning."

"Sounds good to me, Mr. Kiplinger. It is cold out here."

They settled at a far table in the corner of the plush, red velvet salon. Markus surveyed the room. When he was convinced that nobody could possibly overhear them, he leaned forward, his elbows on the table.

Markus did not notice the slight movement behind the heavy velvet draperies, shielding the galley door from the salon. Jennifer smiled to herself as she craned her ears to listen. She had counted on her father's habit during the long voyage, of using one particular corner in the salon for his private talks with Lester Cowan.

He had always underestimated her, thinking she would meekly follow his command, like one of his underlings. Her precious daddy was up to something besides going after Nash Foster, and Jennifer planned to find out what.

Markus retrieved a set of keys from his pocket and tossed them on the table. "Go down to the hold and get my daughter's dark green velvet dress, and all the matching accessories that go with it."

"But I'll have to pick through all those trunks of hers to do that," Lester complained. Secretly, the thought of touching and fingering all those intimate feminine frilly things he knew the girl wore against her private places excited Lester.

"You will stay down there until you find what she needs, understand?"

Keeping the aroused grin off his face, Lester shifted in his seat. "I'll stay until I'm finished."

"Good. And while you are down there, open one of the long wooden crates stacked on the port side. I shall require a sample of the merchandise to make a proper impression tomorrow. And do be careful that no one sees you bring it to my cabin. Discretion is most important in this deal we have been discussing."

"You can count on me, Mr. Kiplinger."

"Yes, I know I can. Just remember, that your reward for success will be beyond your wildest dreams."

Lester smiled. Of course, the old man did not know that Lester's wildest dreams had been focused on Miss Jennifer Kiplinger for close to a year now. And once Lester got paid for doing Kiplinger's bidding, he was going to claim his reward.

"The men don't want to wait any longer. They don't want to wait until you put Foster to the test," Jack Tarley complained to a brooding Villamoore. "Further, my spies tell me that Foster was visiting Titus Baranoff, and he isn't as bad off as everybody thought. The river girl is a real cozy guest on Foster's paddle wheeler, too, if you know what I mean."

Tarley waited in the dimly lit dining room for Villamoore to face him and respond. But the man just continued to sit and stare at his portrait, as he had since the girl shot it.

Tarley cleared his throat. "You hear what I said about those Baranoffs and Foster, boss?" He waited. "You all right?"

"Do I look all right?" Villamoore's face was a study in black hatred when he swivelled around to face Tarley.

"You look like it's time to stop playing games and get serious," Jack managed.

Villamore's lips did not crack a smile when he

sneered, "Go back and tell the men to be ready. I have already made a decision." He shot a glance back at his unmanned portrait. "Tomorrow is going to be the beginning of the end for that river girl and Foster."

Chapter Thirty-five

Columbia sat at the rail with her boots up, sure it was the beginning of the end of her independence. Why had she accepted that poor facsimile of a proposal Nash had made? It certainly could not be considered a declaration of his undying love.

It took more than the extraordinary pleasure of mating to make a marriage, and she wished that he loved her. Then she smiled to herself. She was not going to admit it to another living soul, but in spite of his lack of love, she had accepted the proposition because if she were going to marry anyone, it was going to be that incredible man.

"Excuse me, Miz Columbia," Little John said, breaking into her musings about Nash.

His arms were ladened with baskets of food, and he was trying to get past her. Columbia dropped her feet and slid her chair backwards, allowing the harried man to pass.

Except for Nash, Dolly had drafted everyone even remotely connected with the paddle wheeler. They were scurrying around like rats up an anchor cable.

Columbia got up and strolled amidst the organized chaos. She tried to sneak a glimpse inside the salon, but was shooed away by Dolly with firm instructions not to peek before the ceremony.

"Why don't you go take a walk and check on how your paddle wheeler is coming along," a chafed Dolly recommended. "That's it. Go oversee the repair workers. They'll keep you busy."

Columbia stuffed her hands in her pockets and headed down the gangplank toward her wreck of a boat. The clouds were starting to part, letting the blue sky of the coming spring break through, as she strolled along the docks of Portland. A great ocean-going ship was just docking, and she stopped to watch the men work the lines and several of the passengers disembark before she moved off to make her way toward the dry dock.

As she approached, she took in the progress already made on the *Columbia's Pride*. Two men who seemed vaguely familiar were striding away from the remnants of the hull, their arms filled with tools. Three men she did not recognize at all were busily nailing new planks to the side, and two others sawed boards newly delivered from the sawmill. She counted over two dozen men hard at work, and her heart could not help but swell. This was Nash's doing. He had salvaged her precious paddle wheeler, and was having it rebuilt for her.

Frank McGee looked up, a hammer in his hand. "Howdy, Columbia, heard your uncle put the word out that you're gettin' hitched."

"That's right," she mumbled.

353

The huge man unfolded his frame and stood facing her squarely. "I'm downright glad you happened by. I was wonderin' if you'd mind much, if GlennieLynn and me come and watch you get hitched?"

"Why would I mind?"

"It's GlennieLynn. She feels a mite peculiar since she dumped Titus. Afraid we wouldn't be welcome."

Columbia thought about how happy her uncle seemed to be around Dolly, and just smiled. "It wouldn't be a proper weddin' without you and GlennieLynn, Francis."

To her surprise the man gave her a bear hug. "Don't you worry about another thing, we'll get this boat runnin' before you get back from your honeymoon."

"Honeymoon?" she gulped.

"It *is* customary," Nash said as he joined her.

Columbia tried to ignore the tingling sensation invading her body from such thoughts. She made a conscious effort to concentrate her attention on a study of his face, in an effort to discern his mood just one day before he was to become a married man. It was unreadable, and she still had a good case of the tingles. "Where'd you come from?"

"The attorney's office. I have all the necessary papers, so nothing can go wrong tomorrow."

"No, nothing." Columbia smiled weakly, too embarrassed in front of Frank McGee to ask to see the legal documents.

"Everything's ahead of schedule with the repairs, sir," Frank announced, and then excused himself to get back to work.

Once they were alone, Nash spread out his arm toward the wreck. "What do ya'll think?"

"You seem to be spendin' a lot of money to put her back in the water. Where you gettin' it?"

Nash hid his disappointment. He had hoped she would be impressed by how much effort he was putting in to the restoration. "Credit has not been a problem."

" 'Cause you're still workin' for Villamoore?"

Nash took her arm and attempted to redirect her attention toward the *Yacht*. "Ya'll are the one I rescued the last time we were all together, if I recall."

"If I recall correctly, I'd say that Villamoore was the one bein' rescued."

He took a more possessive hold of her arm. "Let's not talk about him anymore the day before our wedding."

She agreed to that, but she refused to be herded back to a boat where she was not wanted today. "I can't go back to your paddle wheeler."

Nash lifted a brow. "Can't or won't?"

The expression on his face told her in no uncertain terms that he was annoyed, despite his benign stance. "I'm not plannin' to welch on our agreement to get married, if that's what's got the hair standin' up on the back of your neck."

To her chagrin, he stood gazing into her eyes and laughed. "Columbia, that is the last thing on my mind."

So he was trying to forget he was about to become a married man. It made her more determined than ever not to let him. "I can't go back because Dolly

355

shooed me out of the way. You can go into town with me if you'd like. There's something to wear I ought to buy before tomorrow."

Nash's expression could almost be interpreted as being genuinely pleased. "If it is for the honeymoon, ya'll will not be needing any new clothing," he announced within earshot of six smirking workers.

"Boots! I need a new pair of boots," she blurted out, quickly ushering him back in the direction from which he had just come.

"I suppose boots might prove provocative," he commented, as she dragged him toward the mercantile.

She stopped.

"What is the matter? Are we not going inside to buy ya'll a pair of boots?"

"No. I've changed my mind. I don't need no boots."

Nash just grinned. "Never thought ya'll did." She left him standing one block from the mercantile and swung around. "Sure ya'll do not need anything before tomorrow?"

She was halfway into the Dockside, when she threw back over her shoulder, "Yeah. A dozen good stiff drinks."

Nash caught up with her and ushered her back out of the rough saloon, before she could attempt to order anything from the bar. "Ya'll tried liquor already . . . on Barth. And it put ya'll to sleep. I want ya'll to remain wide-awake now, and tomorrow when we get married, and not be hung over." Two men going into the saloon laughed at the implication.

"All right," she said tightly. She didn't truly want a

drink anyway. But this trying to figure out what to do with herself before the wedding was getting downright difficult. "I can't hang around the dry dock. Can't do any shoppin', which I don't care for anyway. Can't get drunk like a man—"

"Ya'll are not a man, Columbia. And ya'll no longer have to try to act like one. Ya'll are a most desirable woman. And after tomorrow, I shall take responsibility for your battles. So as of right now, ya'll can quit being so tense and ready to fight all the time."

"Does that mean that you'll be fightin' Villamoore after tomorrow, instead of workin' for him?"

"I thought we already decided that we were not going to discuss that man."

"Oh, all right. Then what're we gonna do all day?"

"Barth and I have business a little later. In the meantime, why don't you go into the mercantile and buy the prettiest dress they have? I shall fix it with Dolly to allow ya'll back on board the *Yacht* when you are done shopping."

Columbia frowned. She knew when a man was up to something. "Thought I wasn't gonna need no clothes," she protested.

"The majority of the time, ya'll won't." He pivoted her around and gave her a gentle shove in the direction of the mercantile. "I shall see ya'll later on board."

That's what you think. She would duck into the store long enough to satisfy him, and then tail him. But a moment after she had entered, GlennieLynn converged on her, all abustle over Columbia's wedding, and totally ruined Columbia's plans.

The sun shone in through the porthole in Columbia's room, creating a round glow which framed her face. The bright light caused her to moan in her sleep and cover her head with a pillow. The next thing she knew, the pillow was suddenly pulled from her head.

"Trying to block out the inevitable?" came a deep rich voice.

Columbia opened her eyes. Nash was standing over her, holding her pillow. "Only the inescapable."

Nash tossed the pillow aside and plucked her from the bed into his arms. "Since there will be no avoiding it any longer by pleading ya'll overslept, you might as well get dressed. It is a warm sunny morning outside. And the preacher is already here to do the honors."

At the sensations his touch wrought, Columbia came fully awake. "You ain't supposed to see the bride before the ceremony. What're you doin' in here?"

"Just making sure I am not left at the altar."

"Makin' sure or hopin'?" she asked, wishing he would declare what was in his heart.

"Columbia, I agreed to marry ya'll. The wedding has been arranged. Everyone is here waiting for ya'll."

"But I can't actually go through with it, unless I know that you—you could want me after we're husband and wife," she blurted out.

358

"I want ya'll now," he said thickly.

She pushed him away. "No. That ain't what . . . r, what I meant. Before the weddin' I got to know f—"

"Nash!" Dolly scowled as she fluttered into the abin. "You were only supposed to wake her." She ook hold of his arm to disengage the couple. "Now, one of that until after the ceremony."

"Ya'll do not have to shove, Dolly." Nash went to he door and stopped to wink at Columbia. "I shall e waiting for ya'll."

Once the door closed behind Nash, Columbia lunked down on the bed in a rare pout. "Your imin' leaves a lot to be desired."

"What's the matter, Columbia honey?"

"I was just about to ask Nash if he could learn to ove me just a little, once we're married."

Dolly gathered up Columbia's frilly underthings nd tossed them to the girl. Then she picked up the oopskirt that she was loaning to Columbia for the eremony. "Nash *already* loves you, silly girl."

"Did he say as much to you or Barth? After all, his is one of them shotgun weddin's, thanks to Uncle Titus."

"Honey, from what I know of Nash, there is no vay anyone could force that man into nothing, unless t was what he wanted."

Columbia crawled into the first layer of clothing nd frowned at the metal contraption in Dolly's ands. "I just wish he would have said it, is all."

Dolly giggled. "You're a young woman in love, narrying the right man. Quit fretting. Now step into this and let's get you two married, so afterward he can show you exactly what you mean to him."

Columbia stepped into the hoopskirt and sucked in her breath. "He shows well enough. I'd just like to hear the words."

"Honey, just be patient. And remember, he had a pretty tough childhood." Dolly worked the tapes. "He didn't have no role model. And from what Barth said, Nash hasn't never told any woman he loved her. You just listen to me; he'll probably shout it when he's ready."

Dolly twisted, turned, pushed, and pulled, until she was satisfied with Columbia's appearance. "You're beautiful in that white creation. Ready?"

"I was gonna get ready just fine all by myself before you cut in and tied me up in all this squeezin' lady gear. Now I'm not sure I can breathe, much less walk to my own weddin' and say I do."

"Nonsense." Dolly waved off Columbia's wheezing dramatics and swung open the door with great pomp. "You'll catch on real quick."

Titus was waiting outside the door. After giving Dolly an appreciative smile, he offered his arm to Columbia. "You look beautiful, Mary Catherine. Just like the day your ma married your pa."

"You're all spit 'n' polish like a brass beacon on top deck yourself."

Titus shook his head. The girl would never be a lady. But as they headed for the salon, there was a part of him that sang out loud and clear, that it would not matter one bit to Nash Foster.

When they reached the salon, Titus had to hustle

to open the door for the girl, before she could barge into the room. She stepped inside and he offered his arm.

As Columbia glanced around, she was as nervous as the first time she piloted a paddle wheeler, and her fingers dug into her uncle's arm. The spacious salon was decorated with homespun decorations of pine-cones and evergreen boughs, and smelled of the forested hills climbing up from the river that she so loved. Three of the crew were playing mouthpieces, and the room was filled to capacity with friends from the river and town. But Columbia only had eyes for Nash.

He was a handsome devil, in a dark gray jacket and pants, white shirt and black tie. She had never seen him all dressed up before, and her breath caught.

Titus leaned over and whispered, "Don't worry, girl. Just follow my lead and you will be fine. Everyone here loves you, and wants the wedding to go just as planned."

Columbia looked behind her. Dolly nodded in reinforcement. Columbia's gaze shot to Nash. He winked. Despite the screaming tension building inside her, she rasped to a round of laughter, "Let's shove off."

They had not travelled more than ten feet, when a loud high-pitched screech from the door threatened to pierce her eardrums. Columbia stopped and swallowed, instantly wondering if that shriek had come from her.

Chapter Thirty-six

The mouth harp players stopped, women gasped, men stood to gawk, Nash rushed toward her, and Columbia thought she might faint for the first time in her entire life. When Nash strode past her, she finally realized that despite the pounding thunder in her head, she was not the one who had screamed.

Columbia swung around and watched in horror as Nash stood in front of a distinguished white-haired gentleman she had seen disembark yesterday from the newly docked oceangoing vessel. Next to him were two men who had left the ship at the same time. Her gaze shifted, and she caught sight of a gorgeous blond who looked vaguely familiar; the scream must have come from her. Columbia inched closer to learn what was going on.

"Kiplinger. Never realized ya'll would take my departure so personally," Nash drawled, slipping back into a heavier than usual Southern accent. "Ya'll have come a long way just to attend my wedding."

"There is not going to be any wedding, unless it is

to your rightful fiancée," Markus Kiplinger sneered.

Nash's grin did not waver. "Now, I am afraid I beg to differ with ya'll in that regard. But how did ya'll know where to find me?"

"You can thank someone named Dolly for that."

Dolly hung her head. "Sorry, Nash. I put him on to you before we made our peace."

While Nash's back was turned, questioning the redhead, Kiplinger, his face blood red, pulled a pistol from his belt. Columbia grabbed the gun out of the man's hand.

"What the hell's goin' on?" Columbia demanded, her fear of marriage replaced with anger at its interruption.

"You certainly have selected an interesting bride, Nash," Jennifer said drolly. "Shotgun wedding?"

"I'll shotgun weddin' you! Ooh!" Nash grabbed Columbia back from advancing on Jennifer Kiplinger.

"Go join your uncle while I settle this, Columbia," Nash said, his thick accent thinning into anger.

"A family name, of course," Jennifer scoffed.

"Shut up, Jennifer."

"But we have not been properly introduced yet. I am Jennifer Kiplinger, Nash's fiancée from New York. And this is my father Markus Kiplinger. And you, my dear . . . what was the name . . . ? Oh, yes, Columbia. You must be the—how should I put it— blushing bride-to-be? And dressed all in white, too."

"I am warning ya'll, Jennifer," Nash cautioned in a menacing voice.

She pulled a face and stepped back under his deep scowl, and the girl's tightening finger on her daddy's gun. Kiplinger looked ready to kill, as he circled his daughter's shoulders.

"Give me the gun, Columbia," Nash directed. "Then go join your uncle."

"Not on your life," Columbia said between her teeth, but she relinquished the weapon nonetheless.

"Perhaps I was not pushy enough with Nash, Daddy," Jennifer sniped without losing the haughty lift of her chin.

"What're these people to you, Nash?" Columbia demanded.

Markus puffed out his chest. "My daughter is Nash's only rightful fiancée, come all the way from New York to join him."

Columbia turned troubled questioning eyes to Nash. "How could she be your fiancée, when you were married to Dolly?" Columbia quickly scanned the crowd and located Dolly leaning against a corner chair. "Ain't that right, Dolly?"

Swallowing hard, Dolly lowered her head and moved next to Titus.

"Dolly?" When Dolly did not come to the fore, Columbia demanded, "Let me see those divorce papers, Nash."

"We shall discuss it later, Columbia," Nash said. "Now I want—"

"No. I want to see those papers." She flung a hand out.

Determined to keep his cool, Nash pulled the documents from his coat pocket to satisfy her, so he could hurry and dispose of this latest crisis. "I had planned to present them to ya'll in the cabin this morning as part of my wedding gift, but did not have the chance."

Columbia unfolded the document and scanned it. Her face fell.

"What is the matter, forgot you cannot read?" Jennifer ridiculed.

"Oh, I read just fine. And I didn't have to chase a man halfway around the world to show up in time for his weddin' . . . to somebody else."

"Why you!"

Markus grabbed Jennifer by the shoulders. "Jennifer, calm down. I told you I would see everything settled. Trust me."

Everything was getting more complicated when Titus decided it was time to jump in and join the budding fray. He was followed by Dolly, who remained behind him. "And you can trust me, Columbia. If you want, I'll have them tossed out on their butts, so we can get on with this wedding."

"No, Uncle Titus. There's a lot of explainin' to be done before I intend to walk down any more aisles to hitch myself to someone who's either married, divorced, or engaged—which and to who, I ain't sure of anymore."

"Hellfire, Foster told everybody on the docks in Astoria months ago that that woman"—one of the men at Kiplinger's side boldly boomed out, pointing an accusing finger at Dolly—"was his sister."

As a horrified Columbia perused the document again, Barth entered the growing circle at Nash's side. "Hello, Jennifer," he said in an awkward voice.

She gave him a shy nod. "Barth."

Nash was just barely hanging on to his patience. Although he did have to give Columbia credit for her self-confidence. She had not used her command of the English language to try and impress Jennifer Kiplinger. But hell, he was here to get married this morning, not stand in front of half the town and allow Kiplinger and his daughter to ruin this day for Columbia and him.

Columbia opened her mouth, and Nash grabbed her arm and pulled her aside. "Columbia, we shall discuss everything once we are wed."

"No. First, I think you're married, then it's just to help out a friend and you're gettin' divorced. Next, my uncle's got to hold a gun on you after you . . ." she let her voice trail off; she was not going to divulge to half the town that she had been to bed with Nash. "Then on our weddin' day, another woman shows up, claimin' that you're engaged to her. If that ain't enough, somebody declares that you told the world the woman you said you were married to and divorced, was your sister. I wondered how could it be until I read the signature on this paper." She shoved the document at him. "It's signed by Sam Parks, one of Uncle Titus's partners in his past shenanigans. I downright don't know what to think anymore."

He took hold of both her arms and mined the depths of her soul with probing eyes. "Just think about becoming Mrs. Nash Foster today, and nothing else."

If only he had said he loved her. Because now she was starting to fear that he could be using her like he must have used Dolly, to keep that New York woman

366

at bay. And she did not know what to think about Dolly's part in this twisted muddle. The thought made Columbia search her out. Dolly kept her eyes on the floor, refusing to attempt eye contact.

"Just answer me one question. Were you truly married to Dolly, or just pretendin'?"

"Later, Columbia."

His voice was filled with finality. His tight expression warned that he had no intention of disclosing anything about himself in front of all these people leaning forward to get an earful of juicy gossip. She pinched her lips. Her head started to throb. It was all just too entangled and perplexing.

"There ain't gonna be no later." She lifted her voluminous skirts and started for the door.

"You cannot leave yet, missy," Kiplinger jeered. He stood in front of the door, effectively blocking her exit. He smirked. He was about to settle the question of who would be Foster's blushing bride this or any other day.

"Ya'll have said quite enough, Kiplinger," Nash spat. He stepped in front of Columbia, to shield her from the man and his two henchmen. "Either ya'll leave now under your own power, or I am going to be forced to assist you. And I guarantee that ya'll are not going to find it to your liking."

"Do not try to threaten me, Foster," Markus said with a curled lip.

"It is not a threat. It is a fact."

"Threat or fact, we are not leaving until I have finished with you."

Nash took a threatening step forward and Kiplinger snapped his fingers. The two men with him closed ranks in front of Kiplinger. One gave Nash a shove, causing him to throw the first punch.

A scuffle ensued as the three men fell into a helix of arms, fists, and legs. To the surprise of all in attendance, Columbia jumped into the fracas, causing her hoopskirt to flip up.

She ignored the sudden draft and pounded against the men. Two against one just was not fair. One of the men landed a punch, and Columbia suddenly found herself flying backward and slammed against the wall.

Unable to see anything in front of her except the bent hoop, which was blocking her view, Columbia scrambled to her feet and launched herself back into the middle of the brawl. She landed squarely on the big gut of one, throwing his head back against the floor so hard that it knocked him out. Nash made short work of the other one, with a right cross to the jaw.

Nash got to his feet and pulled Columbia up beside him. "Are ya'll right?" he asked. "Ya'll did not break anything, did you?" He began to feel her arms, but she shoved him away.

"I'm fine." A pain under her left eye caused her to flinch and slap a palm over it. "Now get out of my way. I need some meat."

"She is a real animal, meat and all, isn't she?" Jennifer remarked at Columbia's comment.

"It's for my eye. It's going to be black, you silly, empty-headed, society witch," Columbia hissed.

Jennifer heaved, "I will have you know I am no—"

"My God, Columbia, are ya'll right?" Nash cut in and tried to have a look at the swelling.

Columbia was going to have none of his concern. She pushed a temporarily stunned Markus Kiplinger aside and tried to get through the door, but the hoop of her skirt stuck fast.

She was struggling to bend the wire from hell, when her attention suddenly caught on a basket lying just outside the door. It looked like a laundry basket from the size of it. And she peevishly wondered if it were Nash's wash, waiting for the new bride to tend to it. She would be damned first. The cloth jerked and she blinked. A puppy. Someone had brought a puppy as a wedding gift! Now she was just as anxious to extricate herself from what had become a mortifying scene, as she was to find out what was in the basket.

She gave a yank on the wire, which released the hoop and sent her hurtling forward headfirst onto the deck. She hit with a thud. Ignoring the fact that she now sat in a heap and her eye throbbed, Columbia scooted to the basket and lifted the cover.

"What are you doin' out here all alone?" Columbia cooed and picked up the bundle.

"Oh, I see you have found my daughter's wedding gift to Nash," Markus observed with a cold smirk.

Columbia's brows crinkled. "I don't understand."

"It is really simple enough," Markus boasted, now that he had everyone's undivided attention. He bent over and lifted the squirming bundle into his arms. "Nash did not remain in New York long enough to learn that he was going to become a parent."

For dramatic effect, Markus tossed off the blanket covering the baby. "I would have liked to present Ely Markus Foster to his father under different circumstances, but I think the boy will convince everyone, including Foster, that the only rightful bride-to-be today should be the mother of his son."

Columbia stayed on the deck. She knew if she tried to stand, she would fall; her legs suddenly felt like coiled ropes. Feeling like her heart had just been battered in a boat's paddle wheel, her gaze shot over the major players in what had become the hideous unfolding of a tragic play before her. Nash stared at the baby in disbelief. Jennifer Kiplinger had regained her haughty pose. Markus Kiplinger stood the victor, backed up by the two men now licking their wounds. Titus had circled Dolly into his embrace and was shaking his head.

"It is not mine," Nash stated flatly.

In a sudden burst of righteous fury, Jennifer claimed the baby from her father. "Take a closer look, Nash. It could be the very picture of you."

It was then that Columbia suddenly recalled why the woman had seemed familiar. She had seen a daguerreotype of her in Nash's cabin. "My good Lord, it's true," she gasped. Her subdued gaze locked with Nash's furious one. "You are the father of that child."

"No, Columbia."

"How can you deny Ely's birth?" shouted Jennifer, who finally had gained the sympathy of the crowd. Histrionics had always helped her get her own way as a child, and it would serve her well now to show Nash that he was not going to simply think he could

370

walk away from her a second time.

Jennifer mustered up a river of tears, her generous chest heaving as she started to sob uncontrollably. "We have not come all this way to be treated as if—" she leveled a transparent tilt of her chin toward the girl, "we were no more than river trash to be tossed overboard at will."

Columbia did not miss the insult. If the woman had not been holding a baby, Columbia would have leaped off the deck, rope legs or not, and given Jennifer Kiplinger a black eye to match her own.

Instead of doing something rash, for once Columbia pinched her eyes shut to calm down. Then she managed to gain her feet with a new dignity, despite the now ungainly angles in which her skirt draped over the mangled hoop.

"You can cease the poor little rich girl act, Jennifer. I am not impressed," Nash announced. "Columbia—"

She swung her back to him. There was nothing more left to say, not when a child was involved.

She had only taken two steps toward the gangplank, to disengage herself from this latest disaster, when all of a sudden a mighty explosion erupted.

Chapter Thirty-seven

"My God, no!" Columbia screamed. "No!"

Columbia lifted her skirts and sprinted toward the black, billowing smoke and shooting flames from the dock. A stitch in her side threatened to slow her down, but she had to hurry. She grabbed her side and kept running, only to come to an abrupt halt a short time later.

Her wreck of a paddle wheeler was rapidly becoming engulfed in flames. She grabbed a bucket, filled it at the pump, and tossed it on the fire, as Nash, followed by the wedding guests, arrived.

He snatched the bucket out of her hands and put his arms around her. "Please," she pleaded, "please help me save my boat."

Nash took one look at the spreading inferno and knew any effort would be in vain. But he quickly handed Columbia over to Dolly's care, shed his jacket, and organized a bucket brigade.

Columbia watched in despair as all the finely dressed men fought to save her paddle wheeler, wondering what had caused it to explode in the first place. The voracious blaze was engulfing the paddle wheel, dancing between it and the hull in fiery conquest.

Another explosion sent burning boards soaring into the sky, and raining down like flaming arrows. Everyone dived for cover behind the crates stacked along the dock. The second explosion brought Columbia out of her gloom. There had not been anything left on board that could have caused an explosion of such magnitude, much less two of them. The troubling deduction caused her to recall the two men heading away from her paddle wheeler yesterday. She remembered where she knew them from. She had once seen one of them lurking near Villamoore's office.

"The dirty bastard," she snarled.

"What are you grumbling about, honey?" Dolly questioned. "The men are working as hard as they can to save your boat."

Columbia patted Dolly's arm. "I know they are. But no one would have to be tryin' to save a boat already lost, if it weren't for that bastard Villamoore."

Columbia got up as far as one knee before Dolly grabbed for her. "You can't help. Stay back here with me, where it's safe."

Columbia disengaged herself and stood up. "I've got some unfinished business to settle. And this time I aim to see it through once 'n' for all."

Dolly watched Columbia stomp toward Nash's paddle wheeler. Columbia could almost be considered a comical sight, in her ruined white gown smudged with soot, except that her hands were balled into angry fists, and her bent elbows worked back and forth as her determined strides carried her away from Dolly's safekeeping.

"Oh, my Lord," Dolly cried. She leaped to her feet and ran for Titus, who despite his bandages, was carrying a sloshing bucket toward the fire. "Titus! Titus!"

She grabbed his arms, throwing him off balance and causing the bucket to lose its contents down the front of him. "Crissakes, woman, the water's for the fire, not me. Although I got to admit, when I'm near you, you make me feel like I could burn right up. I need a good dousing, I get so hot."

"You don't understand." She had to practically run to keep up with him. "It's Columbia. I think she's really going to get herself in trouble this time."

Titus stopped and handed his bucket to another man. "I don't want nothing happening to you. Let's get you out of the way. Then you can tell me what the girl is getting herself into now."

It seemed an eternity before Titus found the best place, and had Dolly safely settled away from the fire. He turned to leave, and she cried, "Where are you going? We've got to talk. I haven't told you about Columbia yet."

Titus rolled his eyes. "I love that girl, but I've had enough of her shenanigans. The girl is Nash Foster's responsibility now. The minute I see him, I'll send him over to you. He can handle whatever fool stunt she's pulling this time."

374

"But—" Dolly sank back in frustration when he walked away from her, yet she kept her eyes peeled for Nash. She had to locate him and tell him what Columbia was about, before the river girl got herself in really big trouble.

"Daddy, I think we have caused Nash enough trouble for now. Our ship is not going to explode, too, is it? I would like to return to my cabin with Ely and rest, but only if it is safe."

Columbia had been rounding the corner toward Nash's cabin to change clothes, when she heard voices. She dropped back to listen.

"Don't worry, Jennifer child. I can guarantee that our ship will not explode in the same manner. Come along, I shall escort you back to the ship personally. Then, since Foster is going to be busily engaged for some time, Cowan and I have some business matters in town to settle."

"What about the other man, the one who boarded in Astoria?"

"He's already served his purpose. Probably in some saloon drinking the money I paid him."

"Then what he said wasn't true."

"It was true, all right. He heard Foster call that redhead his sister. It just cost me to have him repeat it."

Columbia was disturbed by the confusing conversation, but she had business matters of her own to settle. She waited until the sound of footsteps faded in the distance before she continued to Nash's cabin, changed, grabbed several guns, and charged back down the gangplank.

"What you up to, Miz Columbia?" Little John called from his watch on top deck.

She ignored the gentle giant and commandeered the first horse she found. After what Villamoore had done to her paddle wheeler, she had no intention of wasting even a moment locating the bastard. He may not have dirtied his own hands directly, but he was responsible nonetheless. There was not one doubt in her mind, as she spurred the piebald up the hill toward the man's house.

Not allowing time for second thoughts once she arrived, Columbia burst through the door. Villamoore was sitting in his dining room, staring up at the portrait she had shot.

"Ain't you moved from that spot, since I left you with that retouched picture?"

Villamoore slowly swiveled his chair around to face the girl. His smile was unperturbed. "And what about you? Didn't you have anywhere else to go since that paddle wheeler of yours blew up? Poor homeless girl, and with a black eye, too. My men just brought me the news. Looks as if you're out of business. Pity you did not sell when you had the chance."

"You bastard!" she spat and aimed the gun, ignoring her wounded eye.

His gaze briefly darted past her, before it settled on her once again. "Some have doubted my parentage, but not for long."

376

She cocked the gun. "Funny thing. I ain't got no doubts. Why'd you blow my boat?"

"Thought I just answered that. You wouldn't sell. What else could I do under the circumstances?"

Her face turned fury red. "You are a son of a bitch."

He lifted a spoon from the table and toyed with it. "My, my, such language. That uncle of yours should have taught you better, my dear girl. Now, aren't you going to pull the trigger? You are beginning to bore me."

Columbia brought the hammer back. But at the same moment she was grabbed from behind, sending the gunfire into the ceiling and causing a chandelier to crash onto the middle of the table. "Let go of me."

Columbia struggled but was no match for the men, who had her bound in record time to a nearby chair.

"Damn bitch! She kicked me in the balls," Jack Tarley moaned in anguish, as he curled into a painful knot.

"Don't give it another thought, Tarley. I shall personally see that she pays for her crimes." Villamoore again glanced at his portrait. "By the time I am finished with her, she is going to become intimately acquainted with, shall we say, that portion of a man's anatomy. When I am finished, you can have her."

Jack and Barney grinned. "Hope it won't take you too long. We still got to set the dynamite on Foster's boat." Columbia raised her chin in defiance. "You two shouldn't have to hang around long."

While the men fought to stifle chuckles and slipped

out the side doors, Villamoore bounded to his feet, raised his hand to backhand her for the unfavorable implication toward his performance as a man, and advanced toward her. "I am going to make you wish you had shot off the real thing, instead of defiling my portrait. You bitch! When I—"

Villamoore suddenly stopped and stood very still with his arm in the air.

"What is the matter, Villamoore?" Nash questioned from the doorway, a gun in his hand. "Don't ya'll intend on finishing what you began, or have your plans suddenly changed?" Nash untied Columbia.

Villamoore slowly lowered his arm. "Guess you flunked the test. Coming here like Tarley said you would after the mishap at the docks just proves that nobody is infallible. Even Southerners. Pity, I liked you, Foster. But I'd say you just are not the kind of man I am looking for after all."

"Guess not. Now, sit down before ya'll find yourself on the floor, flat."

"Watch out!" Columbia screamed, as the two men who had attacked her set upon Nash.

Villamoore lunged for Columbia, but soon realized he had taken on more than a man his size could easily handle. He tried to hold her off while he stretched for the nearby gun, but the girl kicked him squarely in the rear, sending him flat on his face. When he tried to pick himself up, he found a foot between his shoulders blades, the cold metal of a gun in his back.

Nash chuckled as the pair who had taken him on scrambled from the house. "Villamoore did not realize what he was taking on in ya'll."

Columbia nodded awkwardly as she noticed two men heading across the lawn outside the French doors.

"Nash, what are—?" Markus Kiplinger took a breath. "I am glad we got here in time. The moment I heard what was going on, I summoned one of my crew and came immediately—"

Nash had that same strange feeling of déjà vu as he listened to Kiplinger. It was just like the first time he had stood inside Villamoore's house.

"—although it appears that you have things well in hand."

Nash's attention was diverted when Columbia said, "Nash, we got to talk." Her eyes trailed to Markus Kiplinger.

"Later, we shall talk later."

"But—"

"We shall straighten everything out in time, Columbia. I promise."

Maybe she was jumping to conclusions, and was mistaken about Kiplinger and his daughter. Then she remembered Jack Tarley, and what he and his accomplice were about. "Yeah, well, I got to go." She dashed from the house. Nash headed after her.

"Let her go, Nash. We need to take care of matters here first," Markus advised.

Nash watched Columbia mount the horse she had taken and gallop off through the trees. He smiled to himself. Columbia would insist she had just *borrowed* the animal.

When Nash turned around, he came face to face with the barrel of a gun. "I wondered how ya'll found Villamoore's place."

"My, my, my, now you know," Villamoore scoffed. "Looks as if you find yourself at a disadvantage, Foster."

Kiplinger was smirking ear to ear, while his crew member and Villamoore held guns pointed directly at Nash. He glanced around the room and it suddenly hit him. "Ya'll know, the first time I came here I had the strangest feeling, as if I had been here before. Now I realize why. This house is a miniature of your country house, Kiplinger."

"You are observant, Foster. Pity you had to go and get my daughter pregnant, or I would kill you without further delay." He heaved a bored sigh. "But since you did, you are going to marry Jennifer so you can make her a widow, instead of just another wealthy whore with a bastard son."

Nash took a seat and crossed his legs. "Since I am about to become a member of the family — even if for such a short duration — mind filling me in on the family secret? Ya'll did not sail all the way from New York merely to see your daughter married, did you?"

Markus laughed. "Pity you are so smart, because you have outsmarted yourself this time. I wanted Jennifer to marry you. Wanted a Southerner in the family. You see, I have always had an affinity for the South.

"There is a war coming, Foster. And I intend to be a leader once the South emerges as the victor. To that end, a group of us has been at work for some time, shipping and storing supplies, money, guns. Whatever will be needed.

"I even sent John here," Markus motioned toward Villamoore, "to set up operations and take control of the profitable commerce and portage out here on the frontier. The Columbia River, just like the mighty Mississippi, will be a valuable asset to the South. And to my good fortune, *you* ended up here, giving me the perfect excuse to check on my investments."

"All the pieces of the puzzle fit now. Ya'll have masterminded a complex conspiracy, Kiplinger," Nash commented dryly, remembering he had come to Oregon because he had heard someone at one of Kiplinger's parties speak of it. "Mind if I finish it for ya'll?"

"Be my guest, if you think you have it all figured out."

"Both houses are patterned after the same Southern plantation house. I should have picked up on that quicker."

"That is what separates us, Foster. You see, I have seen to all the details."

"Did ya'll *see to* the guns lost from the warehouse at Lower Cascades that Villamoore had sent upriver?" Kiplinger frowned at Villamoore, unhappy at losing any of the merchandise sent from New York. "That may or may not be the first detail ya'll missed, Kiplinger."

"Villamoore has been systematically taking control of all the shipping out of Portland. Must have galled ya'll, Villamoore, when Columbia and her uncle refused to cooperate." Villamoore remained silent. Kiplinger's frown deepened and Nash grinned. "There is another chink in your *detailed* armor, so to speak.

"I met part of your contingent at the statehood celebration; men ya'll had recruited to take up the cause. Really quite ingenious of you, Kiplinger. Although what is it that is said about trust and zealots?

"You even used Jennifer's convenient pregnancy as an excuse, or I should say cover, to sail after the wayward captain who had 'done her wrong,' when what ya'll were actually planning was to check on your investment. Did ya'll arrange her pregnancy, too? Maybe the trained gorilla ya'll brought with you today obliged?"

"That was your doing, Foster, which is why I am sparing your life long enough to marry her," Kiplinger insisted in a raised voice, suddenly very annoyed and uncomfortable at finding himself on the defensive although his cronies held the guns.

Nash ignored the old man's remark. "Ya'll needed to make sure control of the river and recruitment were proceeding according to schedule. Is it? Have ya'll seen to every detail? I think not."

"What else haven't I seen to?" Markus sneered. But he was starting to sweat.

"Trust is such an important commodity in a conspiracy such as yours, since your very life depends on it. Ya'll would be hanged if found out, I believe. Did ya'll trust Villamoore to travel so far out of your reach and handle things for you? Can ya'll trust the men indebted to Villamoore? Bet ya'll do not trust that one either. Is that why ya'll brought him along?"

Villamoore and Cowan's faces filled with questions, and they took their concentration off Nash and toward Kiplinger.

It was the moment Nash had been waiting for. He charged the two men holding guns.

Chaos erupted in the room as shots blasted out.

Chapter Thirty-eight

Villamoore's dining room turned into a chaotic scene. Soldiers in blue pounced on Villamoore and Cowan. One of the ricocheting bullets hit the nail holding Villamoore's prized portrait. The monstrosity crashed down onto Villamoore, imprisoning him within the gilded frame and transforming what had been a flat, smiling likeness into three-dimensional fury.

Nash quickly subdued Cowan, then got up and brushed himself off. Kiplinger had not even bothered to unfold himself from his chair.

"You all right, Foster?" General Shallcross questioned, stepping over the broken china and overturned chairs.

"Fine now. Guess I am fortunate ya'll happened by when you did."

"Fortune had nothing to do with it. We were on maneuvers, heading toward the billowing smoke coming from the docks, when Columbia stopped us. She informed us the smoke was from her boat, and said that something was not quite right at Villamoore's, and we'd better have a check. Although that girl has a reputation for starting a lot of the trouble surrounding Villamoore, this time there was a different tone in her voice, so we came to have a look. Oh, by the way, she—"

Markus got to his feet and offered his hand. "Markus Kiplinger is the name. I am so happy you arrived in time. Saved me from being forced to continue with my acting performance in order to rescue Foster."

General Shallcross started to take the distinguished older man's hand, but Nash interceded. "It is not going to work, Kiplinger. This is the man from New York that I mentioned to ya'll yesterday, General. The one I learned is at the bottom of the plot to gain control of the river. The conspiracy is more widespread than ya'll originally thought. Captain Youngston was right, Villamoore was working for someone higher up."

General Shallcross fixed Youngston, who was standing next to Villamoore, with a nod of approval. "Looks as if that promotion that you have been after, to start recruitment for your own unit of the First Oregon Volunteers, is guaranteed, Captain."

The captain's sly gray eyes gleamed. "Yes, sir."

"And I thought you were one of us, Youngston. You are nothing but a traitor to the Southern cause," Villamoore sneered. "There are those in these parts who won't forget what you have done."

"Thanks to the list Foster procured from Villamoore's desk after the statehood celebration, my men

385

will shortly be rounding all of them up. Good of you to cooperate, Villamoore."

Kiplinger gave a disgusted look down his nose at Villamoore, and smiled through his teeth. "I never did trust short, baldheaded men who try to hide underneath ill-fitting wigs. Your undersized type always has something to prove. And usually you are shortsighted and full of shortcomings, just like your height."

"You didn't fare any better, *Mr. Big-time Leader* Kiplinger," Villamoore mocked, then bellowed, "Get this picture frame off me."

"Oh, I don't know. Actually, I think it never looked better," Nash quipped. Then he turned serious. "Ya'll can remain as you are until ya'll unburden yourself. Once ya'll do, we shall be pleased to remove the frame."

Nash spent the next half hour filling the soldiers in on the details of the conspiracy and the events which had brought them to Villamoore's, as well as answering the general's question about how Columbia got the black eye. Villamoore finally confessed to everything, including blowing up the *Columbia's Pride*. Kiplinger remained sullen.

"Guess we can relieve you of that expensive picture frame shortly, Villamoore. Ya'll will not need it where you are going." Nash made another perusal of the hideous canvas with a glowering Villamoore standing in the middle of it. "Looks as if Columbia is going to get the last laugh after all. Except ya'll are not smiling now like you were in the portrait. Pity she is not here to see this." A thought struck Nash.

"General, Columbia was headed back to check on her burning paddle wheeler, you said?"

The general's long somber face grew longer. "Actually, as I started to mention before Kiplinger interrupted me, Columbia was rather in a rush. Mumbled something about two men heading toward your boat for some reason."

Nash raked his fingers through his tousled black waves. "Christ, if I did not love that crazy young woman, I would wring her neck." For a moment Nash was startled that he had just put voice to a feeling he had refused to acknowledge heretofore. He beat down the realization. He did not have time now to explore the ramifications of such a disclosure.

"Best hurry and clamp the old ball and chain around her ankle. That might slow her down a bit."

Nash rolled his eyes at the general's attempts at humor. "Somehow I doubt it. As I told ya'll, I tried to do that very thing earlier this morning — until Kiplinger intruded. Since ya'll have things here well in hand, I had best catch up with Columbia, before she gets herself in the middle of yet another mess."

The general and captain chuckled as they watched Foster fast-talk one of the soldiers out of a horse and speed away from the house. "Good thing Foster came to town, or God only knows who in these parts would have been man enough to have taken on the likes of Columbia Baranoff," Captain Youngston said.

"It definitely would take someone crazy enough to bring a paddle wheeler all the way from New York to match wits with her," bantered the general, who appreciated Foster's mettle.

While the two men the general ordered to remove the heavy frame and take Villamoore and Kiplinger into custody were busy carrying out the directives, Lester Cowan saw his chance to escape and took it. He slipped out the open French doors and scurried into the dense cover of pines.

Cowan headed toward the docks. His dreams of collecting riches had been dashed, but his dreams of another kind were still on board the ship, and he intended to collect. He stumbled into a clearing overlooking the docks and noted Foster's horse below kicking up clods of dirt as the son of a bitch rushed to that damned river girl's side.

The closer Nash came to the docks, the more worried he got. Columbia's paddle wheeler was little more than smoldering ash and a few patches of flaring flames. Most of the men had gone, and Titus and Dolly were nowhere to be seen. He drove the mighty beast past Kiplinger's ship toward his own.

"Dammit!" Nash cursed when he reached the empty slip where his paddle wheeler should have been docked.

Little John heard a string of loud expletives and came out of a nearby warehouse. "Captain Foster, sir. I got something you ought to see first.

"Come see," he repeated.

There was a note of pride in the gentle giant's voice. So Nash headed toward him, determined to find out where his paddle wheeler was while he obliged the man, since he had the distinct sinking feeling that it had to have something to do with Columbia.

Inside the building crates were stacked from floor to ceiling. "Well, make this quick. I want to know where my boat is," Nash warned.

Little John shoved a pannier aside to reveal two morose men, bruised, bound together, and gagged. "These two were trying to plant dynamite on board your boat, when Miz Columbia and me surprised them. Hell, Captain Foster, sir, they didn't have no chance to do no dirty work at all, we was so fast. And you should have seen Miz Columbia."

"Right in the middle of the fracas, no doubt," Nash commented dryly.

"How'd you know?" Nash merely remained silent, his face deadpan. "Well, we got 'em all tied up real pretty, and waiting for Titus to bring the sheriff to tote 'em off to jail."

Nash stood with his arms crossed over his chest, his feet planted wide apart. "Good work, Little John. But—"

"Thanks, Captain Foster, sir." Little John bobbed his head like a pleased schoolboy. "We make a good t—"

"Little John, where is Columbia now?" Nash questioned, somehow knowing yet fearing the answer.

Little John's triumphant grin drooped, and he shuffled his foot in an effort to get his thoughts together before answering the man.

"Little John?" Nash prodded.

"Ah gosh, Captain Foster, sir, after your wedding went sour, and then the *Columbia's Pride* burnt all to hell, Miz Columbia said she needed to get away to think about what she wanted to do with her life, so she took—"

"In which direction did she go?"

Little John shrank under the fierce stare. "East. But you don't got to worry. She's got a good crew with her."

Nash was already stomping from the warehouse when Little John anxiously called out, "She said you had given her your permission."

"She would." Nash just shook his head and kept on going.

Little John was in a sudden panic. It was he who had sworn to Miz Columbia's latest story in front of the crew. He felt the weight of responsibility, and he had to be part of the solution. "Looks like you fellers are going to have to get comfortable by yourselves 'til the sheriff gets here. At least you got each other to keep company with."

Jack Tarley and Barney's eyes went wide, and fear that they might be forgotten about was reflected by the retreating bulk of Little John as he ran after Foster.

"Captain Foster, sir, wait up. I can be of help."

"I would say ya'll have already helped enough," Nash spat. He kept on going, and despite Little John's size, the man was having trouble keeping up with him.

"I can help find you a boat so you can follow her."

"I do not need your help. Kiplinger's ship will do just fine. She cannot have gone too far, and the steamer will be able to overtake her before she does."

"Please, Captain Foster, sir, lemme help."

"Come along, if ya'll must. But ya'll had best

stand back when I catch up with Columbia."

"Yes, sir, Captain Foster. But you won't hurt her, will you?" he asked, as they stormed up the gangplank to Kiplinger's ship.

"I am not going to hurt her, only wring her neck," Nash threatened. But inside what he truly wanted was to take her into his embrace and whisper in her ear that he loved her, while he demonstrated how he felt.

The captain of the ship rushed out to intercept the intruders. "What are you doing on board? This ship belongs to Mr. Markus Kiplinger."

"Not anymore. Now fire up the engines or I shall have my friend here" — Nash thumbed toward Little John — "toss your carcass overboard."

The captain took one look at the giant and sagely decided the river was much too cold for swimming this time of year. "Yes sir."

Nash went up to the wheelhouse and prepared to cast off, after directing Little John to accompany the captain. They had barely gotten underway when Nash was joined by Barth.

"Nash, Little John told me you were here. I was wondering where you'd disappeared to after Titus spoke to you earlier. But I must say, I am rather surprised to see you at the helm of Kiplinger's ship, heading upriver."

"Since ya'll know Columbia, I am disappointed that you would be surprised by anything."

Barth suppressed a grin at his friend's dour mood. "Mind if I ask where we are going?"

"After that little hellion; where else?"

"And do I dare ask why you chose this particular ship?" Barth asked, although he suspected the answer.

"Because she commandeered, or shall I say *borrowed* mine."

Barth could no longer help himself. He burst forth laughing, although he tried to stop at Nash's glower. "Hell, I am sorry, friend. It is just that three of Kiplinger's armed thugs could not wrest that paddle wheeler from you back in New York, but one hundred-pound young woman took it right out from under your very nose. And she was not even armed."

"I would not be so sure of that," Nash grumbled.

"You mean that she took it by force of arms?" Barth asked in disbelief.

"Since she has continued to wield that luscious mouth of hers like a weapon, I presume ya'll could say so."

Barth was sure he was going to double over trying not to roar with laughter.

"She has got to be one of the spunkiest females you have ever encountered."

"Considering that she tried unsuccessfully to seduce ya'll—only you could not take your liquor and passed out—I wouldn't be so glib, if I were ya'll."

Barth could no longer help himself. He broke out in a hearty round of laughter again. "Nash, my friend, if I had not passed out, you would have killed me! So I would say that luck was on my side, since the young lady in question can be most difficult—if not impossible—to ignore."

"Impossible definitely fits Miss Mary Catherine Columbia Baranoff, I would say."

392

In between chuckles, Barth managed, "Just like trying to ignore her uncle's gun."

Nash did not deign to answer his friend's latest jab. Instead he kept his eyes on the river and guided the ship through the current and past a snag, as he filled Barth in on all the details involved with Columbia's most recent excursion to Villamoore's residence and the suspected conspiracy. When the identical Southern plantation homes, along with Kiplinger's name, was connected with the conspiracy, Barth quickly sobered.

"What's the matter, Barth? Ya'll do not find Columbia's antics particularly amusing any longer?"

Barth swallowed and rubbed his cheeks with the palms of his hands. Taking a deep breath, he sat on the stool to the right of the wheel. "I had not counted on Kiplinger being involved, much less the head man. Hell, are you sure? The man came all the way from New York."

Nash's brows lifted. "As I just told ya'll, the conspiracy has been years in the planning. But what has gotten into you all of a sudden? I did not think ya'll believed that phony pillar-of-the-community image Kiplinger has always tried to project. It does not surprise me at all. Just the length of time it took to figure it out."

Nash worked the controls, calling for more speed, while Barth sat in mute contemplation. "By the way, Barth, just what are ya'll doing aboard Kiplinger's ship?"

Chapter Thirty-nine

Although the day was partially overcast with
compressed glimmer of sun glistening across th
river, Barth broke out in a sweat. His mind worke
furiously to come up with a plausible explanation a
to why he was on board Kiplinger's ship. But luc
was with Barth, as they neared the large island in th
middle of the Columbia River.

Barth vaulted from his stool and waved a pointin
finger toward the island. "Your paddle wheeler
Ahead. Just off shore there. I'm sure of it."

Even as Barth spoke, Nash was spinning the whee
and working the controls to overtake the *Yacht.* "I se
her."

"She seems to be putting in at that island. Yo
don't suppose the paddle wheeler finally broke down
do you? We still have not taken the time to make th
repairs needed when we arrived in Portland," Bart
offered.

"God only knows why Columbia does what sh
does."

Barth did not laugh this time. He was too relieve

that Nash's attention had been diverted. "Maybe she ran out of firewood. The island is heavily forested. It would be a good place to replenish the chopped cord wood."

"Looks like I shall soon find out."

Nash navigated the ship around the far side of the island. After instructing Barth to captain the ship back to Portland and wait for him there, Nash took one of the dinghies and rowed to shore.

He made his way through the thick stands of trees, stopping behind a huge tree trunk. Barth was right. The crew was chopping fuel wood. He waited until he caught sight of Columbia. Despite her plaid shirt, jacket, trousers, and heavy boots, she caused his desire to rise as she directed the crews' efforts. He waited until she moved closer in his direction, then he stepped from behind the tree.

"I see ya'll impetuously *borrowed* my paddle wheeler, as seems to be your usual method of operation when you require transportation not belonging to ya'll."

Columbia's head snapped up, her eyes growing as big with surprise as waves during a storm. "Nash?"

He lifted a brow. "Some might consider your latest actions pirating. Ya'll do know the penalty for piracy."

"How did you get here?" she asked, ignoring the mention of piracy. After all, she had merely borrowed the paddle wheeler. "W-where did you come from?"

"Your worst nightmare, darlin'," Nash drawled.

She smiled weakly. "I ain't never had any nightmares with you in them before."

"Is that why ya'll saw fit to lie to Little John and the crew, so you could steal my paddle wheeler?"

"I didn't exactly lie or steal," she insisted.

Little John moved out into the clearing beside Nash. "Sorry, Captain Foster, sir, but since the girl's taking your boat was partly my fault, I had to follow you and help put things right."

Columbia pulled Little John by his heavy jacket to her side. "I'm glad you came along, Little John. Now you can assure Nash that I didn't steal or pirate his precious paddle wheeler."

Nash did not intend to continue to stand in front of his gaping crew and argue with the girl. He swooped her up in his arms.

She took a swing at him.

He easily pinned her arms at her sides. "If ya'll are trying to give me a black eye to match yours, darlin', forget it."

Columbia opened her mouth to protest, but Nash's glare and the tension exuding from his body warned her to let him have his say.

"Little John, have the crew bring enough provisions ashore for three days, then shove off. I am putting ya'll in charge. Once back at Portland, give the men shore leave before ya'll return for us."

"No!" Columbia cried. "Little John, you ain't gonna let him kidnap me, are you?"

"Miz Columbia, we all know how you got here. Besides, seems to me kidnapping and piracy go hand 'n hand in this case."

Columbia swung beseeching eyes toward the crew, but Nash announced in a honey-thick Southern drawl, "If ya'll want to keep your jobs, ya'll will get a move on. My lady and I want to be alone."

Columbia had learned enough about Nash Foster

to know that when he reverted to that sickeningly sweet Southern accent, she had best watch out. But the "my lady" warmed her heart, despite her determination to put distance between them.

"I'm not stayin' here on this island with you," she rasped.

"Wrong." He directed, "Get a move on, Little John. I am going to take Columbia for a walk amongst the trees. When we return, ya'll and the paddle wheeler best be on your way downriver."

With Columbia in his arms, Nash headed toward the center of the island. She did not say one word to him until he sat her down on a fallen log. She crossed her arms over her chest and lifted her chin. "I may be stuck here with you, but that doesn't mean I'm gonna talk to you."

"Talk is not what I had in mind. And it looks as if that is not what ya'll have on your mind either. The way your chin in raised, it puts your lips in the best position to be kissed." His voice suddenly became a caressing whisper. "Do ya'll want to be kissed, Columbia?"

"No," she protested feebly. She was not going to admit it, but being near him was wreaking havoc with her innards, even if she *was* put out with him.

"Yes," he murmured in response, placing a hand on each side of her and leaning over so his lips were very close to hers.

Nash took her chin in his hand and dipped his head to kiss her. Columbia panicked and shoved him away from her. "Don't you understand? I can't kiss you," she cried and scrambled off the log.

Nash started toward her. She backed away. "Why

not, Columbia? Don't ya'll trust yourself to kiss me?"

"Yes. I mean, no. No, I don't. If I kiss you, I won't be able to stop." She was trembling. "I'll want more, and I can't have more."

She stumbled backward, and then suddenly broke for the beach before he could try to change her mind. She ran flat out, hoping that the paddle wheeler had not left her stranded in the middle of the river with the one man who drove her wild; the one man whom she could never hope to have.

Nash followed after her at a distance, deciding that he would let her tire before he overtook her. The paddle wheeler had to be on its way by now, and she had nowhere she could run from him. If nothing else, in the next three days, he was going to force her to listen to him . . . one way or another.

By the time he reached the river's edge, Columbia had waded into the icy waters and was frantically waving toward the disappearing paddle wheeler.

"Ya'll are only going to be wet and cold, Columbia," he observed in a calm voice.

She fixed him a stony glare, slogged back to shore, plunked down on a rock, and pulled off her wet boots. She was surprised when he kneeled before her, a cloth from the stores in his hand, and began to dry her feet and ankles.

"I can take care of myself."

"I have no doubt of it." He continued with his ministrations.

Despite a determination not to, Columbia shivered. Her trousers were wet halfway up her thighs, and the wind had picked up. Not to mention the part his touch had played in her goose bumps.

"Better get those pants off, before ya'll catch your death," Nash advised.

She jumped to her feet and headed toward the provisions, before tossing back over her shoulder, "Not on your life."

Nash joined her and merely smiled. "I have always believed that it did not matter how long it took, if I want something bad enough, darlin', I am going to have it."

"Well, you're not gonna have me again," she said in an unconvinced voice. "I was mistaken. I thought you were bein' kind, but you're just like a man. You only wanted to get my pants off."

"I am a man, Columbia. But that is *not* why I suggested ya'll remove your trousers. Can't ya'll accept an act of concern as genuine?"

"Humph!" She grabbed up a good portion of the supplies and tromped off to look for a shelter.

In exasperation Nash gathered up the remaining stores and followed after. "My God, woman, am I always going to be following after ya'll?"

She stopped and pivoted around. "You can stop right now."

Nash shrugged, undaunted. "Good idea." He dropped his load and grabbed for her, causing her burden to tumble from her arms.

She swallowed hard. "What're you gonna try doin' this time?"

He tried to probe the depths of her soul, but it was closed. She was keeping part of herself shut off from him. He relinquished his hold on her. "It looks like a storm is heading in, so we had best set up camp before we are caught in it."

A part of Columbia experienced grievous disappointment, as she helped pitch a makeshift shelter and drag the foodstuffs inside. There was not much room to escape him once they climbed in together. It had already started to sprinkle, and unless she wanted to get the rest of herself as wet as her trouser legs, she had no choice but to remain huddled side by side with him.

And huddle was what they did for two days, since the storm did not abate once it had begun. The only concession she had made on the second day was to finally remove her trousers in exchange for a blanket. But other than that she remained firm. She let him fill her in on Villamoore's fall and Kiplinger's role in it. But she absolutely refused to discuss what, if anything, was bothering her.

Night was rapidly approaching, and she felt a mixture of sadness and relief that tomorrow the paddle wheeler would return for them. Nash seemed frustrated by her refusals to fall victim to his disarming Southern charm, although he tried to hide it. But she had frustrations of her own, which plagued her at being so close to him.

"Coffee is ready," he announced, intruding into her troubling thoughts.

"Thanks." She took the cup and sipped the warming brew. He was watching her, like a predator does its prey, patiently awaiting the right moment. "Guess I ain't been the best of company," she finally admitted in a weak moment.

He took a position next to her, his leg leaning against hers. "Your trousers are not dry yet," he said.

"Oh." She heard herself sigh. "Guess I'll have to put

400

them back on in the mornin' wet or dry."

"Guess so."

The tension at being so near him burgeoned. She could feel the heat of his thigh through the blanket. It was almost unbearable; she wanted him so much she ached. "I got an ache," she said, before she thought better of it.

Concern and something else — hunger — filled his face. "Where do ya'll hurt?"

This was it. It was now or never. He had just provided another opening for telling him what was bothering her. She searched his face in the light of the small fire he had built. Flames danced in his eyes. His face appeared heated. Her heart beat as fast and loudly as the rain on the tarp. It joined in protesting her self-imposed isolation. In silence she was now fighting a desperate battle on another front.

"Columbia, this is our last night alone together. I am not going to deny that I thought things between us were going to turn out differently. And I am not going to deny that I want ya'll, because right now I am hurting so bad myself, that I may have to go stand out in the rain. Despite the urges I have felt, I have not tried to force ya'll, and I never will. I do not know if ya'll are hurting from the same cause I am, but — "

He broke off, got up, and had made it as far as the edge of the shelter, before Columbia's voice stopped him. "Don't go."

He pivoted around and stood perfectly still, staring at her, waiting for her to call him back.

Columbia lost the battle.

She reached out for him. "Come back. Please."

Nash did not wait for further invitation. He tossed his cup aside, disposed of hers, and had her in his arms in record time. "Oh God, Columbia."

His mouth came down on hers in a passionate frenzy before unknown to him. His lips devoured hers, and he rained kisses over her face and down her neck.

Then suddenly he was unbuttoning her shirt, a heated hand caressed her breasts, and he was consuming them. Her lacy underwear fell away before she knew they had been tossed aside.

"Hmm, ya'll are still wearing lace. Always wear lace, Columbia."

"But it's cold in the winter," she protested, at feeling a sudden cold gust.

"I shall be there to keep ya'll warm," he murmured, and his body pressed along hers, cutting off the cold. His fingers dipped into her.

She held him so close, his magical fingers driving her beyond herself. The searing heat and fevered friction inspired her to make her own exploration, as if it would be the last time. She put the unexpected sobering thought out of her mind, and let the pure sensation of what he was doing to her take over.

He groaned, his chest heaving against hers. She was squeezing him with scorching hands that rode up and down him, until he thought he was going to erupt. He kneeled over her. "I am going to explode if I do not get inside ya'll *now*."

"Then what're you waitin' for?"

With one hard plunge he entered her. Their bodies combined, she arched to receive his pounding thrusts, responding with her own. Wanton desire paired with a clamoring delirium as pressure built within her, until she climaxed with such fierce pulsations that she cried out and clung to him.

Columbia experienced Nash's release in spasm after burning spasm, reveling in the male essence of him. She wished she could prolong the sensations. At least they would be preserved in her mind forever, burned there for all time. She reached up and pulled his head down to her, kissing him with such desperation that he broke the kiss and gazed into her heavy-lidded eyes.

"I have never felt this way about a woman before. I love you, Columbia. Ya'll are the first—"

"What about Jennifer Kiplinger?" The question had just seemed to rush out of her mouth before she could control it, despite the sharp stab his words of love had wrought to her heart.

Nash had expected her to return his words of love. "Is that what has been bothering ya'll?"

She hesitated before she said, "Not so much her. But, Nash, she is the mother of your child. A baby deserves to know its pa." Tears formed in her eyes and threatened to spill down her cheeks at the remembrance of the loss of her own parents, and the loneliness of not having them there while she grew up. "He's got to have a name. You can't let a child go through this world without a name."

For an instant Nash was sure she had just leaped up and kicked him in the gut. How could he combat the naked truth of an innocent baby, when he himself must have been a bastard, neatly disposed of at that foundling home in Nashville? He took a deep breath, his nerves suddenly frayed with fears of losing Columbia.

With the pads of his thumbs, he wiped the tears pooling on her lower lids. "Columbia, we shall work it out just as soon as we get back to Portland, I promise ya'll."

She lowered her head. "It ain't something that can be worked out, Nash."

He circled her in the protective crook of his arm, and leaned her head against his shoulder. She did not attempt to say another word or pull away, and neither did he. They sat together silently listening to the beat of the rain. But Nash's mind was spinning.

Her body belonged to him, just as his belonged to her. But there was something missing. The inner sense that they shared not only body, but souls, without reservations.

Columbia was withholding a part of herself. Nash knew she would never commit to him, if he did not first resolve the issue of his possible parenthood. He might very well be a father. It was a distinct possibility. And Nash intended to honor that responsibility, if indeed it were true. He would never allow the same thing to happen to a child of his that had happened to him. But he loved only one woman, and there was only one way to untangle the predicament.

Chapter Forty

By the time Nash and Columbia returned to Portland, the tension crackled like lightning, it was so intense. Little John had retrieved the pair with a hopeful smile. But the moment he made the mistake of asking if everything had been settled, their differing answers exposed the underlying strain that could explode to the surface.

"Where do ya'll think you are going?" Nash demanded as Columbia marched toward the gangplank.

"To get on with my life."

"I thought I told ya'll that I would work things out."

Her eyes were sparkling when she spat, "And I told you that there ain't no way. That baby is real. You can't work it out. It needs a pa and you're it."

Nash moved so fast, that before she realized it, Nash had grabbed her arm and was practically dragging her toward Kiplinger's ship.

"What the hell do you think you're doin'? Ain't you listened to a word I said?"

"Not any more than ya'll listened to what *I* said! I love you, you hellion," he shouted.

"And I love you, too," she shouted back, her heart aching. If the situation had not been so hopeless, she would have smiled as she recalled that Dolly had said Nash would eventually shout his love for her. "But it don't matter," she said in a quieter voice.

"Like hell."

He dragged her past gawking dockworkers, who smirked at the sight. Titus had informed them that the wedding had merely been postponed, and would go through without a hitch soon. For years Columbia had been the one doing the dragging; it was about time she met her match.

Barth was standing on deck as they approached the ship. He furrowed his brows. "I see the last three days have not tempered her nature any."

"We are not here to discuss Columbia's merits," Nash snapped.

"Then what are you here for?" Barth's voice humbled considerably. He had realized too late that he should have known better than to say something less than glowing about Columbia. He and Nash may be friends, but Columbia was the woman Nash intended to have as his own.

"I might ask ya'll the same question, but I do not have the time right now. Where is Jennifer?"

Barth grew uneasy. "Resting. Why don't you come back later?"

Nash shot Barth a questioning glance, then pushed past his friend, dragging Columbia along behind him. He stomped forward, determined to settle things with the spoiled debutante.

"Okay," Barth said grudgingly, and moved into the forefront. "Follow me."

Nash noted how strangely his friend was acting, but he had a single-minded determination to resolve the most pressing problem first. Then he would get to the bottom of why Barth was behaving so out of character.

Barth stopped in front of a heavy door and put his hand on the knob. "I'll knock and see if Jennifer is prepared to receive visitors."

"Like hell you will," Nash spat. He shouldered Barth aside and swung open the door.

"Barth, is it y—?" Jennifer's blond head snapped up. "Oh, it is Nash and the girl with the black eye. How is the eye, Columbia? It is Columbia, isn't it?"

Columbia's fingers went to her eye. It was already turning from black and blue to deep hues of green and purple. But she was not going to give that snooty woman the courtesy of an answer.

"Ya'll never did learn how to be civil, Jennifer," Nash drawled.

Jennifer's voice was full of indignation when she asked, "What do you want?"

"The truth." Nash pulled Columbia further into the cabin. Columbia stiffened. Barth moved in behind her, quietly bringing up the rear.

Jennifer splayed her fingers out and studied her nails a moment before responding. "And what truth would that be? That you are the one responsible for my daddy being imprisoned at Fort Vancouver? That you left New York after refusing to marry me? Or possibly that you are frightened that Ely is yours, and your little riverboat girl will not marry you if you have a responsibility to me and your son?"

Jennifer gave a sly laugh.

Columbia gasped.

Nash started toward Jennifer.

Barth moved to shield Jennifer from Nash's wrath.

It was a strange course of events that brought Nash and Barth face to face. "Ya'll and I have been friends a long time, Barth. But I am warning ya'll, get out of my way. Jennifer and I have business to settle and no one . . . I repeat . . . no one is going to stop me from settling it."

"You are right. We have been friends — brothers — for a long time. And I even share the feelings about a child without a real family, remember? But to get to Jennifer, you are going to have to go through me first."

Nash was astonished by the vehemence in his friend's voice. Suddenly a thought hit him. "Have ya'll been working for Kiplinger?"

Columbia wasn't sure who threw the first punch, but the next thing she knew Nash and Barth were tussling on the floor. They scuffled, knocking over a table and lamp before Nash gained the upper hand.

Nash was straddling Barth, his fist drawn back about to land a blow, when Jennifer screamed and grabbed Nash's arm. "No! Please. Do not hurt him. I love him."

Columbia had been about to pounce on the woman when she had grabbed Nash, but Columbia stood statue-still at Jennifer's confession. Nash's anger seemed to have been spent, and he climbed off Barth. Jennifer knelt down and kissed Barth's bloodied cheek as he sat up.

"I think explanations are rather overdue, don't ya'll, Barth?"

Barth curved an arm around Jennifer's shoulders and pulled her to him. "Although you have always been the consummate ladies' man, Nash, you have not always won the girl when we used to compete.

"In answer to your question, no, I have never worked for Kiplinger. As a matter of fact, I just finished helping General Shallcross confiscate the guns in the ship's hold. He filled me in on Kiplinger's conspiracy. And to reply to the question on your face, I fell in love with Jennifer, and she with me."

Columbia stepped forward. "Then why'd you kick up such a fuss, Jennifer?"

"That was Daddy's doing." Jennifer glanced at Barth, and he patted her arm in support. "You know how narrow-minded Daddy can be. When Nash jilted me in public, then left New York, and I discovered I was pregnant, Daddy told everyone that we had been secretly wed." She shrugged. "So I thought I had no choice. Appearances have always been important to Daddy."

"Well, he will not have to worry about that anymore," Nash grunted.

"I know. There is not much we can do to help Daddy. But I still love him." She paused. "I apologize to you, Columbia, for my behavior. And I am sorry about the wedding, Nash," she said for Barth's bene-

409

fit. She did love Barth. "But I am not going to deny that it gave me a certain measure of gratification, after the embarrassment you caused me back in New York when you refused to marry me in front of all my friends, not to mention taking Barth half a world away from me."

Nash made no comment, although he questioned Barth's wisdom for falling in love with such a self-centered young woman. He listened patiently as they described how they fell in love. Barth explained that he had grudgingly gone to Oregon to forget, since he thought Jennifer had wanted Nash after all. Then they met face to face the day of the wedding, and finally got together and sorted everything out.

Columbia listened, too, and her heart softened toward the woman, hearing such a love story. But when no mention of Ely was forthcoming, she could not restrain herself any longer. "What about the baby?"

"Ely?" Jennifer answered.

"My God, there ain't another, is there?"

Jennifer and Barth laughed. Nash remained stone-faced. Columbia's heart raced with fear, and she crossed her fingers.

"There is only one son. I suppose you are wondering who the father is?"

Columbia clasped her hands behind her back and rocked on her heels. "Suppose so."

Jennifer glanced at Nash, then at Barth, then back at Nash. "You can breathe a sigh of relief, Nash. The boy is Barth's."

"True enough?" Columbia questioned.

"True enough, Columbia. Barth and I plan to be married and return to New York, at Daddy's urging, as soon as arrangements can be made."

Jennifer kept her smile bright and self-assured, despite an inner sadness over her father. She explained the plans she and Barth had, but inside a single doubt assailed her. Although she could never be sure of Ely's parentage, no one else on earth would ever share that secret. Not all concealments were meant to be, or should be, shared. For the benefit of everyone involved — especially Ely — Jennifer silently promised to take that secret to the grave with her.

"Oh, and Nash, before we leave, I shall make sure you hold the legal ownership papers to your paddle wheeler."

"Nash could become godfather to Ely," Barth offered in a hopeful voice.

"You will, won't you?" Jennifer quickly seconded.

For an instant Nash wanted to question her enthusiasm, but chalked it up to her desire to please Barth. Nash offered his hand. "It would be an honor, but only if ya'll will allow me to be best man at your wedding first, and then only if Columbia is godmother . . . as my wife."

All eyes turned to Columbia. She shrugged, holding back a smile for nearly five seconds. "Oh, posh, how can I refuse when we have ended up with matchin' black eyes, after all?"

Nash's fingers flew to his eye. Then he threw back his head and laughed. "Barth, you threw the luckiest punch of my life." They all laughed, and Nash swept Columbia off her feet and hugged her.

411

After a round of congratulations, Jennifer said, "If you will excuse me, I should go look in on Ely. He must be waking now and will be hungry."

A few moments after Jennifer had excused herself, a high-pitched scream pierced through the door. Barth and Nash rushed from the cabin, followed by Columbia.

Lester Cowan was holding a knife at Jennifer's throat. "Don't come any closer, or I'll kill her."

The man's attention was focused on the two men as he backed up, forcing Jennifer with him. Columbia fell back. She made her way around deck behind them. A life ring raised high in her hands, she crashed it down over the fat man. Barth caught Jennifer as she fell forward, and Nash sent a blow to Cowan's chin. The force of the blow knocked him backward with such force, that it sent him spinning over the rail.

Barth left Jennifer's side and ran to the rail. "If I remember our last night in New York Harbor correctly, that man can't swim."

Nash joined him. "True. But thanks to Columbia, he was wearing a life ring when he abandoned ship."

Barth laughed. "Good choice of words."

"No doubt the soldiers will pick him up before he gets too far downriver. If not, the navy can pick him up out at sea."

"If he ain't frozen stiff first," Columbia added, joining Nash to peer over the side.

Jennifer had disappeared during the chaos, and now returned carrying Ely. "I hate to intrude, but it is time for Ely to eat. Barth, you said you wanted to help feed him."

"I sure do. You will excuse us, Nash?"

Left together on deck, Columbia took Nash's hand and started down the gangplank. "I hope ya'll intend to whisk me off to some hideout away from all humanity," he chuckled.

"You already tried that on the island. No. We got to go tell Uncle Titus the news. Unless I miss my guess, he's probably worryin' his head off in that room over the Dockside."

Although Nash did not argue, visiting with Uncle Titus was not what he had on his mind.

Columbia did not bother to knock when they arrived. She barged through the door and came to an abrupt halt. Titus was in bed with Dolly, and from what Columbia could see, they were as naked as two rutting jaybirds.

Columbia gasped.

As the pair scrambled to cover themselves, Nash came up behind her. Hiding a grin, he said, "I had a sneaking suspicion ya'll meant to have her. So, my soon-to-be uncle, looks like there may be a need for a shotgun wedding. Shall we set the date?"

Titus sat up, amused annoyance on his creased face. "Too late. Dolly and me got hitched yesterday. Now, will you two get out of here, and let a man and his woman enjoy their honeymoon in peace, since I hear you two already had yours on the island. And don't interrupt us again until your wedding."

"We shall be in touch," Nash said, in a way that would let Titus know that there would be another wedding soon.

"But—" Nash grabbed Columbia's arm, and cutting her off, pulled her from the room and shut the door.

"We are going to leave them to their privacy."

Columbia nodded, and as they headed toward his paddle wheeler, she suddenly stopped. "Nash, what you said to Uncle Titus. Those were practically the same words Uncle Titus said to you, when he burst into *your* cabin. Gosh, you got a good memory."

He took her in his arms. "I remember a lot of things. Like the soft feel of your lap, when I rested my head there while we were in that crate. The silky feel of your skin, the salty sweet taste of your flesh. All the times we have been together." He held her from him and delved into her eyes. "Why don't we go back to *our* paddle wheeler, and refresh my memory on any details I may have forgotten?"

"We could *borrow* a couple of horses and get there faster."

"No more borrowing. If ya'll are going to become the first licensed female riverboat pilot on the Columbia River, ya'll cannot have a criminal record—even if it *is* for just *borrowing.*"

Her heart swelled with incredible joy. He had remembered her precious goal, and planned to provide support while she achieved it. She cast him her widest grin.

"Then I guess it'll take us longer before we can start refreshin' your memory."

He laughed, and with her hand in his, began to hasten toward the paddle wheeler. "Not if we run."

DISCOVER DEANA JAMES!

CAPTIVE ANGEL (2524, $4.50/$5.50)
Abandoned, penniless, and suddenly responsible for the biggest
tobacco plantation in Colleton County, distraught Caroline Gillard had no time to dissolve into tears. By day the willowy redhead labored to exhaustion beside her slaves . . . but each night
left her restless with longing for her wayward husband. She'd
make the sea captain regret his betrayal until he begged her to
take him back!

MASQUE OF SAPPHIRE (2885, $4.50/$5.50)
Judith Talbot-Harrow left England with a heavy heart. She was
going to America to join a father she despised and a sister she
distrusted. She was certainly in no mood to put up with the insulting actions of the arrogant Yankee privateer who boarded her
ship, ransacked her things, then "apologized" with an indecent,
brazen kiss! She vowed that someday he'd pay dearly for the liberties he had taken and the desires he had awakened.

SPEAK ONLY LOVE (3439, $4.95/$5.95)
Long ago, the shock of her mother's death had robbed Vivian
Marleigh of the power of speech. Now she was being forced to
marry a bitter man with brandy on his breath. But she could not
say what was in her heart. It was up to the viscount to spark the
fires that would melt her icy reserve.

WILD TEXAS HEART (3205, $4.95/$5.95)
Fan Breckenridge was terrified when the stranger found her nearnaked and shivering beneath the Texas stars. Unable to remember
who she was or what had happened, all she had in the world was
the deed to a patch of land that might yield oil . . . and the fierce
loving of this wildcatter who called himself Irons.

*Available wherever paperbacks are sold, or order direct from the
Publisher. Send cover price plus 50¢ per copy for mailing and
handling to Zebra Books, Dept. 3847, 475 Park Avenue South,
New York, N.Y. 10016. Residents of New York and Tennessee
must include sales tax. DO NOT SEND CASH. For a free Zebra/
Pinnacle catalog please write to the above address.*

FEEL THE FIRE IN CAROL FINCH'S ROMANCES!

BELOVED BETRAYAL   (2346, $3.95)

Sabrina Spencer donned a gray wig and veiled hat before blackmailing rugged Ridge Tanner into guiding her to Fort Canby. But the costume soon became her prison—the beauty had fallen head over heels in love!

LOVE'S HIDDEN TREASURE   (2980, $4.50)

Shandra d'Evereux felt her heart throb beneath the stolen map she'd hidden in her bodice when Nolan Elliot swept her out onto the veranda. It was hard to concentrate on her mission with that wily rogue around!

MONTANA MOONFIRE   (3263, $4.95)

Just as debutante Victoria Flemming-Cassidy was about to marry an oh-so-suitable mate, the towering preacher, Dru Sullivan flung her over his shoulder and headed West! Suddenly, Tori realized she had been given the best present for a bride: a night of passion with a real man!

THUNDER'S TENDER TOUCH   (2809, $4.50)

Refined Piper Malone needed bounty-hunter, Vince Logan to recover her swindled inheritance. She thought she could coolly dismiss him after he did the job, but she never counted on the hot flood of desire she felt whenever he was near!